0503572

MONTVILLE TWP. PUBLIC LIBRARY
90 HORSENECK ROAD
MONTVILLE, NJ 07045

P9-DGK-928

ON LINE

JFICTION
Batma

Batman adventures
Rogues gallery /

Montville Township Public Library
90 Horseneck Road
Montville, N.J. 07045-9626
973-402-0900
<u>Library Hours</u>

Monday	10 a.m.-9 p.m.
Tuesday	10 a.m.-9 p.m.
Wednesday	1 p.m.- 9 p.m.
Thursday	10 a.m.- 9 p.m.
Friday	10 a.m.- 5 p.m.
Saturday	10 a.m.- 5 p.m.
Sunday	1 p.m.- 5 p.m.

Closed Sundays July & August
see website   www.montvillelib.org

ON LINE

BATMAN ADVENTURES

ROGUES GALLERY

Written by:

Scott Peterson

Dan Slott

Ty Templeton

Colored by:

Lee Loughridge

Illustrated by:

Terry Beatty

Rick Burchett

Tim Levins

Ty Templeton

Lettered by:

Albert T. De Guzman

Phil Felix

Dan DiDio
VP-Editorial

Joan Hilty
Editor-original series

Harvey Richards
Assistant Editor-original series

Scott Nybakken
Editor-collected edition

Robbin Brosterman
Senior Art Director

Paul Levitz
President & Publisher

Georg Brewer
VP-Design & Retail Product
Development

Richard Bruning
Senior VP-Creative Director

Patrick Caldon
Senior VP-Finance & Operations

Chris Caramelis
VP-Finance

Terri Cunningham
VP-Managing Editor

Alison Gill
VP-Manufacturing

Rich Johnson
VP-Book Trade Sales

Hank Kanalz
VP-General Manager, WildStorm

Lillian Laserson
Senior VP & General Counsel

Jim Lee
Editorial Director-WildStorm

David McKillips
VP-Advertising & Custom Publishing

John Nee
VP-Business Development

Gregory Noveck
Senior VP-Creative Affairs

Cheryl Rubin
VP-Brand Management

Bob Wayne
VP-Sales & Marketing

BATMAN ADVENTURES VOL. 1: ROGUES GALLERY
Published by DC Comics. Cover and compilation copyright © 2004
DC Comics. All Rights Reserved. Originally published in single magazine
form as BATMAN: GOTHAM ADVENTURES 50 and BATMAN ADVENTURES
1-4. Copyright © 2002, 2003 DC Comics. All Rights Reserved. All characters,
their distinctive likenesses and related elements featured in this publication
are trademarks of DC Comics. The stories, characters and incidents featured
in this publication are entirely fictional. DC Comics does not read or accept
unsolicited submissions of ideas, stories or artwork.

CARTOON NETWORK and its logo are trademarks of Cartoon Network.

DC Comics, 1700 Broadway, New York, NY 10019
A Warner Bros. Entertainment Company.
Printed in Canada. First Printing.
ISBN: 1-4012-0329-9
Cover illustration by Bruce Timm
Publication design by John J. Hill

0 1021 0196929 7

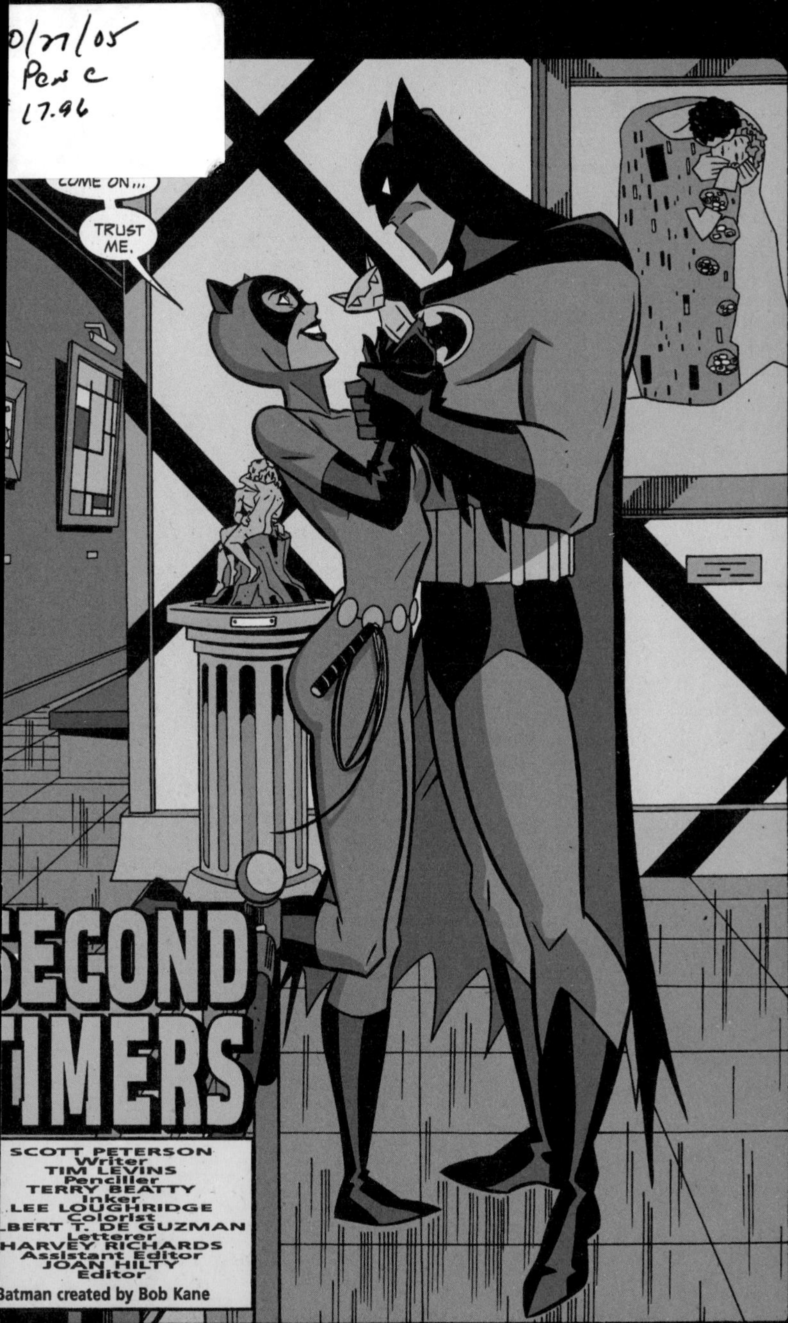
COME ON...
TRUST ME.
SECOND
IMERS
SCOTT PETERSON
Writer
TIM LEVINS
Penciller
TERRY BEATTY
Inker
LEE LOUGHRIDGE
Colorist
LBERT T. DE GUZMAN
Letterer
HARVEY RICHARDS
Assistant Editor
JOAN HILTY
Editor
Batman created by Bob Kane

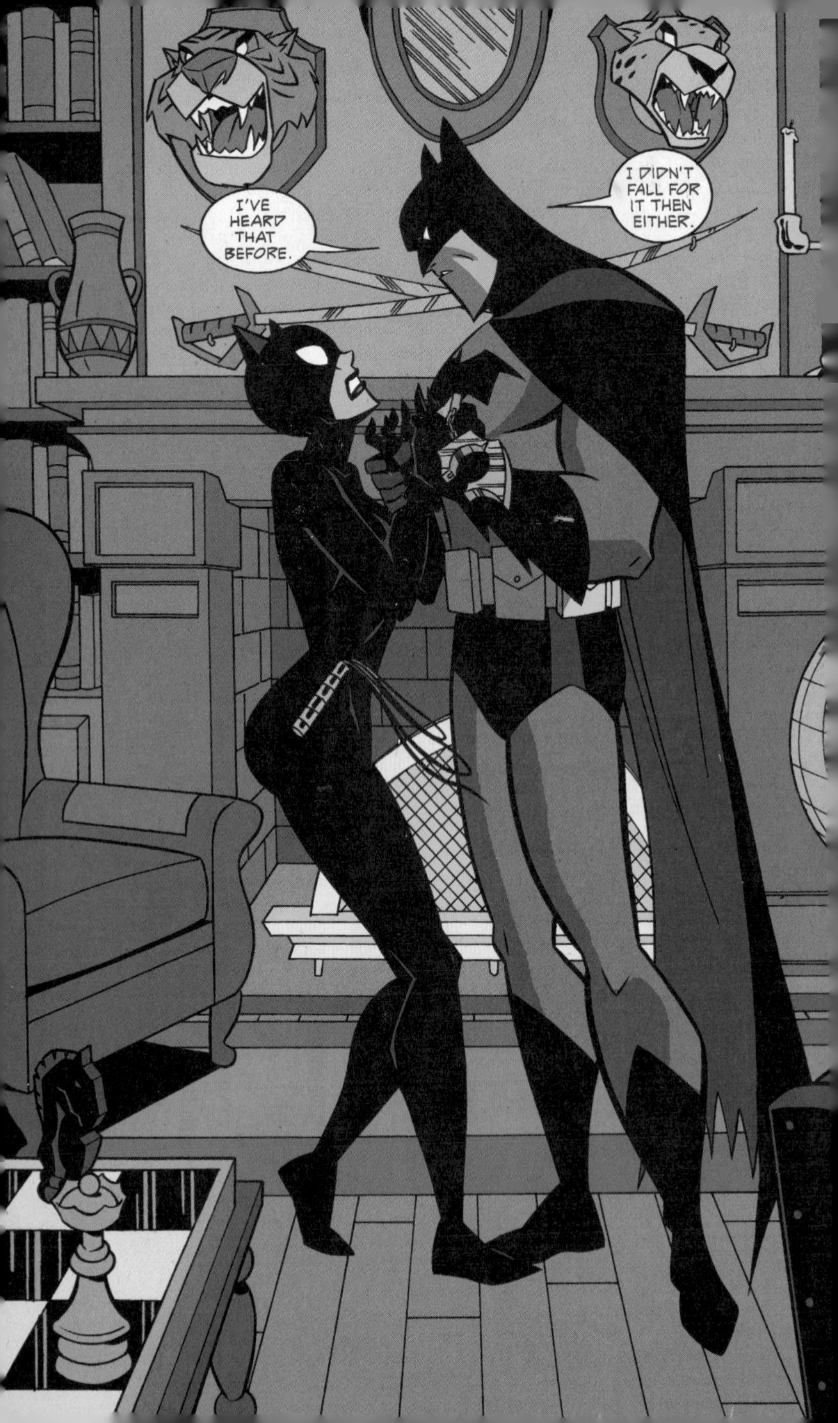
I'VE HEARD THAT BEFORE.
I DIDN'T FALL FOR IT THEN EITHER.

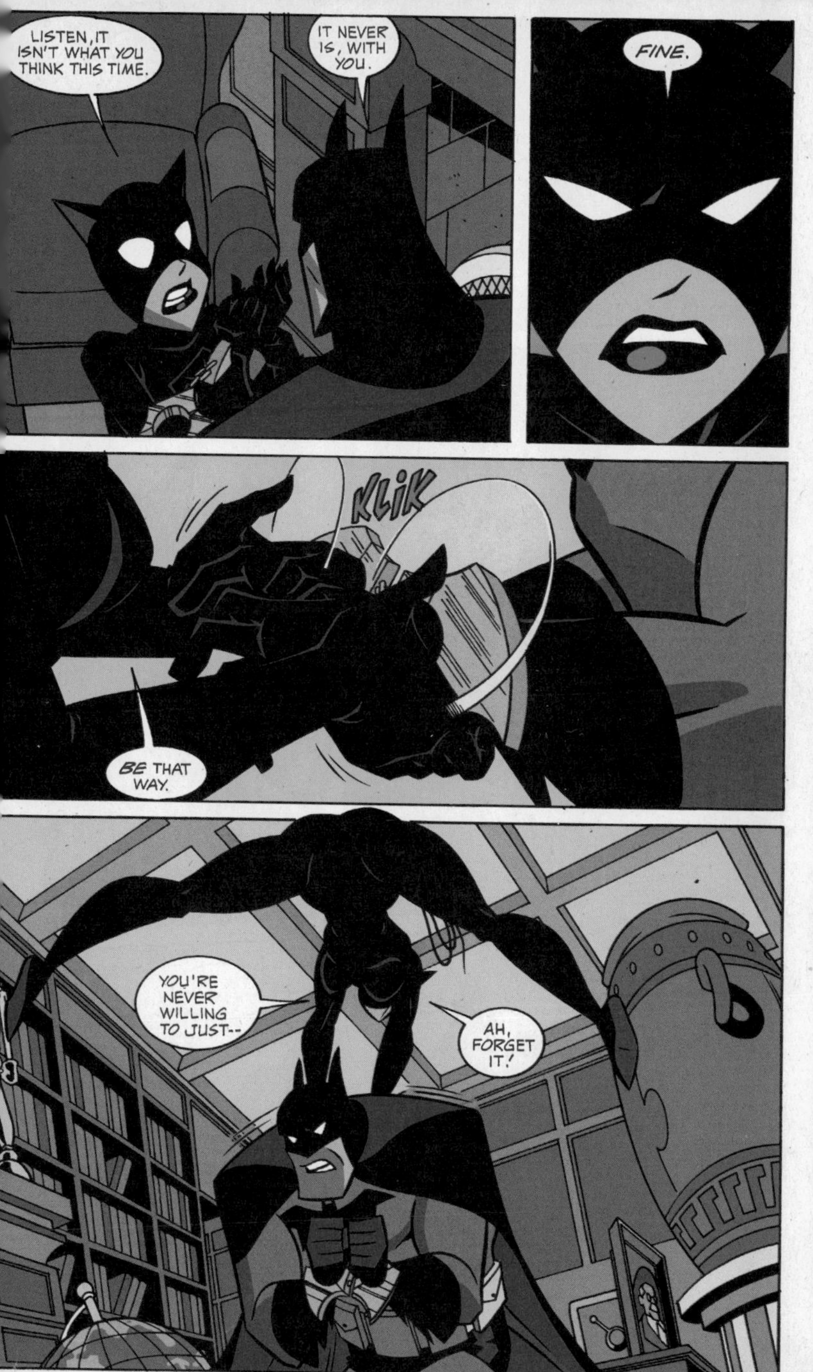
LISTEN, IT ISN'T WHAT YOU THINK THIS TIME.
IT NEVER IS, WITH YOU.
FINE.
KLIK
BE THAT WAY.
YOU'RE NEVER WILLING TO JUST--
AH, FORGET IT!

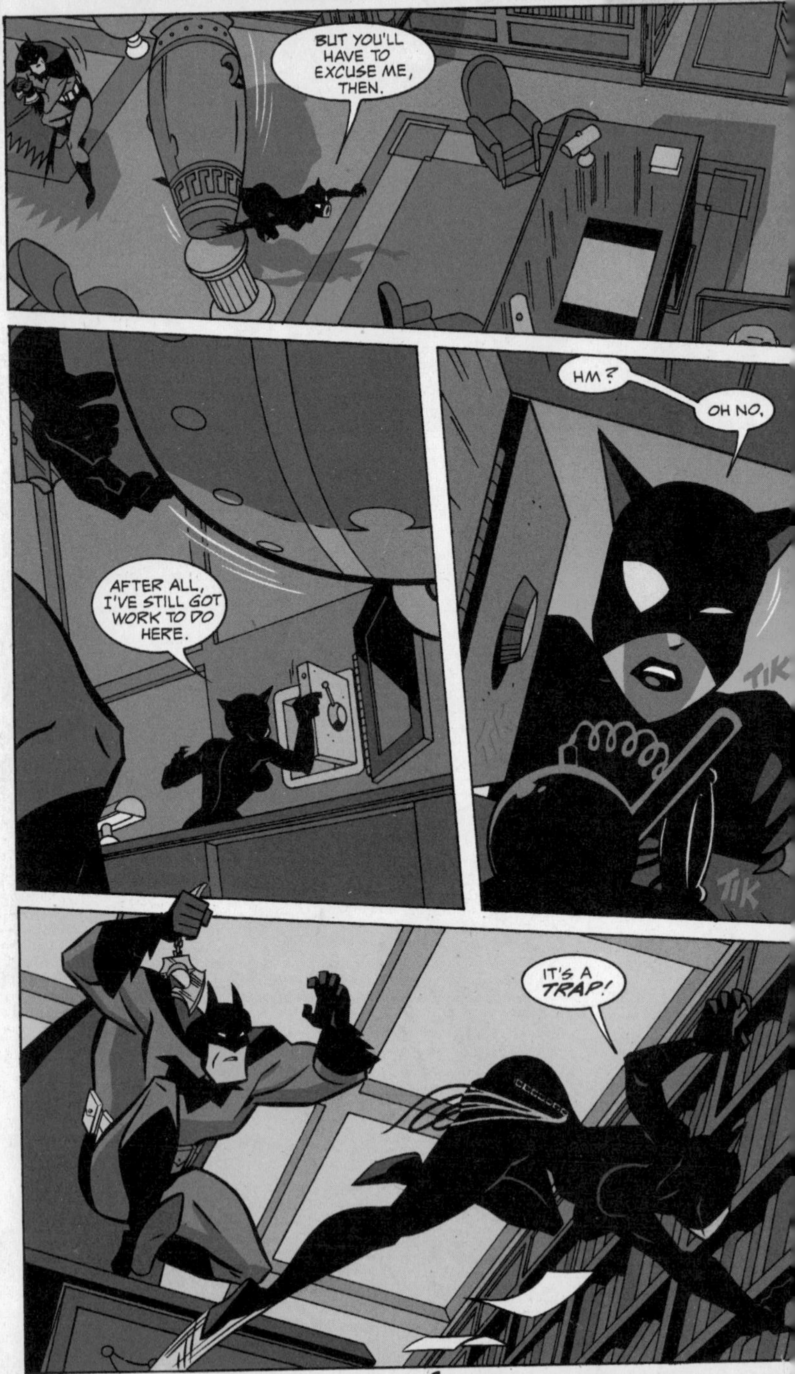

BUT YOU'LL HAVE TO EXCUSE ME, THEN.
AFTER ALL, I'VE STILL GOT WORK TO DO HERE.
HM?
OH NO.
TIK
TIK
TIK
IT'S A TRAP!

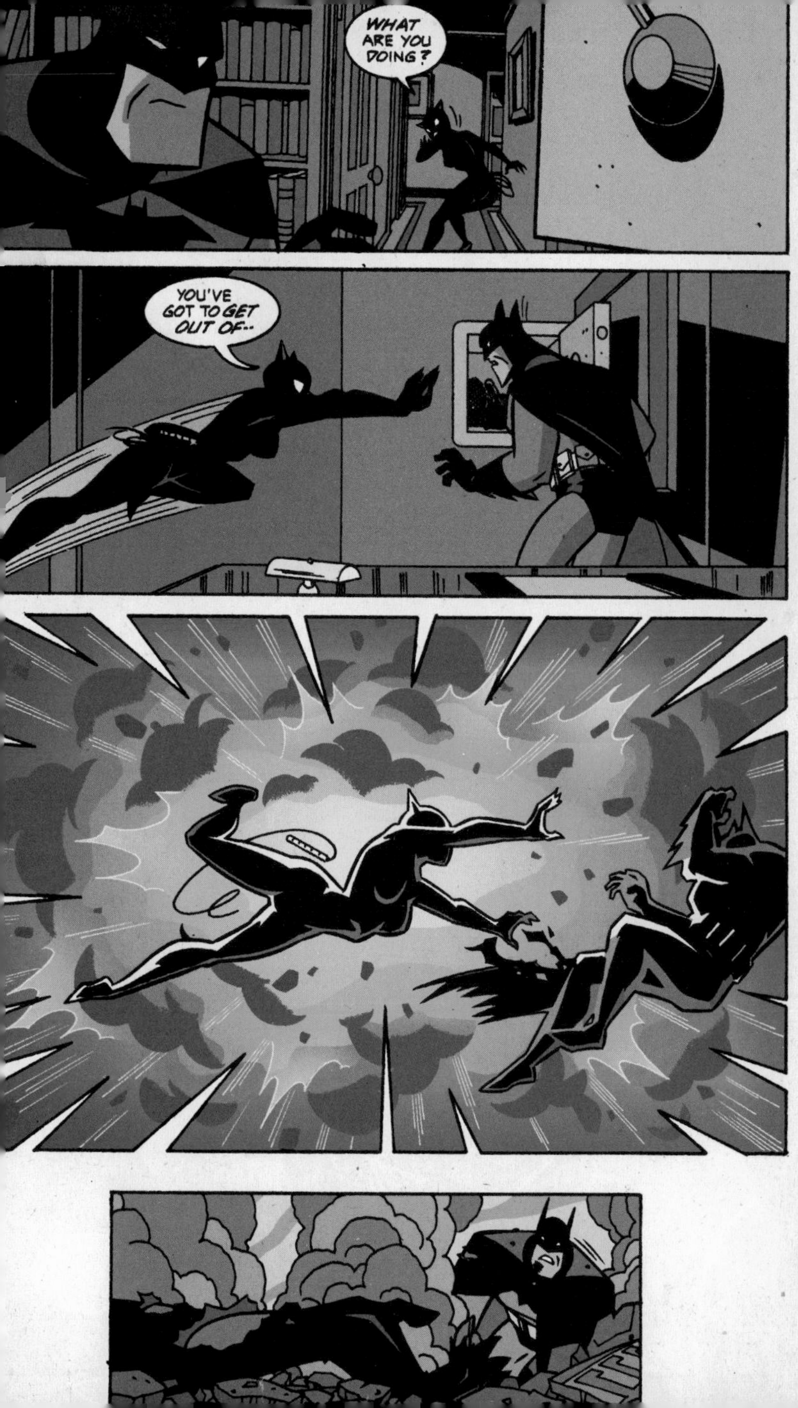
WHAT ARE YOU DOING?
YOU'VE GOT TO GET OUT OF--

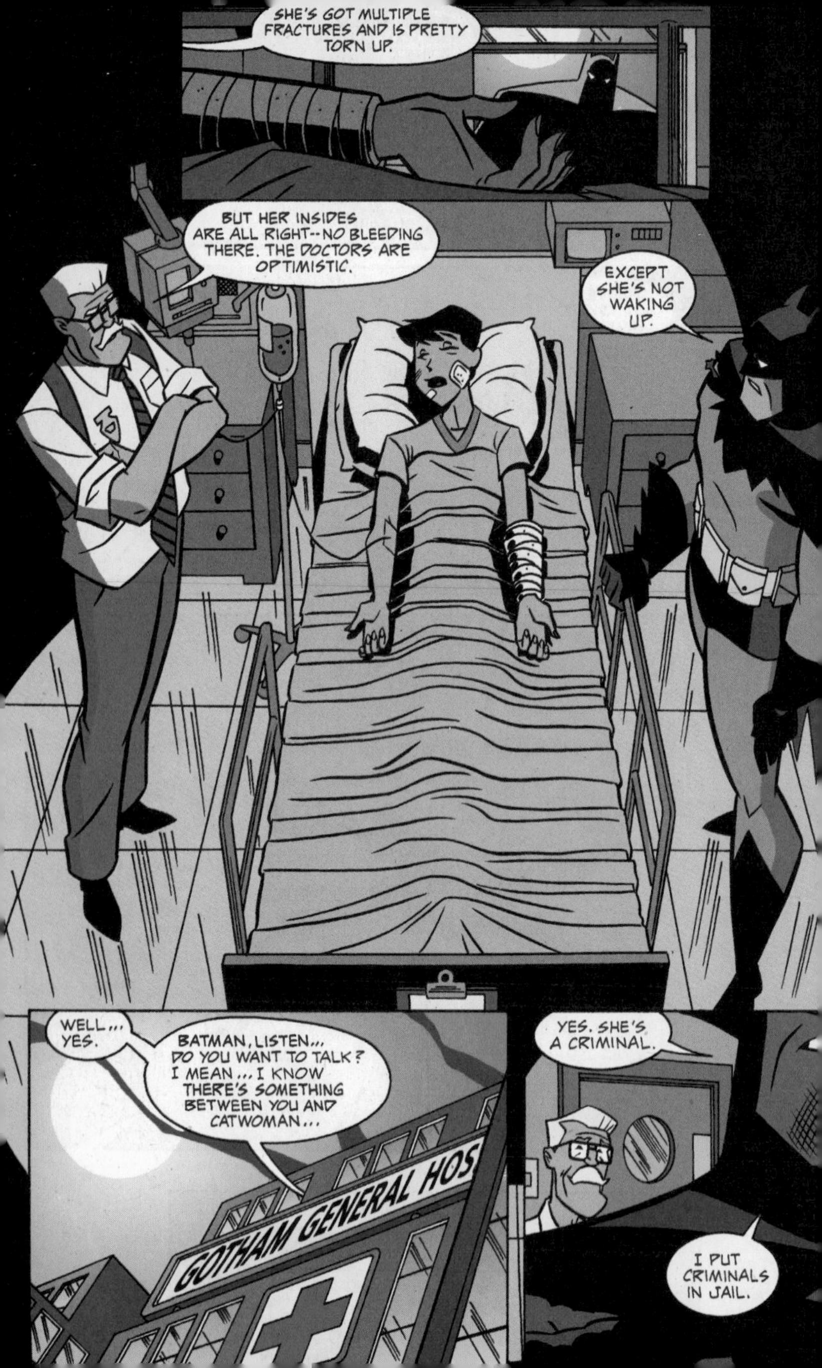
SHE'S GOT MULTIPLE FRACTURES AND IS PRETTY TORN UP.
BUT HER INSIDES ARE ALL RIGHT--NO BLEEDING THERE. THE DOCTORS ARE OPTIMISTIC.
EXCEPT SHE'S NOT WAKING UP.
WELL... YES.
BATMAN, LISTEN... DO YOU WANT TO TALK? I MEAN... I KNOW THERE'S SOMETHING BETWEEN YOU AND CATWOMAN...
GOTHAM GENERAL HOS
YES. SHE'S A CRIMINAL.
I PUT CRIMINALS IN JAIL.

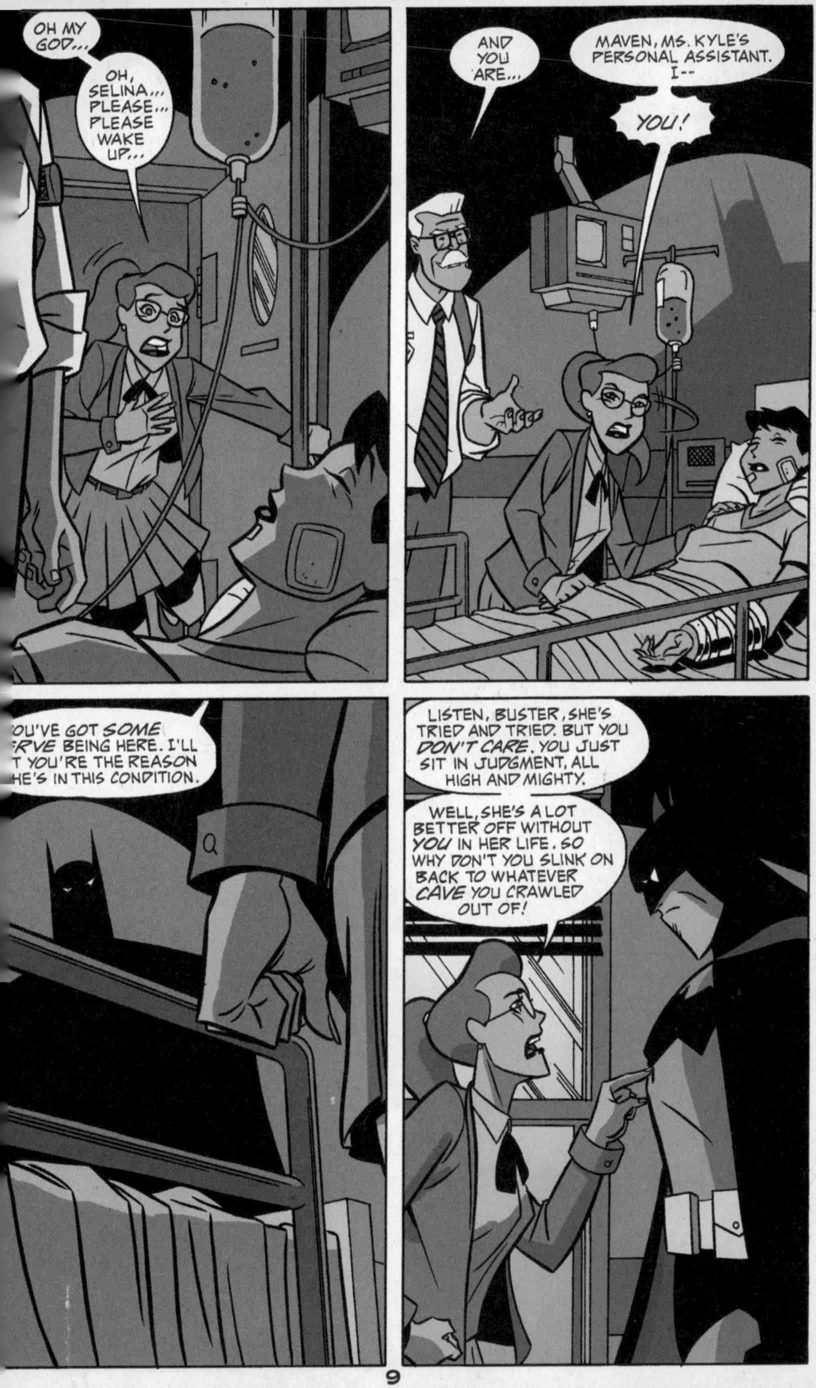
OH MY GOD...
OH, SELINA... PLEASE... PLEASE WAKE UP...
AND YOU ARE...
MAVEN, MS. KYLE'S PERSONAL ASSISTANT. I--
YOU!
OU'VE GOT SOME ERVE BEING HERE. I'LL T YOU'RE THE REASON HE'S IN THIS CONDITION.
LISTEN, BUSTER, SHE'S TRIED AND TRIED. BUT YOU DON'T CARE. YOU JUST SIT IN JUDGMENT, ALL HIGH AND MIGHTY.
WELL, SHE'S A LOT BETTER OFF WITHOUT YOU IN HER LIFE. SO WHY DON'T YOU SLINK ON BACK TO WHATEVER CAVE YOU CRAWLED OUT OF!

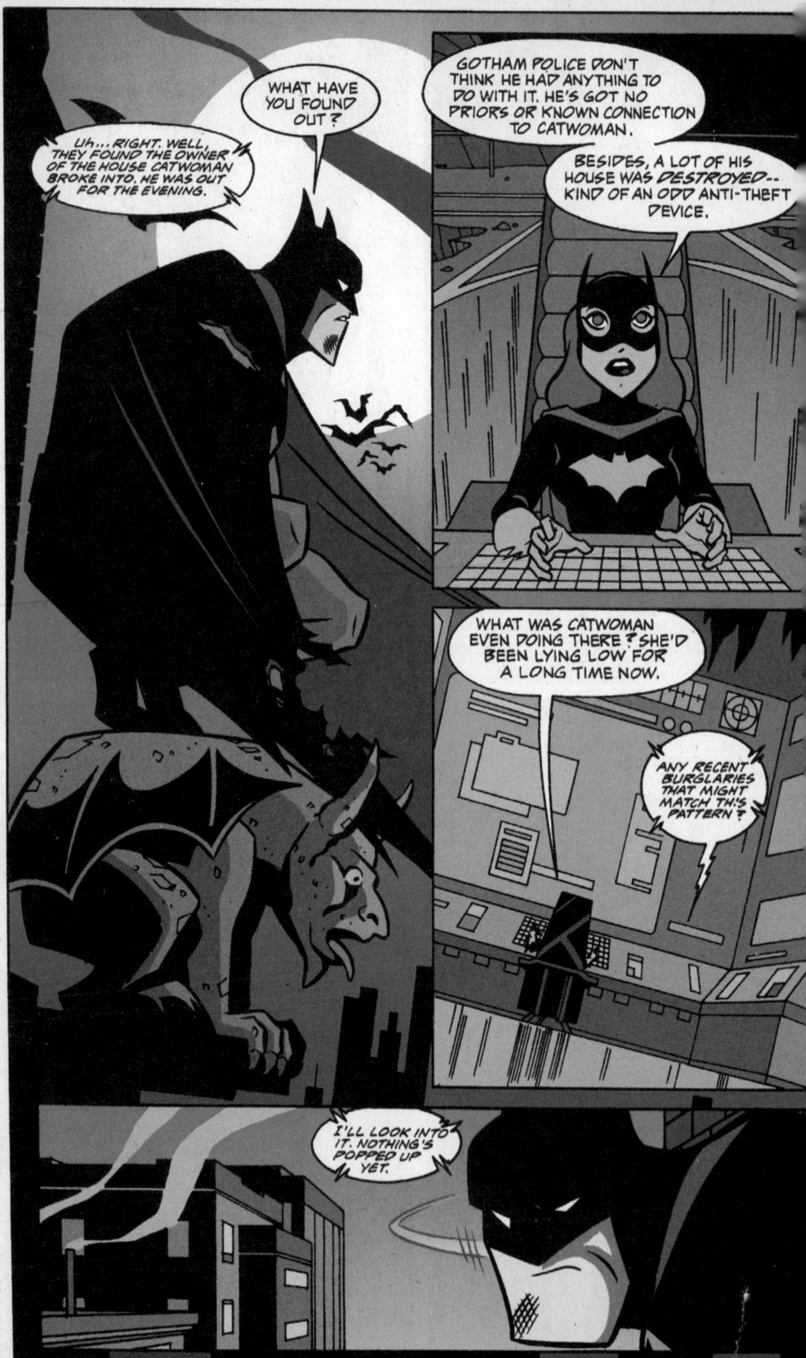
UH... RIGHT. WELL, THEY FOUND THE OWNER OF THE HOUSE CATWOMAN BROKE INTO. HE WAS OUT FOR THE EVENING.
WHAT HAVE YOU FOUND OUT?
GOTHAM POLICE DON'T THINK HE HAD ANYTHING TO DO WITH IT. HE'S GOT NO PRIORS OR KNOWN CONNECTION TO CATWOMAN.
BESIDES, A LOT OF HIS HOUSE WAS DESTROYED-- KIND OF AN ODD ANTI-THEFT DEVICE.
WHAT WAS CATWOMAN EVEN DOING THERE? SHE'D BEEN LYING LOW FOR A LONG TIME NOW.
ANY RECENT BURGLARIES THAT MIGHT MATCH THIS PATTERN?
I'LL LOOK INTO IT. NOTHING'S POPPED UP YET.

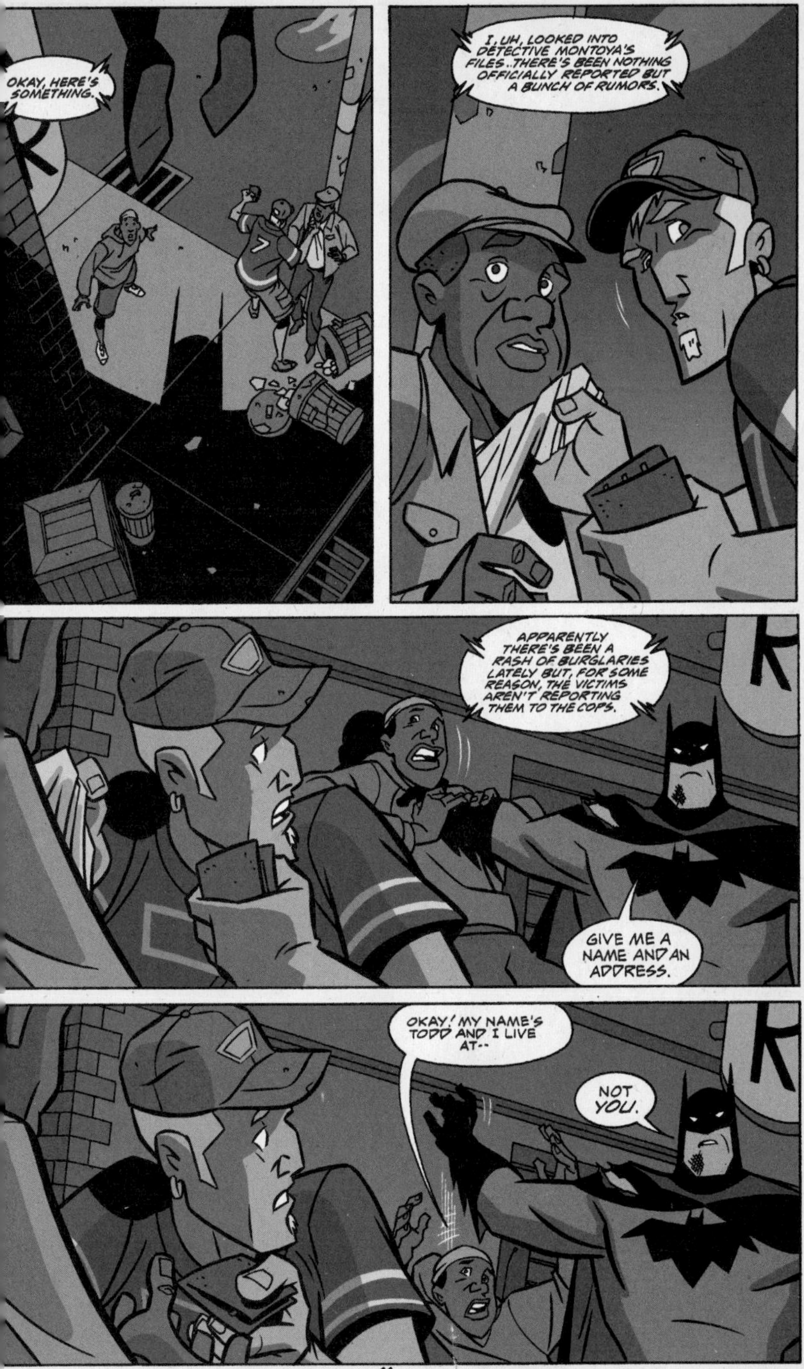
OKAY, HERE'S SOMETHING.
I, UH, LOOKED INTO DETECTIVE MONTOYA'S FILES..THERE'S BEEN NOTHING OFFICIALLY REPORTED BUT A BUNCH OF RUMORS.
APPARENTLY THERE'S BEEN A RASH OF BURGLARIES LATELY BUT, FOR SOME REASON, THE VICTIMS AREN'T REPORTING THEM TO THE COPS.
GIVE ME A NAME AND AN ADDRESS.
OKAY! MY NAME'S TODD AND I LIVE AT--
NOT YOU.

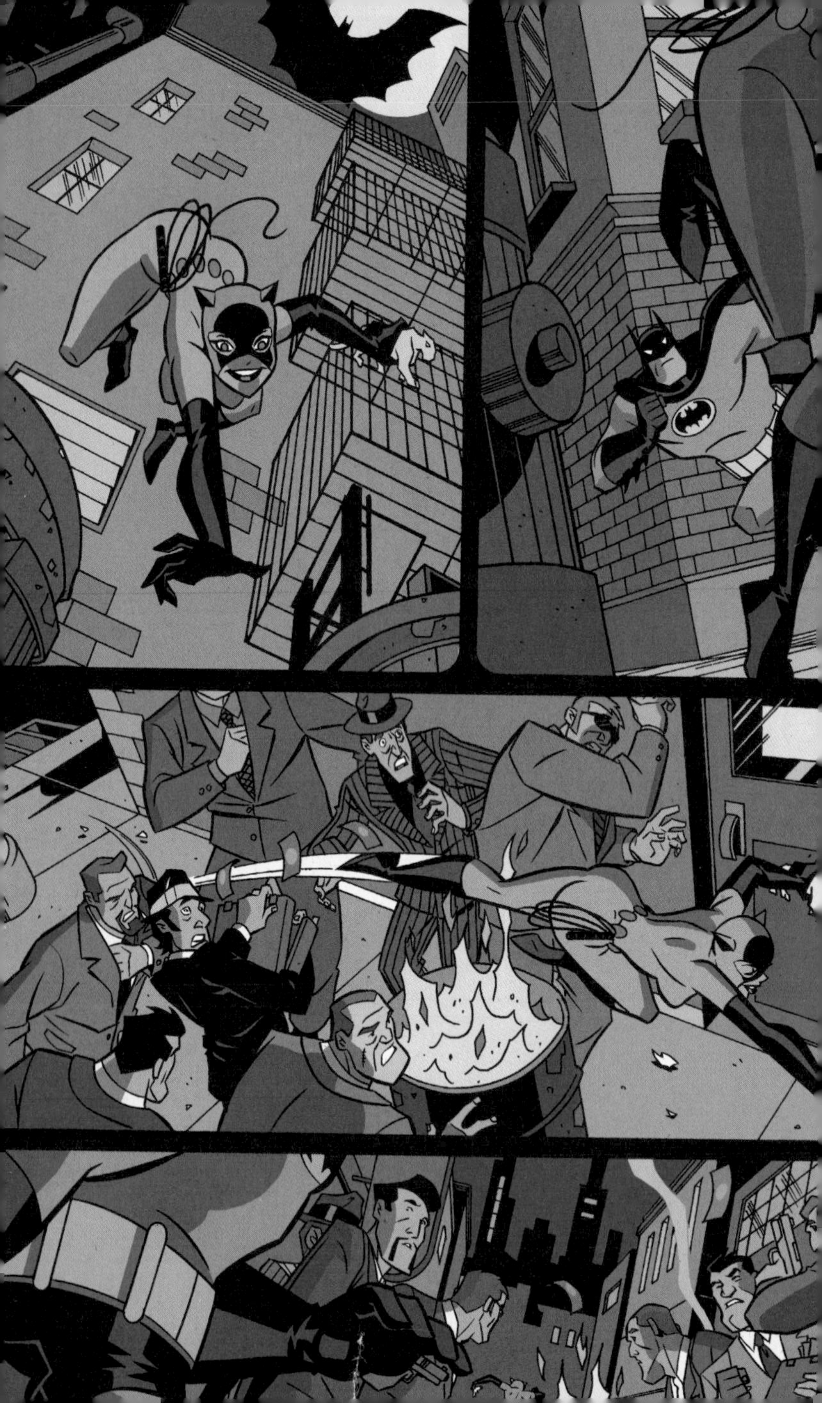

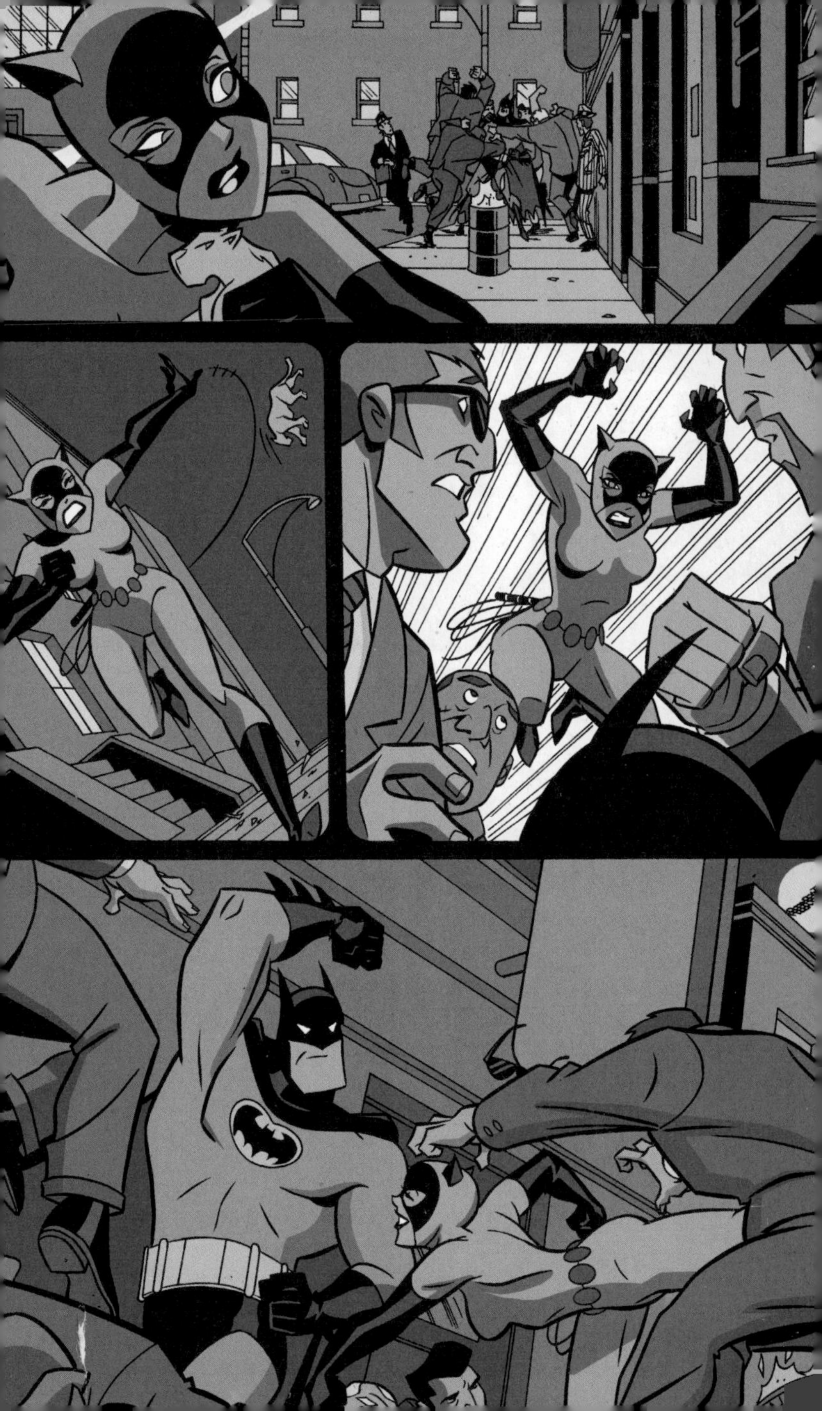

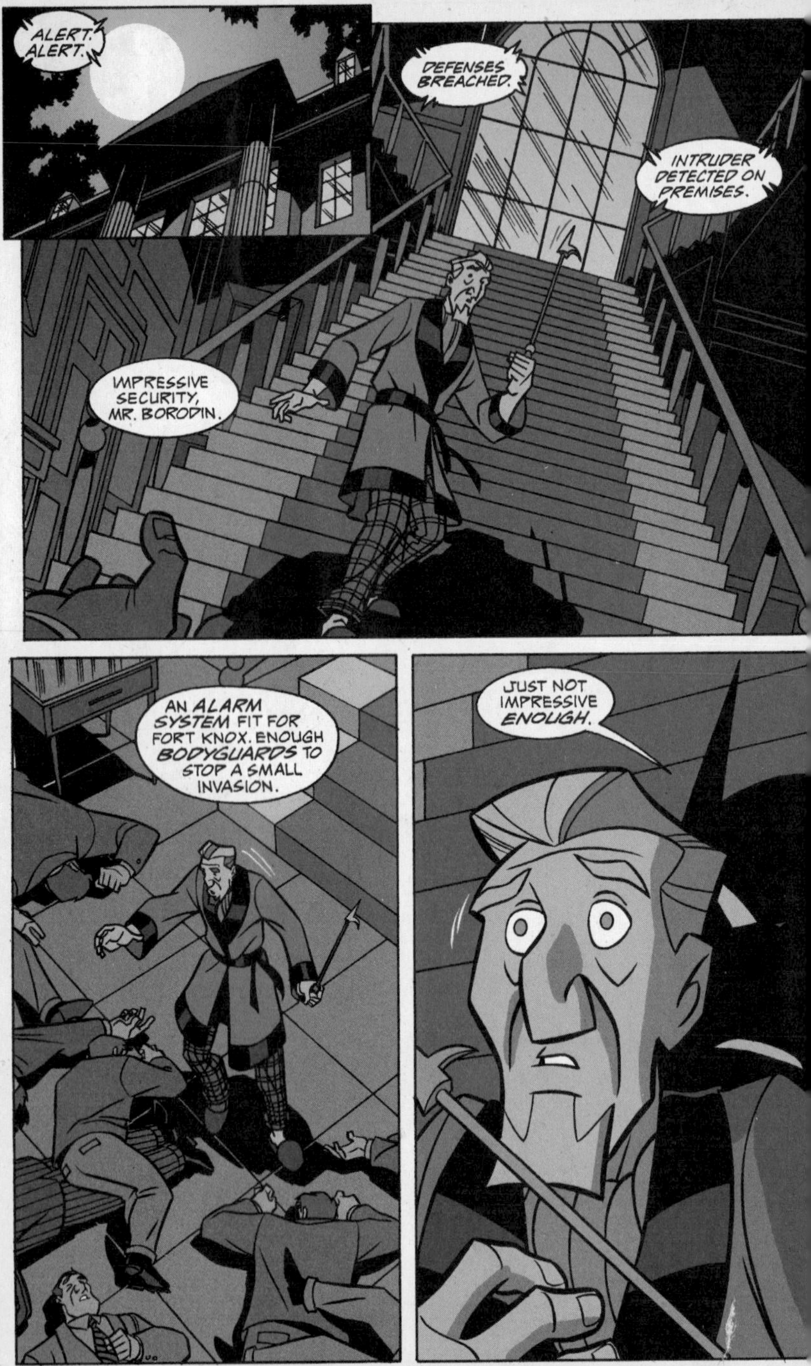
ALERT. ALERT.
DEFENSES BREACHED.
INTRUDER DETECTED ON PREMISES.
IMPRESSIVE SECURITY, MR. BORODIN.
AN *ALARM SYSTEM* FIT FOR FORT KNOX. ENOUGH *BODYGUARDS* TO STOP A SMALL INVASION.
JUST NOT IMPRESSIVE *ENOUGH*.

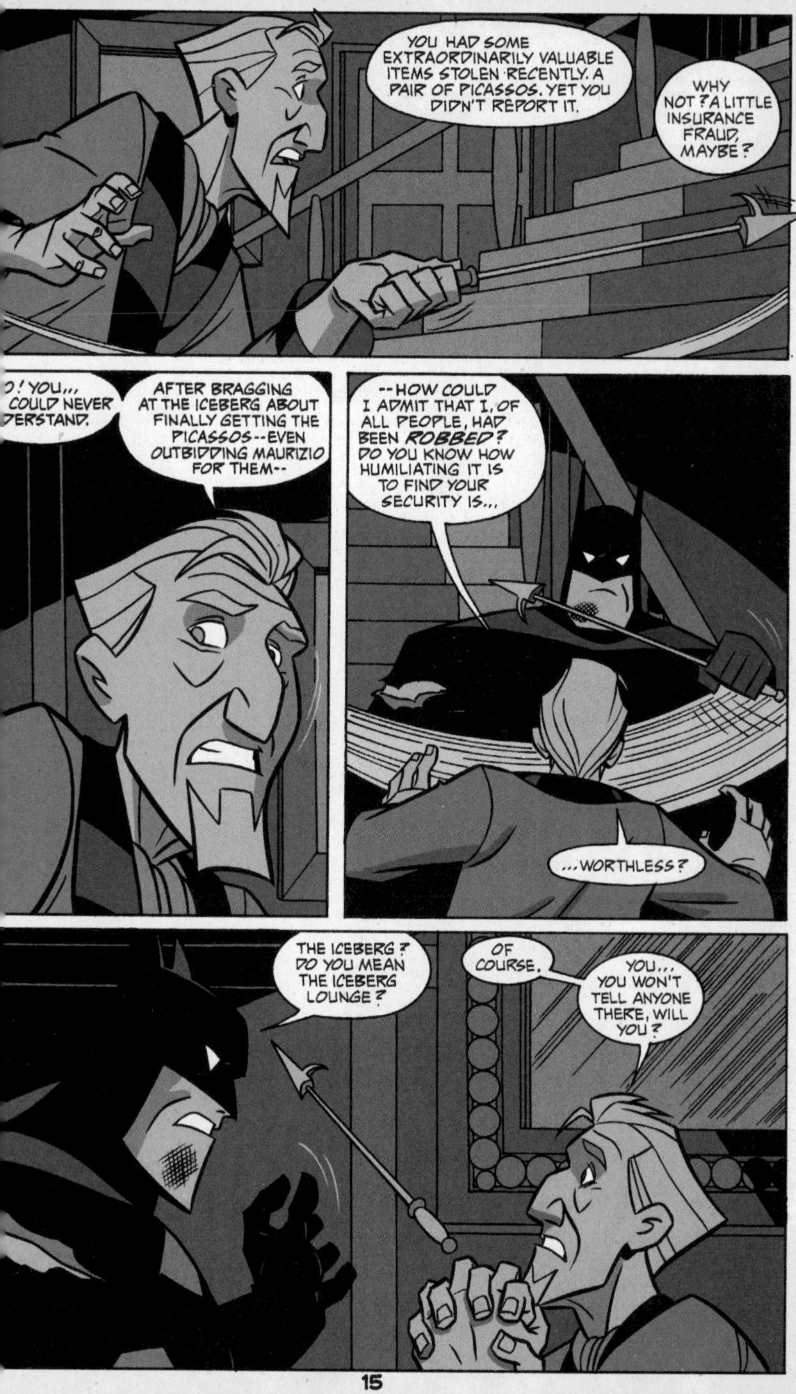

YOU HAD SOME EXTRAORDINARILY VALUABLE ITEMS STOLEN RECENTLY. A PAIR OF PICASSOS. YET YOU DIDN'T REPORT IT.
WHY NOT? A LITTLE INSURANCE FRAUD, MAYBE?
COULD NEVER
AFTER BRAGGING AT THE ICEBERG ABOUT FINALLY GETTING THE PICASSOS--EVEN OUTBIDDING MAURIZIO FOR THEM--
--HOW COULD I ADMIT THAT I, OF ALL PEOPLE, HAD BEEN *ROBBED*? DO YOU KNOW HOW HUMILIATING IT IS TO FIND YOUR SECURITY IS...
...WORTHLESS?
THE ICEBERG? DO YOU MEAN THE ICEBERG LOUNGE?
OF COURSE.
YOU... YOU WON'T TELL ANYONE THERE, WILL YOU?

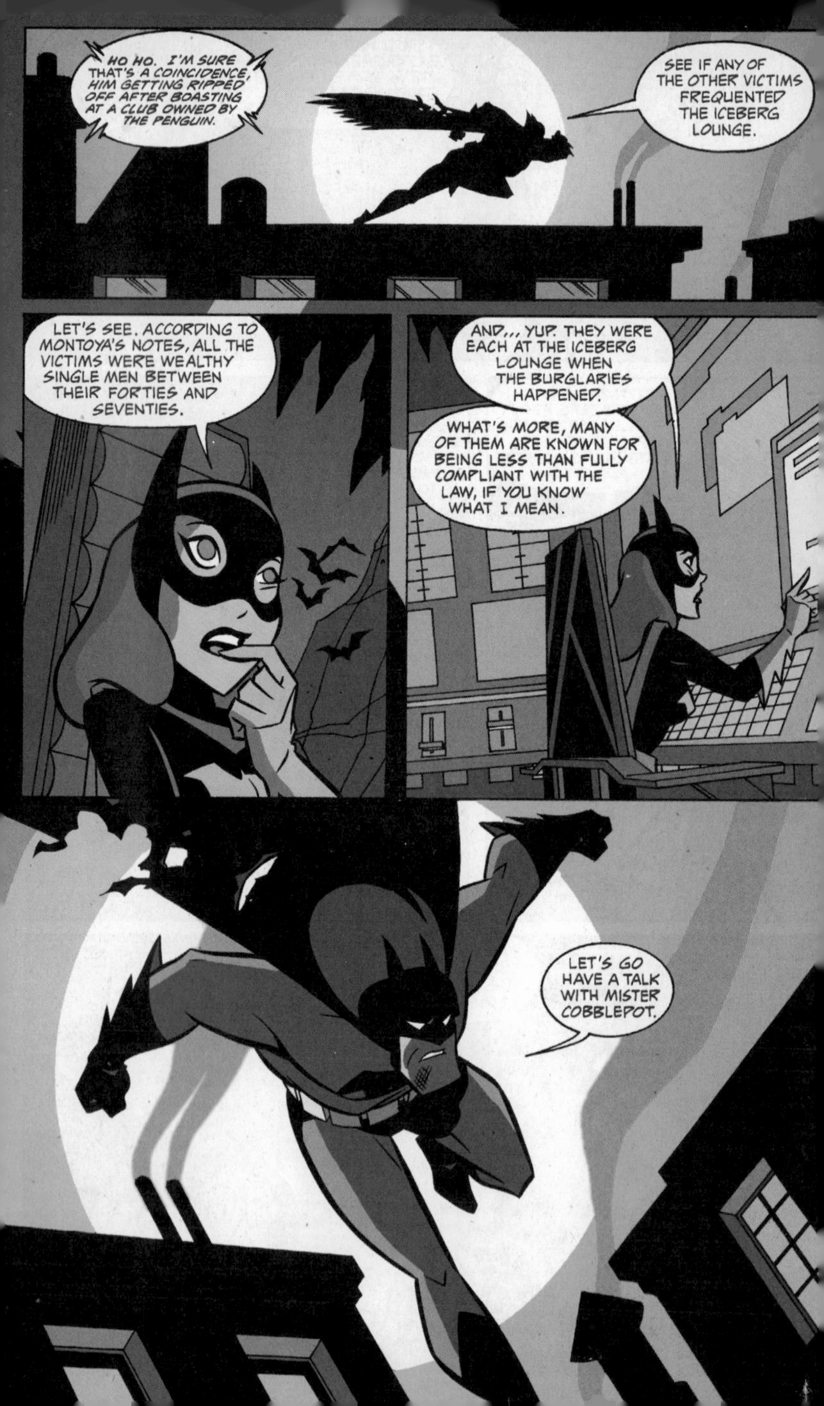
HO HO. I'M SURE THAT'S A COINCIDENCE, HIM GETTING RIPPED OFF AFTER BOASTING AT A CLUB OWNED BY THE PENGUIN.
SEE IF ANY OF THE OTHER VICTIMS FREQUENTED THE ICEBERG LOUNGE.
LET'S SEE. ACCORDING TO MONTOYA'S NOTES, ALL THE VICTIMS WERE WEALTHY SINGLE MEN BETWEEN THEIR FORTIES AND SEVENTIES.
AND... YUP. THEY WERE EACH AT THE ICEBERG LOUNGE WHEN THE BURGLARIES HAPPENED.
WHAT'S MORE, MANY OF THEM ARE KNOWN FOR BEING LESS THAN FULLY COMPLIANT WITH THE LAW, IF YOU KNOW WHAT I MEAN.
LET'S GO HAVE A TALK WITH MISTER COBBLEPOT.

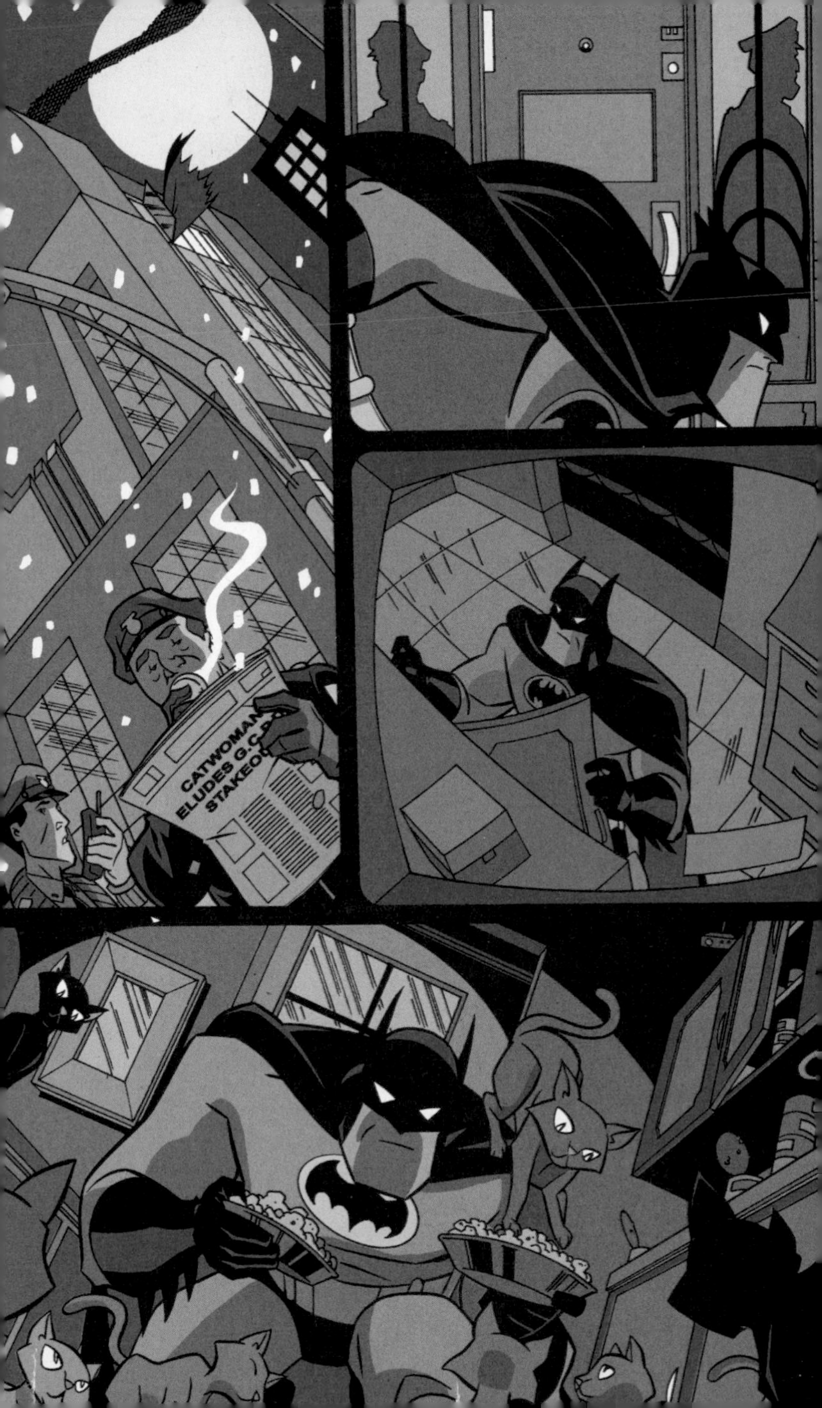
CATWOMAN
ELUDES G.C.P
STAKEO

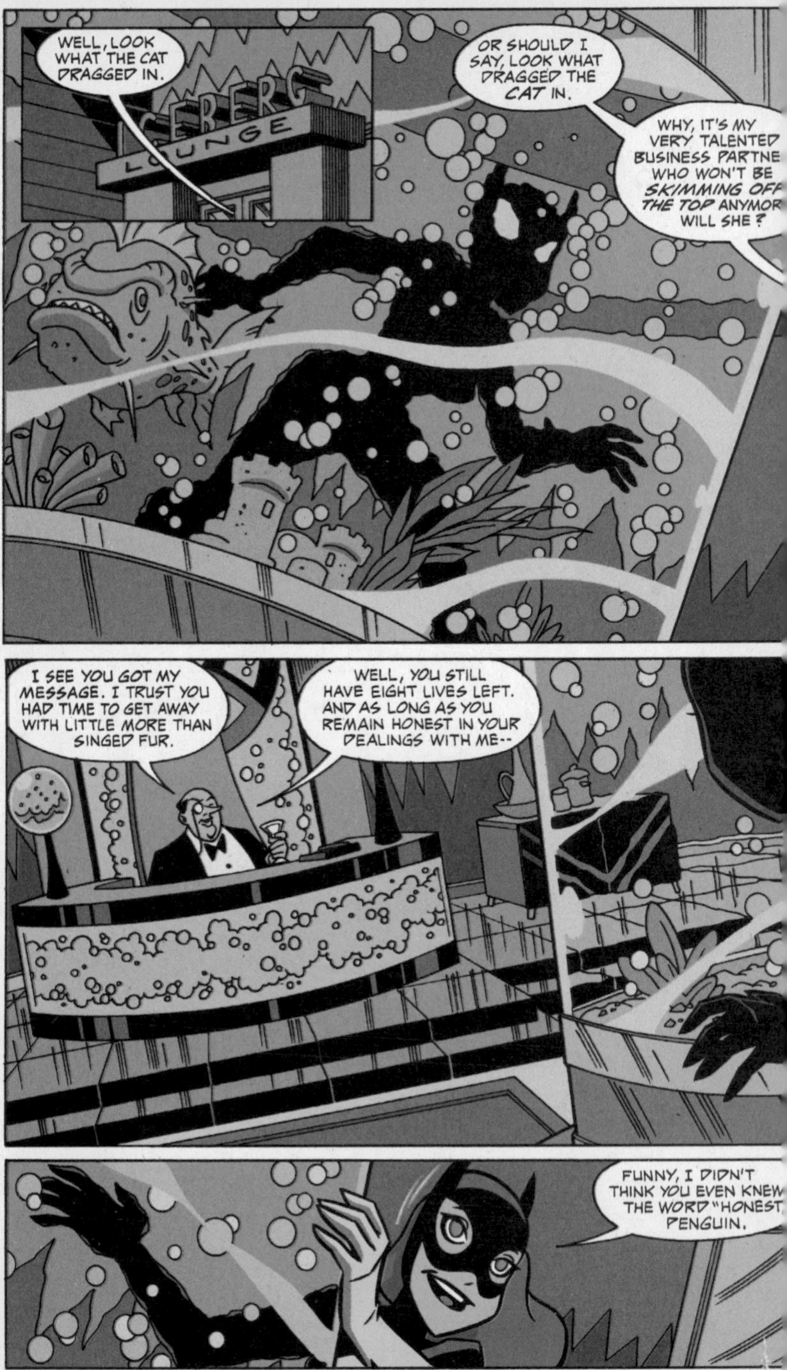

WELL, LOOK WHAT THE CAT DRAGGED IN.
ICEBERG LOUNGE
OR SHOULD I SAY, LOOK WHAT DRAGGED THE *CAT* IN.
WHY, IT'S MY VERY TALENTED BUSINESS PARTNE WHO WON'T BE *SKIMMING OFF THE TOP* ANYMOR WILL SHE?
I SEE YOU GOT MY MESSAGE. I TRUST YOU HAD TIME TO GET AWAY WITH LITTLE MORE THAN SINGED FUR.
WELL, YOU STILL HAVE EIGHT LIVES LEFT. AND AS LONG AS YOU REMAIN HONEST IN YOUR DEALINGS WITH ME--
FUNNY, I DIDN'T THINK YOU EVEN KNEW THE WORD "HONEST PENGUIN.

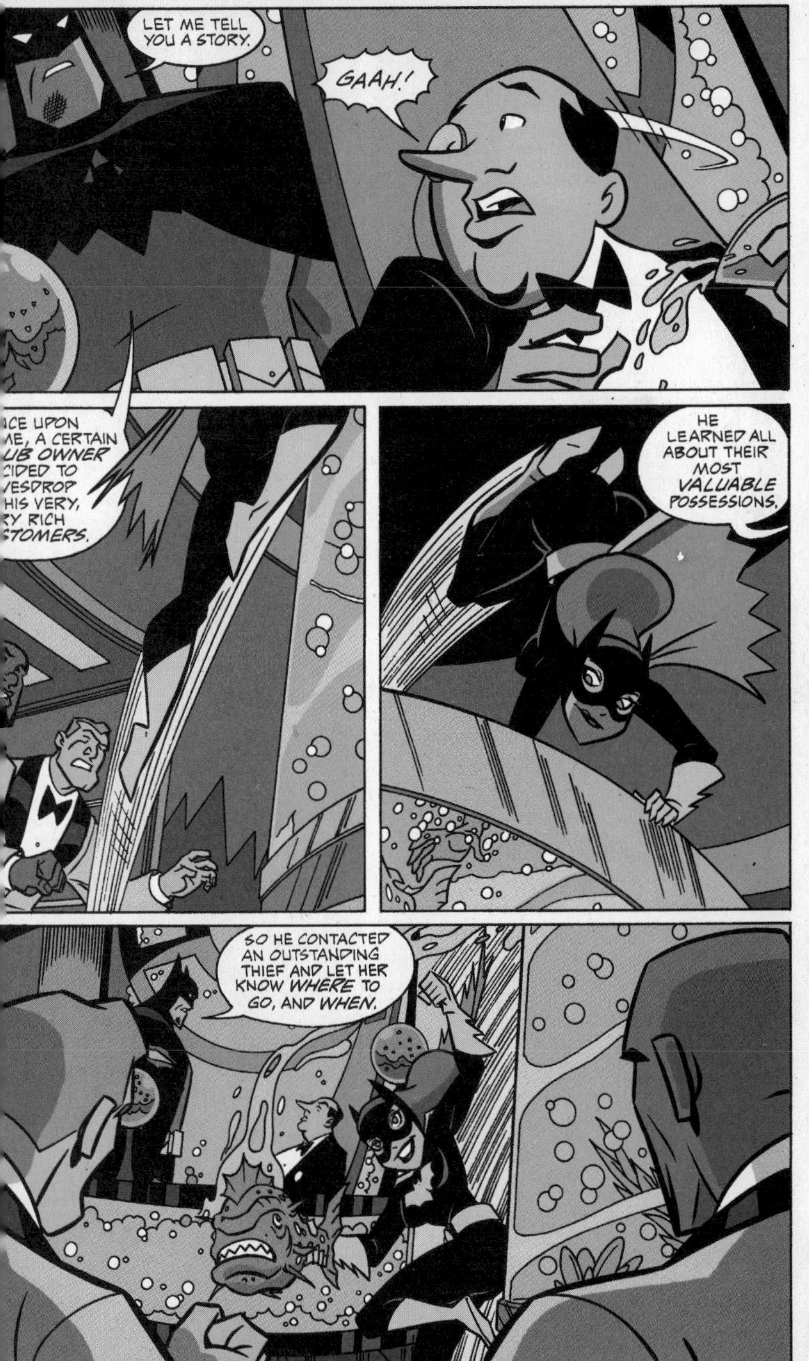
LET ME TELL YOU A STORY.
GAAH!
HE LEARNED ALL ABOUT THEIR MOST VALUABLE POSSESSIONS.
SO HE CONTACTED AN OUTSTANDING THIEF AND LET HER KNOW WHERE TO GO, AND WHEN.

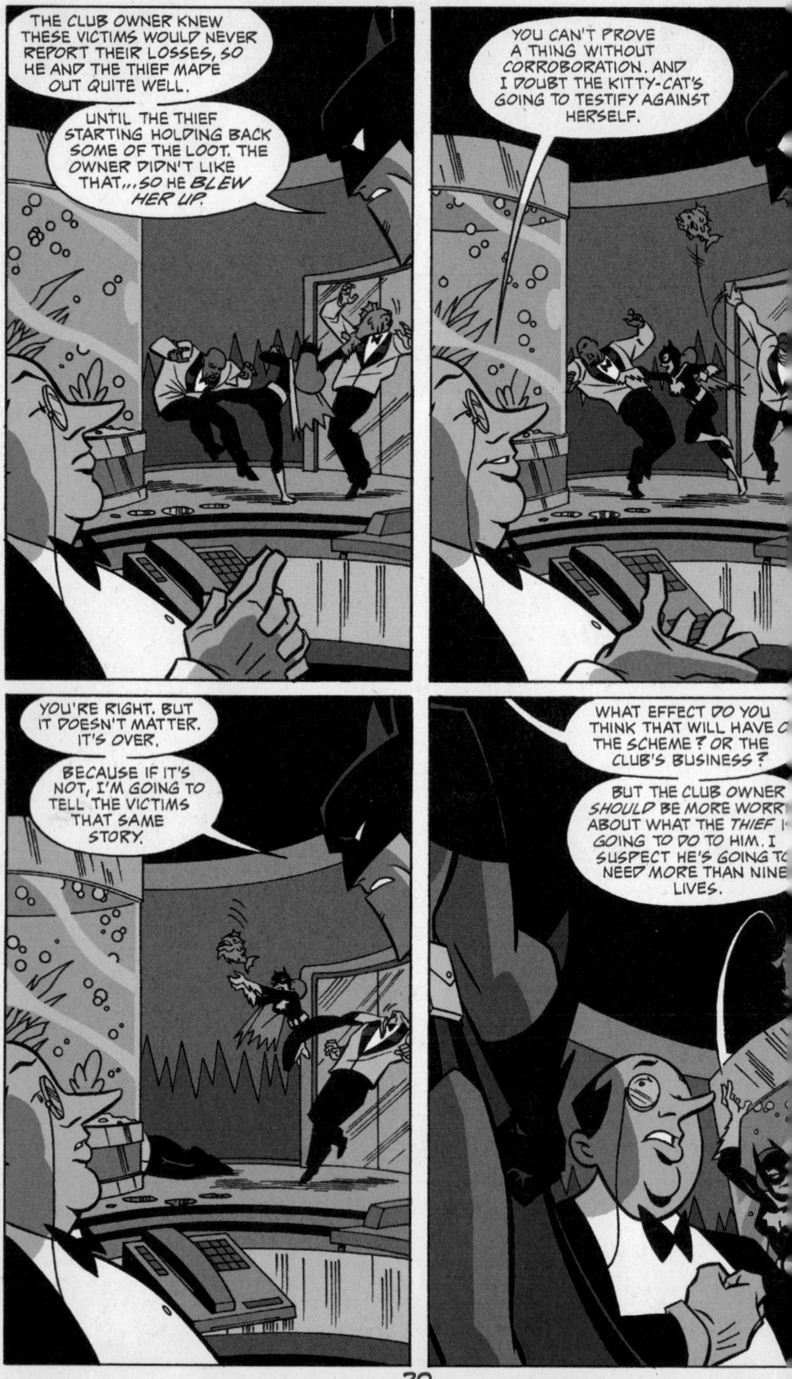
THE CLUB OWNER KNEW THESE VICTIMS WOULD NEVER REPORT THEIR LOSSES, SO HE AND THE THIEF MADE OUT QUITE WELL.
UNTIL THE THIEF STARTING HOLDING BACK SOME OF THE LOOT. THE OWNER DIDN'T LIKE THAT...SO HE *BLEW HER UP.*
YOU CAN'T PROVE A THING WITHOUT CORROBORATION. AND I DOUBT THE KITTY-CAT'S GOING TO TESTIFY AGAINST HERSELF.
YOU'RE RIGHT. BUT IT DOESN'T MATTER. IT'S OVER.
BECAUSE IF IT'S NOT, I'M GOING TO TELL THE VICTIMS THAT SAME STORY.
WHAT EFFECT DO YOU THINK THAT WILL HAVE
THE SCHEME? OR THE CLUB'S BUSINESS?
BUT THE CLUB OWNER *SHOULD* BE MORE
ABOUT WHAT THE *THIEF*
GOING TO DO TO HIM. I SUSPECT HE'S GOING
NEED MORE THAN NINE
LIVES.

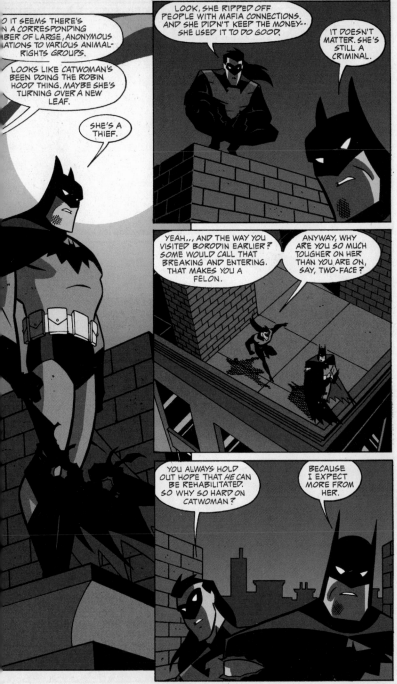

SO IT SEEMS THERE'S
BEEN A CORRESPONDING
NUMBER OF LARGE, ANONYMOUS
DONATIONS TO VARIOUS ANIMAL-
RIGHTS GROUPS.

LOOKS LIKE CATWOMAN'S
BEEN DOING THE ROBIN
HOOD THING. MAYBE SHE'S
TURNING OVER A NEW
LEAF.

SHE'S A
THIEF.

LOOK, SHE RIPPED OFF
PEOPLE WITH MAFIA CONNECTIONS.
AND SHE DIDN'T KEEP THE MONEY--
SHE USED IT TO DO GOOD.

IT DOESN'T
MATTER. SHE'S
STILL A
CRIMINAL.

YEAH... AND THE WAY YOU
VISITED BORODIN EARLIER?
SOME WOULD CALL THAT
BREAKING AND ENTERING.
THAT MAKES YOU A
FELON.

ANYWAY, WHY
ARE YOU SO MUCH
TOUGHER ON HER
THAN YOU ARE ON,
SAY, TWO-FACE?

YOU ALWAYS HOLD
OUT HOPE THAT HE CAN
BE REHABILITATED.
SO WHY SO HARD ON
CATWOMAN?

BECAUSE
I EXPECT
MORE FROM
HER.

21

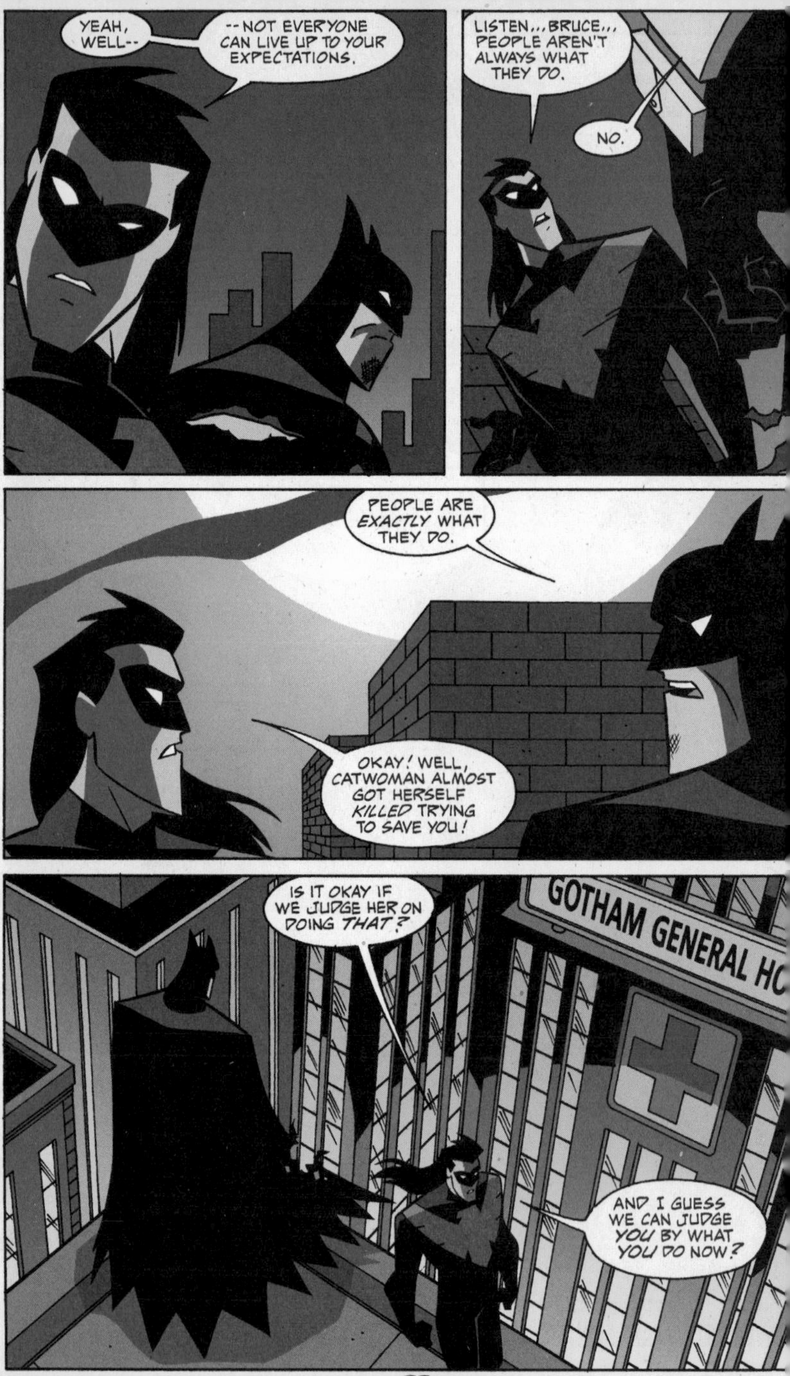
YEAH, WELL--
--NOT EVERYONE CAN LIVE UP TO YOUR EXPECTATIONS.
LISTEN... BRUCE... PEOPLE AREN'T ALWAYS WHAT THEY DO.
NO.
PEOPLE ARE *EXACTLY* WHAT THEY DO.
OKAY! WELL, CATWOMAN ALMOST GOT HERSELF *KILLED* TRYING TO SAVE YOU!
IS IT OKAY IF WE JUDGE HER ON DOING *THAT*?
GOTHAM GENERAL HO
AND I GUESS WE CAN JUDGE *YOU* BY WHAT *YOU* DO NOW?

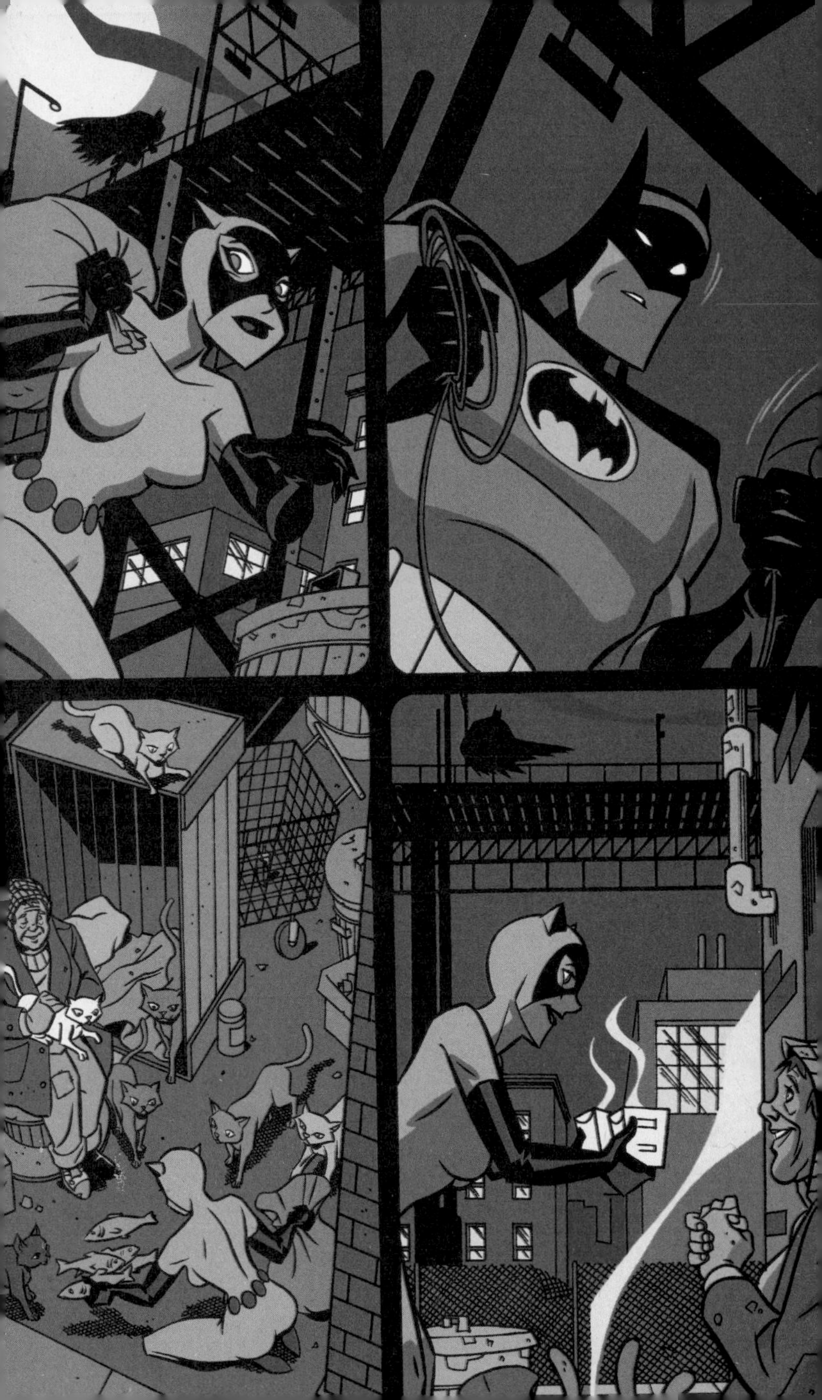

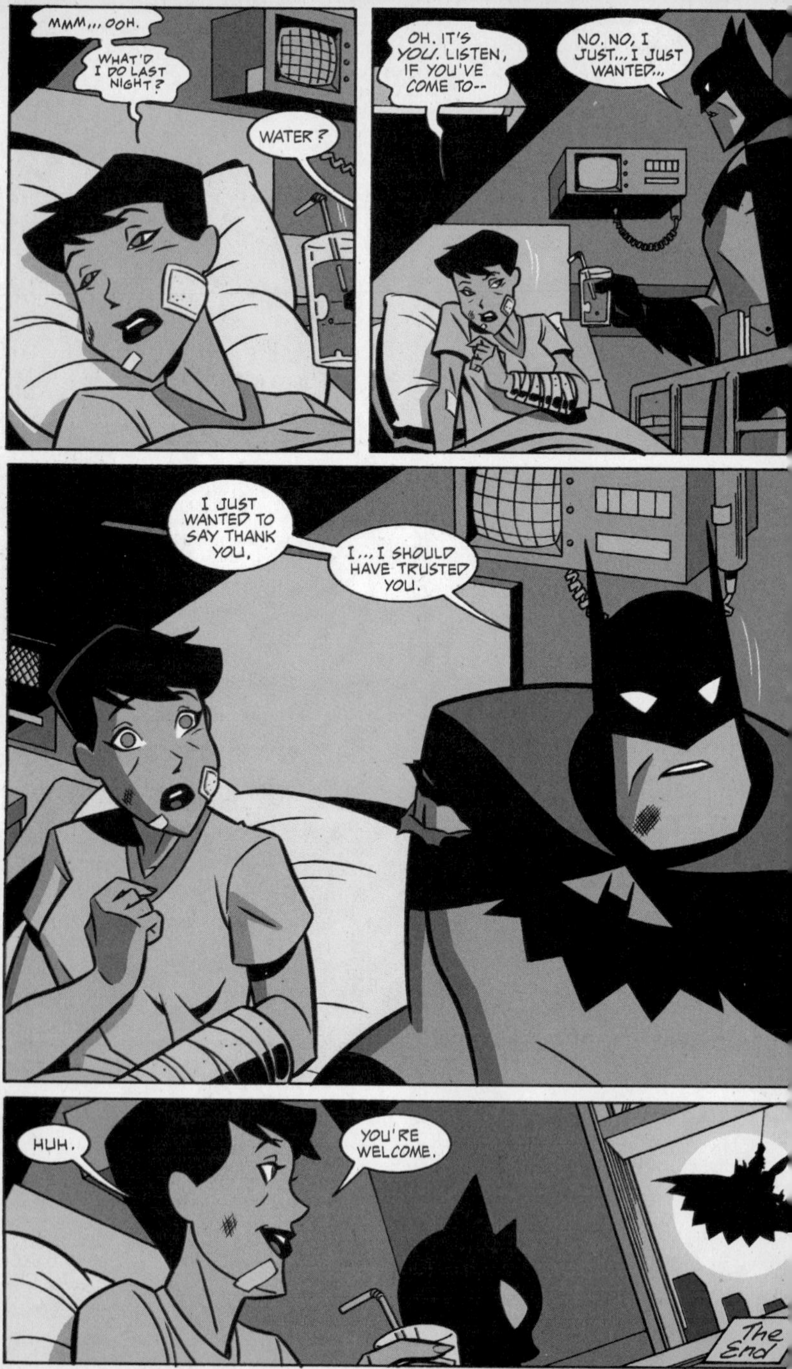
MMM... OOH.
WHAT'D I DO LAST NIGHT?
WATER?
OH. IT'S YOU. LISTEN, IF YOU'VE COME TO--
NO. NO, I JUST... I JUST WANTED...
I JUST WANTED TO SAY THANK YOU.
I... I SHOULD HAVE TRUSTED YOU.
HUH.
YOU'RE WELCOME.
The End

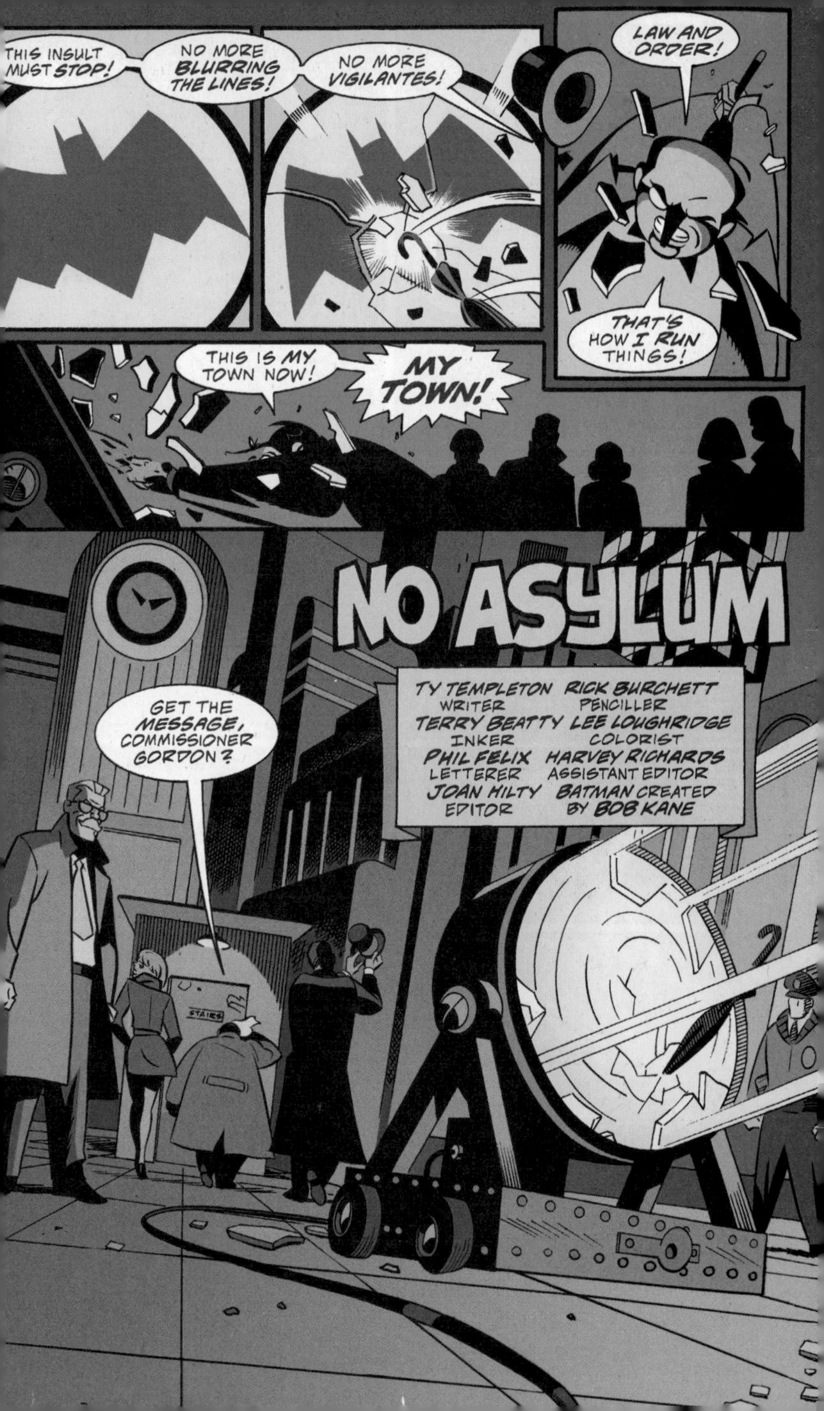
THIS INSULT MUST STOP!
NO MORE BLURRING THE LINES!
NO MORE VIGILANTES!
LAW AND ORDER!
THAT'S HOW I RUN THINGS!
THIS IS MY TOWN NOW!
MY TOWN!
NO ASYLUM
TY TEMPLETON WRITER
RICK BURCHETT PENCILLER
TERRY BEATTY INKER
LEE LOUGHRIDGE COLORIST
PHIL FELIX LETTERER
HARVEY RICHARDS ASSISTANT EDITOR
JOAN HILTY EDITOR
BATMAN CREATED BY BOB KANE
GET THE MESSAGE, COMMISSIONER GORDON?
STAIRS

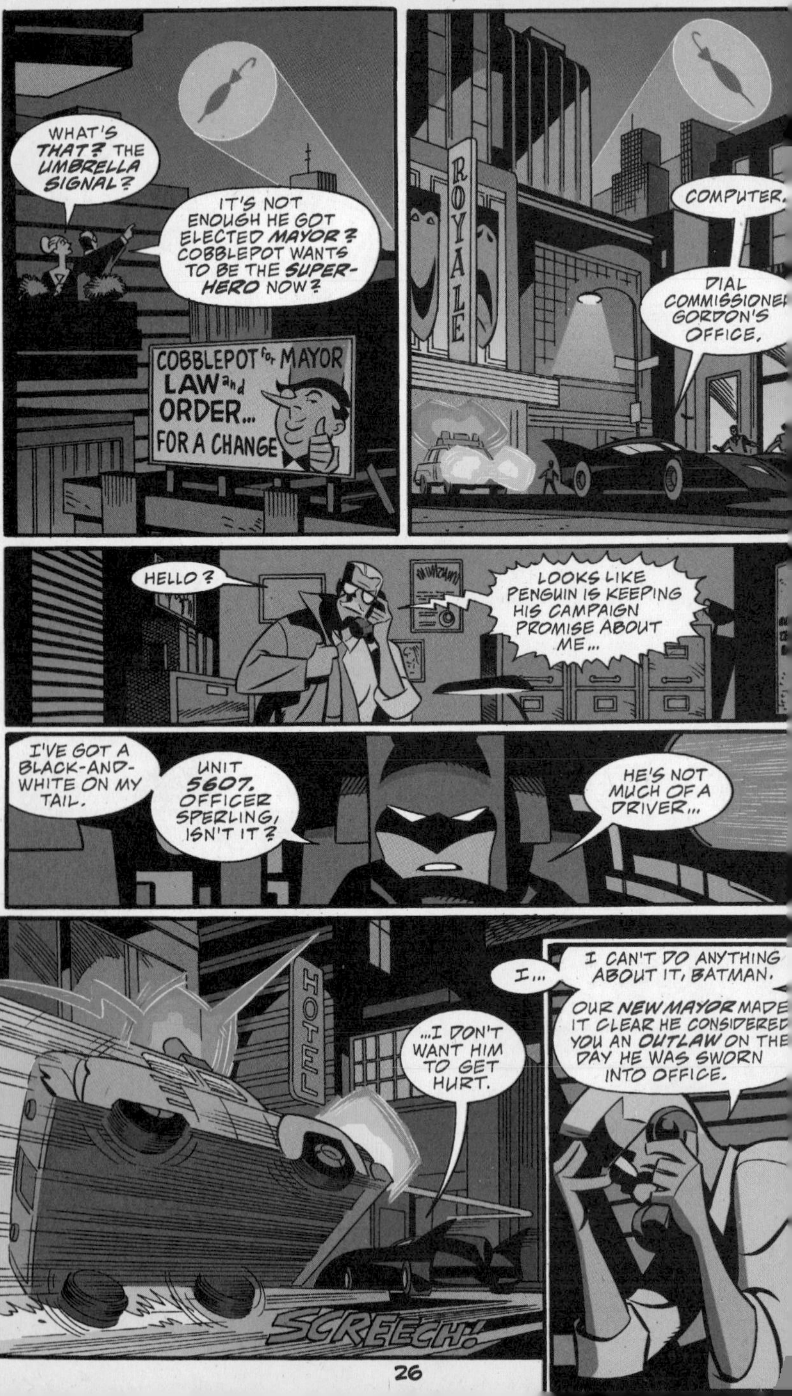

WHAT'S THAT? THE UMBRELLA SIGNAL?
IT'S NOT ENOUGH HE GOT ELECTED MAYOR? COBBLEPOT WANTS TO BE THE SUPER-HERO NOW?
COBBLEPOT for MAYOR LAW and ORDER... FOR A CHANGE
ROYALE
COMPUTER.
DIAL COMMISSIONER GORDON'S OFFICE.
HELLO?
LOOKS LIKE PENGUIN IS KEEPING HIS CAMPAIGN PROMISE ABOUT ME...
I'VE GOT A BLACK-AND-WHITE ON MY TAIL.
UNIT 5607. OFFICER SPERLING, ISN'T IT?
HE'S NOT MUCH OF A DRIVER...
HOTEL
...I DON'T WANT HIM TO GET HURT.
SCREECH!
I...
I CAN'T DO ANYTHING ABOUT IT, BATMAN.
OUR NEW MAYOR MADE IT CLEAR HE CONSIDERED YOU AN OUTLAW ON THE DAY HE WAS SWORN INTO OFFICE.

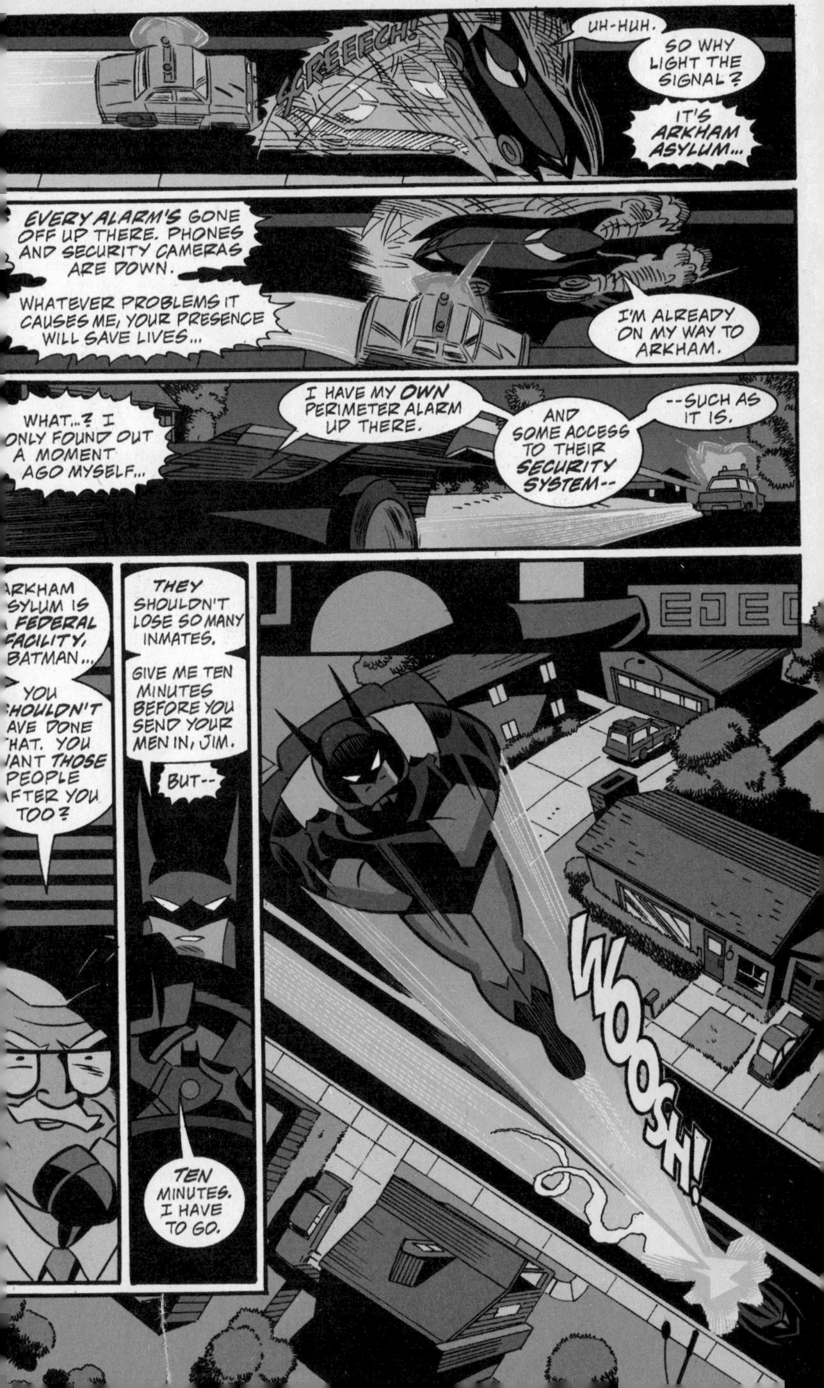
SCREEECH!
UH-HUH.
SO WHY LIGHT THE SIGNAL?
IT'S ARKHAM ASYLUM...
EVERY ALARM'S GONE OFF UP THERE. PHONES AND SECURITY CAMERAS ARE DOWN.
WHATEVER PROBLEMS IT CAUSES ME, YOUR PRESENCE WILL SAVE LIVES...
I'M ALREADY ON MY WAY TO ARKHAM.
WHAT...? I ONLY FOUND OUT A MOMENT AGO MYSELF...
I HAVE MY OWN PERIMETER ALARM UP THERE.
AND SOME ACCESS TO THEIR SECURITY SYSTEM--
--SUCH AS IT IS.
RKHAM SYLUM IS FEDERAL FACILITY, BATMAN...
YOU HOULDN'T AVE DONE HAT. YOU ANT THOSE PEOPLE FTER YOU TOO?
THEY SHOULDN'T LOSE SO MANY INMATES.
GIVE ME TEN MINUTES BEFORE YOU SEND YOUR MEN IN, JIM.
BUT--
TEN MINUTES. I HAVE TO GO.
WOOSH!

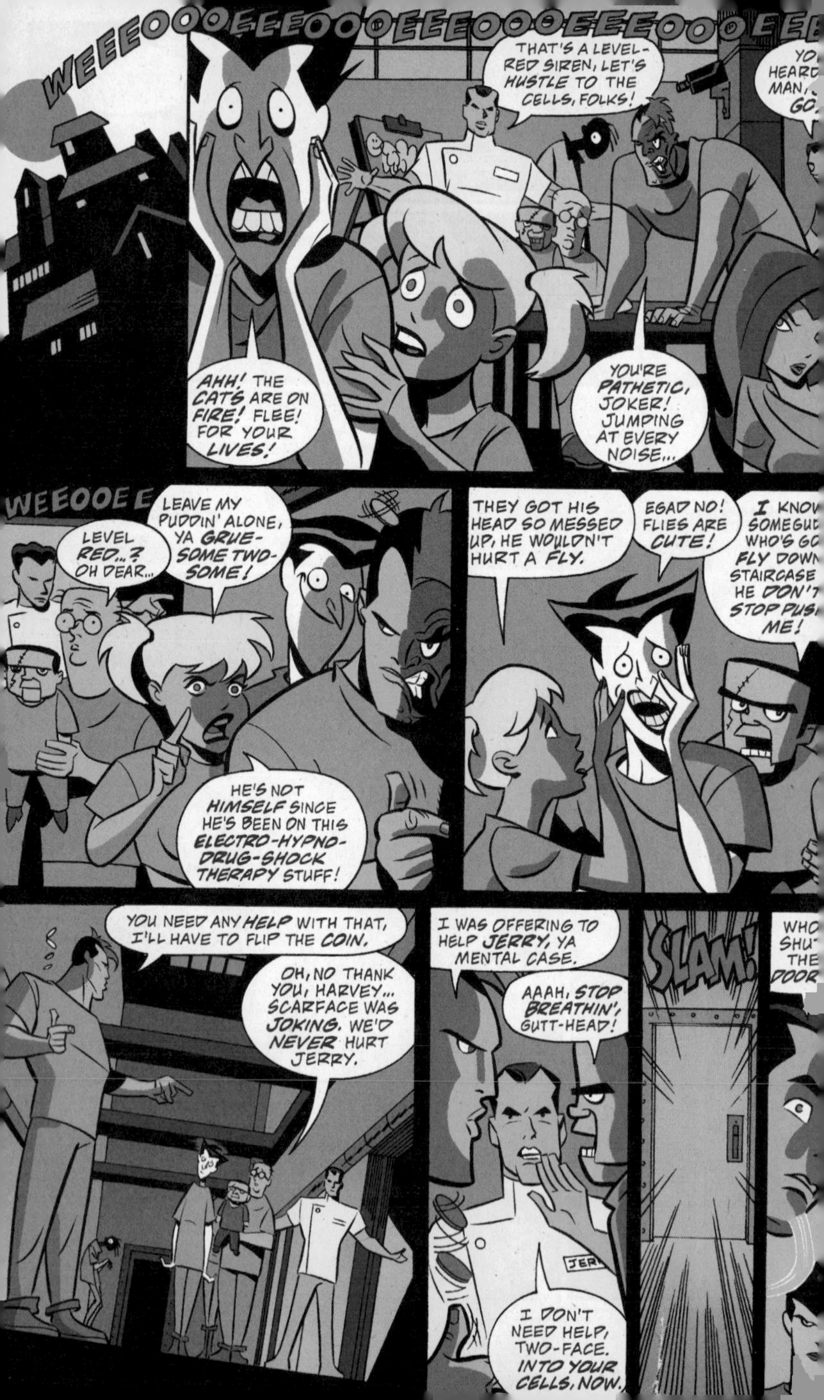
WEEEOOOEEEOOOEEEOOOEEEOOOEEE
THAT'S A LEVEL-RED SIREN, LET'S HUSTLE TO THE CELLS, FOLKS!
AHH! THE CATS ARE ON FIRE! FLEE! FOR YOUR LIVES!
YOU'RE PATHETIC, JOKER! JUMPING AT EVERY NOISE...
WEEOOEE
LEVEL RED...? OH DEAR...
LEAVE MY PUDDIN' ALONE, YA GRUESOME TWOSOME!
HE'S NOT HIMSELF SINCE HE'S BEEN ON THIS ELECTRO-HYPNO-DRUG-SHOCK THERAPY STUFF!
THEY GOT HIS HEAD SO MESSED UP, HE WOULDN'T HURT A FLY.
EGAD NO! FLIES ARE CUTE!
YOU NEED ANY HELP WITH THAT, I'LL HAVE TO FLIP THE COIN.
OH, NO THANK YOU, HARVEY... SCARFACE WAS JOKING. WE'D NEVER HURT JERRY.
I WAS OFFERING TO HELP JERRY, YA MENTAL CASE.
AAAH, STOP BREATHIN', GUTT-HEAD!
I DON'T NEED HELP, TWO-FACE. INTO YOUR CELLS, NOW.
SLAM!

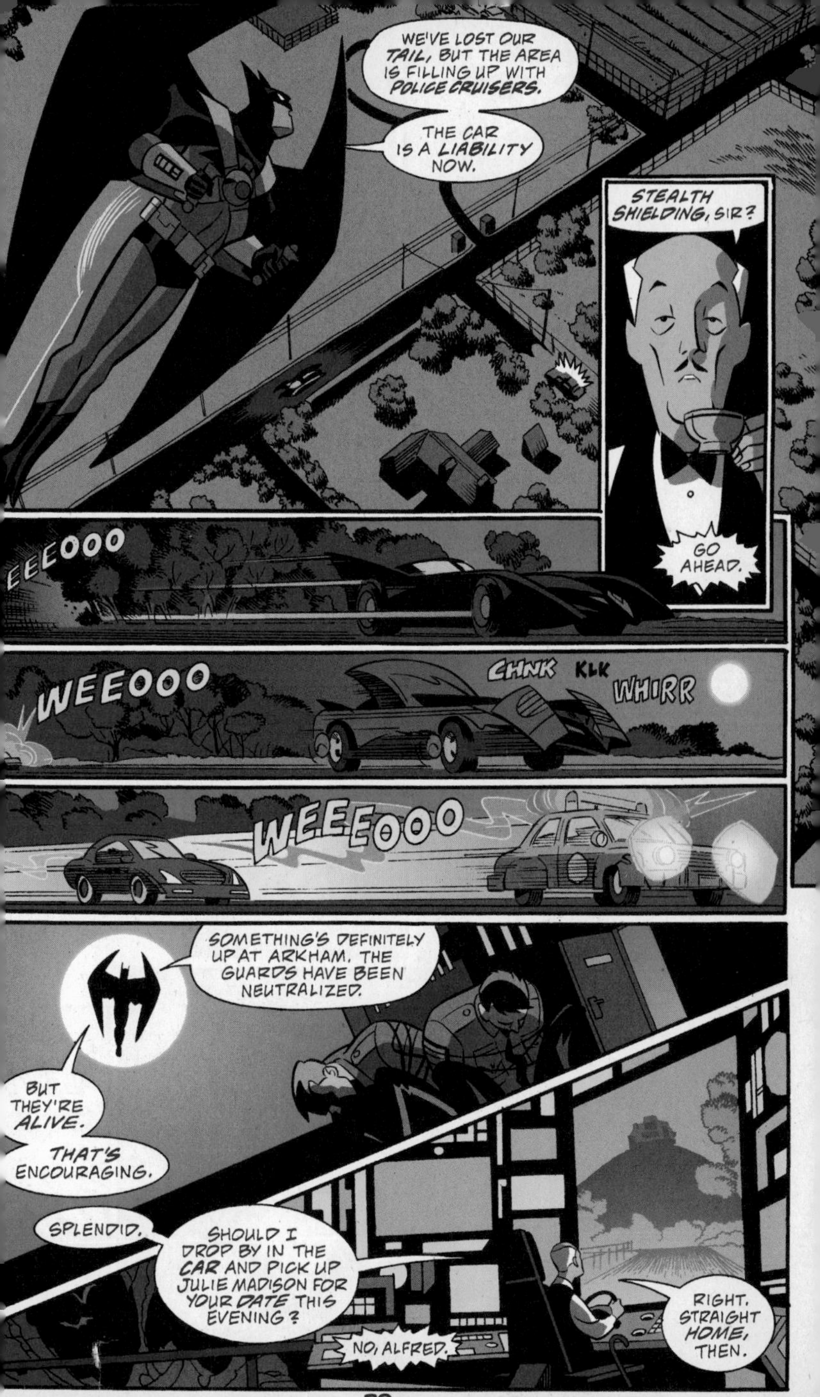
WE'VE LOST OUR TAIL, BUT THE AREA IS FILLING UP WITH POLICE CRUISERS.
THE CAR IS A LIABILITY NOW.
STEALTH SHIELDING, SIR?
GO AHEAD.
EEEOOO
WEEOOO
CHNK KLK WHIRR
WEEEOOO
SOMETHING'S DEFINITELY UP AT ARKHAM. THE GUARDS HAVE BEEN NEUTRALIZED.
BUT THEY'RE ALIVE.
THAT'S ENCOURAGING.
SPLENDID.
SHOULD I DROP BY IN THE CAR AND PICK UP JULIE MADISON FOR YOUR DATE THIS EVENING?
NO, ALFRED.
RIGHT. STRAIGHT HOME, THEN.

I WANT OUT! I WANT OUT!

THIS IS GOOD!

I NEVER SEE YOU AFRAID LIKE THIS, JERRY! THIS IS SO GOOD!

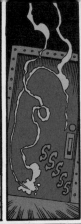

SSSSS

BEHIND YOU THOSE ARE M... PEOPLE COMIN... IN! YOU BETTE... STEP BACK

THOOM

OOH, LOOKS LIKE BAD GUYS. BAD LUCK FOR THE STAFF!

ANYONE ORDER A BREAK-OUT?

SCARE-CROW?

NOT ONE OF MINE...

I DON'T KNOW THESE GUYS EITHER--

--BUT GIVE ME A MINUTE AND THAT'LL CHANGE.

POISON IVY--

--YOU ARE FIRST!

IIIVY

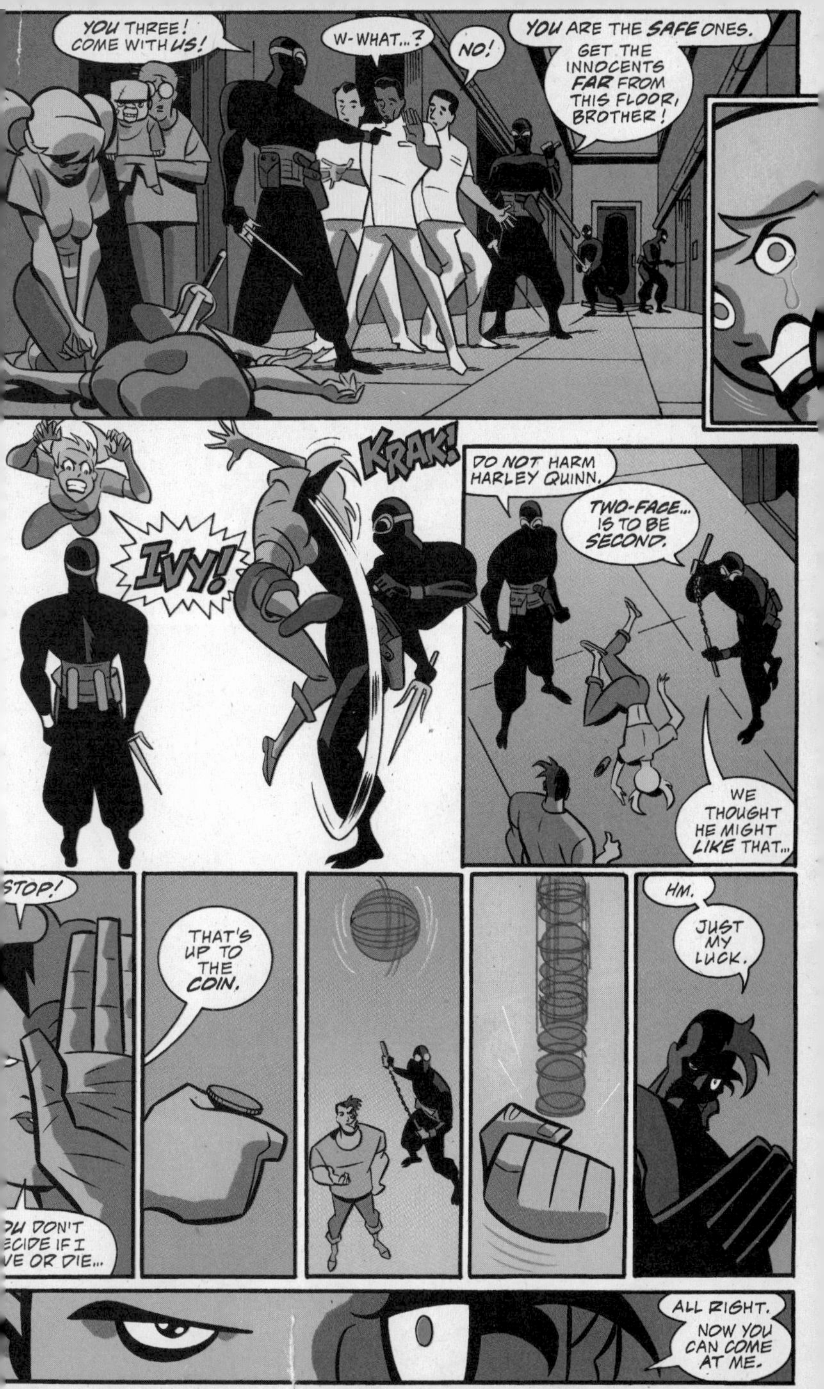
YOU THREE! COME WITH US!
W-WHAT...?
NO!
YOU ARE THE SAFE ONES.
GET THE INNOCENTS FAR FROM THIS FLOOR, BROTHER!
KRAK!
IVY!
DO NOT HARM HARLEY QUINN.
TWO-FACE... IS TO BE SECOND.
WE THOUGHT HE MIGHT LIKE THAT...
STOP!
YOU DON'T DECIDE IF I LIVE OR DIE...
THAT'S UP TO THE COIN.
HM.
JUST MY LUCK.
ALL RIGHT.
NOW YOU CAN COME AT ME.

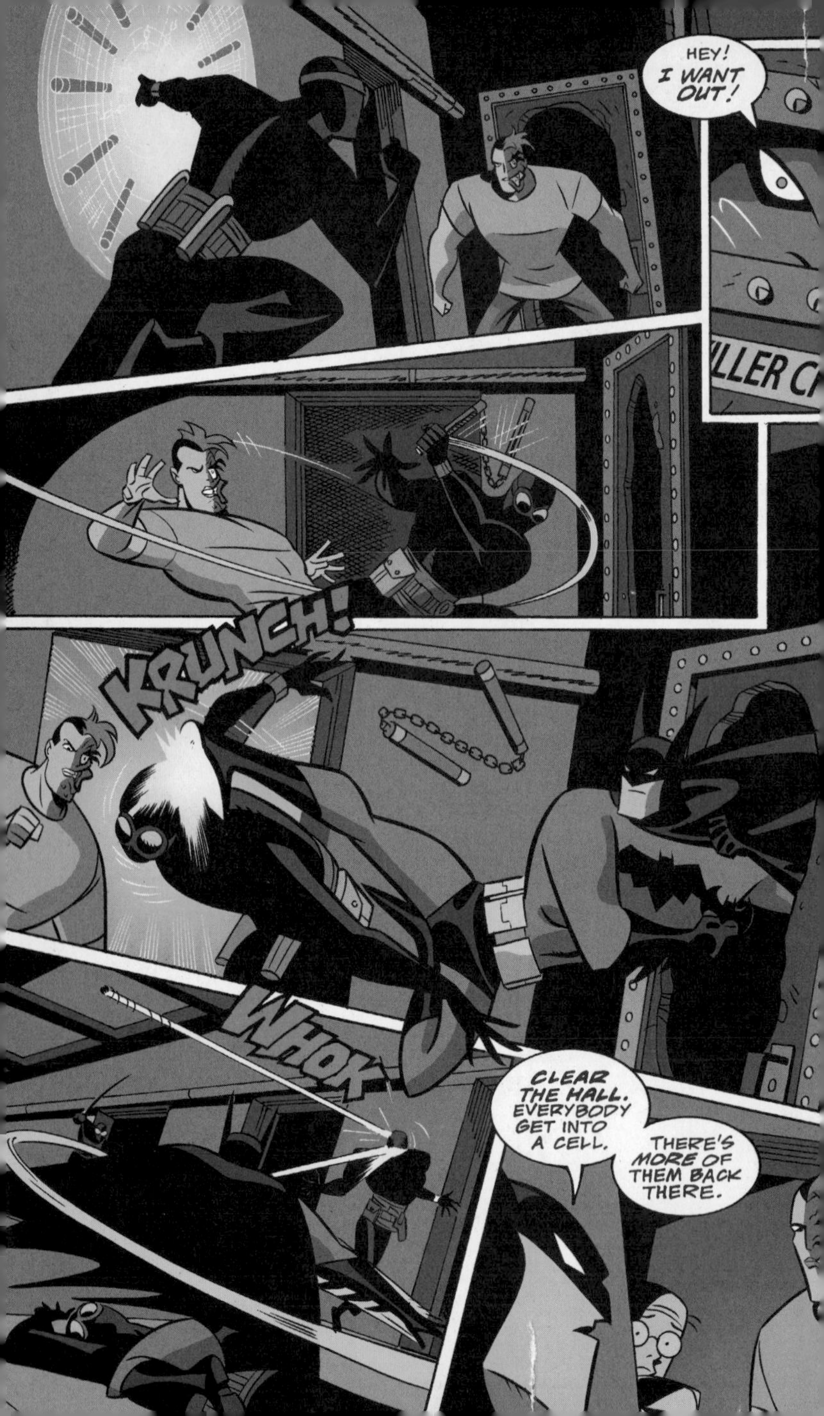
HEY! I WANT OUT!
ILLER CR
KRUNCH!
WHOK
CLEAR THE HALL. EVERYBODY GET INTO A CELL.
THERE'S MORE OF THEM BACK THERE.

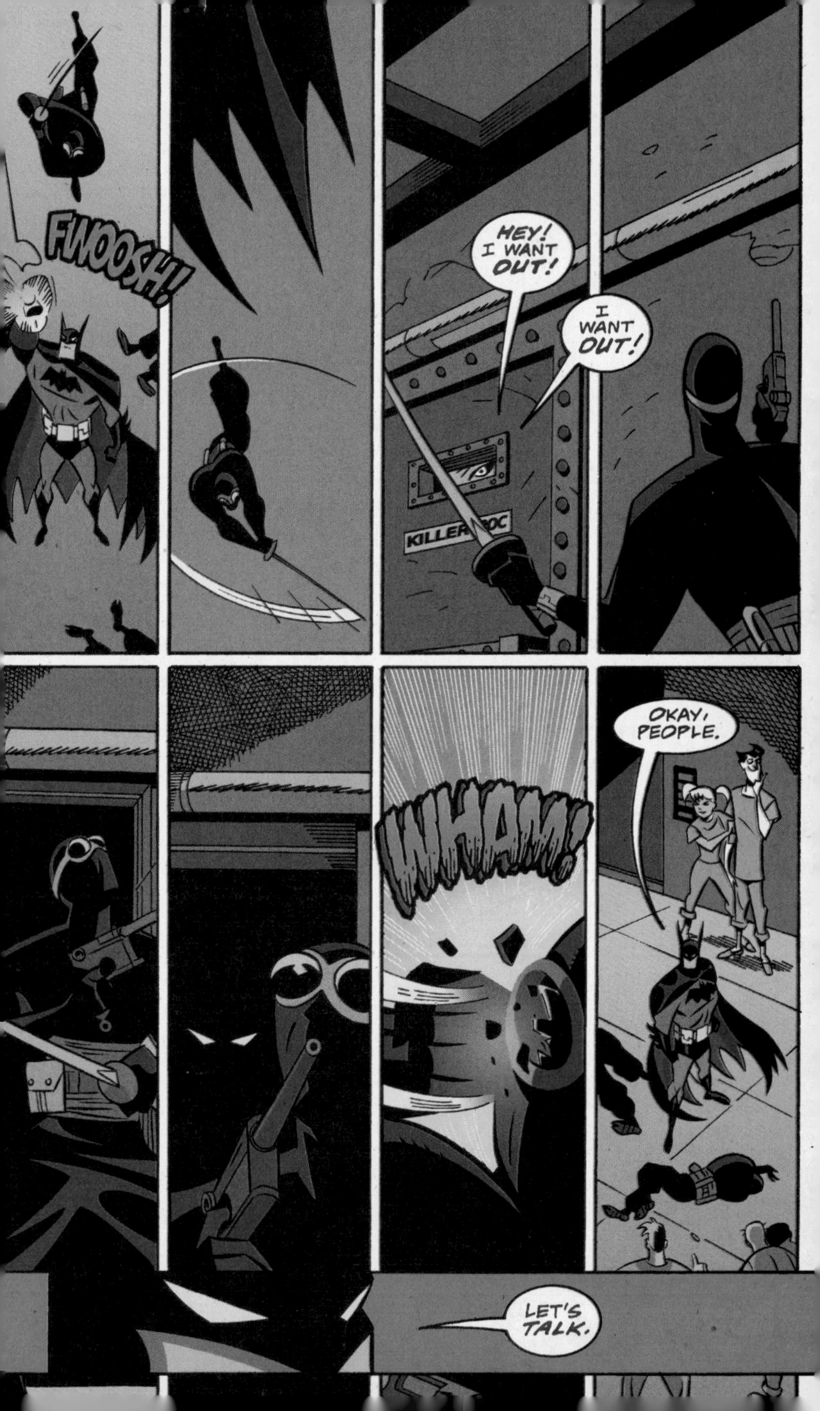
FWOOSH!
HEY! I WANT OUT!
I WANT OUT!
KILLER CROC
WHAM!
OKAY, PEOPLE.
LET'S TALK.

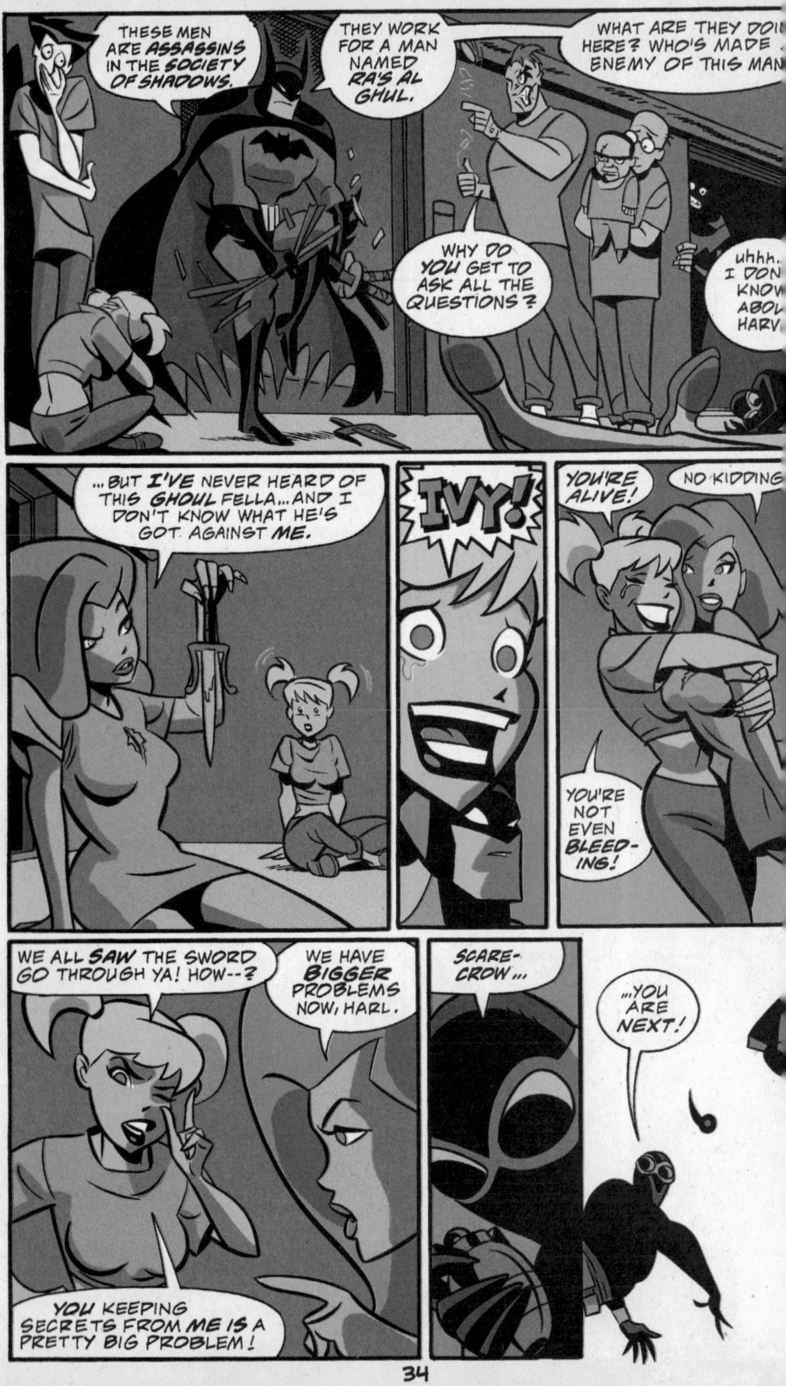

THESE MEN ARE ASSASSINS IN THE SOCIETY OF SHADOWS.
THEY WORK FOR A MAN NAMED RA'S AL GHUL.
WHAT ARE THEY DOI HERE? WHO'S MADE ENEMY OF THIS MAN
WHY DO YOU GET TO ASK ALL THE QUESTIONS?
uhhh. I DON KNOW ABOU HARV
...BUT I'VE NEVER HEARD OF THIS GHOUL FELLA... AND I DON'T KNOW WHAT HE'S GOT AGAINST ME.
IVY!
YOU'RE ALIVE!
NO KIDDING
YOU'RE NOT EVEN BLEEDING!
WE ALL SAW THE SWORD GO THROUGH YA! HOW--?
WE HAVE BIGGER PROBLEMS NOW, HARL.
YOU KEEPING SECRETS FROM ME IS A PRETTY BIG PROBLEM!
SCARECROW...
...YOU ARE NEXT!

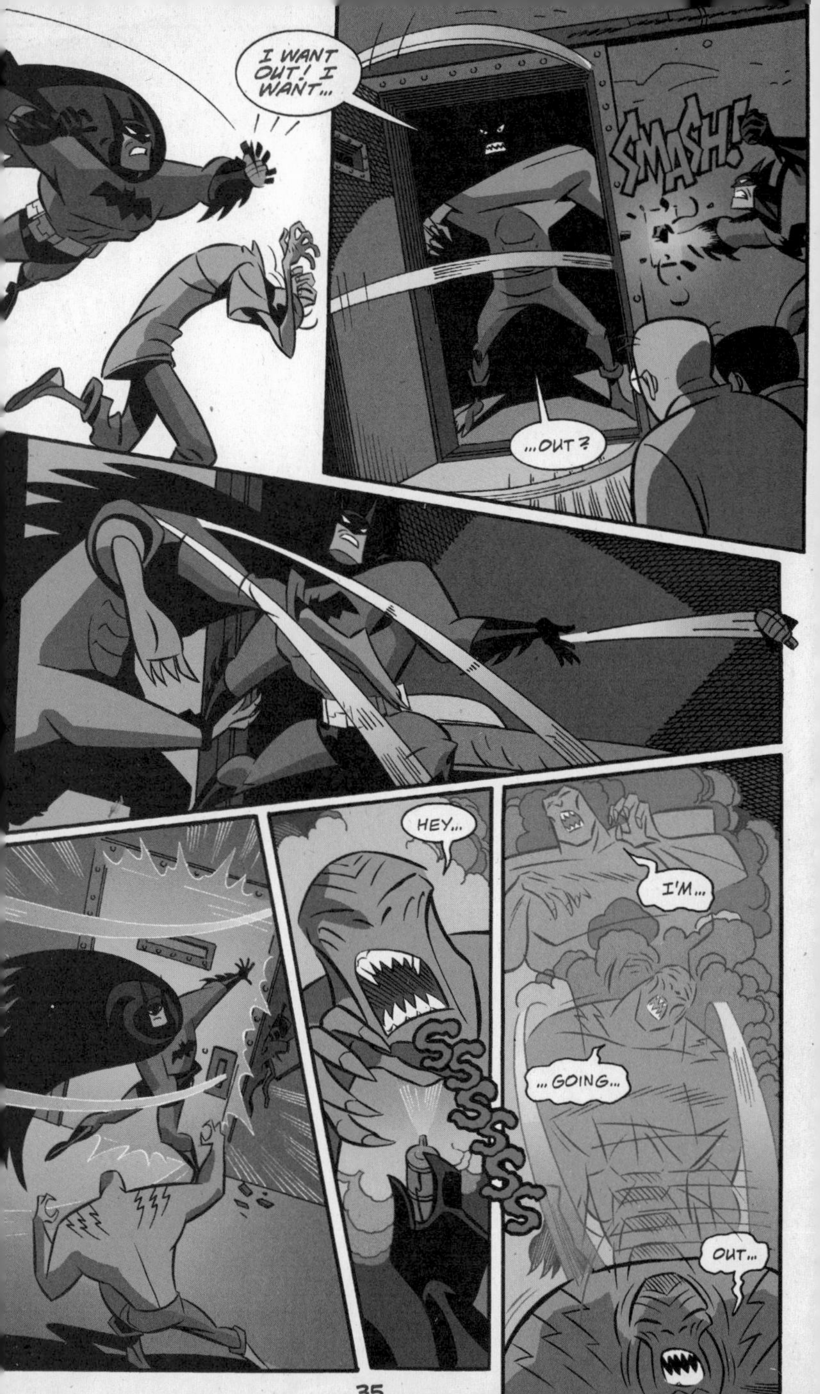
I WANT OUT! I WANT...
SMASH!
...OUT?
HEY...
SSSSSSS
I'M...
...GOING...
OUT...

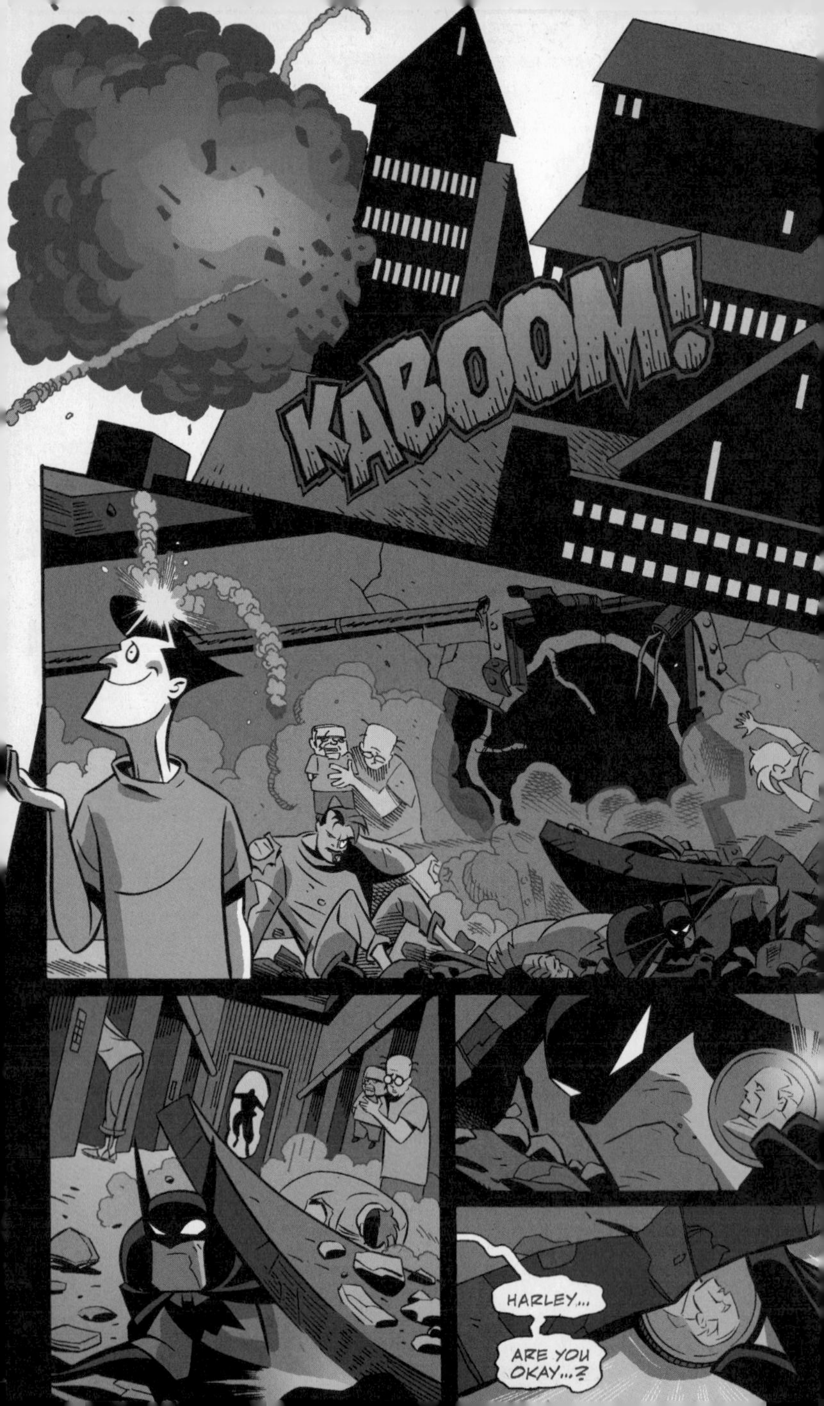

KABOOM!
HARLEY...
ARE YOU OKAY...?

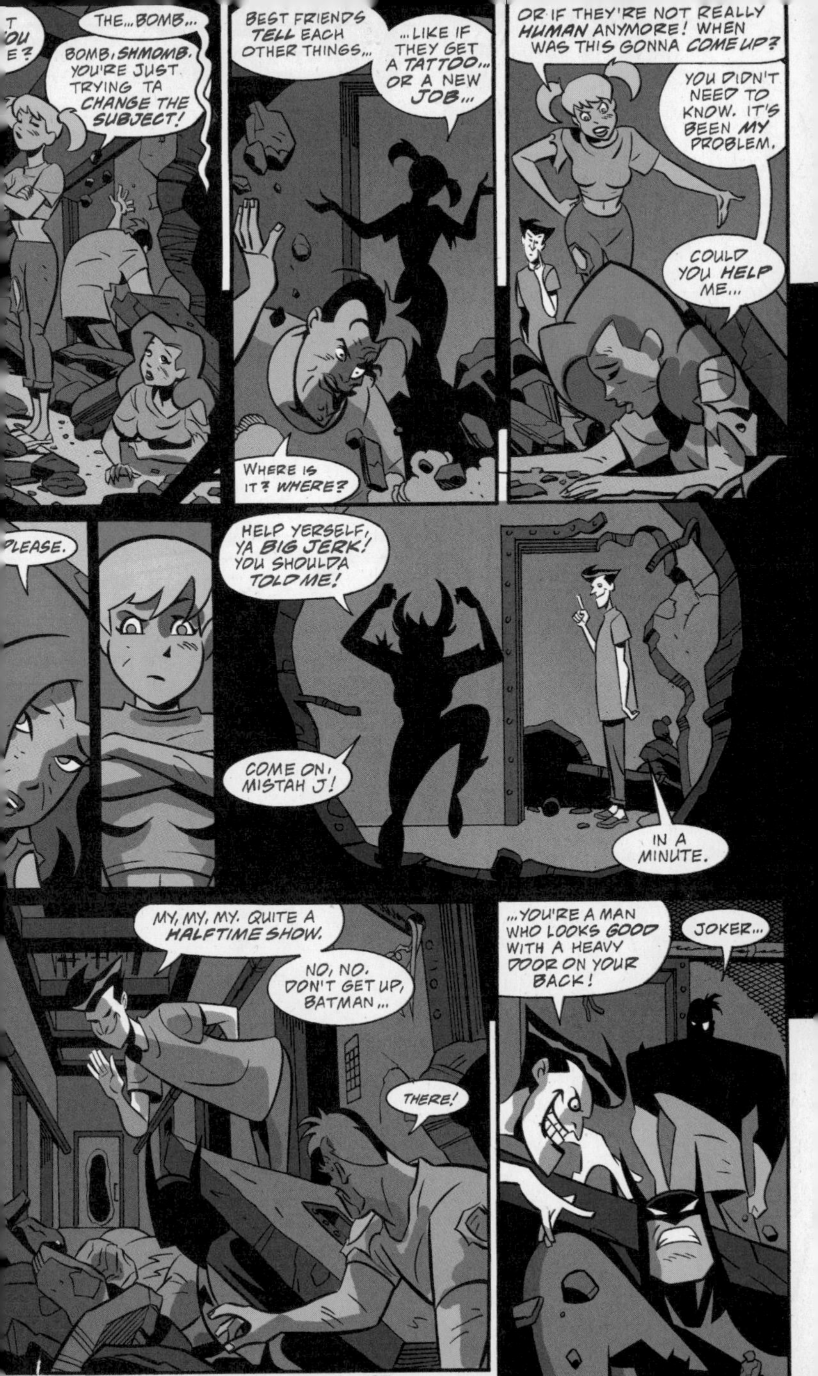

THE...BOMB...
BOMB, SHMOMB. YOU'RE JUST TRYING TA CHANGE THE SUBJECT!
BEST FRIENDS TELL EACH OTHER THINGS...
...LIKE IF THEY GET A TATTOO... OR A NEW JOB...
WHERE IS IT? WHERE?
OR IF THEY'RE NOT REALLY HUMAN ANYMORE! WHEN WAS THIS GONNA COME UP?
YOU DIDN'T NEED TO KNOW. IT'S BEEN MY PROBLEM.
COULD YOU HELP ME...
HELP YERSELF, YA BIG JERK! YOU SHOULDA TOLD ME!
COME ON, MISTAH J!
IN A MINUTE.
MY, MY, MY. QUITE A HALFTIME SHOW.
NO, NO. DON'T GET UP, BATMAN...
THERE!
...YOU'RE A MAN WHO LOOKS GOOD WITH A HEAVY DOOR ON YOUR BACK!
JOKER...

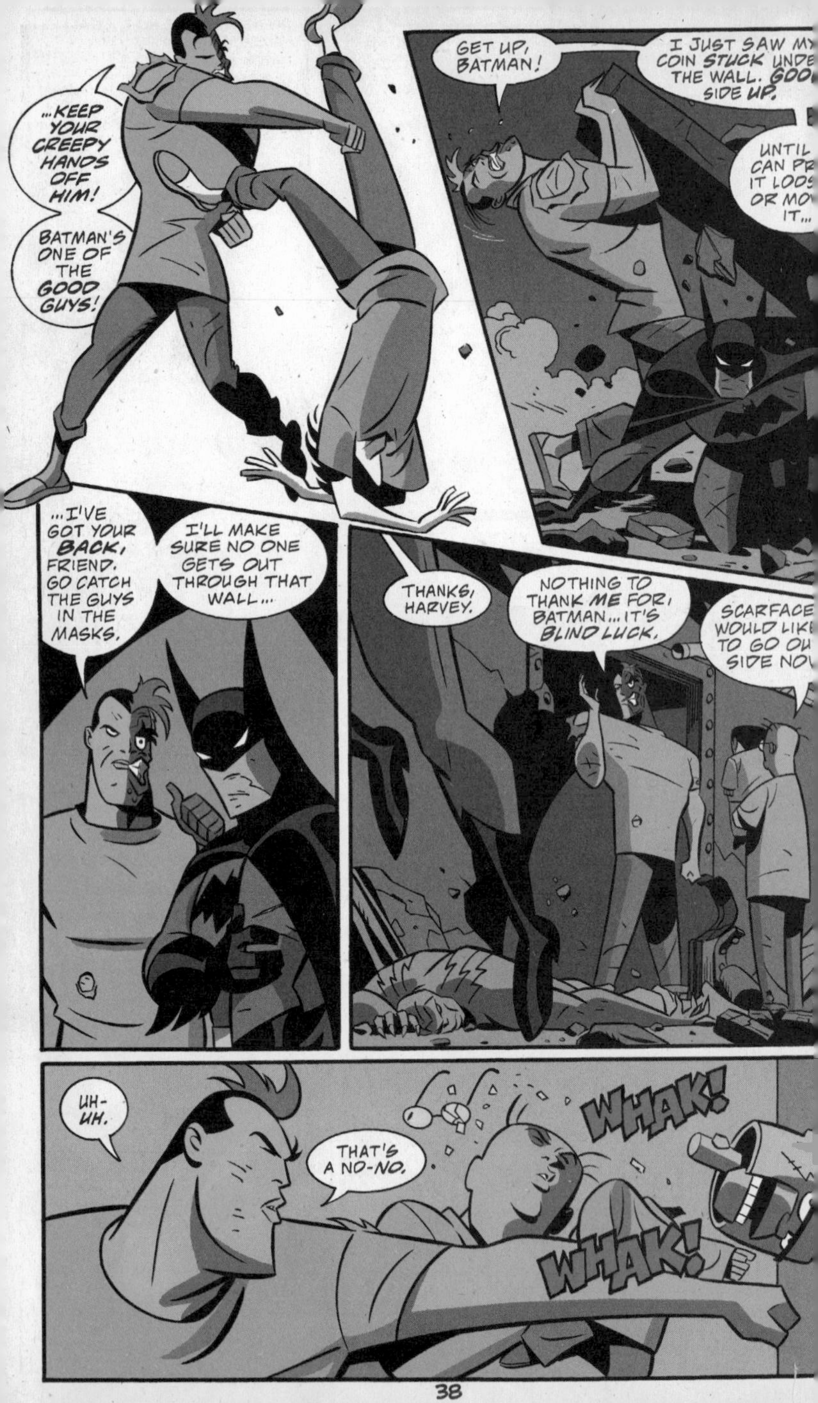

...KEEP YOUR CREEPY HANDS OFF HIM!
BATMAN'S ONE OF THE GOOD GUYS!
GET UP, BATMAN!
I JUST SAW MY COIN STUCK UNDE THE WALL. GOO SIDE UP.
UNTIL CAN PR IT LOOS OR MO IT...
...I'VE GOT YOUR BACK, FRIEND. GO CATCH THE GUYS IN THE MASKS.
I'LL MAKE SURE NO ONE GETS OUT THROUGH THAT WALL...
THANKS, HARVEY.
NOTHING TO THANK ME FOR, BATMAN... IT'S BLIND LUCK.
SCARFACE WOULD LIK TO GO OU SIDE NO
UH-UH.
THAT'S A NO-NO.
WHAK!
WHAK!

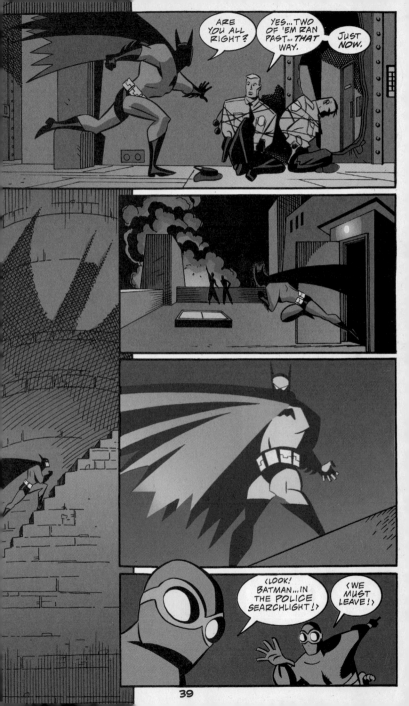

ARE YOU ALL RIGHT?

YES... TWO OF 'EM RAN PAST... *THAT* WAY.

JUST NOW.

⟨LOOK! BATMAN... IN THE POLICE SEARCHLIGHT!⟩

⟨WE MUST LEAVE!⟩

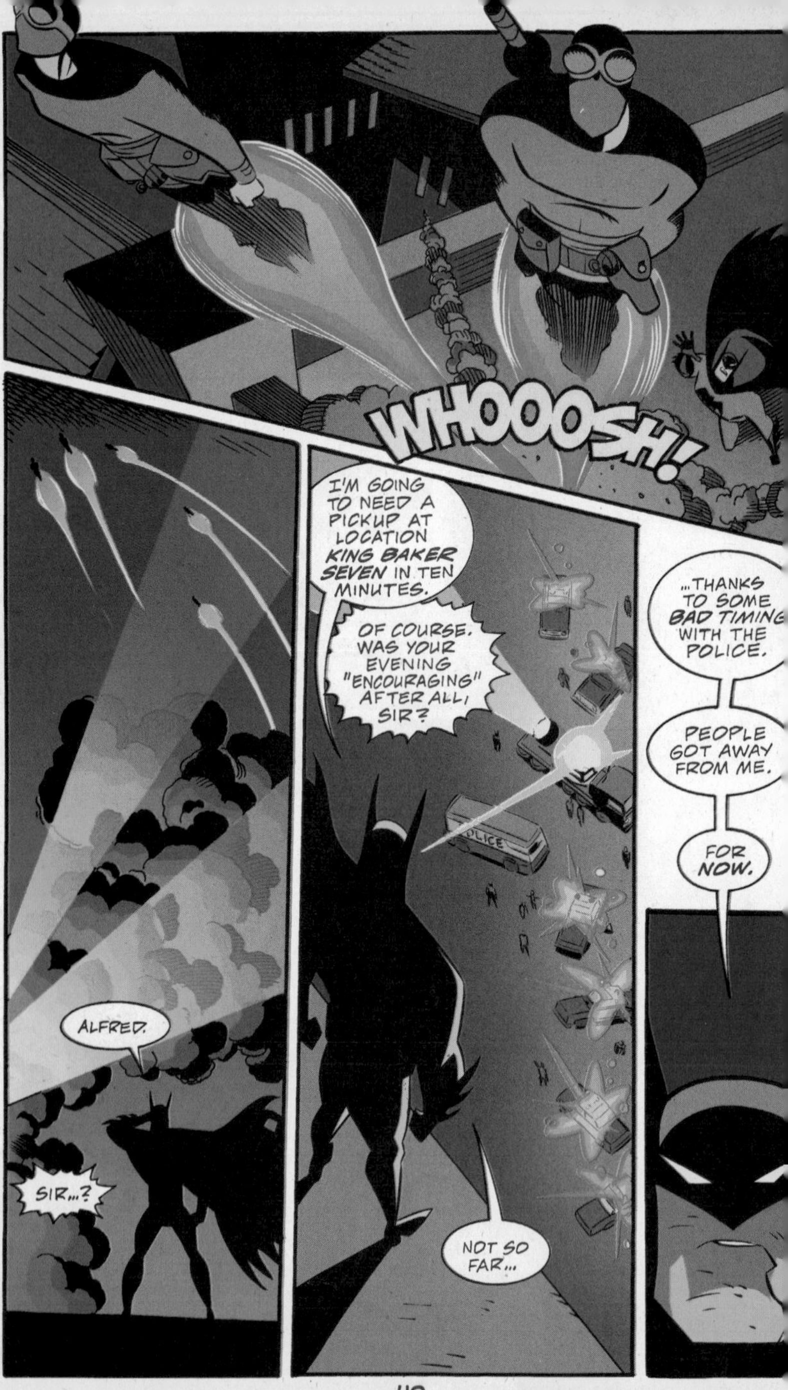
WHOOOSH!
I'M GOING TO NEED A PICKUP AT LOCATION KING BAKER SEVEN IN TEN MINUTES.
OF COURSE. WAS YOUR EVENING "ENCOURAGING" AFTER ALL, SIR?
...THANKS TO SOME BAD TIMING WITH THE POLICE.
PEOPLE GOT AWAY FROM ME.
FOR NOW.
ALFRED.
SIR...?
NOT SO FAR...
POLICE

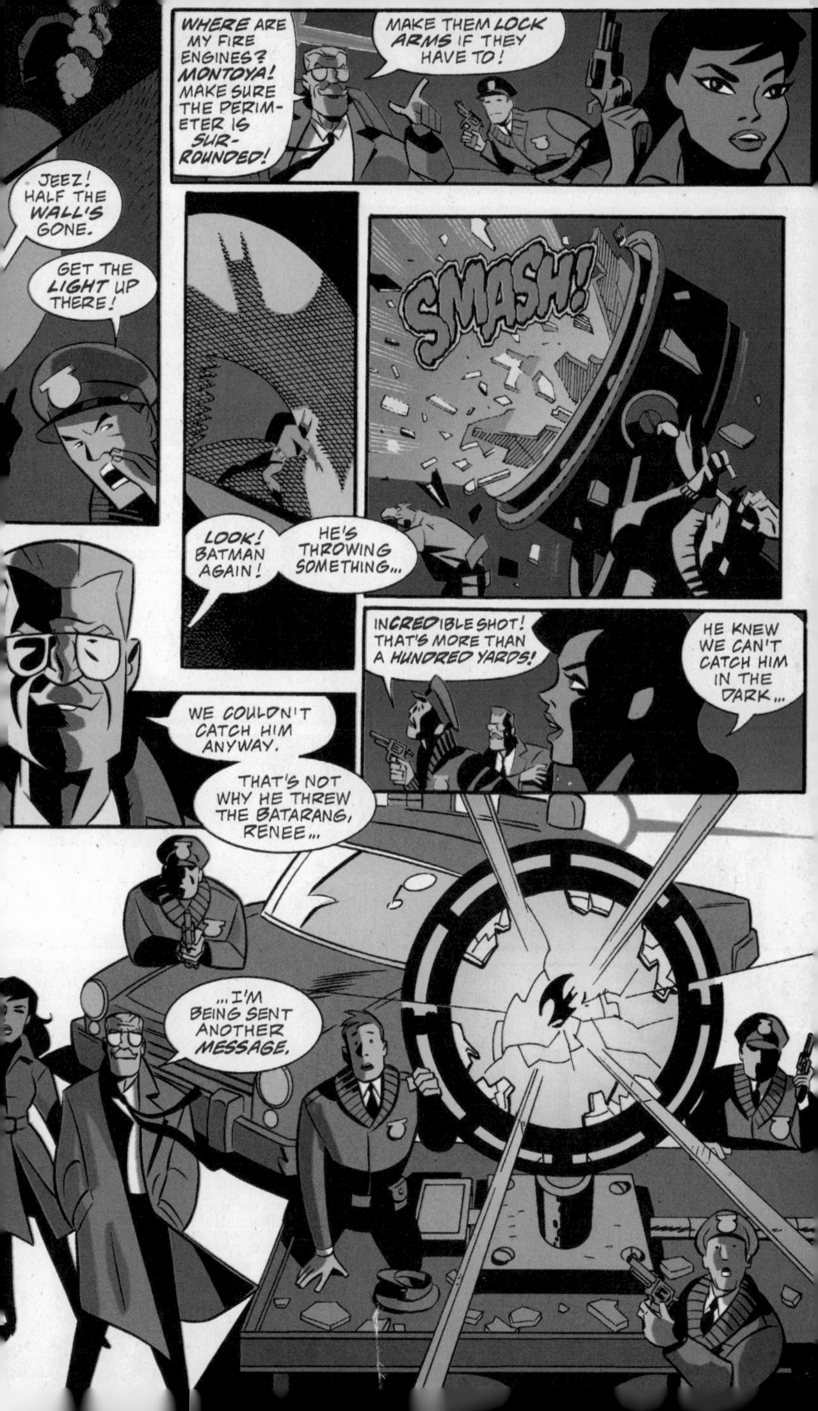
WHERE ARE MY FIRE ENGINES? MONTOYA! MAKE SURE THE PERIMETER IS SURROUNDED!
MAKE THEM LOCK ARMS IF THEY HAVE TO!
JEEZ! HALF THE WALL'S GONE.
GET THE LIGHT UP THERE!
SMASH!
LOOK! BATMAN AGAIN!
HE'S THROWING SOMETHING...
INCREDIBLE SHOT! THAT'S MORE THAN A HUNDRED YARDS!
HE KNEW WE CAN'T CATCH HIM IN THE DARK...
WE COULDN'T CATCH HIM ANYWAY.
THAT'S NOT WHY HE THREW THE BATARANG, RENEE...
...I'M BEING SENT ANOTHER MESSAGE.

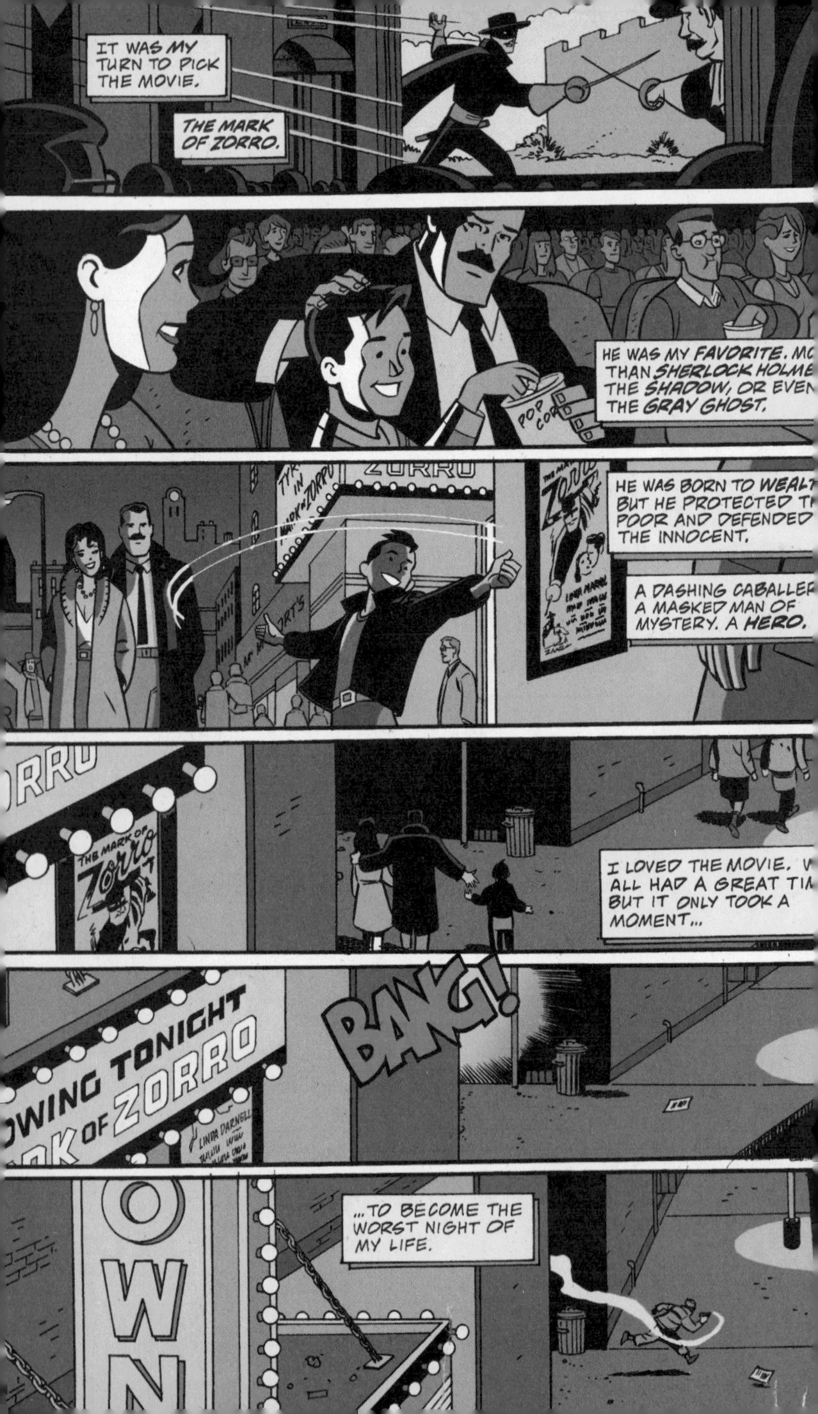
IT WAS MY TURN TO PICK THE MOVIE.
THE MARK OF ZORRO.
HE WAS MY FAVORITE. MO THAN SHERLOCK HOLME THE SHADOW, OR EVEN THE GRAY GHOST.
POP COR
ZORRO
HE WAS BORN TO WEALT BUT HE PROTECTED T POOR AND DEFENDED THE INNOCENT.
A DASHING CABALLER A MASKED MAN OF MYSTERY. A HERO.
RRO
THE MARK OF Zorro
I LOVED THE MOVIE. W ALL HAD A GREAT TIM BUT IT ONLY TOOK A MOMENT...
BANG!
OWING TONIGHT
OK OF ZORRO
LINDA DARNELL
...TO BECOME THE WORST NIGHT OF MY LIFE.

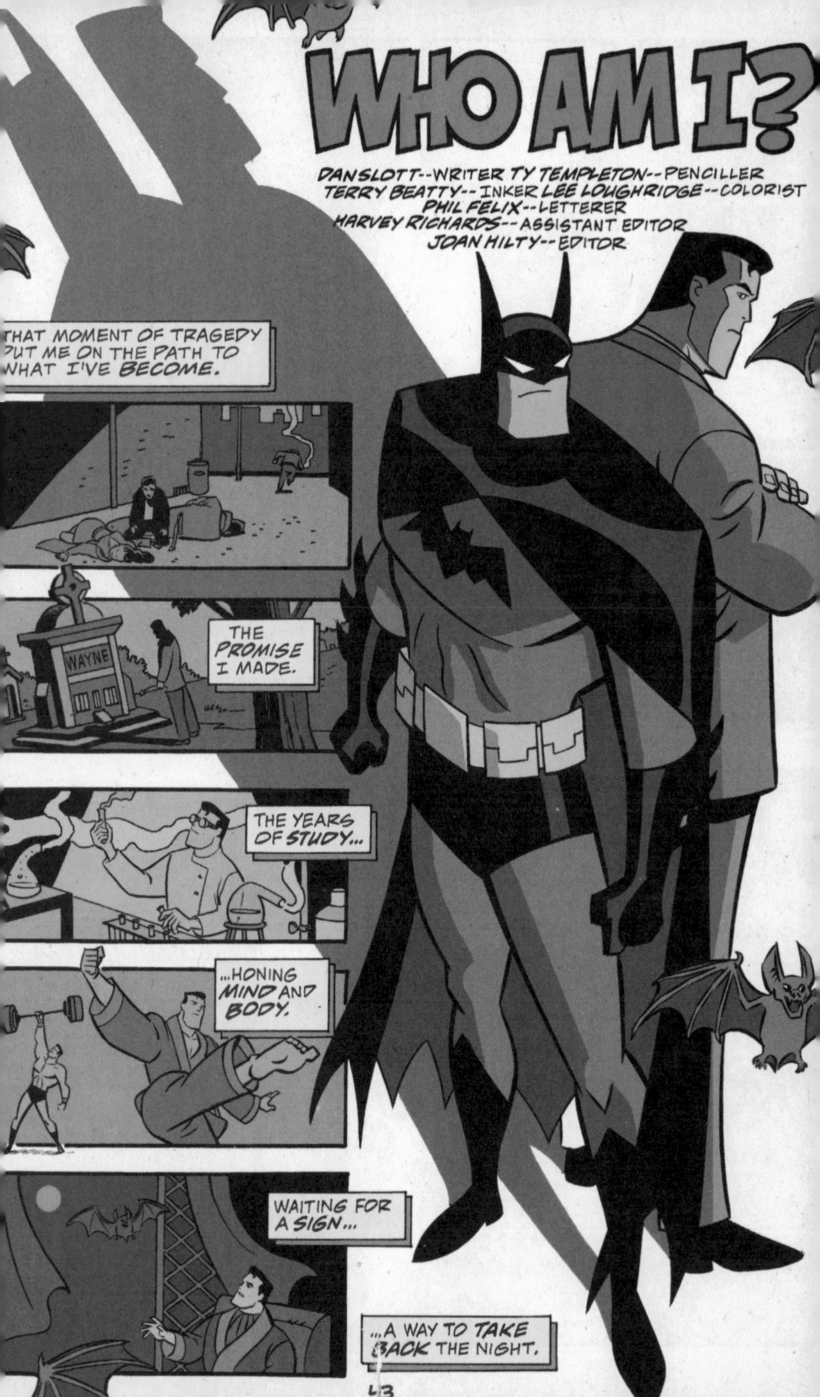
WHO AM I?
DAN SLOTT--WRITER TY TEMPLETON--PENCILLER
TERRY BEATTY--INKER LEE LOUGHRIDGE--COLORIST
PHIL FELIX--LETTERER
HARVEY RICHARDS--ASSISTANT EDITOR
JOAN HILTY--EDITOR
THAT MOMENT OF TRAGEDY PUT ME ON THE PATH TO WHAT I'VE BECOME.
WAYNE
THE PROMISE I MADE.
THE YEARS OF STUDY...
...HONING MIND AND BODY.
WAITING FOR A SIGN...
...A WAY TO TAKE BACK THE NIGHT.

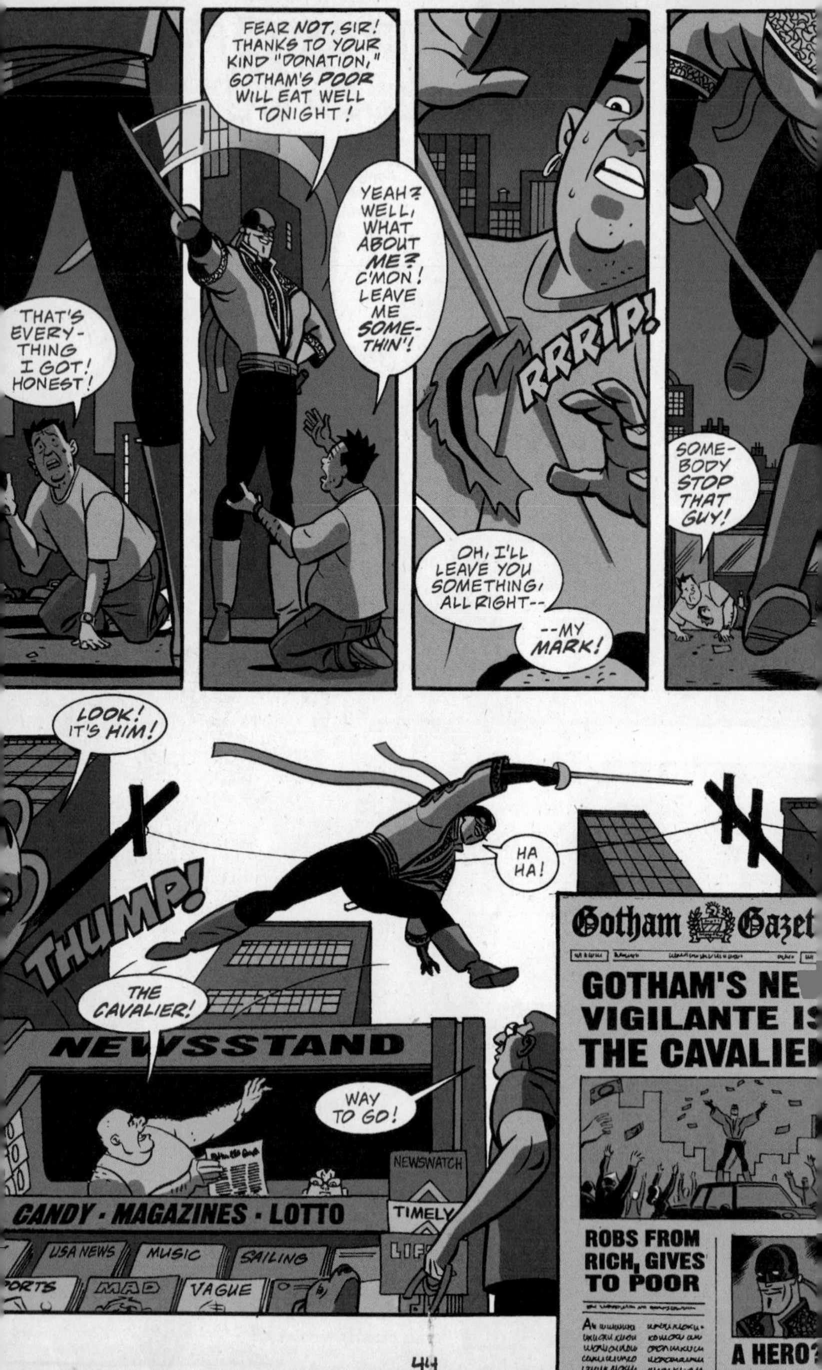
THAT'S EVERY-THING I GOT! HONEST!
FEAR NOT, SIR! THANKS TO YOUR KIND "DONATION," GOTHAM'S POOR WILL EAT WELL TONIGHT!
YEAH? WELL, WHAT ABOUT ME? C'MON! LEAVE ME SOME-THIN'!
RRRIP!
OH, I'LL LEAVE YOU SOMETHING, ALL RIGHT--
--MY MARK!
SOME-BODY STOP THAT GUY!
LOOK! IT'S HIM!
THUMP!
HA HA!
THE CAVALIER!
NEWSSTAND
WAY TO GO!
NEWSWATCH
TIMELY
CANDY · MAGAZINES · LOTTO
USA NEWS
MUSIC
SAILING
VAGUE
MAD
Gotham Gazet
GOTHAM'S NE
VIGILANTE I
THE CAVALIE
ROBS FROM RICH, GIVES TO POOR
A HERO?

HEY, CAVALIER! IN *HERE*, MAN!

WE GOT YOUR *BACK*, C!

WEEEOOO

...ND ONCE AGAIN, THE CAVALIER SLIPS AWAY...

...THANKS TO HIS *ADORING PUBLIC*!

THAT'S QUITE A *SCAM* YOU'VE GOT!

...AND KEEPING *MOST* FOR *YOURSELF*!

BATMAN!

YOUR *PAYOFFS* MAY ENDEAR YOU TO THE *STREET SCUM* OF GOTHAM--

WAK!

--BUT NOT TO *ME*. YOU'RE *NOTHING* MORE THAN A *COMMON THIEF*.

ROBBING FROM THE *RICH*, GIVING TO THE *POOR*...

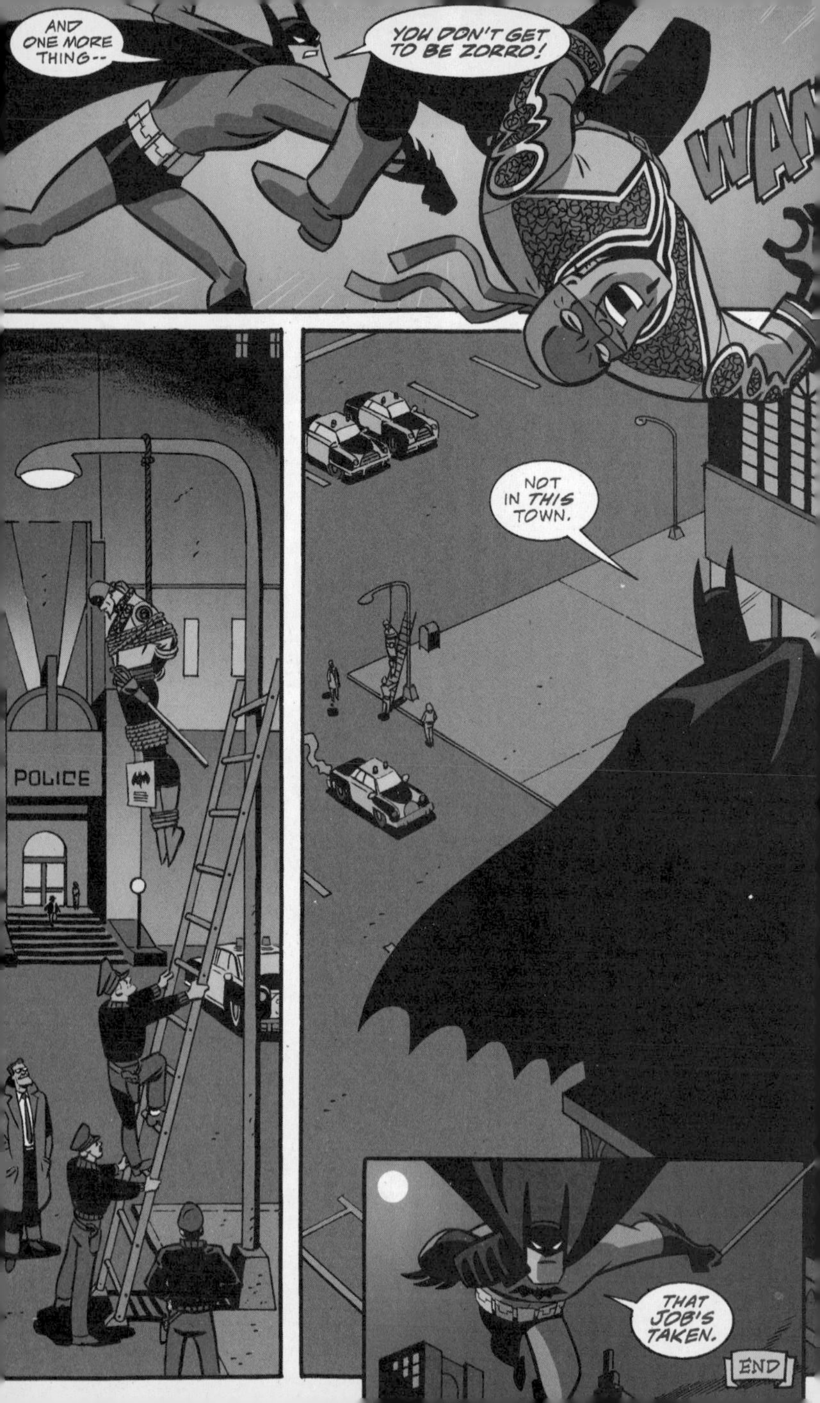
AND ONE MORE THING--
YOU DON'T GET TO BE ZORRO!
WAM
POLICE
NOT IN THIS TOWN.
THAT JOB'S TAKEN.
END

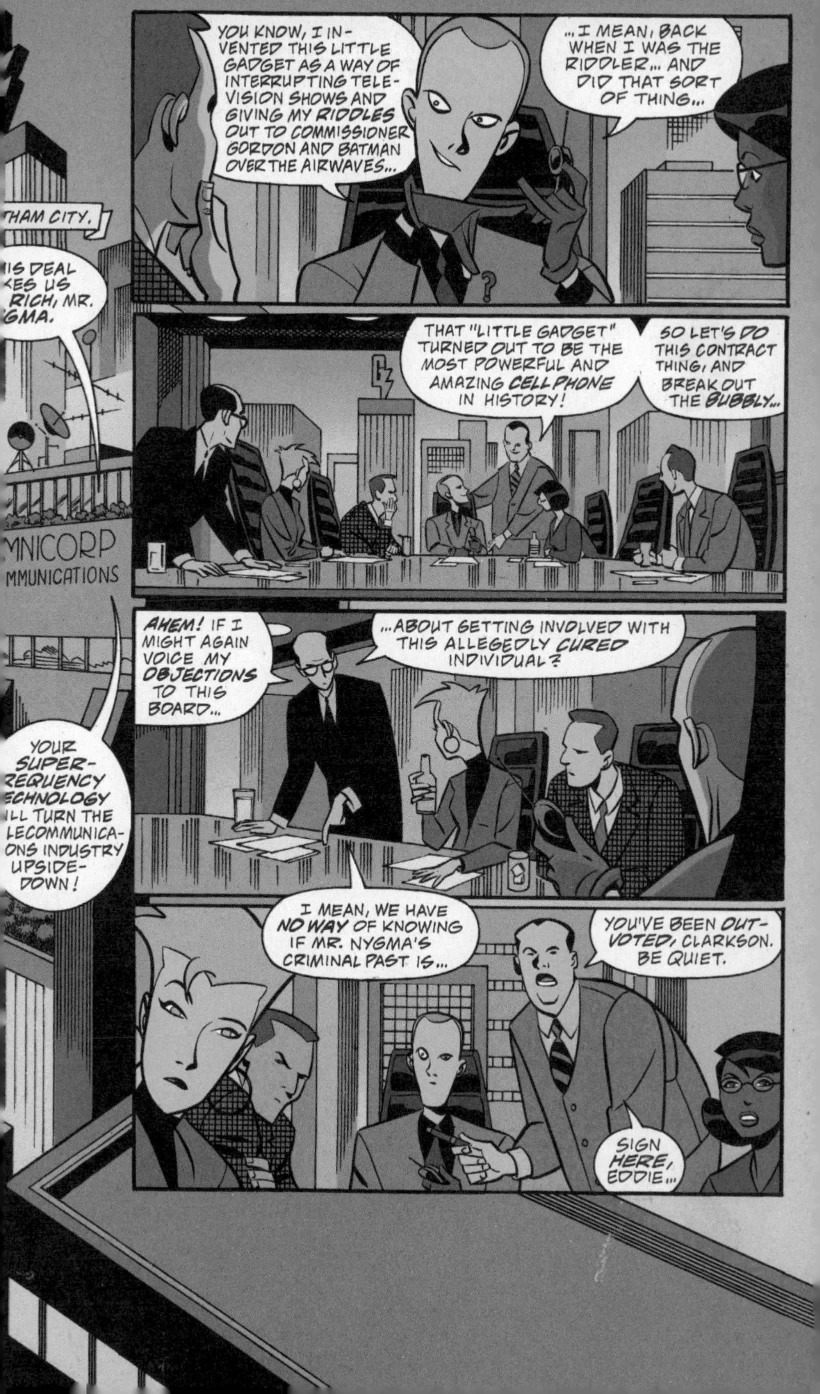

THAM CITY.
IS DEAL
KES US
RICH, MR.
GMA.
YOU KNOW, I INVENTED THIS LITTLE GADGET AS A WAY OF INTERRUPTING TELEVISION SHOWS AND GIVING MY RIDDLES OUT TO COMMISSIONER GORDON AND BATMAN OVER THE AIRWAVES...
...I MEAN, BACK WHEN I WAS THE RIDDLER... AND DID THAT SORT OF THING...
MNICORP
MMUNICATIONS
THAT "LITTLE GADGET" TURNED OUT TO BE THE MOST POWERFUL AND AMAZING CELL PHONE IN HISTORY!
SO LET'S DO THIS CONTRACT THING, AND BREAK OUT THE BUBBLY...
YOUR SUPER-
REQUENCY
ECHNOLOGY
LL TURN THE
LECOMMUNICA-
ONS INDUSTRY
UPSIDE-
DOWN!
AHEM! IF I MIGHT AGAIN VOICE MY OBJECTIONS TO THIS BOARD...
...ABOUT GETTING INVOLVED WITH THIS ALLEGEDLY CURED INDIVIDUAL?
I MEAN, WE HAVE NO WAY OF KNOWING IF MR. NYGMA'S CRIMINAL PAST IS...
YOU'VE BEEN OUT-VOTED, CLARKSON. BE QUIET.
SIGN HERE, EDDIE...

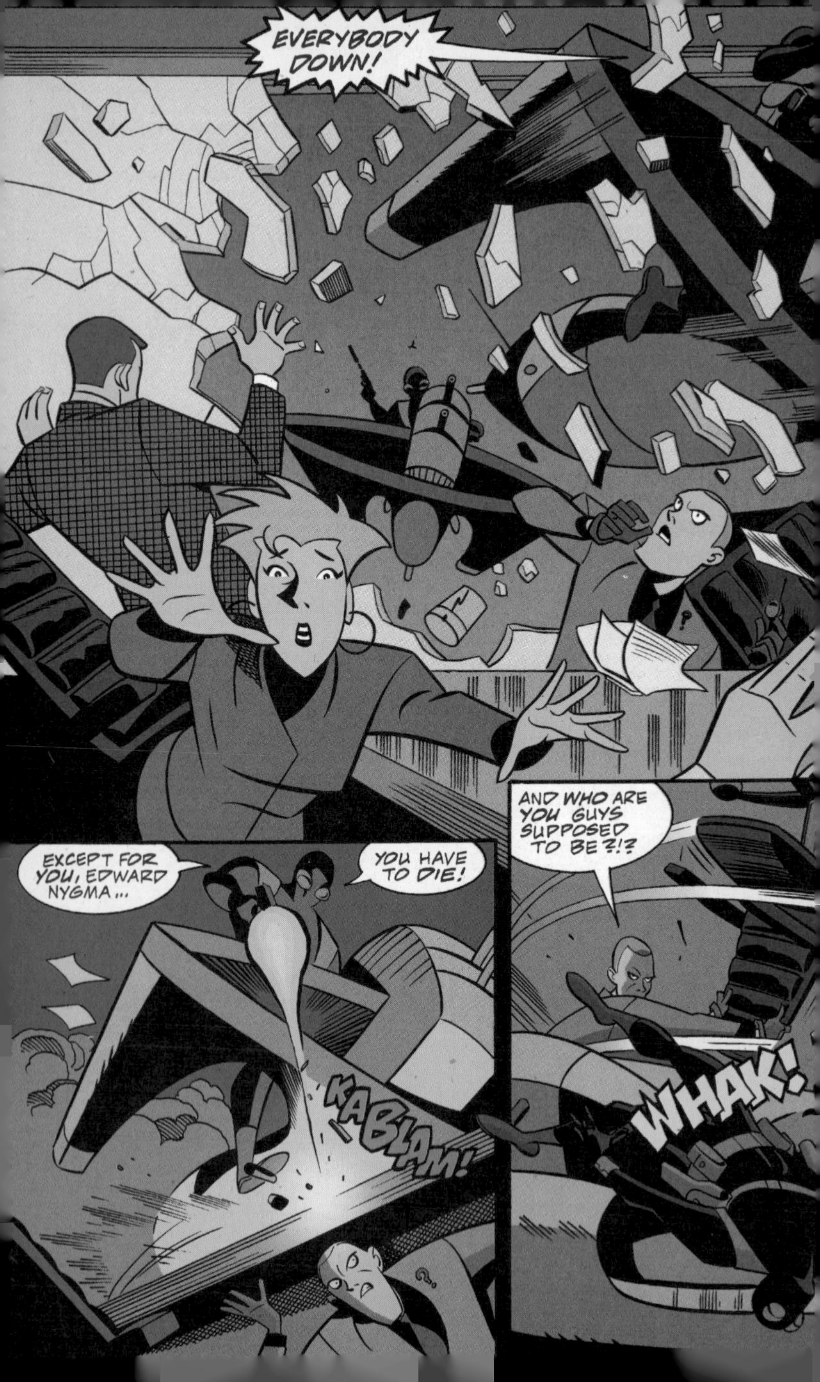
EVERYBODY DOWN!
EXCEPT FOR YOU, EDWARD NYGMA...
YOU HAVE TO DIE!
KABLAM!
AND WHO ARE YOU GUYS SUPPOSED TO BE?!?
WHAK!

FREE MAN

...NOBODY HAS TO BE HURT!

TY TEMPLETON
WRITER
RICK BURCHETT
PENCILLER
TERRY BEATTY
INKER
LEE LOUGHRIDGE
COLORIST
PHIL FELIX
LETTERER
HARVEY RICHARDS
ASSISTANT EDITOR
JOAN HILTY
EDITOR

BATMAN CREATED BY BOB KANE

...E LAST HING YOU'LL VER EE.

THAT'S ALL YOU NEED TO KNOW.

NOT IF I CAN HELP...

...ITAIIIIEEEE!

I WARNED YOU ABOUT THIS, SIR.

THIS IS GOTHAM CITY, AFTER ALL...

VOOM!

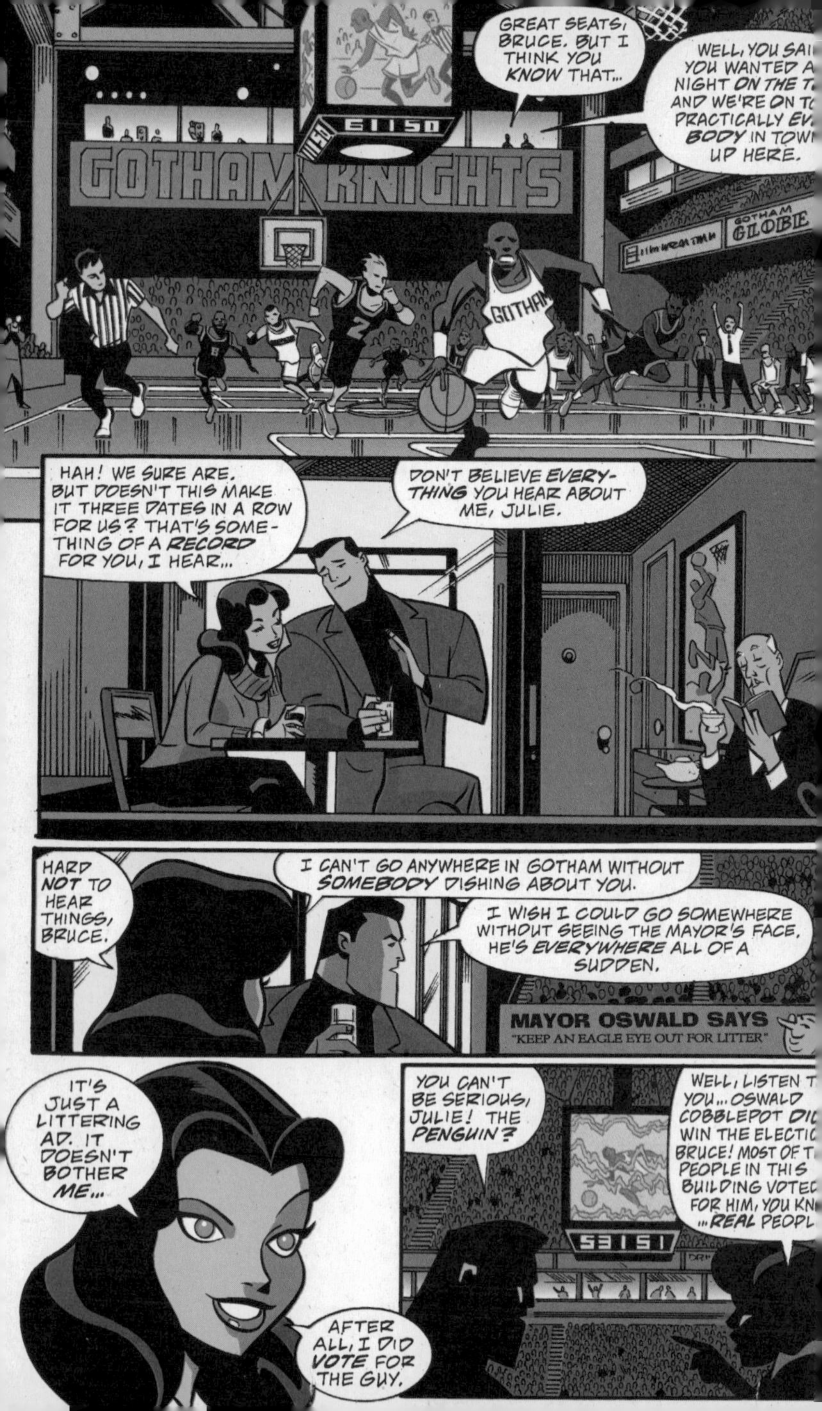
GREAT SEATS, BRUCE. BUT I THINK YOU *KNOW* THAT...
WELL, YOU SAI YOU WANTED A NIGHT *ON THE T* AND WE'RE ON TO PRACTICALLY *EV* *BODY* IN TOWN UP HERE.
GOTHAM KNIGHTS
GOTHAM GLOBE
GOTHAM
HAH! WE SURE ARE. BUT DOESN'T THIS MAKE IT THREE DATES IN A ROW FOR US? THAT'S SOMETHING OF A *RECORD* FOR YOU, I HEAR...
DON'T BELIEVE *EVERYTHING* YOU HEAR ABOUT ME, JULIE.
HARD *NOT* TO HEAR THINGS, BRUCE.
I CAN'T GO ANYWHERE IN GOTHAM WITHOUT *SOMEBODY* DISHING ABOUT YOU.
I WISH I COULD GO SOMEWHERE WITHOUT SEEING THE MAYOR'S FACE. HE'S *EVERYWHERE* ALL OF A SUDDEN.
MAYOR OSWALD SAYS
"KEEP AN EAGLE EYE OUT FOR LITTER"
IT'S JUST A LITTERING AD. IT DOESN'T BOTHER *ME*...
AFTER ALL, I DID *VOTE* FOR THE GUY.
YOU CAN'T BE SERIOUS, JULIE! THE *PENGUIN*?
WELL, LISTEN T YOU... OSWALD COBBLEPOT *DI* WIN THE ELECTI BRUCE! MOST OF T PEOPLE IN THIS BUILDING VOTED FOR HIM, YOU KN ...*REAL* PEOPL

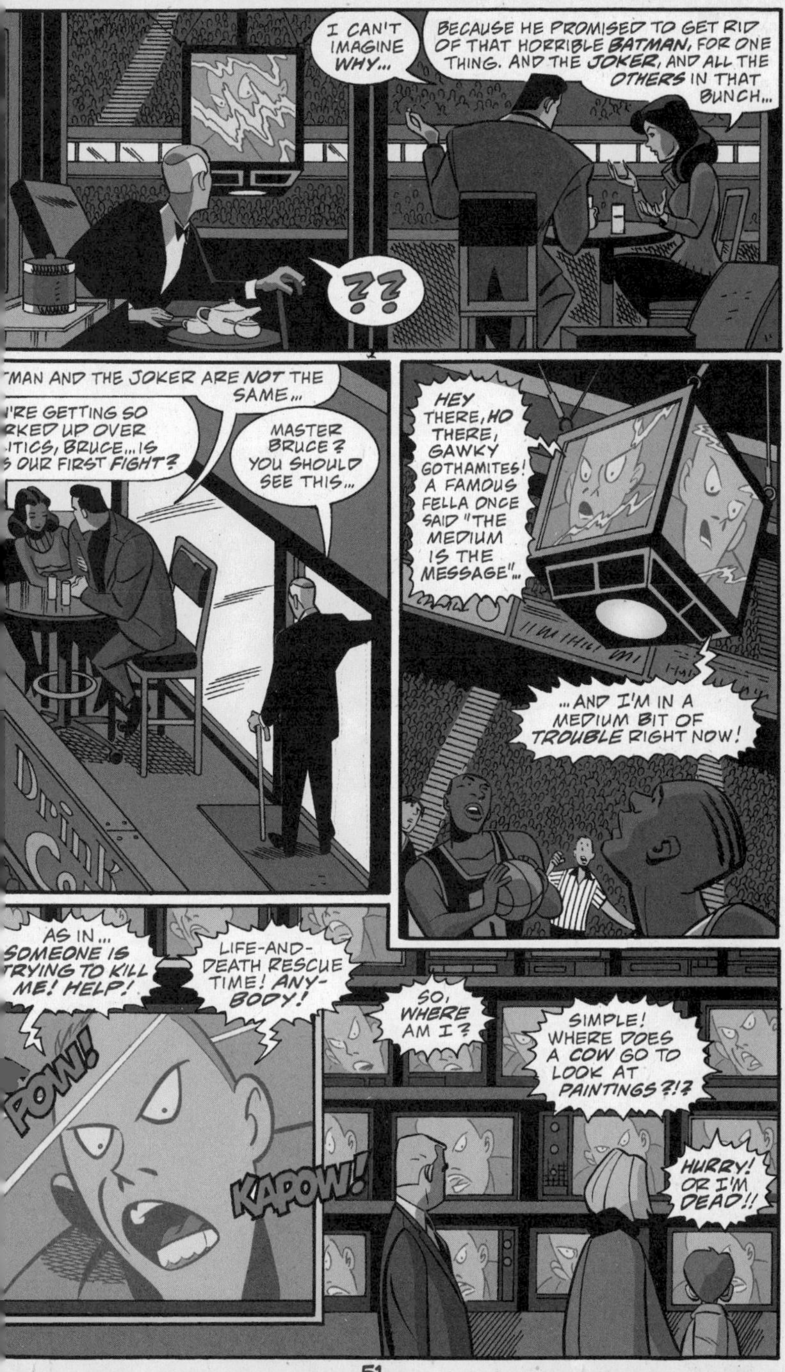

I CAN'T IMAGINE WHY...
BECAUSE HE PROMISED TO GET RID OF THAT HORRIBLE BATMAN, FOR ONE THING. AND THE JOKER, AND ALL THE OTHERS IN THAT BUNCH...
??
TMAN AND THE JOKER ARE NOT THE SAME...
'RE GETTING SO RKED UP OVER ITICS, BRUCE... IS S OUR FIRST FIGHT?
MASTER BRUCE? YOU SHOULD SEE THIS...
HEY THERE, HO THERE, GAWKY GOTHAMITES! A FAMOUS FELLA ONCE SAID "THE MEDIUM IS THE MESSAGE"...
...AND I'M IN A MEDIUM BIT OF TROUBLE RIGHT NOW!
AS IN... SOMEONE IS TRYING TO KILL ME! HELP!
LIFE-AND-DEATH RESCUE TIME! ANY-BODY!
POW!
KAPOW!
SO, WHERE AM I?
SIMPLE! WHERE DOES A COW GO TO LOOK AT PAINTINGS?!?
HURRY! OR I'M DEAD!!

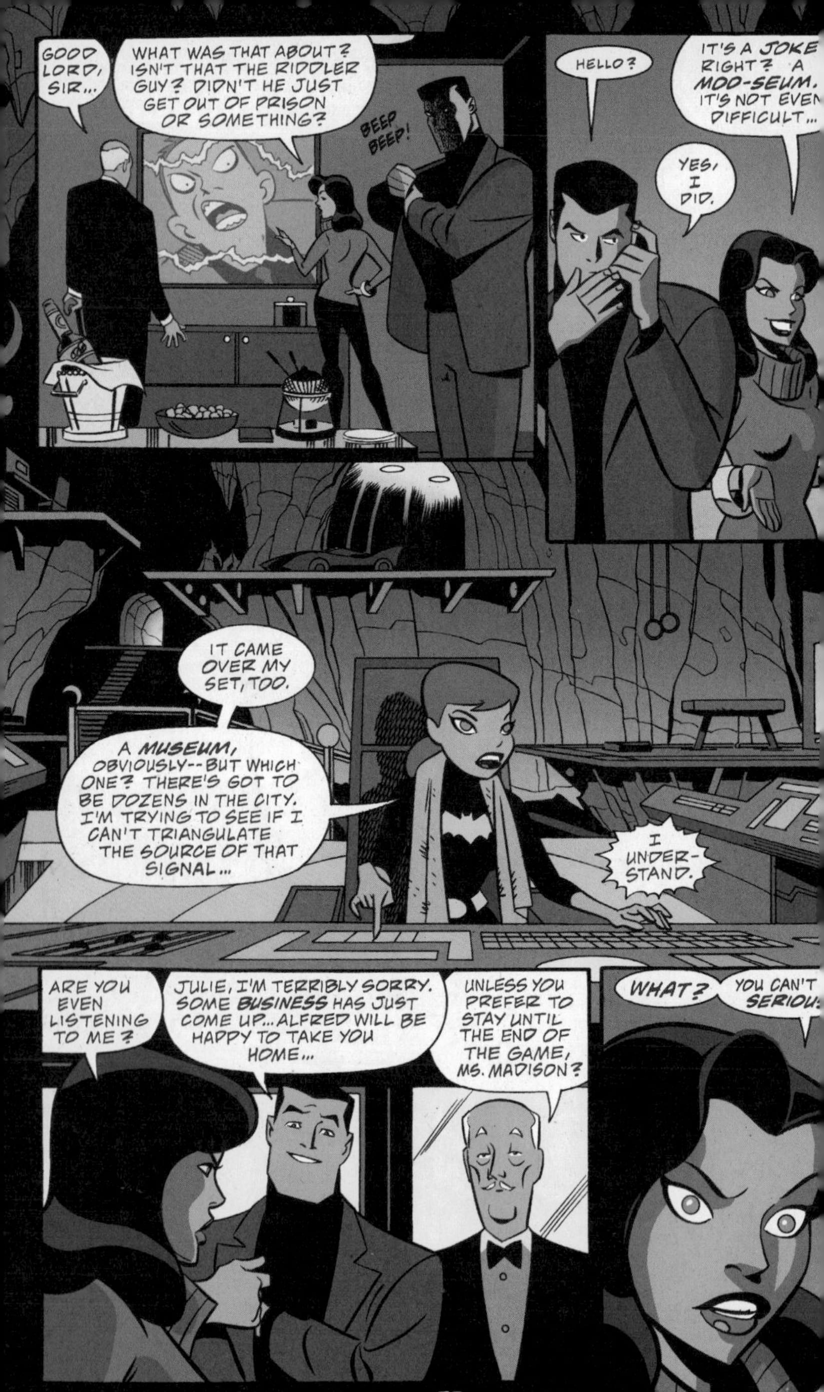

GOOD LORD, SIR...
WHAT WAS THAT ABOUT? ISN'T THAT THE RIDDLER GUY? DIDN'T HE JUST GET OUT OF PRISON OR SOMETHING?
BEEP BEEP!
HELLO?
IT'S A JOKE RIGHT? A MOO-SEUM. IT'S NOT EVEN DIFFICULT...
YES, I DID.
IT CAME OVER MY SET, TOO.
A MUSEUM, OBVIOUSLY--BUT WHICH ONE? THERE'S GOT TO BE DOZENS IN THE CITY. I'M TRYING TO SEE IF I CAN'T TRIANGULATE THE SOURCE OF THAT SIGNAL...
I UNDER-STAND.
ARE YOU EVEN LISTENING TO ME?
JULIE, I'M TERRIBLY SORRY. SOME BUSINESS HAS JUST COME UP... ALFRED WILL BE HAPPY TO TAKE YOU HOME...
UNLESS YOU PREFER TO STAY UNTIL THE END OF THE GAME, MS. MADISON?
WHAT?
YOU CAN'T SERIOU

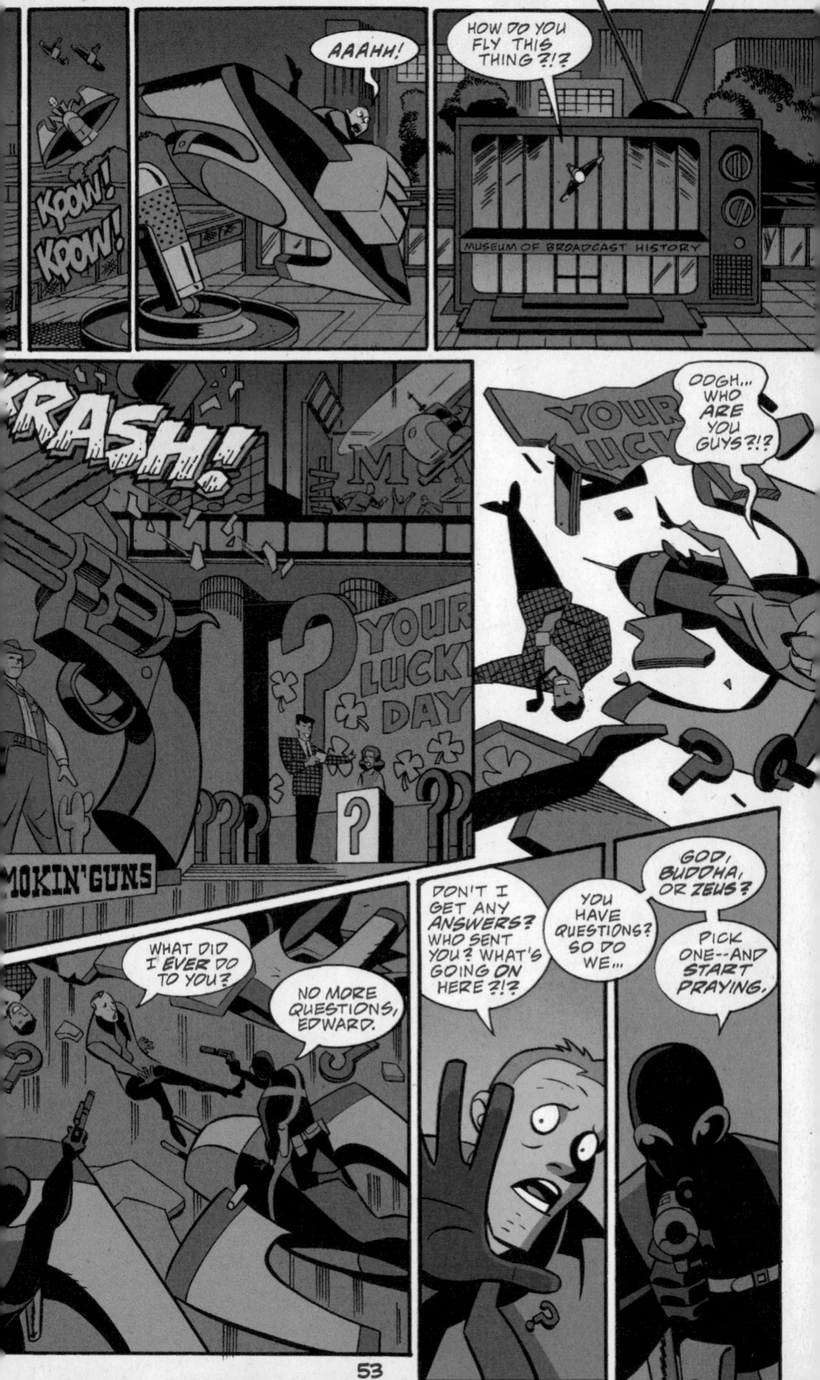

KPOW!
KPOW!
AAAHH!
HOW DO YOU FLY THIS THING?!?
MUSEUM OF BROADCAST HISTORY
RASH!
YOUR LUCKY DAY
MOKIN' GUNS
OOGH... WHO ARE YOU GUYS?!?
WHAT DID I EVER DO TO YOU?
NO MORE QUESTIONS, EDWARD.
DON'T I GET ANY ANSWERS? WHO SENT YOU? WHAT'S GOING ON HERE?!?
YOU HAVE QUESTIONS? SO DO WE...
GOD, BUDDHA, OR ZEUS?
PICK ONE--AND START PRAYING.

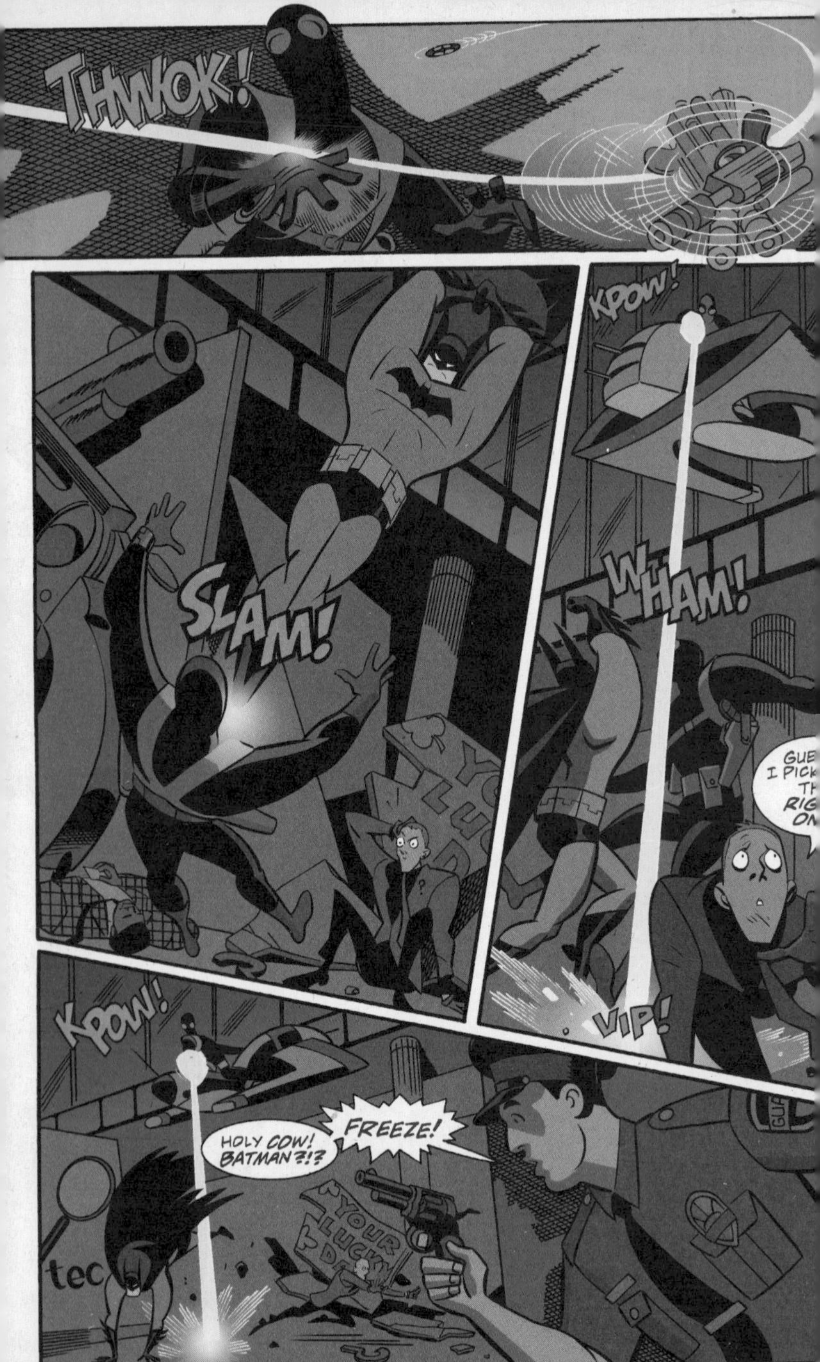
THWOK!
SLAM!
KPOW!
WHAM!
GUE I PICK TH RIG ON
VIP!
KPOW!
HOLY COW! BATMAN?!?
FREEZE!
tec

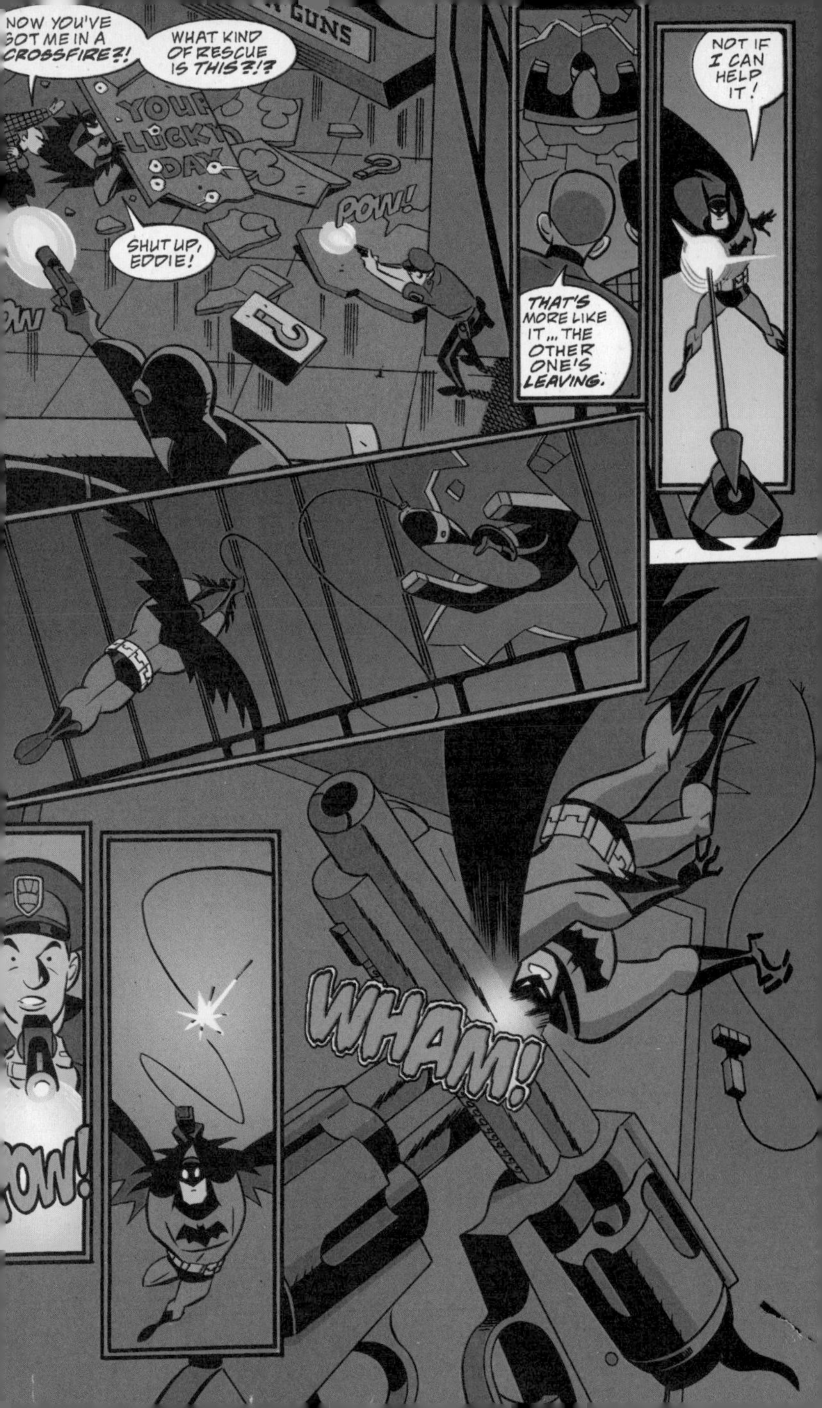

NOW YOU'VE GOT ME IN A CROSSFIRE?!
WHAT KIND OF RESCUE IS THIS?!?
YOUR LUCKY DAY
SHUT UP, EDDIE!
POW!
THAT'S MORE LIKE IT... THE OTHER ONE'S LEAVING.
NOT IF I CAN HELP IT!
WHAM!

HOLD IT RIGHT THERE, FANCY-PANTS.

EVERYBODY SAYS YOU'RE A *BAD GUY* NOW...

DON'T BELIEVE EVERYTHING YOU HEAR.

STAR TRACK

LET HIM GO, EDDIE! HE'S JUST DOING HIS JOB.

WHAT ON *EARTH* IS GOING ON, BATMAN?

THEY WORK FOR A MAN NAMED *RA'S AL GHUL*... AN INTERNATIONAL CULT LEADER. YOU KNOW ANYTHING ABOUT THIS, EDDIE?

THESE MEN ARE *ASSASSINS* IN THE *SOCIETY OF SHADOWS.*

NEW, *AMERICAN* RECRUITS, FROM THE LOOKS OF THEM.

GOOD LORD, NO!

YOU SHOULD FIND A PLACE TO HIDE-- AND STAY THERE!

RA'S HAS TARGETED ALL GOTHAM'S UNDERWORLD FIGURES FOR EXECUTION! ONE OF YOU *KNOWS* SOMETHING YOU SHOULD OR IS A PROBLEM TO RA'S IN SOME WAY...

...AND HE'S WILLING TO KILL YOU *ALL* TO SOLVE IT.

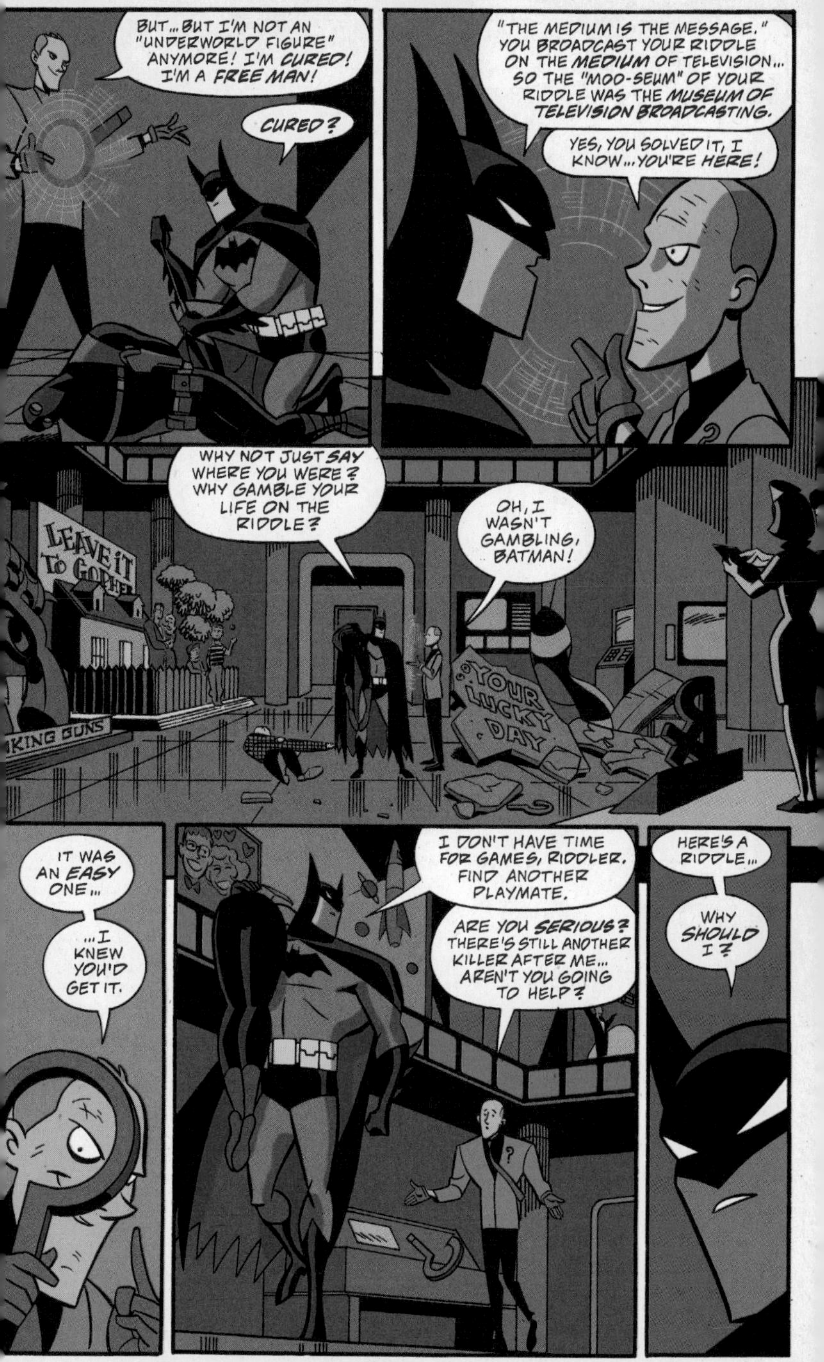
BUT... BUT I'M NOT AN "UNDERWORLD FIGURE" ANYMORE! I'M CURED! I'M A FREE MAN!
CURED?
"THE MEDIUM IS THE MESSAGE." YOU BROADCAST YOUR RIDDLE ON THE MEDIUM OF TELEVISION... SO THE "MOO-SEUM" OF YOUR RIDDLE WAS THE MUSEUM OF TELEVISION BROADCASTING.
YES, YOU SOLVED IT, I KNOW... YOU'RE HERE!
WHY NOT JUST SAY WHERE YOU WERE? WHY GAMBLE YOUR LIFE ON THE RIDDLE?
OH, I WASN'T GAMBLING, BATMAN!
LEAVE IT To GOPHER
KING GUNS
YOUR LUCKY DAY
IT WAS AN EASY ONE...
...I KNEW YOU'D GET IT.
I DON'T HAVE TIME FOR GAMES, RIDDLER. FIND ANOTHER PLAYMATE.
ARE YOU SERIOUS? THERE'S STILL ANOTHER KILLER AFTER ME... AREN'T YOU GOING TO HELP?
HERE'S A RIDDLE...
WHY SHOULD I?

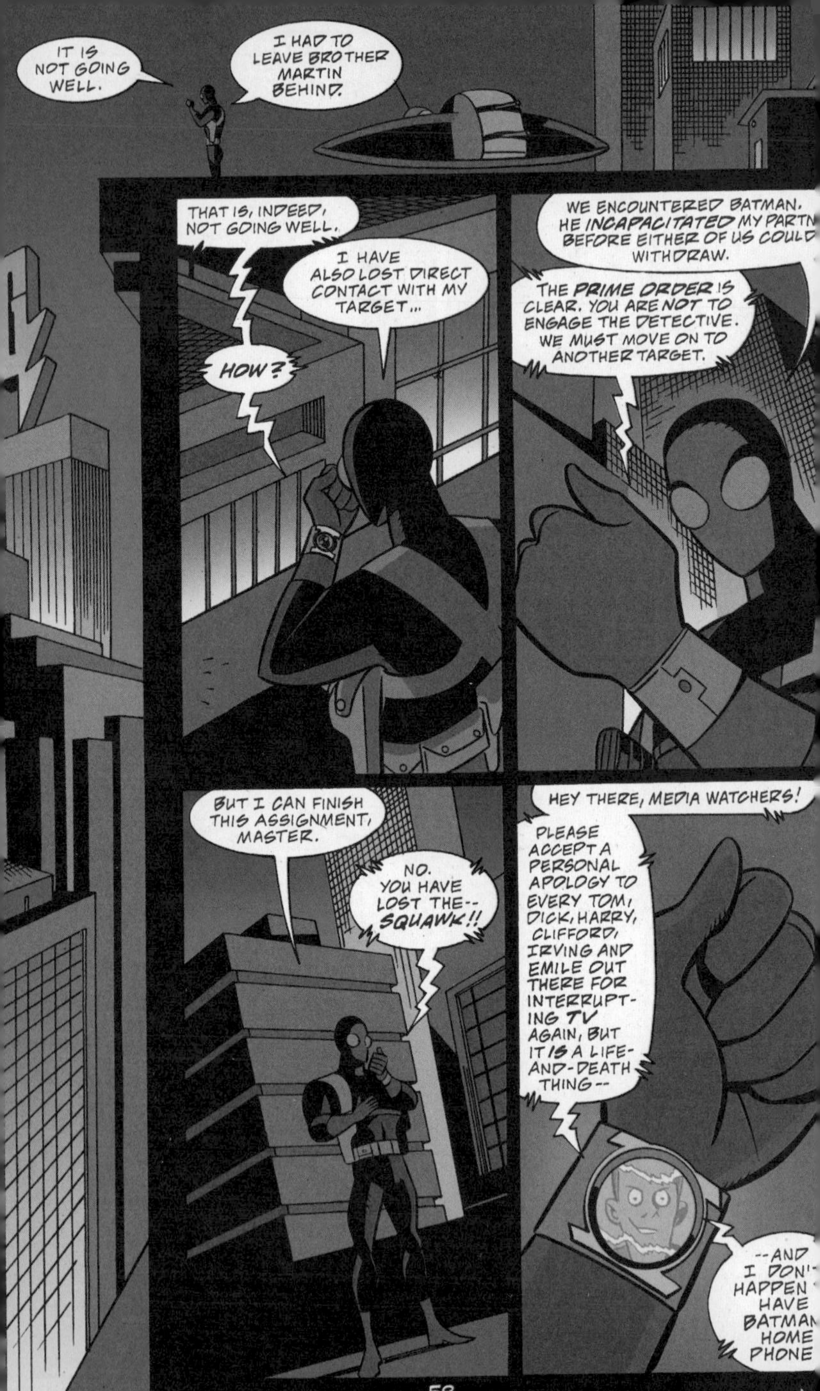
IT IS NOT GOING WELL.
I HAD TO LEAVE BROTHER MARTIN BEHIND.
THAT IS, INDEED, NOT GOING WELL.
I HAVE ALSO LOST DIRECT CONTACT WITH MY TARGET...
HOW?
WE ENCOUNTERED BATMAN. HE INCAPACITATED MY PARTN BEFORE EITHER OF US COULD WITHDRAW.
THE PRIME ORDER IS CLEAR. YOU ARE NOT TO ENGAGE THE DETECTIVE. WE MUST MOVE ON TO ANOTHER TARGET.
BUT I CAN FINISH THIS ASSIGNMENT, MASTER.
NO. YOU HAVE LOST THE-- SQUAWK!!
HEY THERE, MEDIA WATCHERS!
PLEASE ACCEPT A PERSONAL APOLOGY TO EVERY TOM, DICK, HARRY, CLIFFORD, IRVING AND EMILE OUT THERE FOR INTERRUPT-ING TV AGAIN, BUT IT IS A LIFE-AND-DEATH THING--
--AND I DON' HAPPEN HAVE BATMAN HOME PHONE

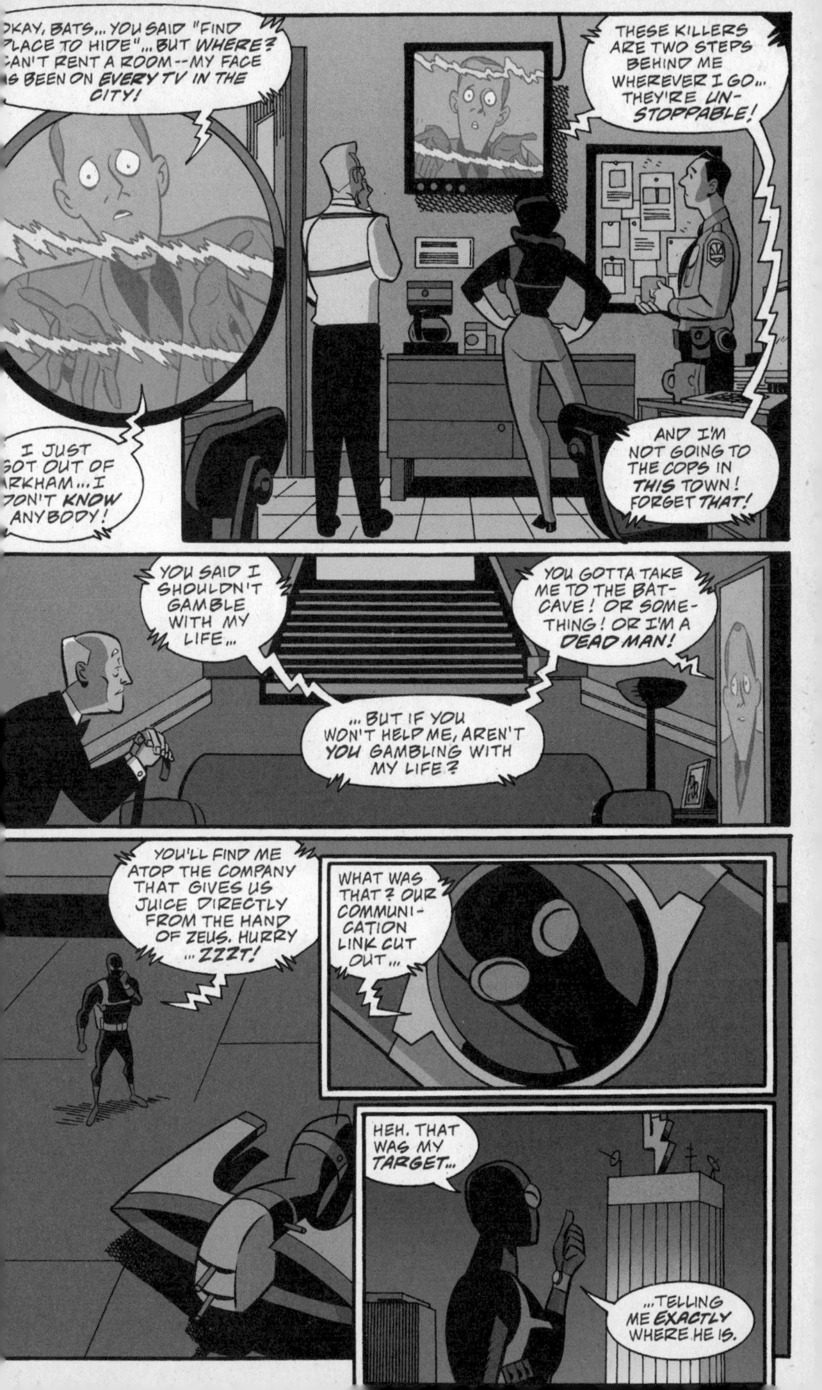
OKAY, BATS... YOU SAID "FIND A PLACE TO HIDE"... BUT WHERE? I CAN'T RENT A ROOM--MY FACE HAS BEEN ON EVERY TV IN THE CITY!
I JUST GOT OUT OF ARKHAM... I DON'T KNOW ANYBODY!
THESE KILLERS ARE TWO STEPS BEHIND ME WHEREVER I GO... THEY'RE UN-STOPPABLE!
AND I'M NOT GOING TO THE COPS IN THIS TOWN! FORGET THAT!
YOU SAID I SHOULDN'T GAMBLE WITH MY LIFE...
YOU GOTTA TAKE ME TO THE BAT-CAVE! OR SOME-THING! OR I'M A DEAD MAN!
...BUT IF YOU WON'T HELP ME, AREN'T YOU GAMBLING WITH MY LIFE?
YOU'LL FIND ME ATOP THE COMPANY THAT GIVES US JUICE DIRECTLY FROM THE HAND OF ZEUS. HURRY ...ZZZT!
WHAT WAS THAT? OUR COMMUNI-CATION LINK CUT OUT...
HEH. THAT WAS MY TARGET...
...TELLING ME EXACTLY WHERE HE IS.

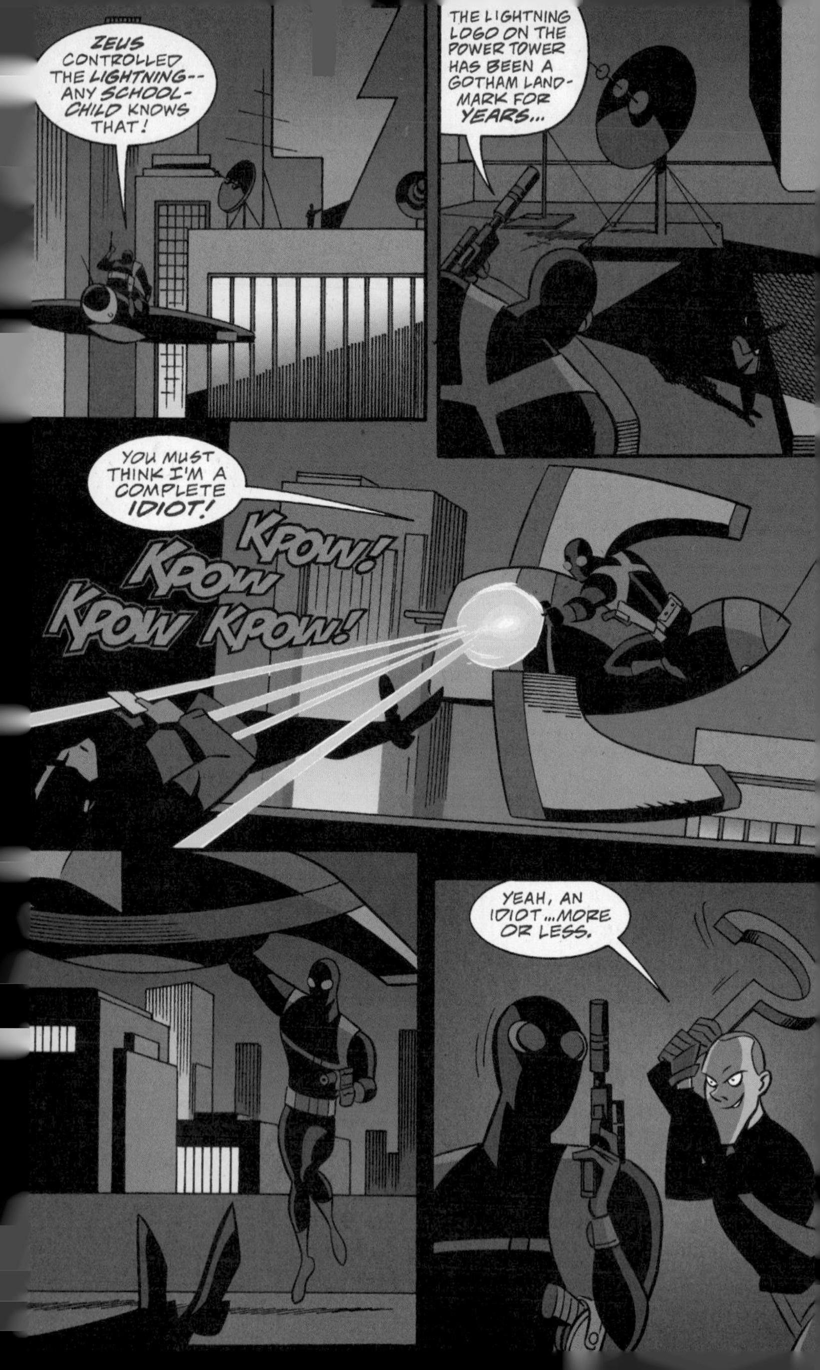

ZEUS CONTROLLED THE LIGHTNING-- ANY SCHOOL-CHILD KNOWS THAT!
THE LIGHTNING LOGO ON THE POWER TOWER HAS BEEN A GOTHAM LAND-MARK FOR YEARS...
YOU MUST THINK I'M A COMPLETE IDIOT!
KPOW! KPOW KPOW KPOW!
YEAH, AN IDIOT...MORE OR LESS.

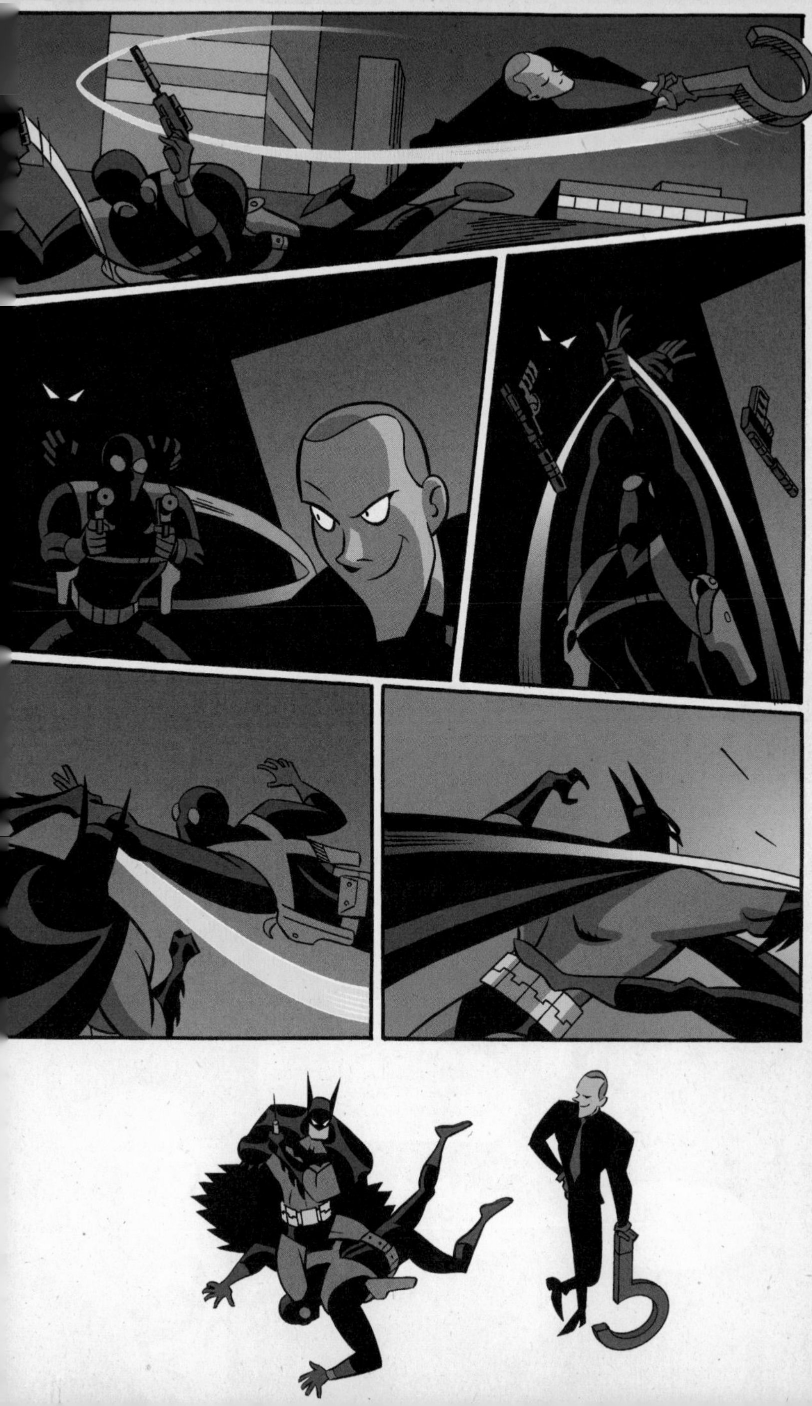

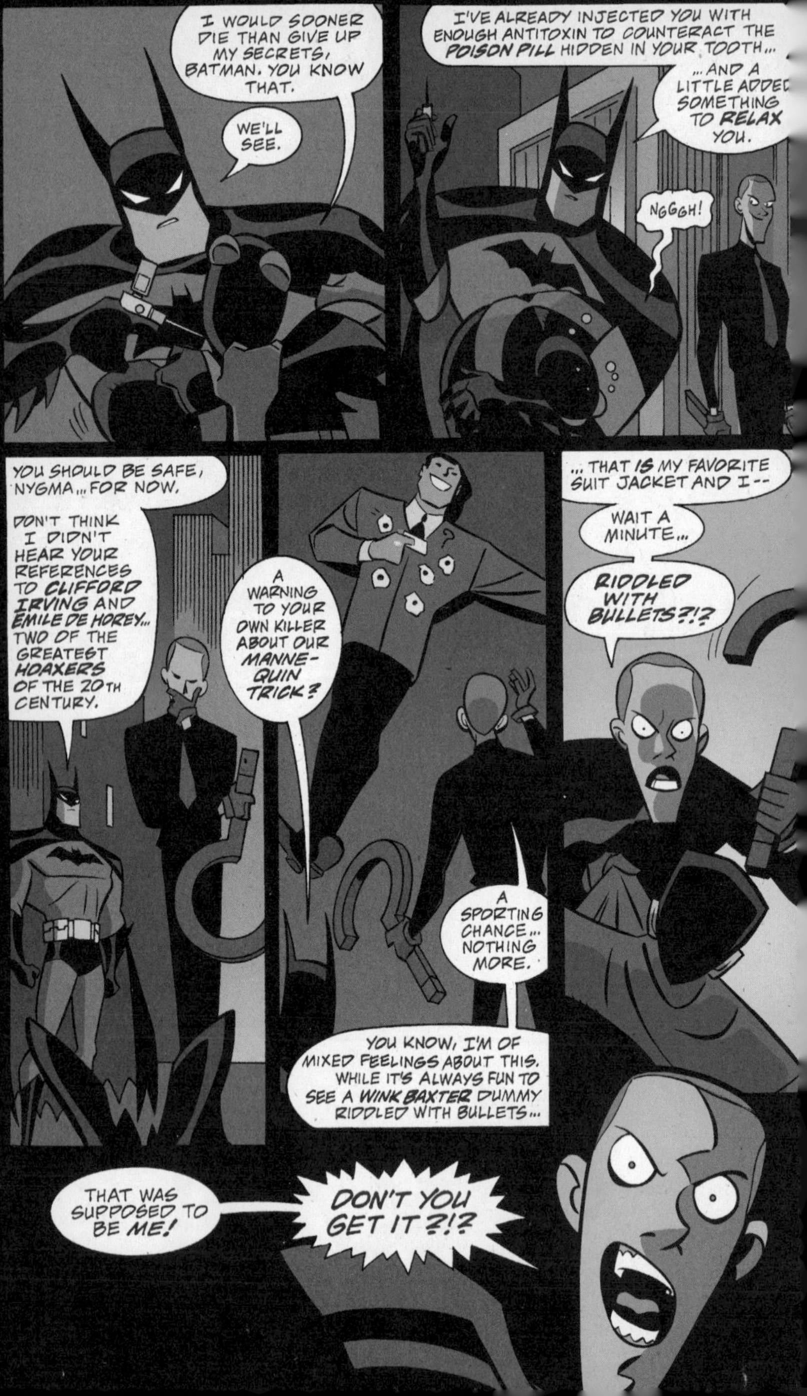

I WOULD SOONER DIE THAN GIVE UP MY SECRETS, BATMAN. YOU KNOW THAT.
WE'LL SEE.
I'VE ALREADY INJECTED YOU WITH ENOUGH ANTITOXIN TO COUNTERACT THE POISON PILL HIDDEN IN YOUR TOOTH...
...AND A LITTLE ADDED SOMETHING TO RELAX YOU.
NGGGH!
YOU SHOULD BE SAFE, NYGMA... FOR NOW.
DON'T THINK I DIDN'T HEAR YOUR REFERENCES TO CLIFFORD IRVING AND EMILE DE HOREY... TWO OF THE GREATEST HOAXERS OF THE 20TH CENTURY.
A WARNING TO YOUR OWN KILLER ABOUT OUR MANNE-QUIN TRICK?
A SPORTING CHANCE... NOTHING MORE.
YOU KNOW, I'M OF MIXED FEELINGS ABOUT THIS. WHILE IT'S ALWAYS FUN TO SEE A WINK BAXTER DUMMY RIDDLED WITH BULLETS...
... THAT IS MY FAVORITE SUIT JACKET AND I--
WAIT A MINUTE...
RIDDLED WITH BULLETS?!?
THAT WAS SUPPOSED TO BE ME!
DON'T YOU GET IT?!?

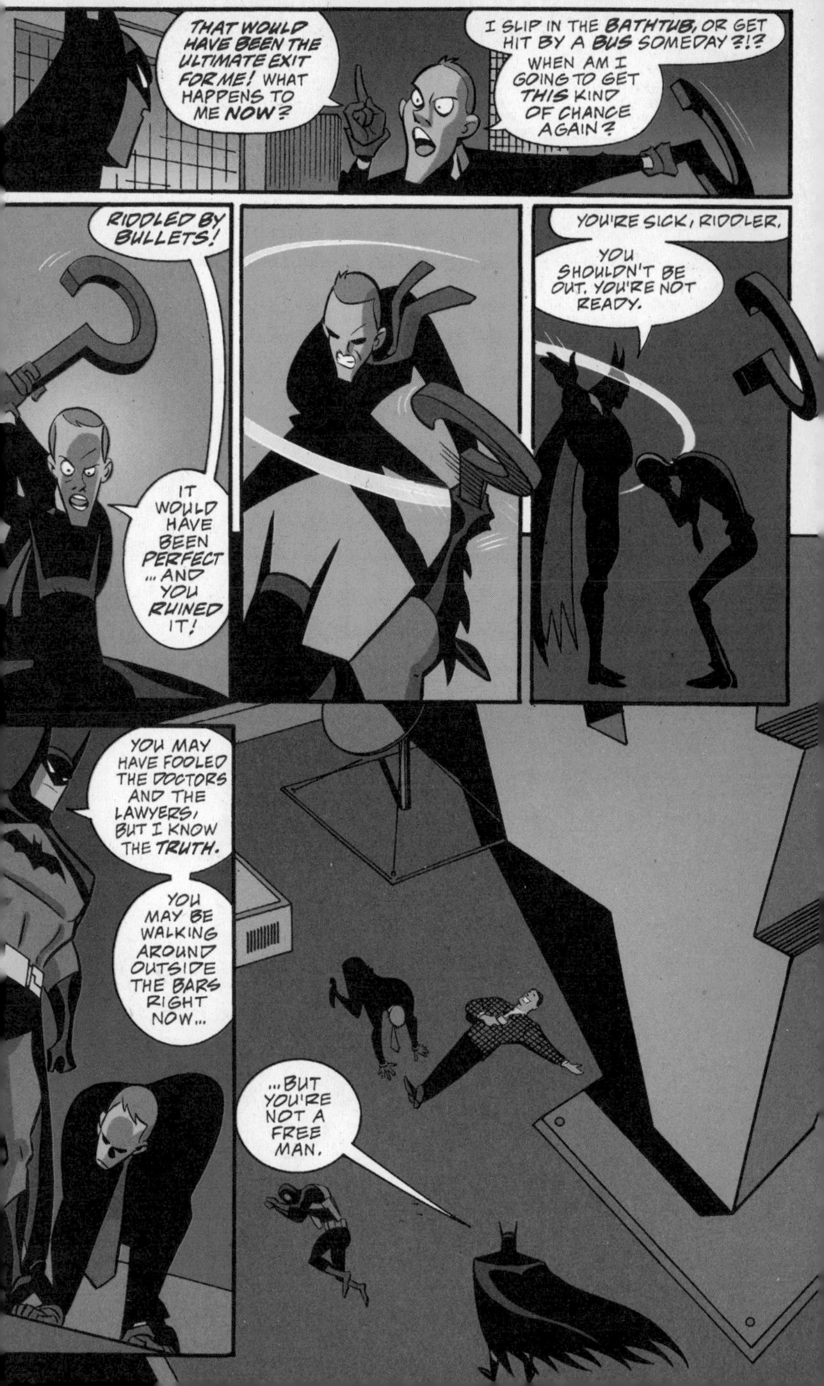
THAT WOULD HAVE BEEN THE ULTIMATE EXIT FOR ME! WHAT HAPPENS TO ME NOW?
I SLIP IN THE BATHTUB, OR GET HIT BY A BUS SOMEDAY?!?
WHEN AM I GOING TO GET THIS KIND OF CHANCE AGAIN?
RIDDLED BY BULLETS!
IT WOULD HAVE BEEN PERFECT ...AND YOU RUINED IT!
YOU'RE SICK, RIDDLER.
YOU SHOULDN'T BE OUT. YOU'RE NOT READY.
YOU MAY HAVE FOOLED THE DOCTORS AND THE LAWYERS, BUT I KNOW THE TRUTH.
YOU MAY BE WALKING AROUND OUTSIDE THE BARS RIGHT NOW...
...BUT YOU'RE NOT A FREE MAN.

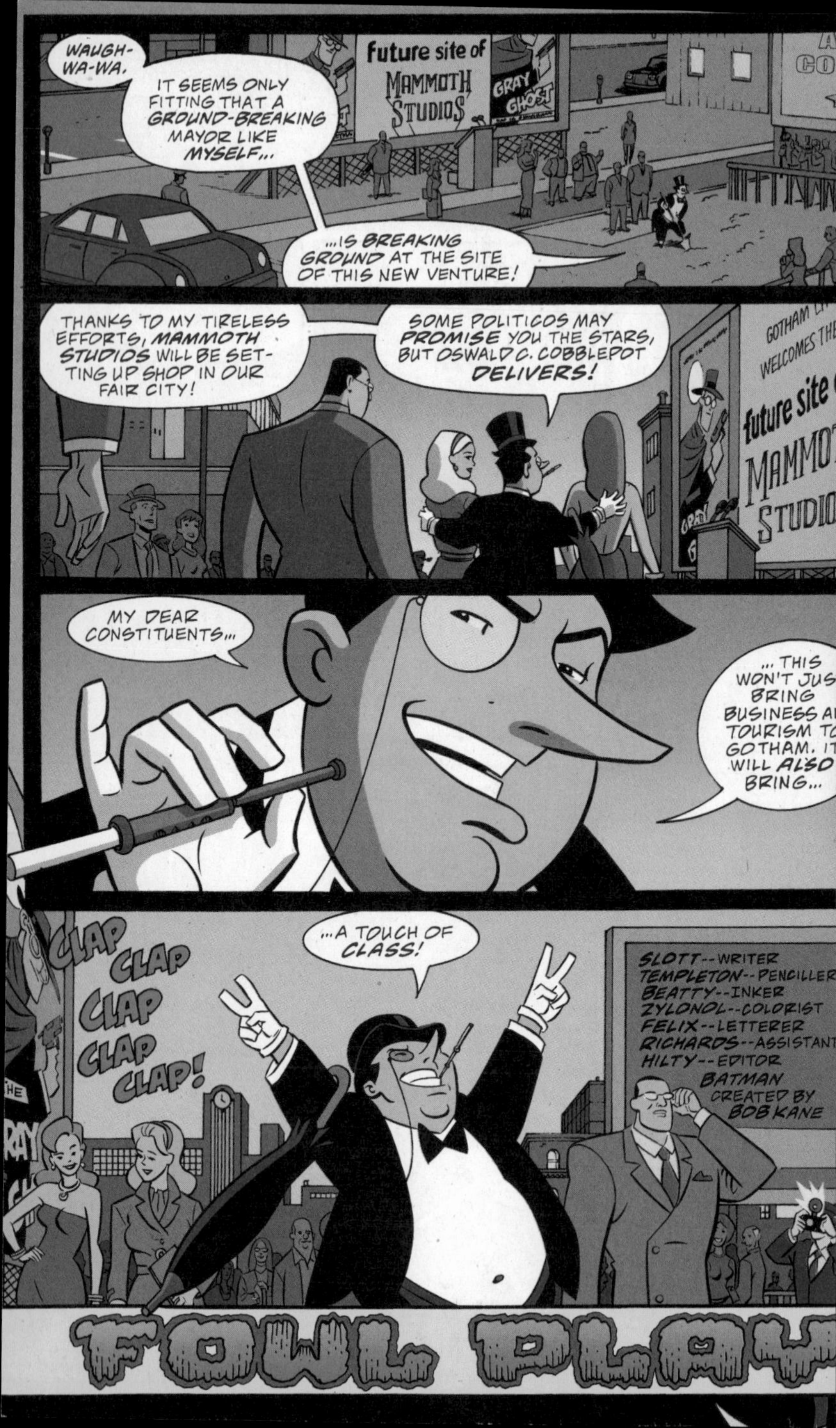

future site of MAMMOTH STUDIOS
GRAY GHOST
WAUGH-WA-WA.
IT SEEMS ONLY FITTING THAT A GROUND-BREAKING MAYOR LIKE MYSELF...
...IS BREAKING GROUND AT THE SITE OF THIS NEW VENTURE!
THANKS TO MY TIRELESS EFFORTS, MAMMOTH STUDIOS WILL BE SETTING UP SHOP IN OUR FAIR CITY!
SOME POLITICOS MAY PROMISE YOU THE STARS, BUT OSWALD C. COBBLEPOT DELIVERS!
WELCOMES THE
future site
MAMMOT
STUDIO
MY DEAR CONSTITUENTS...
... THIS WON'T JUS BRING BUSINESS A TOURISM T GOTHAM. I WILL ALSO BRING...
CLAP CLAP CLAP CLAP CLAP!
...A TOUCH OF CLASS!
SLOTT--WRITER
TEMPLETON--PENCILLER
BEATTY--INKER
ZYLONOL--COLORIST
FELIX--LETTERER
RICHARDS--ASSISTANT
HILTY--EDITOR
BATMAN CREATED BY BOB KANE
FOWL PLAY

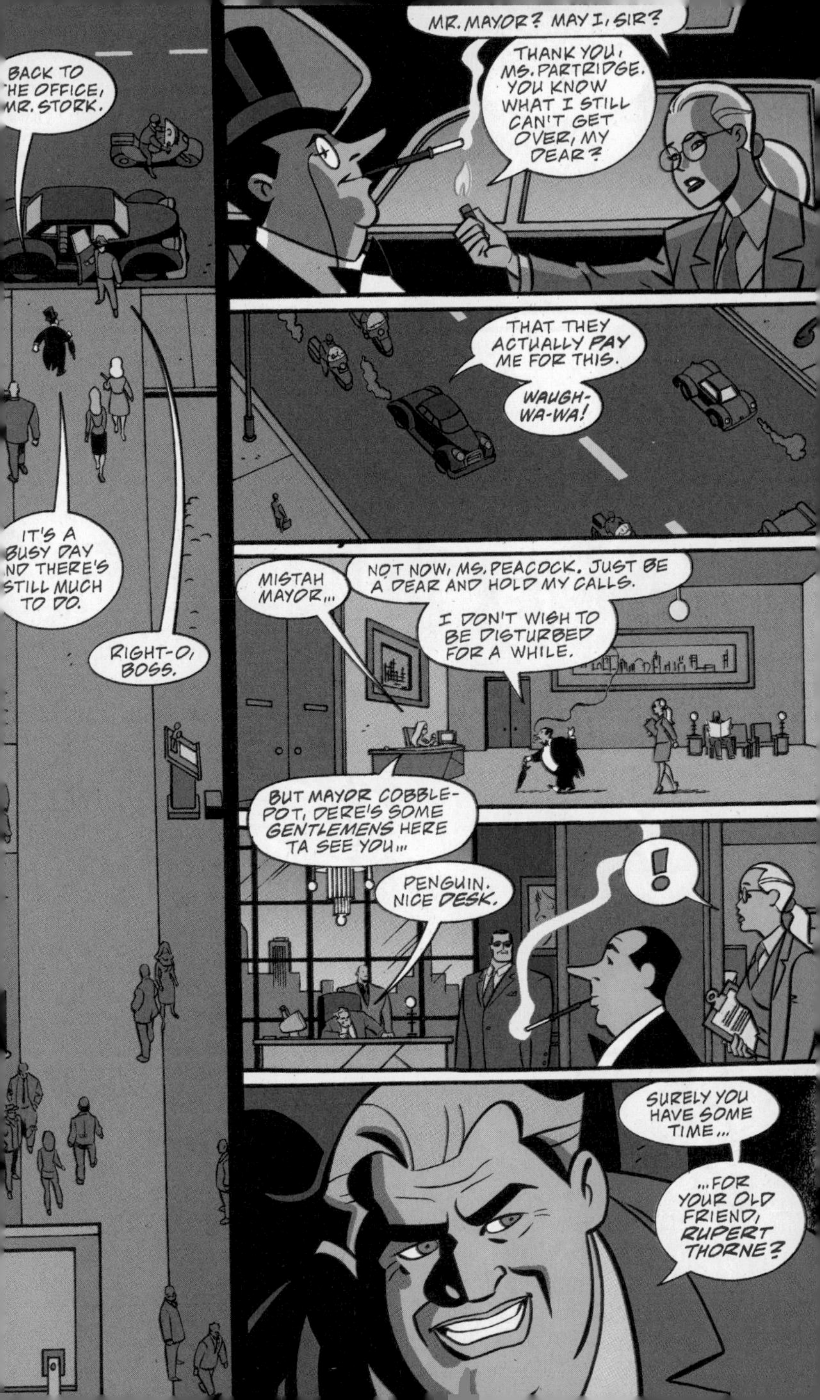
BACK TO THE OFFICE, MR. STORK.
IT'S A BUSY DAY AND THERE'S STILL MUCH TO DO.
RIGHT-O, BOSS.
MR. MAYOR? MAY I, SIR?
THANK YOU, MS. PARTRIDGE. YOU KNOW WHAT I STILL CAN'T GET OVER, MY DEAR?
THAT THEY ACTUALLY PAY ME FOR THIS.
WAUGH-WA-WA!
MISTAH MAYOR...
NOT NOW, MS. PEACOCK. JUST BE A DEAR AND HOLD MY CALLS.
I DON'T WISH TO BE DISTURBED FOR A WHILE.
BUT MAYOR COBBLE-POT, DERE'S SOME GENTLEMENS HERE TA SEE YOU...
PENGUIN. NICE DESK.
!
SURELY YOU HAVE SOME TIME...
...FOR YOUR OLD FRIEND, RUPERT THORNE?

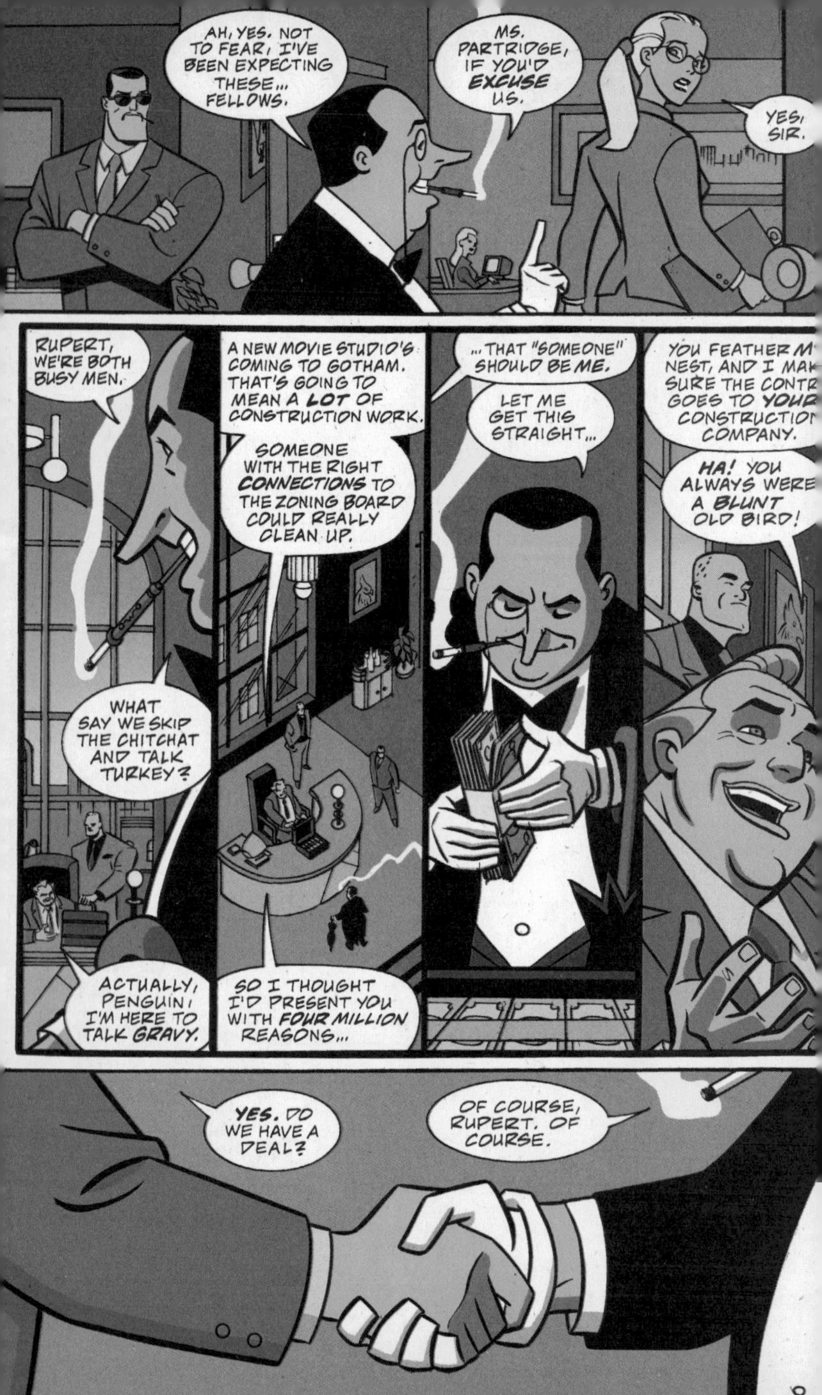
AH, YES. NOT TO FEAR, I'VE BEEN EXPECTING THESE... FELLOWS.
MS. PARTRIDGE, IF YOU'D EXCUSE US.
YES, SIR.
RUPERT, WE'RE BOTH BUSY MEN.
WHAT SAY WE SKIP THE CHITCHAT AND TALK TURKEY?
ACTUALLY, PENGUIN, I'M HERE TO TALK GRAVY.
A NEW MOVIE STUDIO'S COMING TO GOTHAM. THAT'S GOING TO MEAN A LOT OF CONSTRUCTION WORK.
SOMEONE WITH THE RIGHT CONNECTIONS TO THE ZONING BOARD COULD REALLY CLEAN UP.
SO I THOUGHT I'D PRESENT YOU WITH FOUR MILLION REASONS...
...THAT "SOMEONE" SHOULD BE ME.
LET ME GET THIS STRAIGHT...
YOU FEATHER M NEST, AND I MAK SURE THE CONTR GOES TO YOUR CONSTRUCTION COMPANY.
HA! YOU ALWAYS WERE A BLUNT OLD BIRD!
YES. DO WE HAVE A DEAL?
OF COURSE, RUPERT. OF COURSE.

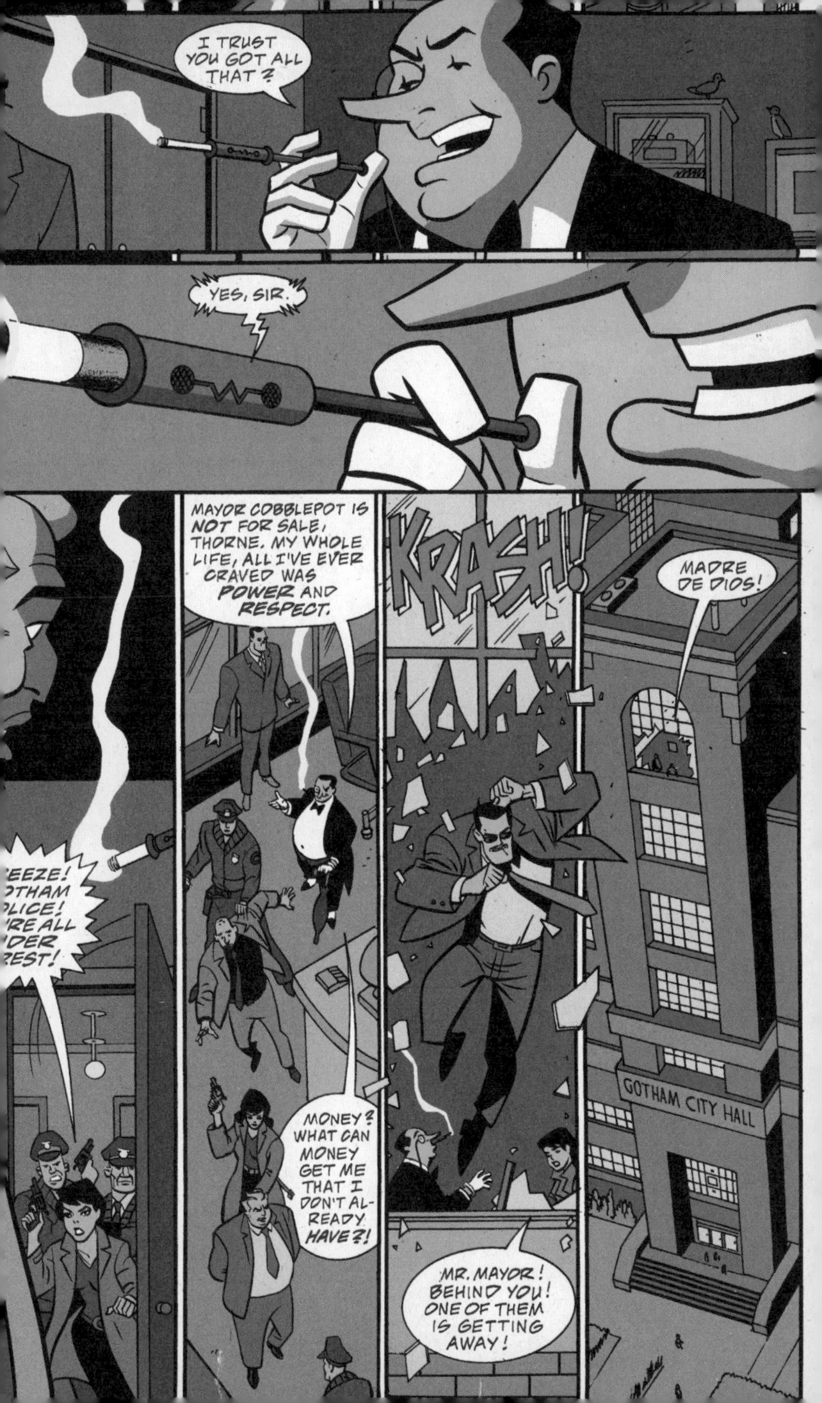

I TRUST YOU GOT ALL THAT?
YES, SIR.
EEZE! OTHAM LICE! RE ALL DER REST!
MAYOR COBBLEPOT IS NOT FOR SALE, THORNE. MY WHOLE LIFE, ALL I'VE EVER CRAVED WAS POWER AND RESPECT.
MONEY? WHAT CAN MONEY GET ME THAT I DON'T AL-READY HAVE?!
KRASH!
MADRE DE DIOS!
GOTHAM CITY HALL
MR. MAYOR! BEHIND YOU! ONE OF THEM IS GETTING AWAY!

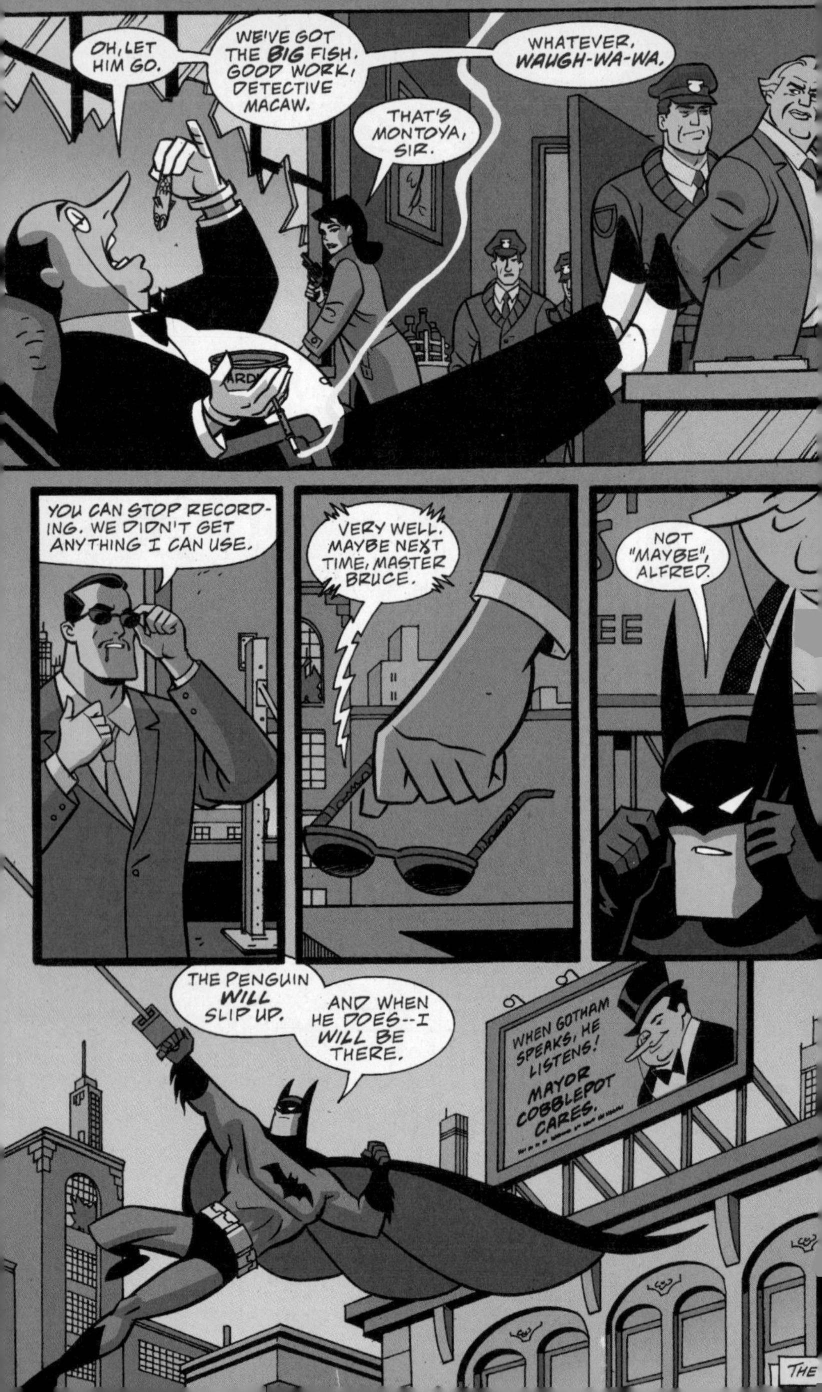
OH, LET HIM GO.
WE'VE GOT THE BIG FISH. GOOD WORK, DETECTIVE MACAW.
WHATEVER, WAUGH-WA-WA.
THAT'S MONTOYA, SIR.
YOU CAN STOP RECORDING. WE DIDN'T GET ANYTHING I CAN USE.
VERY WELL. MAYBE NEXT TIME, MASTER BRUCE.
NOT "MAYBE", ALFRED.
THE PENGUIN WILL SLIP UP.
AND WHEN HE DOES--I WILL BE THERE.
WHEN GOTHAM SPEAKS, HE LISTENS!
MAYOR COBBLEPOT CARES.
THE

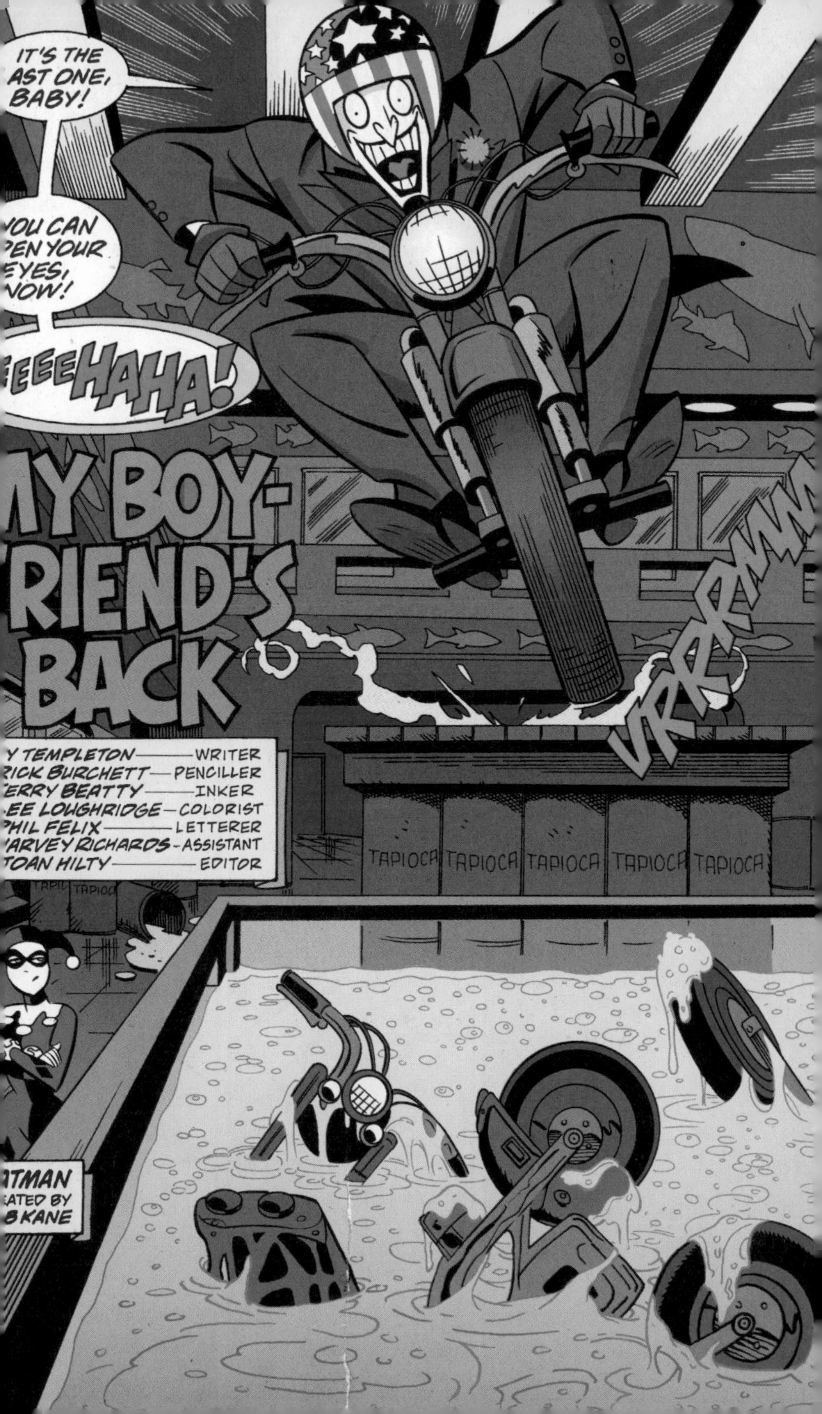
IT'S THE AST ONE, BABY!
OU CAN PEN YOUR EYES, NOW!
EEEEHAHA!
MY BOY-RIEND'S BACK
Y TEMPLETON—WRITER
RICK BURCHETT—PENCILLER
ERRY BEATTY—INKER
EE LOUGHRIDGE—COLORIST
PHIL FELIX—LETTERER
ARVEY RICHARDS-ASSISTANT
JOAN HILTY—EDITOR
VRRRMMM
TAPIOCA TAPIOCA TAPIOCA TAPIOCA TAPIOCA
TMAN EATED BY B KANE

VRRRR GLOOP!

EVIL, MAYBE... KNIEVEL... NOT SO MUCH. YOU'RE *ZERO* FOR *SIX* ON THAT JUMP, JOKER.

NO, NO DON'T Y[...] *GET* IT HONE[...] BUN[...]

TAPIOCA TAPIOCA

OCA

I DROVE A HALF-DOZEN MOTORCYCLES INTO A VAT OF *TAPIOCA* FOR *YOU*, SWEETIE!

IT'S A *HARLEY* PUDDING!

GET IT?!?

THINK OF THE MOTORCYCLES AS *RAISINS!*

IT'S N[...] I S'PO[...]

BUT WH[...] THE ST[...]

THE *MAY*[...]

HMMM? THE DESTRUC-TION! THE COLLAPSE OF CIVILIZATION!

I HOPE YA STOLE THE MOTORCYCLES, AT LEAST...

PERISH THE THOUGHT. I HAD THEM DELIVERED.

TRADED THE HELICOPTER FOR THEM.

WHAT?!?

TROPICAL FISH

I TRADED THE HELICOPTER FOR--

I WAS GONNA DIVE-BOMB CITY HALL WITH THAT ON THURSDAY!

YA CAN'T DIVE-BOMB CITY HALL FROM A STICKY MOTORBIKE--

RD NS I'VE ED!

YOU'RE NOT YOURSELF ANYMORE, MISTAH J.

TAPIOCA

AMMO

NOT SINCE THOSE HEAD-SHRINKING CREEPS AT ARKHAM GAVE YA ALL THAT SHOCK THERAPY AND AVERSION THERAPY AND DRUG THERAPY AND GROUP THERAPY...

AND DIET THERAPY...

I BROKE YOU OUT OF THAT TWO-BIT PRISON THEY STUCK YOU IN...

...FOR THIS?!? FLOWERS AND LOVE POEMS?

THINK FAST!

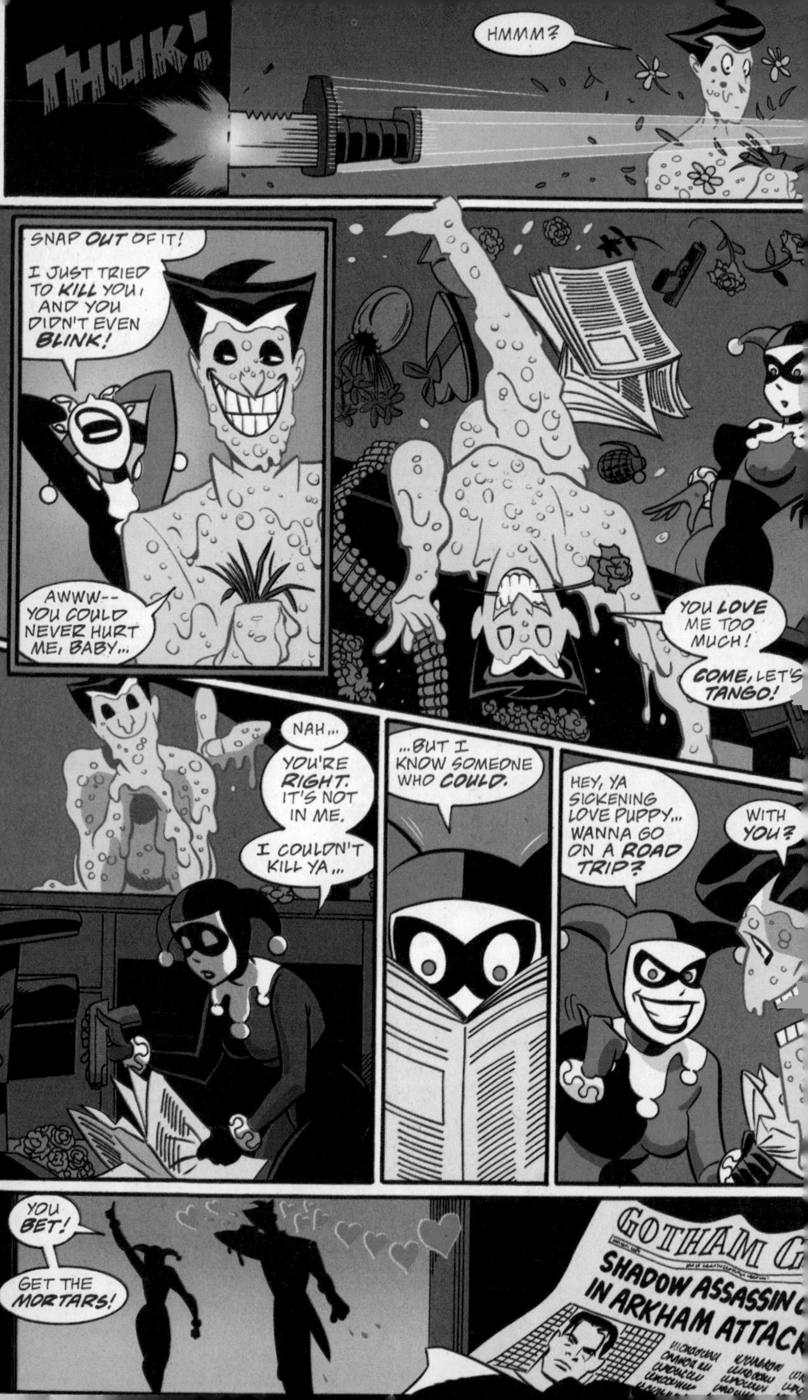
THUK!
HMMM?
SNAP OUT OF IT!
I JUST TRIED TO KILL YOU, AND YOU DIDN'T EVEN BLINK!
AWWW-- YOU COULD NEVER HURT ME, BABY...
YOU LOVE ME TOO MUCH!
COME, LET'S TANGO!
NAH...
YOU'RE RIGHT. IT'S NOT IN ME.
I COULDN'T KILL YA...
...BUT I KNOW SOMEONE WHO COULD.
HEY, YA SICKENING LOVE PUPPY... WANNA GO ON A ROAD TRIP?
WITH YOU?
YOU BET!
GET THE MORTARS!
GOTHAM G
SHADOW ASSASSIN
IN ARKHAM ATTACK

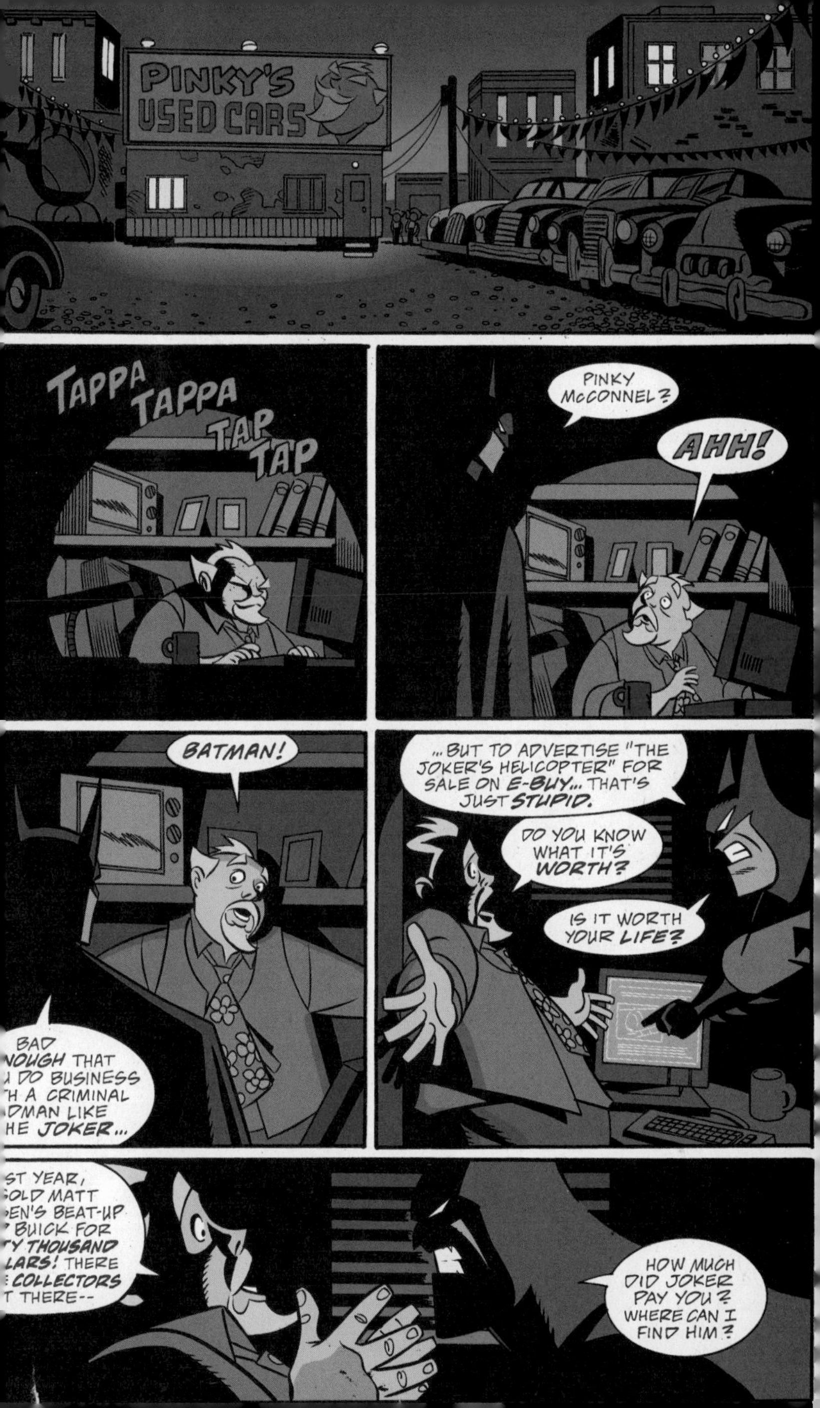
PINKY'S USED CARS
TAPPA TAPPA TAP TAP
PINKY McCONNEL?
AHH!
BATMAN!
BAD
NOUGH THAT
U DO BUSINESS
TH A CRIMINAL
DMAN LIKE
HE JOKER...
...BUT TO ADVERTISE "THE JOKER'S HELICOPTER" FOR SALE ON E-BUY... THAT'S JUST STUPID.
DO YOU KNOW WHAT IT'S WORTH?
IS IT WORTH YOUR LIFE?
ST YEAR,
SOLD MATT
EN'S BEAT-UP
BUICK FOR
TY THOUSAND
LARS! THERE
COLLECTORS
T THERE--
HOW MUCH DID JOKER PAY YOU? WHERE CAN I FIND HIM?

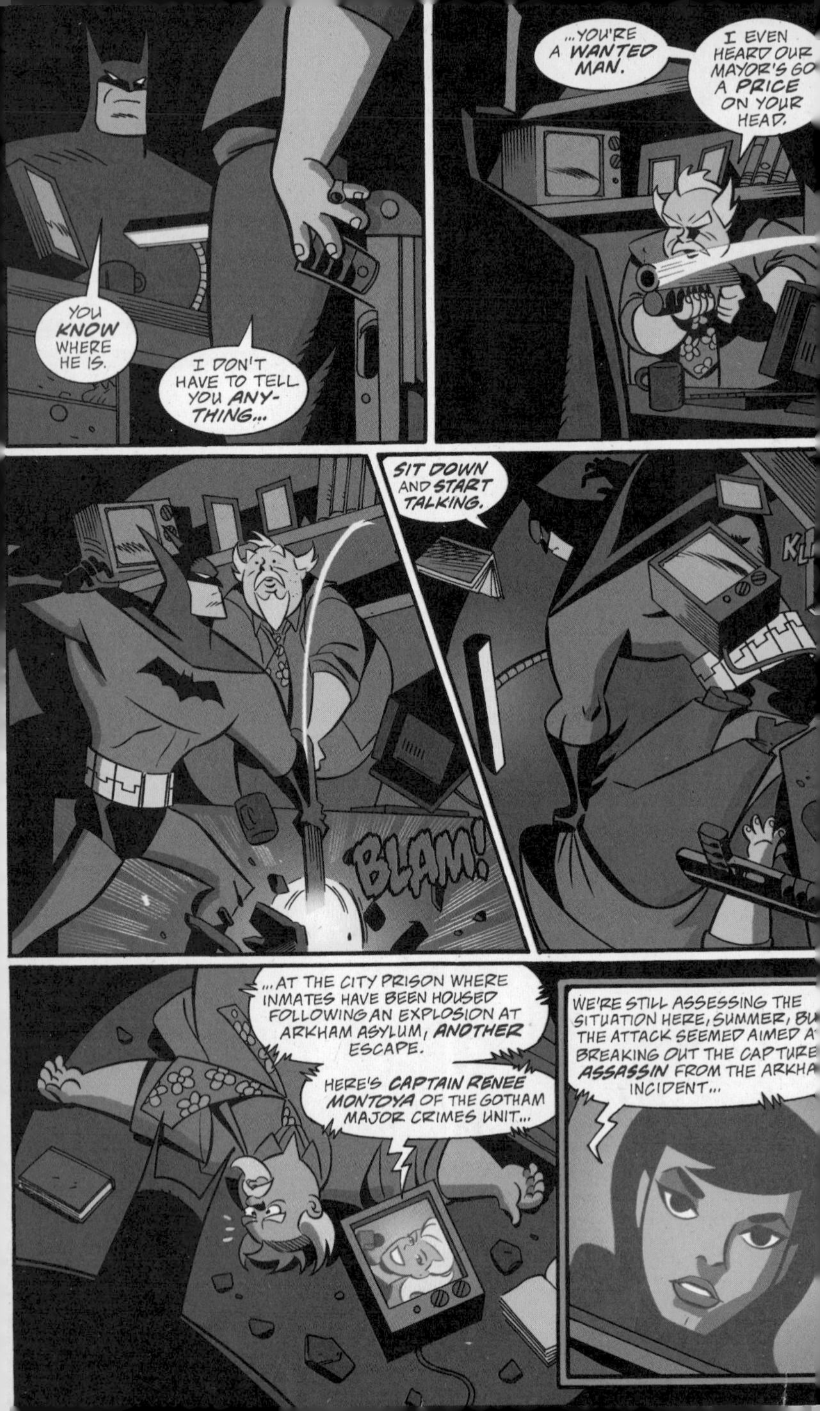
YOU KNOW WHERE HE IS.
I DON'T HAVE TO TELL YOU ANY-THING...
...YOU'RE A WANTED MAN.
I EVEN HEARD OUR MAYOR'S GO A PRICE ON YOUR HEAD.
BLAM!
SIT DOWN AND START TALKING.
...AT THE CITY PRISON WHERE INMATES HAVE BEEN HOUSED FOLLOWING AN EXPLOSION AT ARKHAM ASYLUM, ANOTHER ESCAPE.
HERE'S CAPTAIN RENEE MONTOYA OF THE GOTHAM MAJOR CRIMES UNIT...
WE'RE STILL ASSESSING THE SITUATION HERE, SUMMER, BU THE ATTACK SEEMED AIMED A BREAKING OUT THE CAPTURE ASSASSIN FROM THE ARKHA INCIDENT...

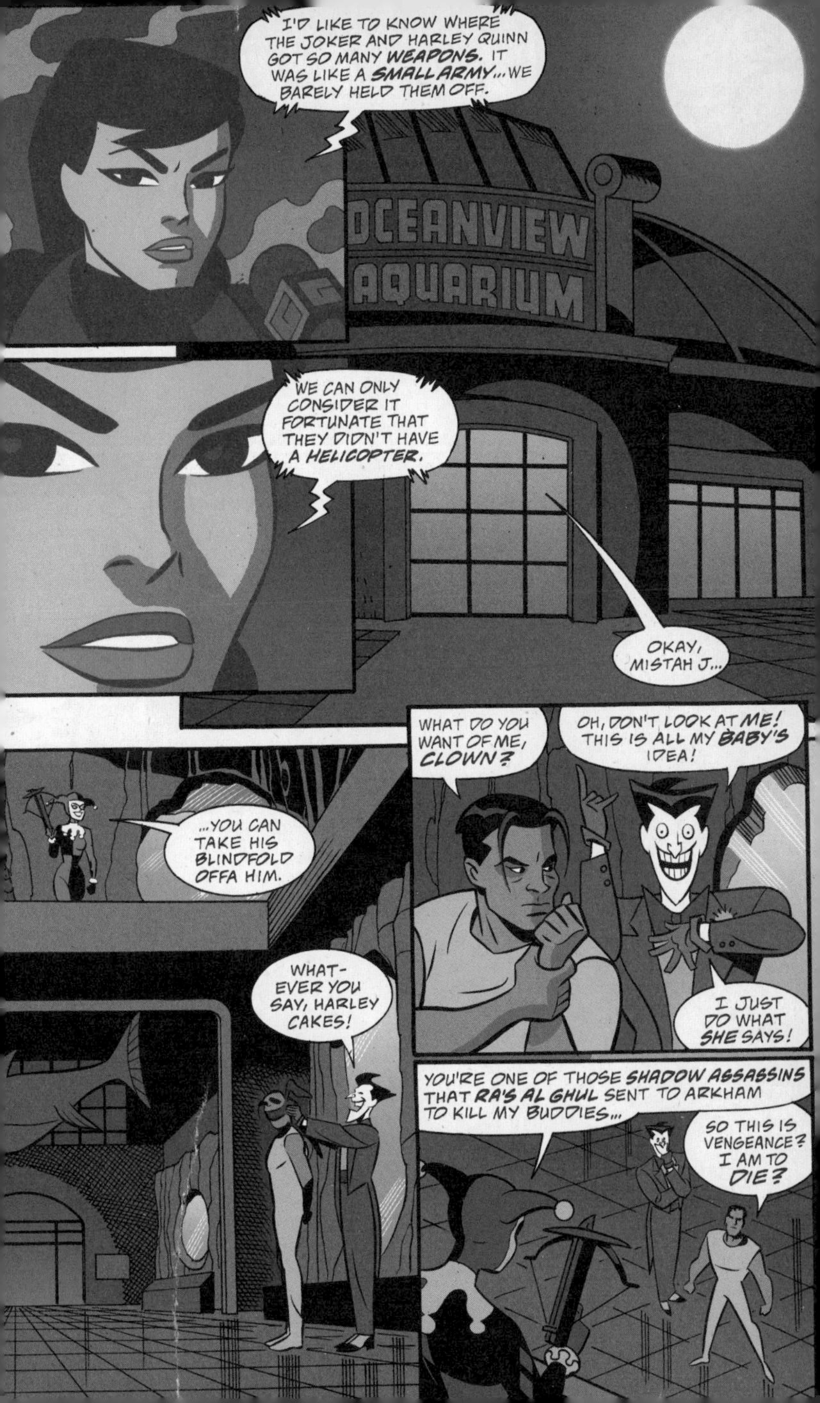
I'D LIKE TO KNOW WHERE THE JOKER AND HARLEY QUINN GOT SO MANY WEAPONS. IT WAS LIKE A SMALL ARMY... WE BARELY HELD THEM OFF.
OCEANVIEW AQUARIUM
WE CAN ONLY CONSIDER IT FORTUNATE THAT THEY DIDN'T HAVE A HELICOPTER.
OKAY, MISTAH J...
...YOU CAN TAKE HIS BLINDFOLD OFFA HIM.
WHAT-EVER YOU SAY, HARLEY CAKES!
WHAT DO YOU WANT OF ME, CLOWN?
OH, DON'T LOOK AT ME! THIS IS ALL MY BABY'S IDEA!
I JUST DO WHAT SHE SAYS!
YOU'RE ONE OF THOSE SHADOW ASSASSINS THAT RA'S AL GHUL SENT TO ARKHAM TO KILL MY BUDDIES...
SO THIS IS VENGEANCE? I AM TO DIE?

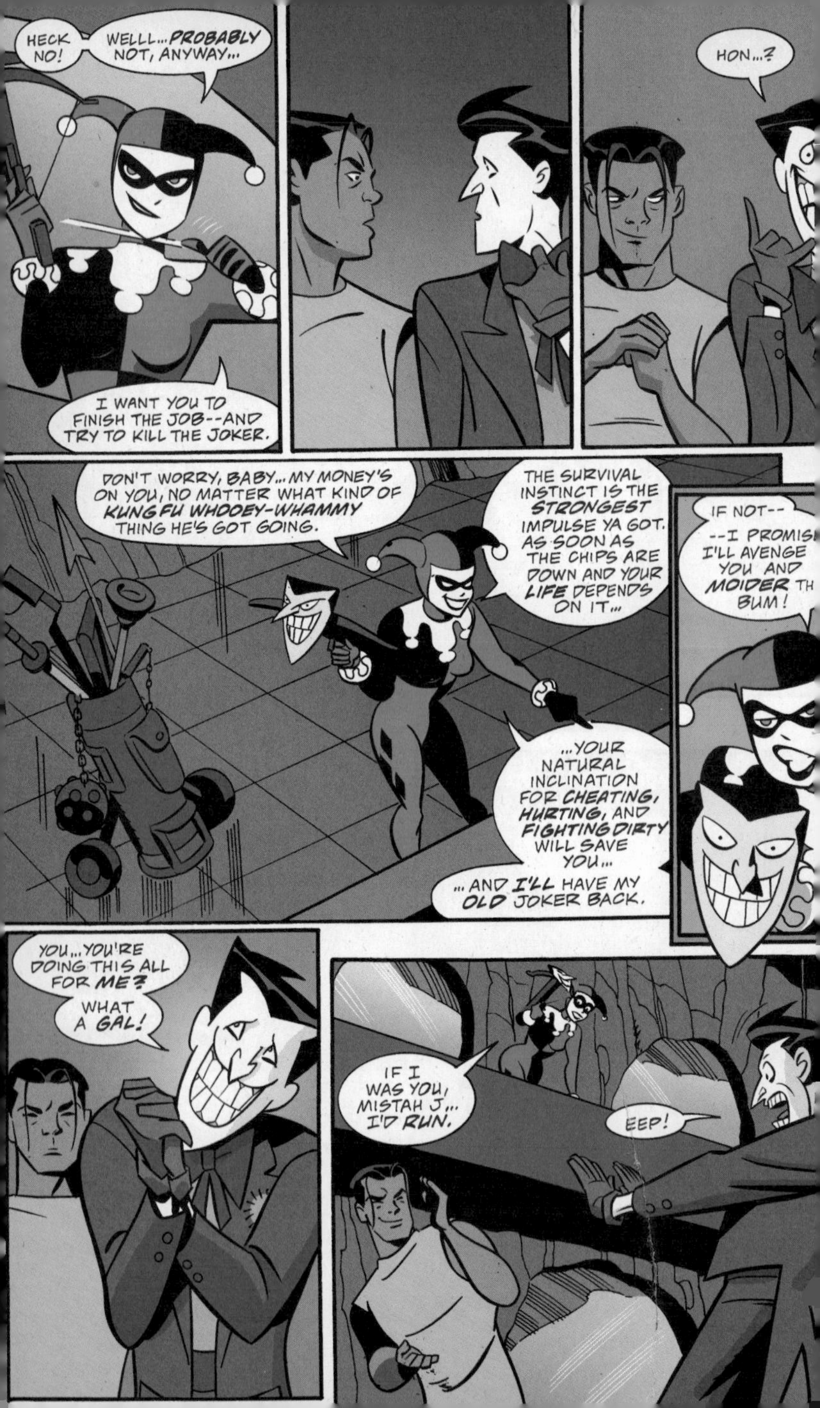
HECK NO!
WELLL... PROBABLY NOT, ANYWAY...
I WANT YOU TO FINISH THE JOB--AND TRY TO KILL THE JOKER.
HON...?
DON'T WORRY, BABY... MY MONEY'S ON YOU, NO MATTER WHAT KIND OF KUNG FU WHOOEY-WHAMMY THING HE'S GOT GOING.
THE SURVIVAL INSTINCT IS THE STRONGEST IMPULSE YA GOT. AS SOON AS THE CHIPS ARE DOWN AND YOUR LIFE DEPENDS ON IT...
...YOUR NATURAL INCLINATION FOR CHEATING, HURTING, AND FIGHTING DIRTY WILL SAVE YOU...
...AND I'LL HAVE MY OLD JOKER BACK.
IF NOT--
--I PROMIS I'LL AVENGE YOU AND MOIDER TH BUM!
YOU... YOU'RE DOING THIS ALL FOR ME?
WHAT A GAL!
IF I WAS YOU, MISTAH J... I'D RUN.
EEP!

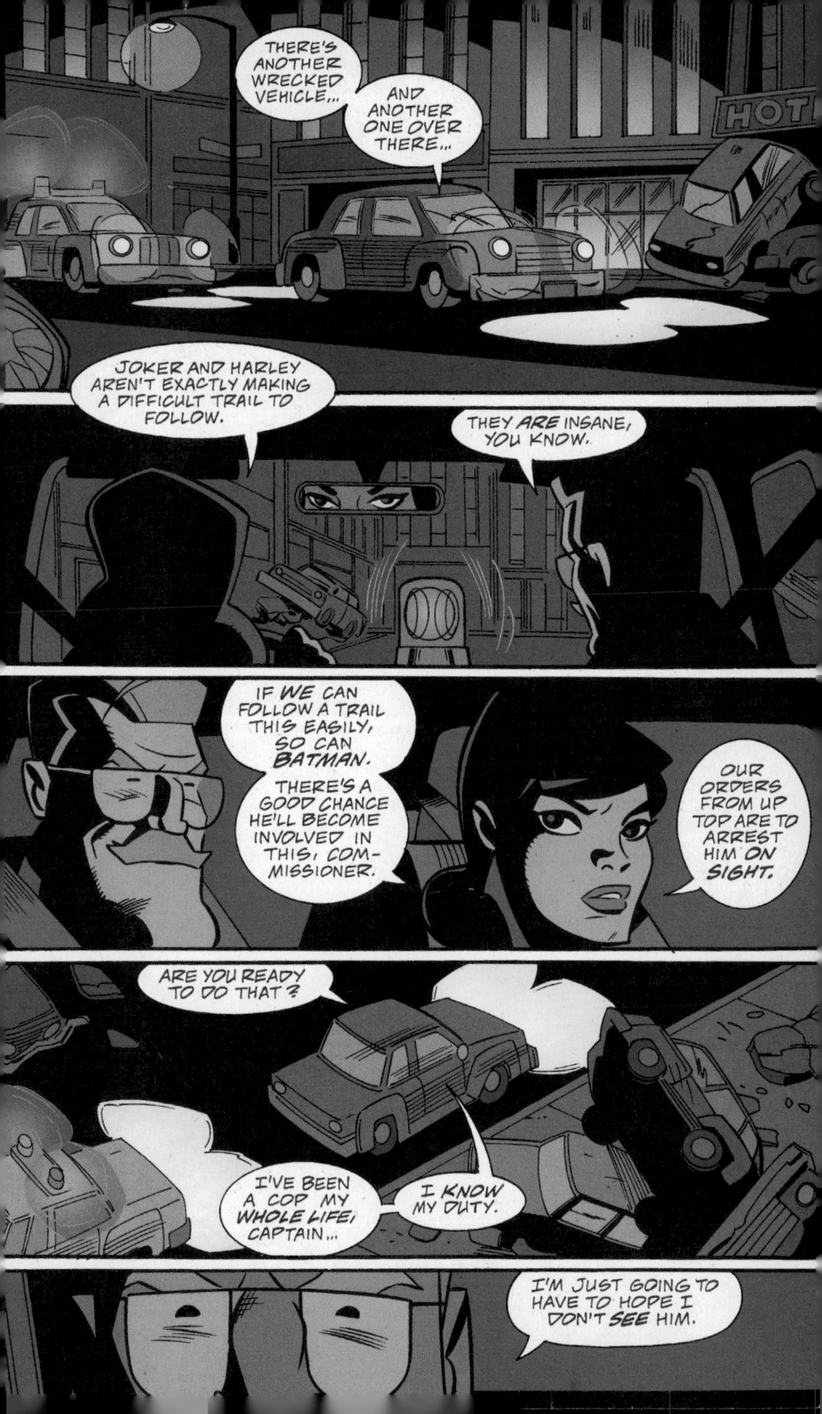
THERE'S ANOTHER WRECKED VEHICLE...
AND ANOTHER ONE OVER THERE...
HOT
JOKER AND HARLEY AREN'T EXACTLY MAKING A DIFFICULT TRAIL TO FOLLOW.
THEY *ARE* INSANE, YOU KNOW.
IF *WE* CAN FOLLOW A TRAIL THIS EASILY, SO CAN *BATMAN*.
THERE'S A GOOD CHANCE HE'LL BECOME INVOLVED IN THIS, COM-MISSIONER.
OUR ORDERS FROM UP TOP ARE TO ARREST HIM *ON SIGHT.*
ARE YOU READY TO DO THAT?
I'VE BEEN A COP MY *WHOLE LIFE*, CAPTAIN...
I *KNOW* MY DUTY.
I'M JUST GOING TO HAVE TO HOPE I DON'T *SEE* HIM.

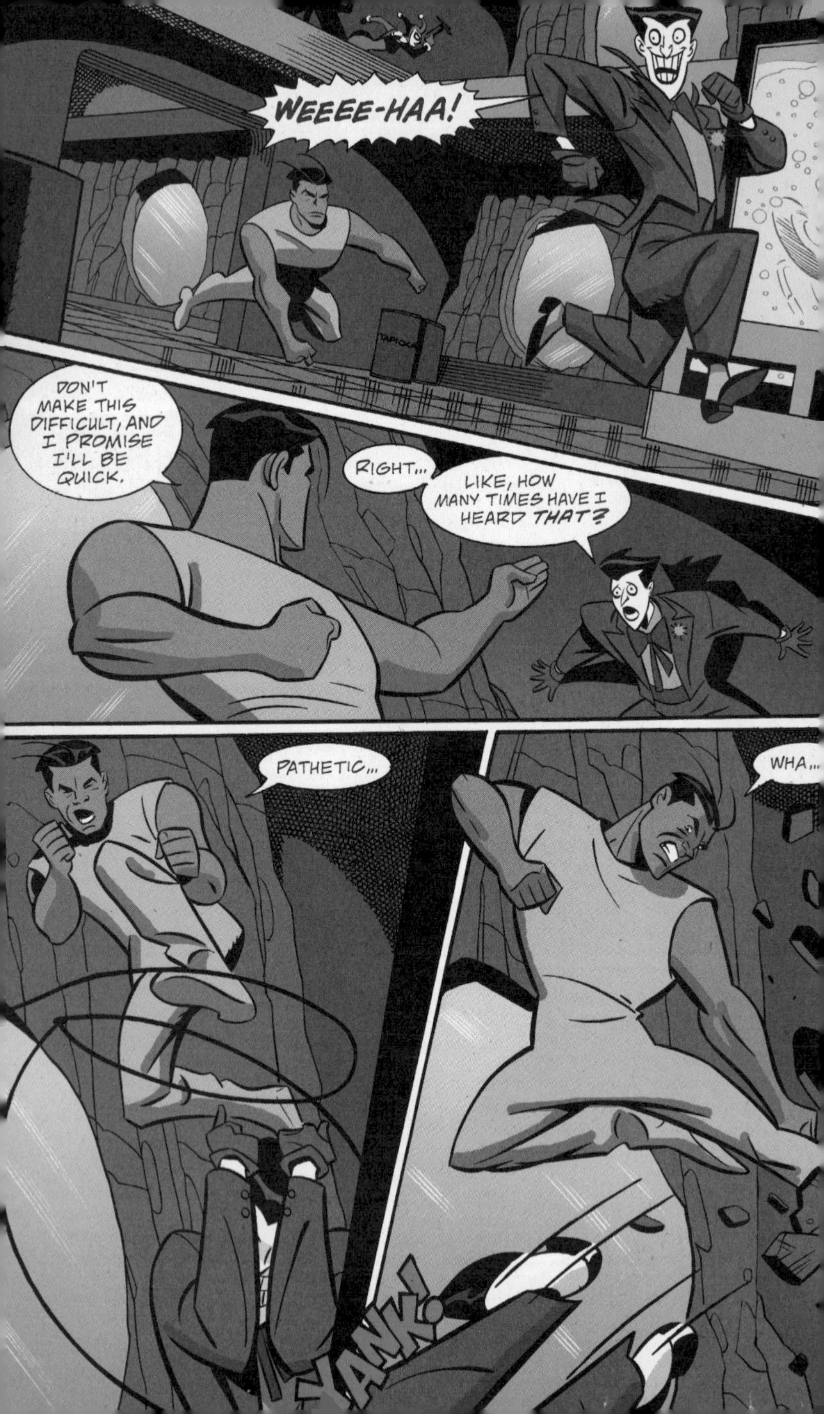
WEEEE-HAA!
DON'T MAKE THIS DIFFICULT, AND I PROMISE I'LL BE QUICK.
RIGHT...
LIKE, HOW MANY TIMES HAVE I HEARD THAT?
PATHETIC...
WHA...

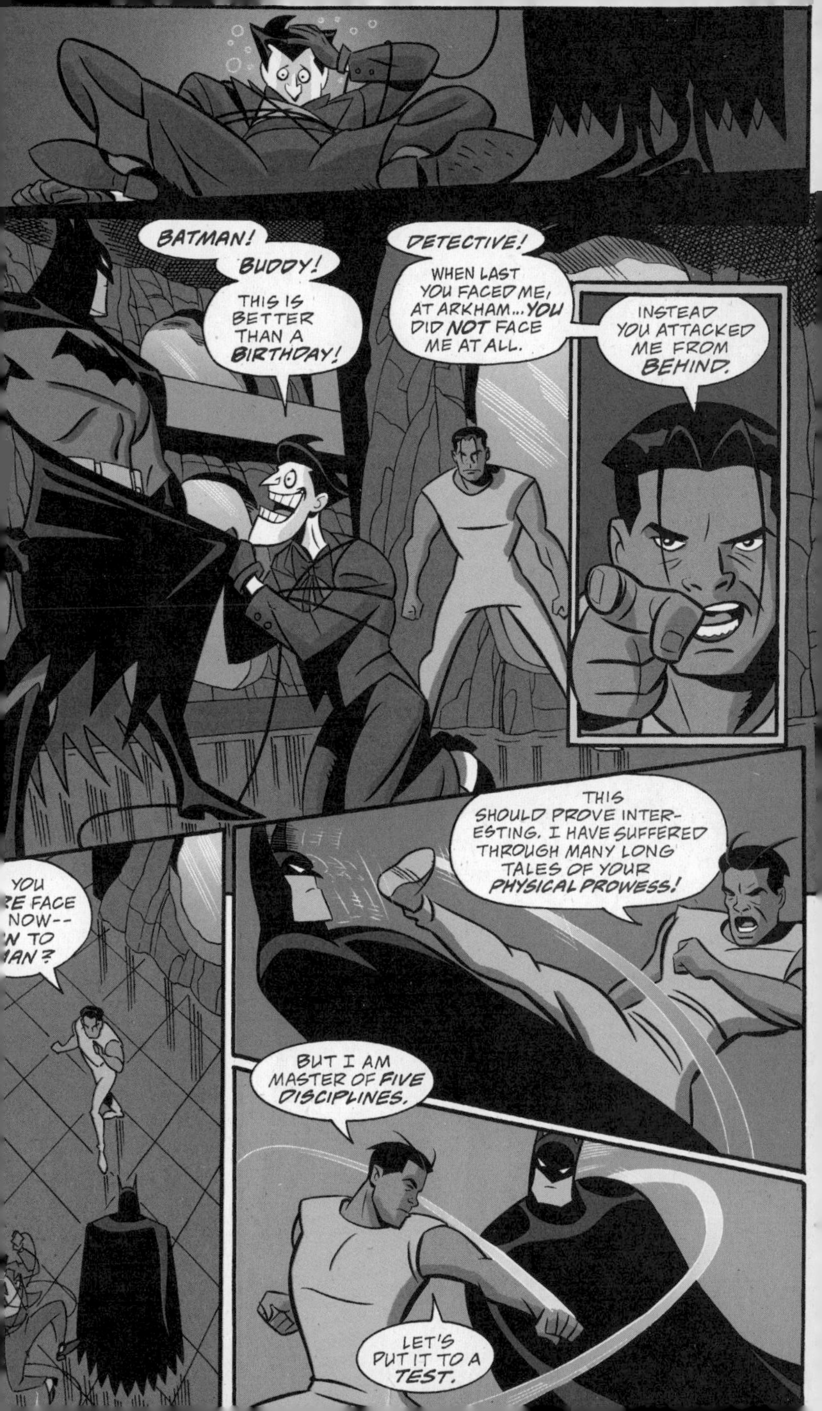
BATMAN!
BUDDY!
THIS IS BETTER THAN A BIRTHDAY!
DETECTIVE!
WHEN LAST YOU FACED ME, AT ARKHAM... YOU DID NOT FACE ME AT ALL.
INSTEAD YOU ATTACKED ME FROM BEHIND.
YOU
FACE NOW--
TO
THIS SHOULD PROVE INTER-ESTING. I HAVE SUFFERED THROUGH MANY LONG TALES OF YOUR PHYSICAL PROWESS!
BUT I AM MASTER OF FIVE DISCIPLINES.
LET'S PUT IT TO A TEST.

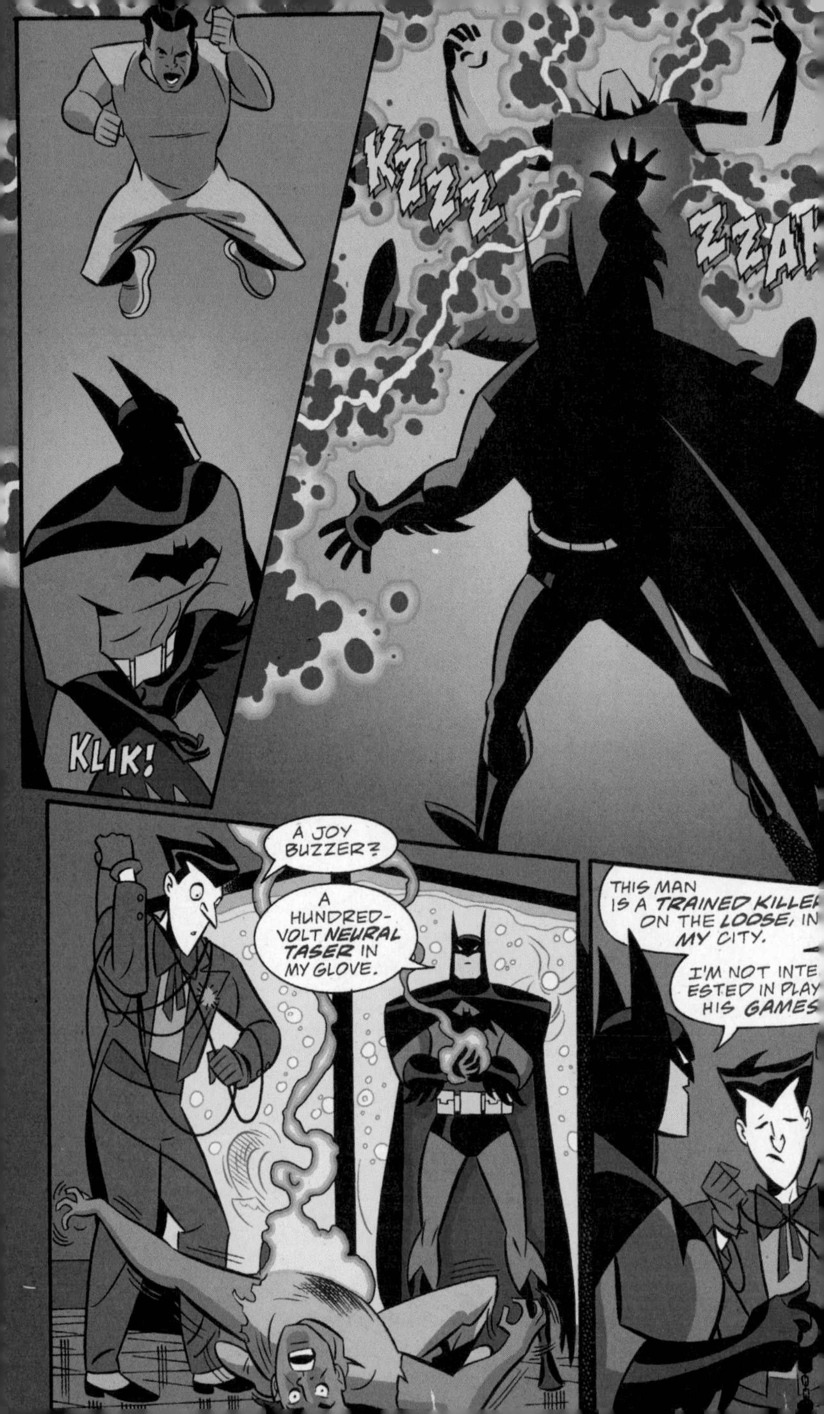
KLIK!
KZZZZ
ZZAK
A JOY BUZZER?
A HUNDRED-VOLT NEURAL TASER IN MY GLOVE.
THIS MAN IS A TRAINED KILLER ON THE LOOSE, IN MY CITY.
I'M NOT INTERESTED IN PLAYING HIS GAMES.

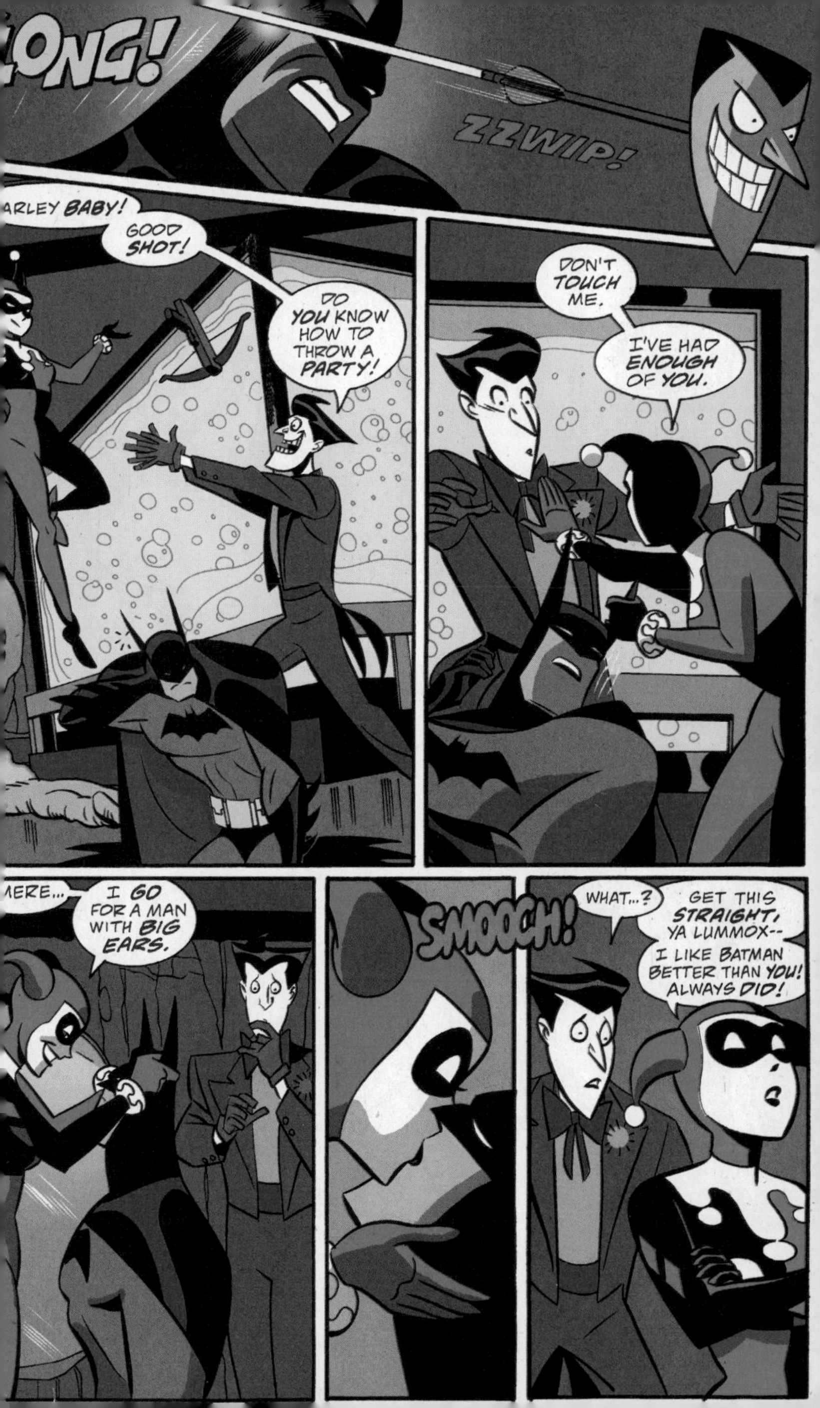

ONG!
ZZWIP!
ARLEY BABY!
GOOD SHOT!
DO YOU KNOW HOW TO THROW A PARTY!
DON'T TOUCH ME.
I'VE HAD ENOUGH OF YOU.
HERE...
I GO FOR A MAN WITH BIG EARS.
SMOOCH!
WHAT...?
GET THIS STRAIGHT, YA LUMMOX-- I LIKE BATMAN BETTER THAN YOU! ALWAYS DID!

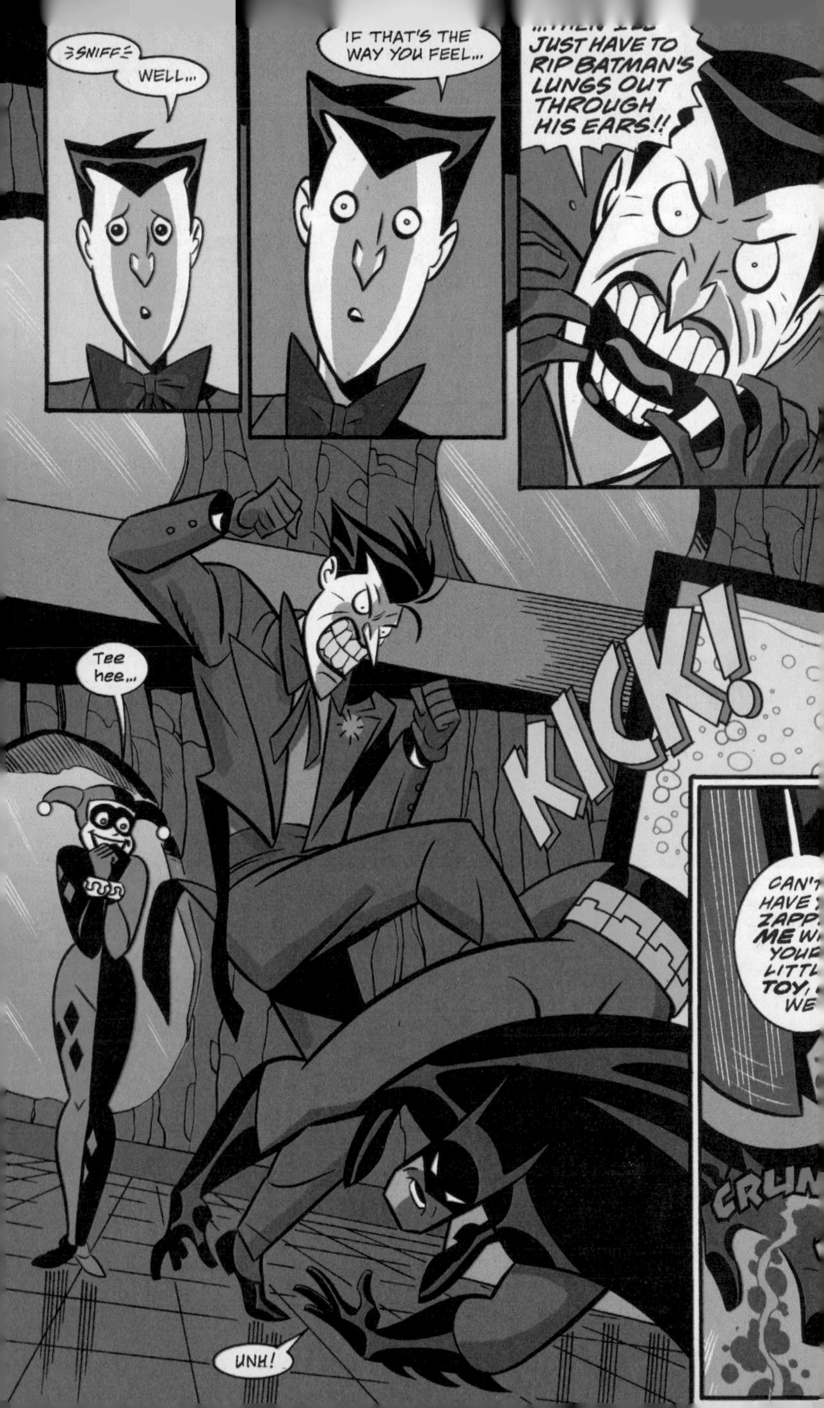

≶SNIFF≶
WELL...
IF THAT'S THE WAY YOU FEEL...
JUST HAVE TO RIP BATMAN'S LUNGS OUT THROUGH HIS EARS!!
Tee hee...
KICK!
UNH!

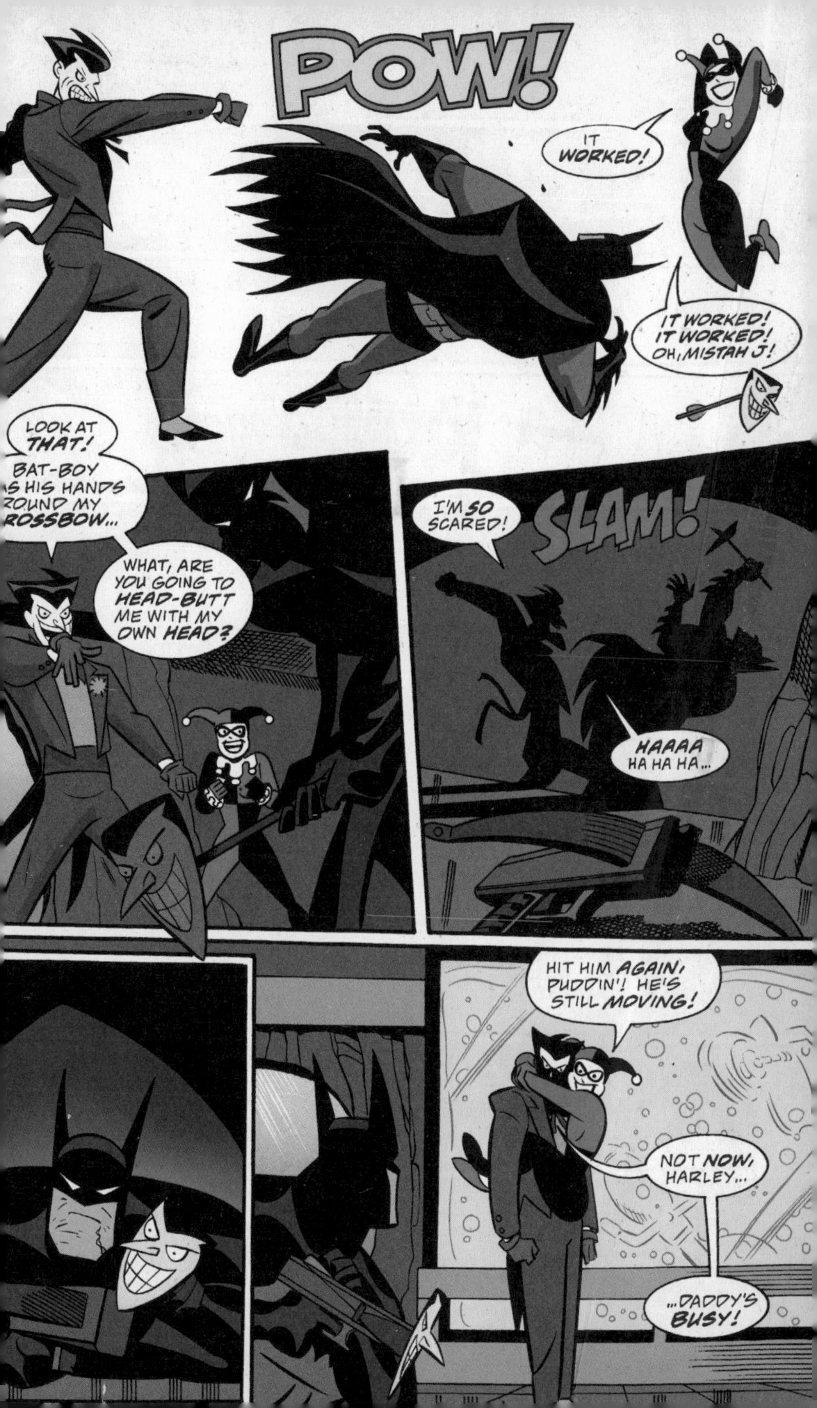
POW!
IT WORKED!
IT WORKED! IT WORKED! OH, MISTAH J!
LOOK AT THAT! BAT-BOY AS HIS HANDS ROUND MY ROSSBOW...
WHAT, ARE YOU GOING TO HEAD-BUTT ME WITH MY OWN HEAD?
I'M SO SCARED!
SLAM!
HAAAA HA HA HA...
HIT HIM AGAIN, PUDDIN'! HE'S STILL MOVING!
NOT NOW, HARLEY...
...DADDY'S BUSY!

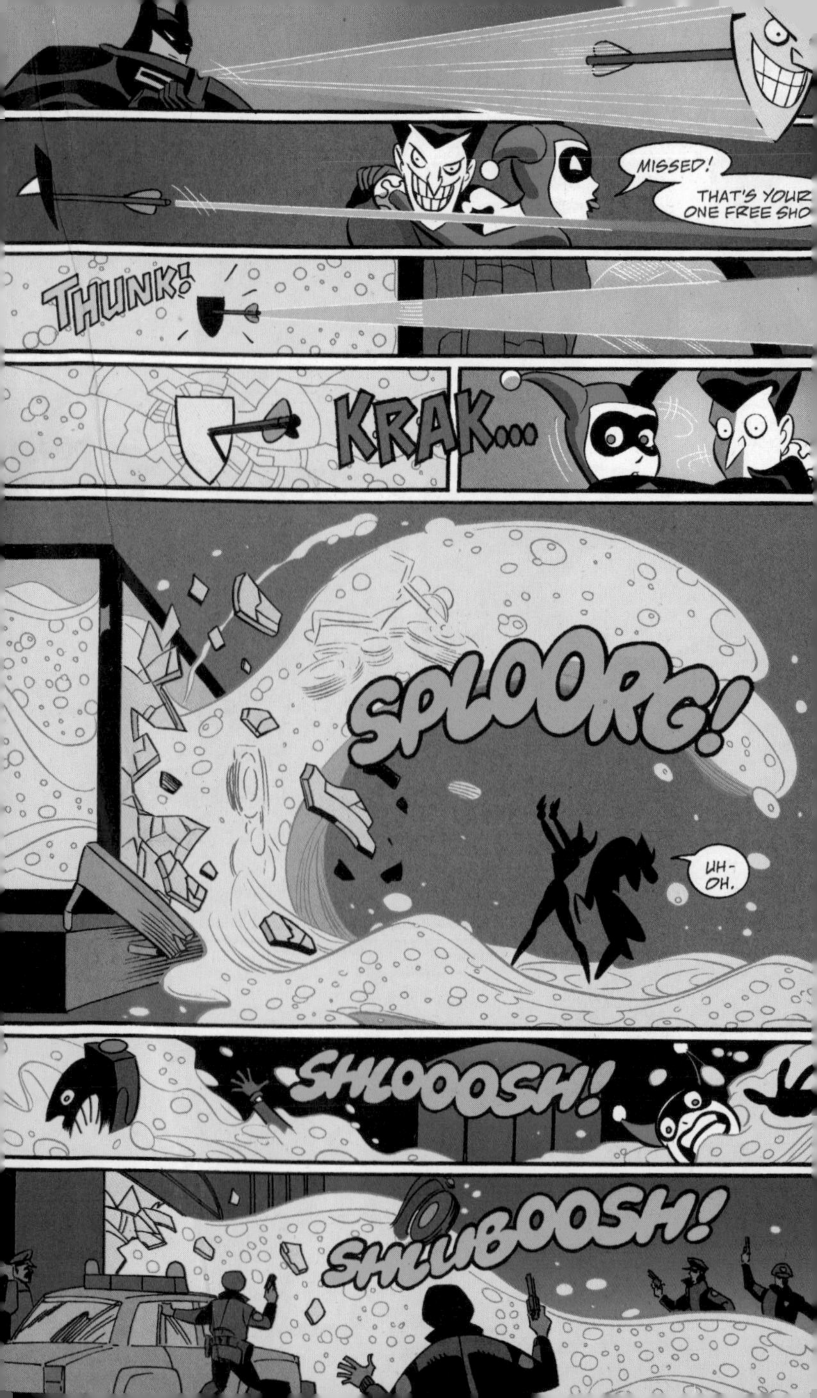

MISSED!
THAT'S YOUR ONE FREE SHO
THUNK!
KRAK...
SPLOORG!
UH-OH.
SHLOOOSH!
SHLUBOOSH!

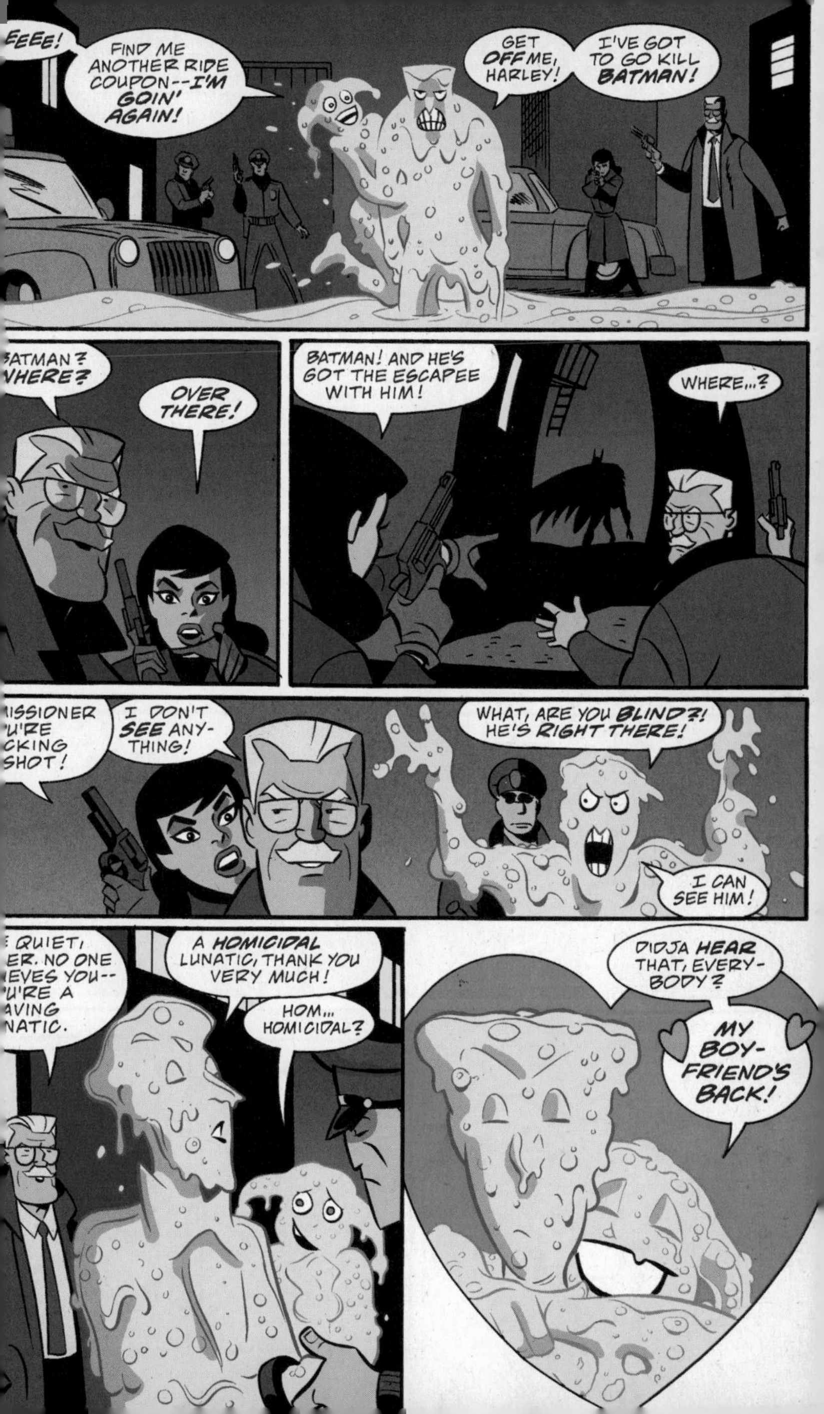
EEEE!
FIND ME ANOTHER RIDE COUPON--I'M GOIN' AGAIN!
GET OFF ME, HARLEY!
I'VE GOT TO GO KILL BATMAN!
BATMAN? WHERE?
OVER THERE!
BATMAN! AND HE'S GOT THE ESCAPEE WITH HIM!
WHERE...?
ISSIONER U'RE CKING SHOT!
I DON'T SEE ANY-THING!
WHAT, ARE YOU BLIND?! HE'S RIGHT THERE!
I CAN SEE HIM!
E QUIET, ER. NO ONE IEVES YOU-- U'RE A AVING NATIC.
A HOMICIDAL LUNATIC, THANK YOU VERY MUCH!
HOM... HOMICIDAL?
DIDJA HEAR THAT, EVERY-BODY?
MY BOY-FRIEND'S BACK!

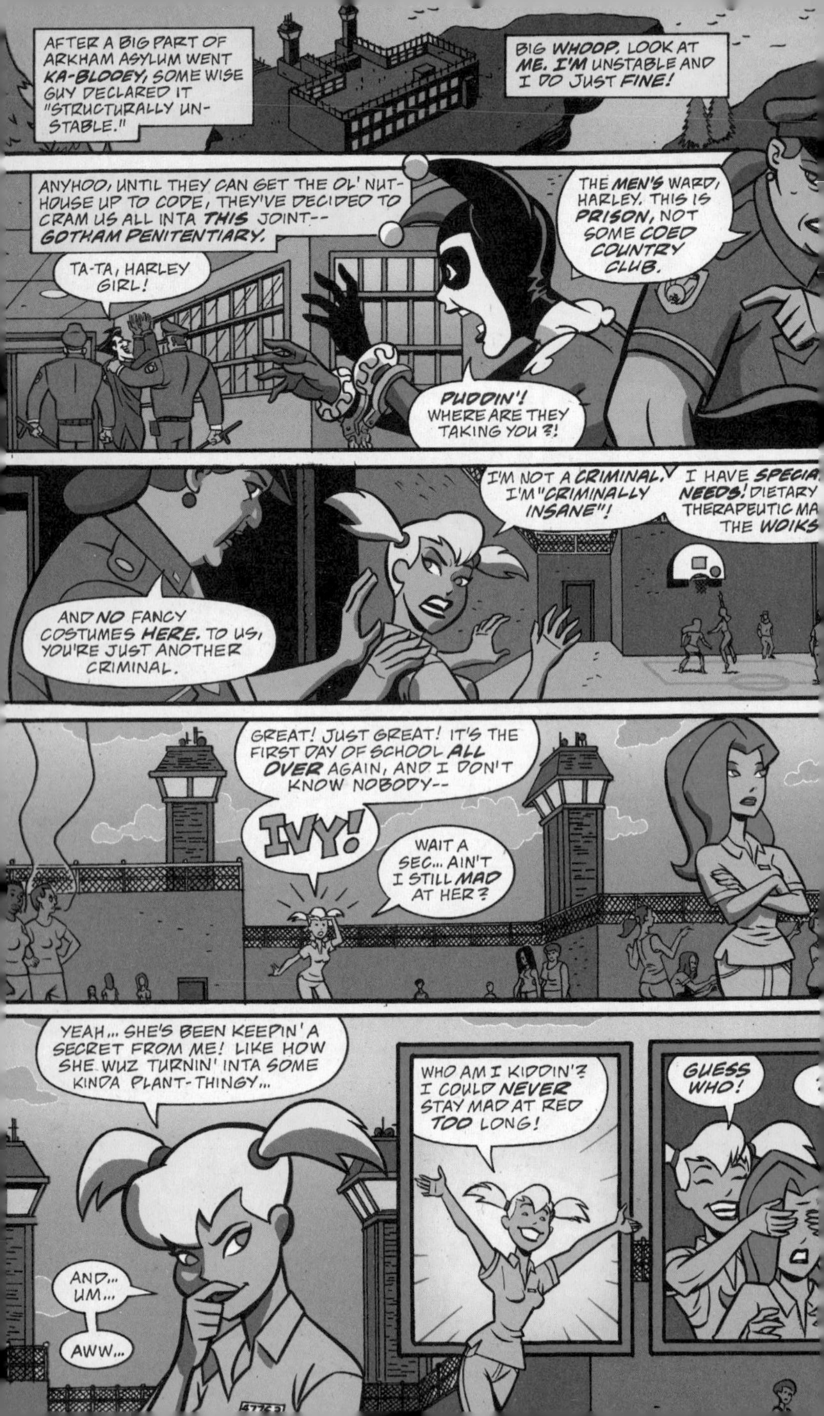

AFTER A BIG PART OF ARKHAM ASYLUM WENT KA-BLOOEY, SOME WISE GUY DECLARED IT "STRUCTURALLY UN-STABLE."
BIG WHOOP. LOOK AT ME. I'M UNSTABLE AND I DO JUST FINE!
ANYHOO, UNTIL THEY CAN GET THE OL' NUT-HOUSE UP TO CODE, THEY'VE DECIDED TO CRAM US ALL INTA THIS JOINT-- GOTHAM PENITENTIARY.
TA-TA, HARLEY GIRL!
PUDDIN'! WHERE ARE THEY TAKING YOU?!
THE MEN'S WARD, HARLEY. THIS IS PRISON, NOT SOME COED COUNTRY CLUB.
AND NO FANCY COSTUMES HERE. TO US, YOU'RE JUST ANOTHER CRIMINAL.
I'M NOT A CRIMINAL, I'M "CRIMINALLY INSANE"!
GREAT! JUST GREAT! IT'S THE FIRST DAY OF SCHOOL ALL OVER AGAIN, AND I DON'T KNOW NOBODY--
IVY!
WAIT A SEC... AIN'T I STILL MAD AT HER?
YEAH... SHE'S BEEN KEEPIN' A SECRET FROM ME! LIKE HOW SHE WUZ TURNIN' INTA SOME KINDA PLANT-THINGY...
AND... UM...
AWW...
WHO AM I KIDDIN'? I COULD NEVER STAY MAD AT RED TOO LONG!
GUESS WHO!

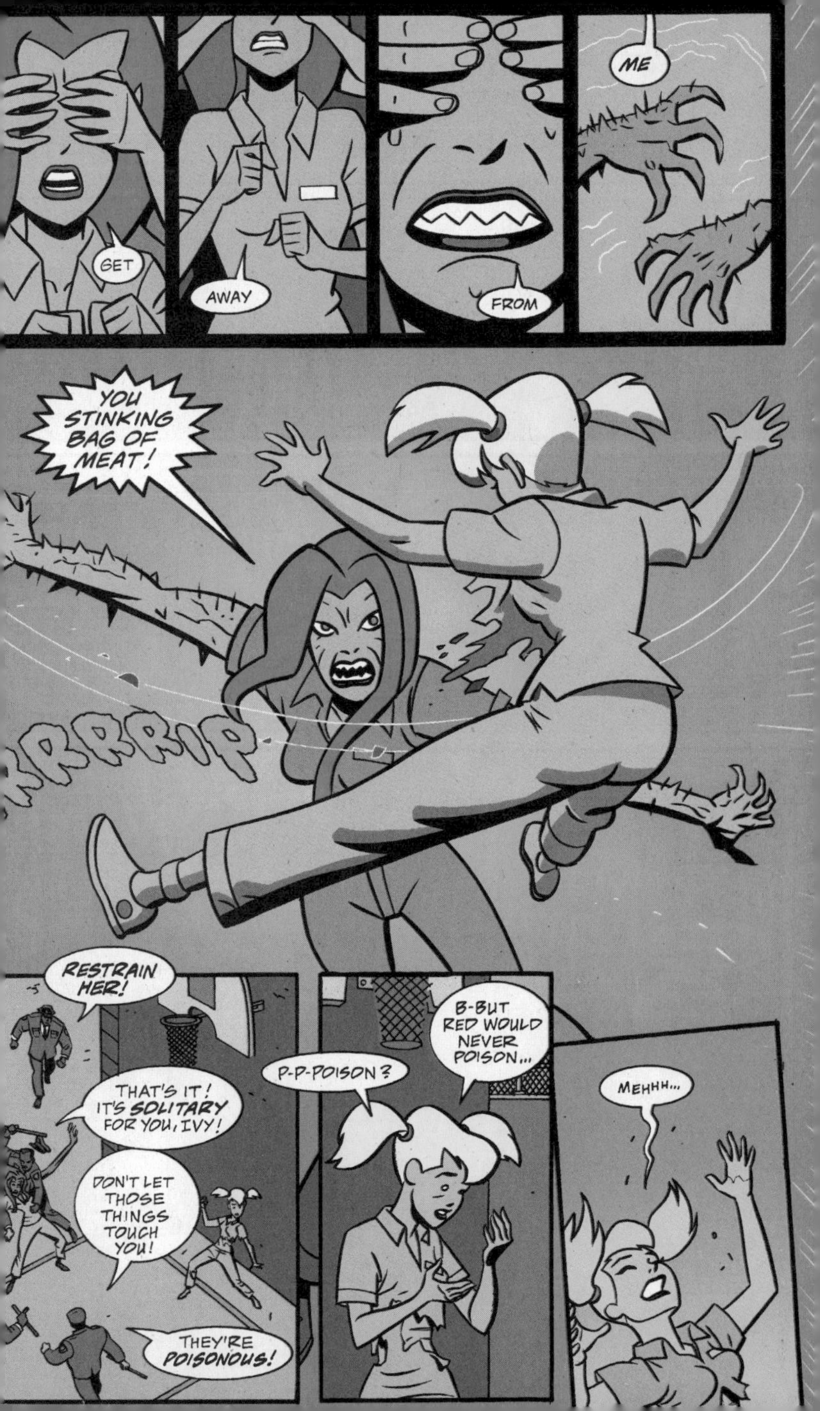
GET
AWAY
FROM
ME
YOU STINKING BAG OF MEAT!
RRRIP
RESTRAIN HER!
THAT'S IT! IT'S SOLITARY FOR YOU, IVY!
DON'T LET THOSE THINGS TOUCH YOU!
THEY'RE POISONOUS!
P-P-POISON?
B-BUT RED WOULD NEVER POISON...
MEHHH...

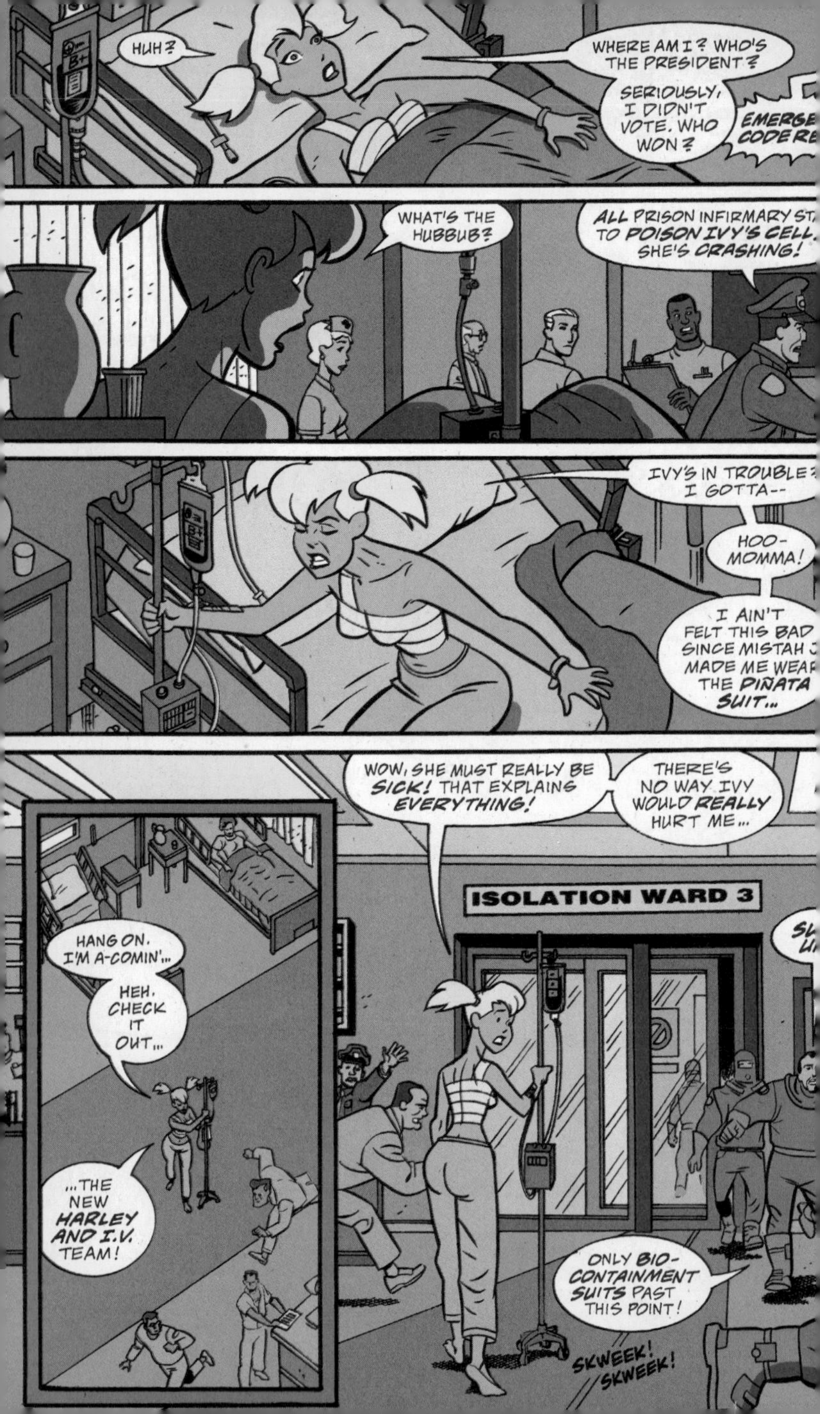

HUH?
WHERE AM I? WHO'S THE PRESIDENT?
SERIOUSLY, I DIDN'T VOTE. WHO WON?
EMERGE CODE RE
WHAT'S THE HUBBUB?
ALL PRISON INFIRMARY ST TO POISON IVY'S CELL. SHE'S CRASHING!
IVY'S IN TROUBLE? I GOTTA--
HOO-MOMMA!
I AIN'T FELT THIS BAD SINCE MISTAH J MADE ME WEAR THE PIÑATA SUIT...
WOW, SHE MUST REALLY BE SICK! THAT EXPLAINS EVERYTHING!
THERE'S NO WAY IVY WOULD REALLY HURT ME...
ISOLATION WARD 3
HANG ON. I'M A-COMIN'...
HEH. CHECK IT OUT...
...THE NEW HARLEY AND I.V. TEAM!
ONLY BIO-CONTAINMENT SUITS PAST THIS POINT!
SKWEEK! SKWEEK!

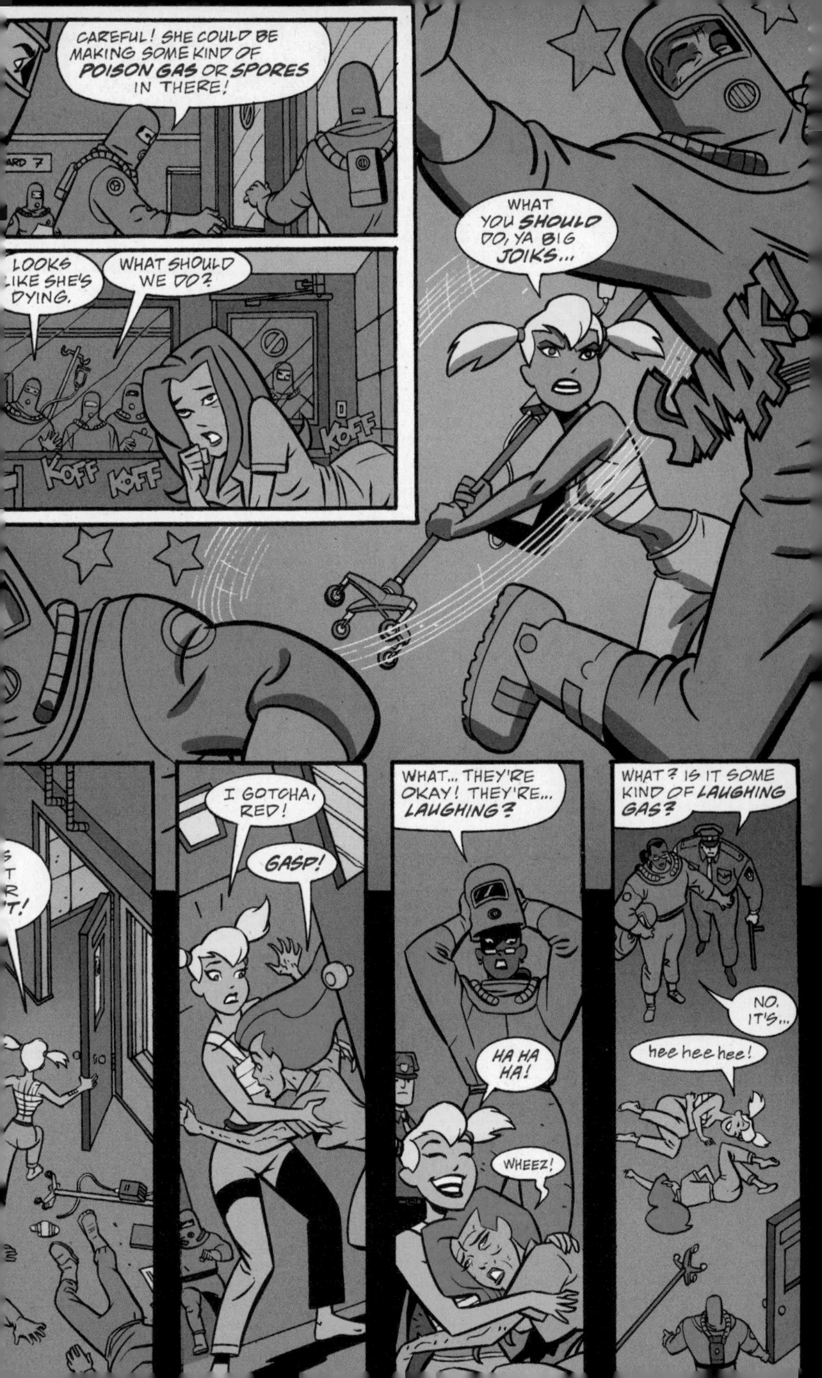

CAREFUL! SHE COULD BE MAKING SOME KIND OF POISON GAS OR SPORES IN THERE!
LOOKS LIKE SHE'S DYING.
WHAT SHOULD WE DO?
KOFF KOFF
KOFF
WHAT YOU SHOULD DO, YA BIG JOIKS...
SMAK!
I GOTCHA, RED!
GASP!
WHAT... THEY'RE OKAY! THEY'RE... LAUGHING?
HA HA HA!
WHEEZ!
WHAT? IS IT SOME KIND OF LAUGHING GAS?
NO. IT'S...
hee hee hee!

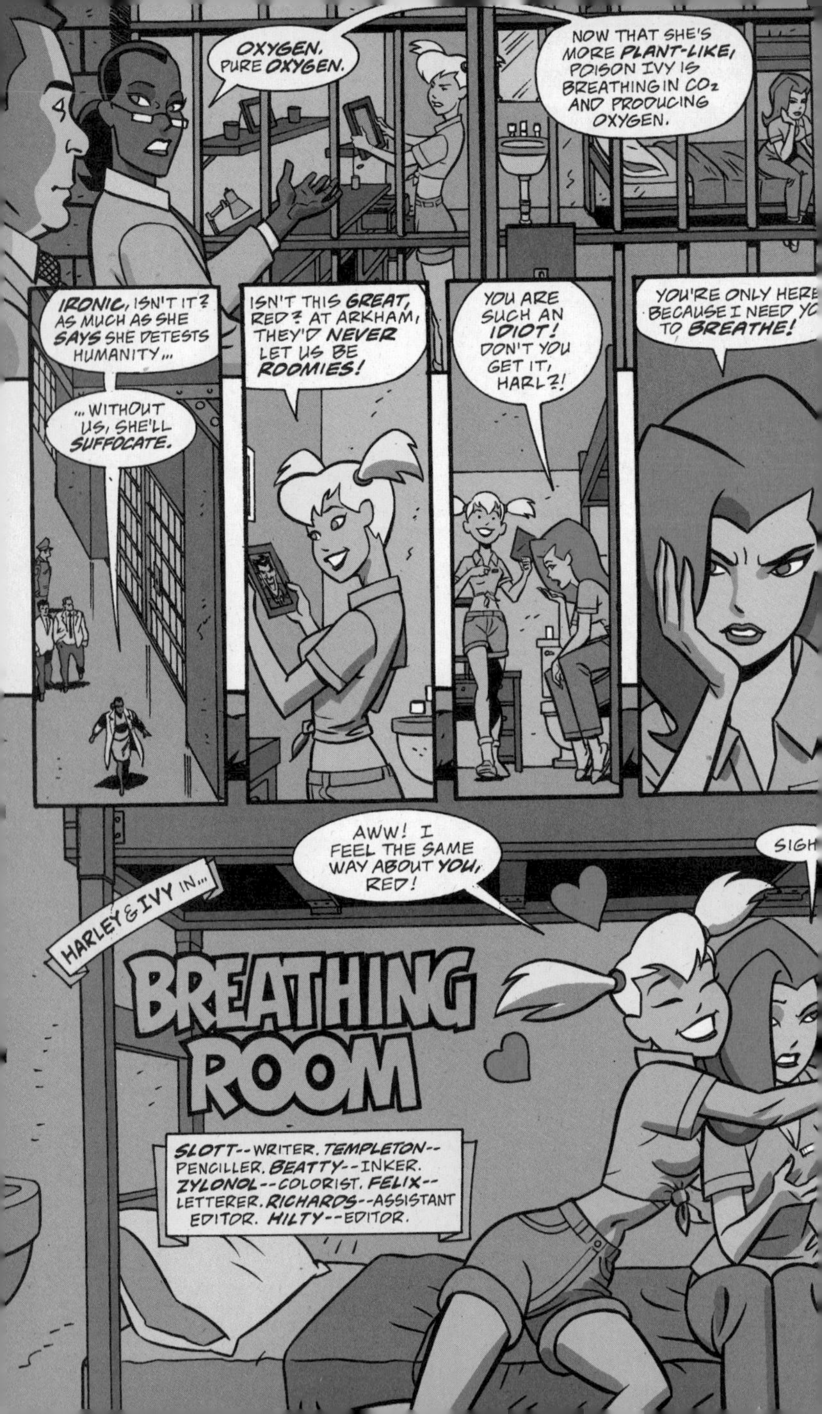

OXYGEN. PURE OXYGEN.
NOW THAT SHE'S MORE PLANT-LIKE, POISON IVY IS BREATHING IN CO_2 AND PRODUCING OXYGEN.
IRONIC, ISN'T IT? AS MUCH AS SHE SAYS SHE DETESTS HUMANITY...
...WITHOUT US, SHE'LL SUFFOCATE.
ISN'T THIS GREAT, RED? AT ARKHAM, THEY'D NEVER LET US BE ROOMIES!
YOU ARE SUCH AN IDIOT! DON'T YOU GET IT, HARL?!
YOU'RE ONLY HERE BECAUSE I NEED YO TO BREATHE!
AWW! I FEEL THE SAME WAY ABOUT YOU, RED!
SIGH
HARLEY & IVY IN...
BREATHING ROOM
SLOTT--WRITER. TEMPLETON--PENCILLER. BEATTY--INKER. ZYLONOL--COLORIST. FELIX--LETTERER. RICHARDS--ASSISTANT EDITOR. HILTY--EDITOR.

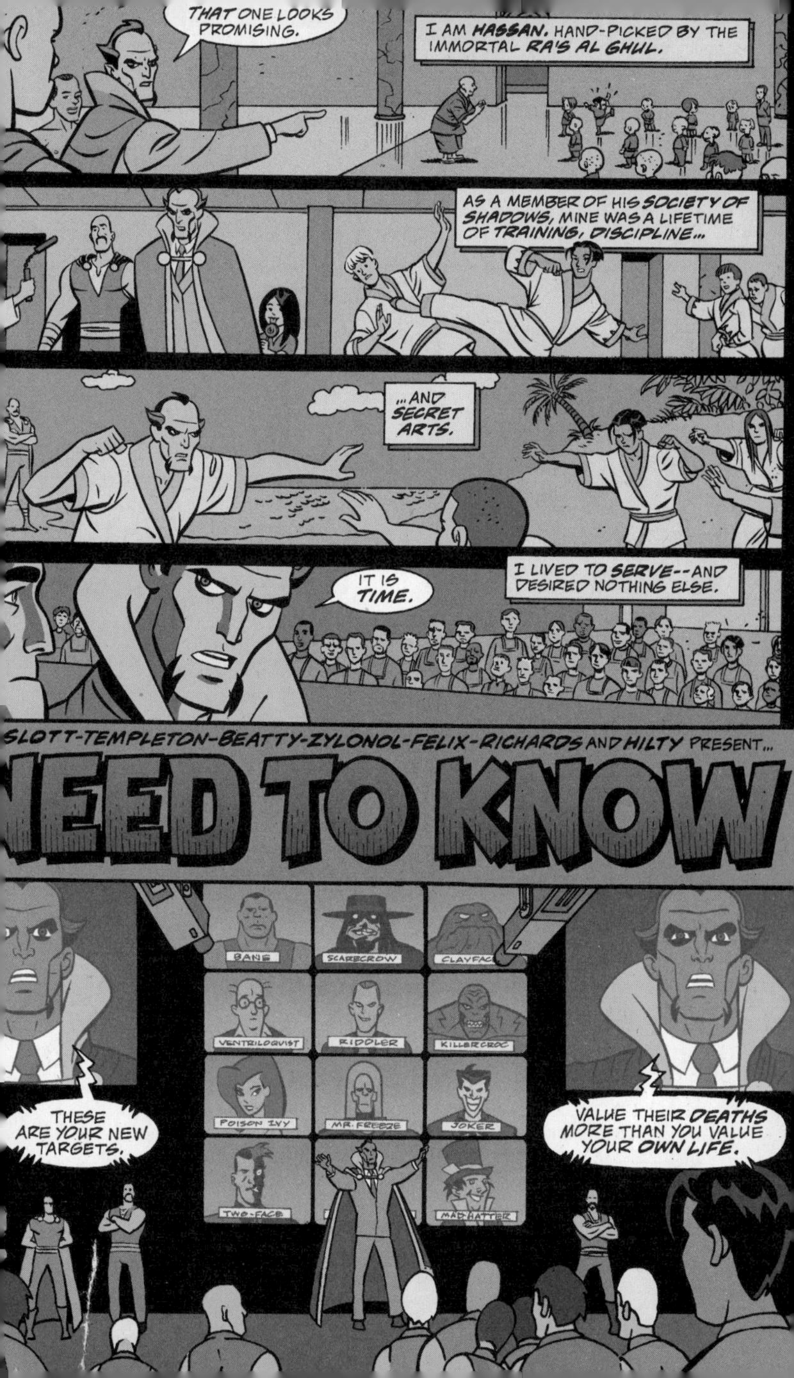
THAT ONE LOOKS PROMISING.
I AM HASSAN. HAND-PICKED BY THE IMMORTAL RA'S AL GHUL.
AS A MEMBER OF HIS SOCIETY OF SHADOWS, MINE WAS A LIFETIME OF TRAINING, DISCIPLINE...
...AND SECRET ARTS.
IT IS TIME.
I LIVED TO SERVE--AND DESIRED NOTHING ELSE.
SLOTT-TEMPLETON-BEATTY-ZYLONOL-FELIX-RICHARDS AND HILTY PRESENT...
NEED TO KNOW
BANE
SCARECROW
VENTRILOQUIST
RIDDLER
KILLER CROC
POISON IVY
MR. FREEZE
JOKER
TWO-FACE
MAD HATTER
THESE ARE YOUR NEW TARGETS.
VALUE THEIR DEATHS MORE THAN YOU VALUE YOUR OWN LIFE.

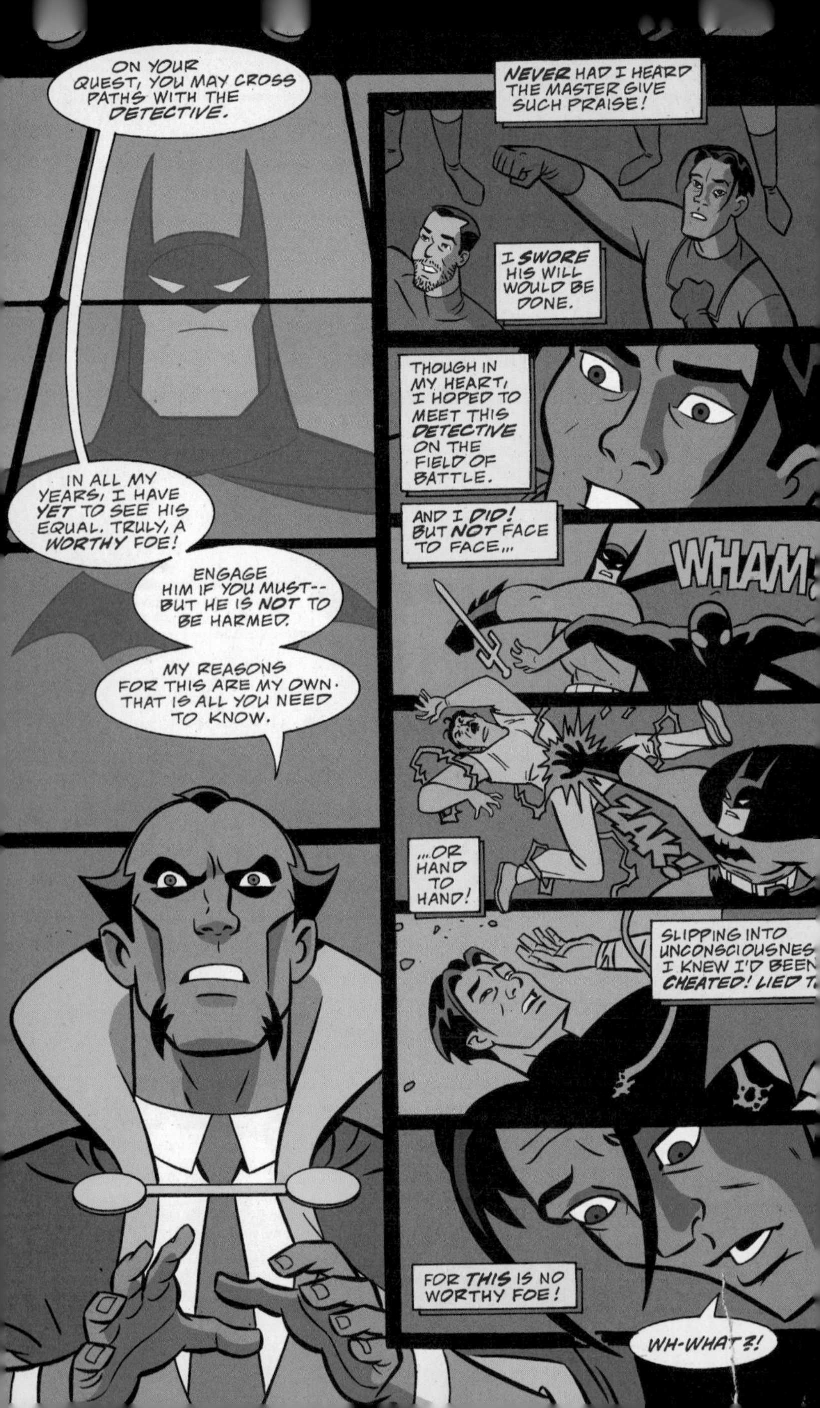

ON YOUR QUEST, YOU MAY CROSS PATHS WITH THE DETECTIVE.
IN ALL MY YEARS, I HAVE YET TO SEE HIS EQUAL. TRULY, A WORTHY FOE!
ENGAGE HIM IF YOU MUST--BUT HE IS NOT TO BE HARMED.
MY REASONS FOR THIS ARE MY OWN. THAT IS ALL YOU NEED TO KNOW.
NEVER HAD I HEARD THE MASTER GIVE SUCH PRAISE!
I SWORE HIS WILL WOULD BE DONE.
THOUGH IN MY HEART, I HOPED TO MEET THIS DETECTIVE ON THE FIELD OF BATTLE.
AND I DID! BUT NOT FACE TO FACE...
WHAM
...OR HAND TO HAND!
ZAK!
SLIPPING INTO UNCONSCIOUSNES
I KNEW I'D BEEN
CHEATED! LIED T
FOR THIS IS NO WORTHY FOE!
WH-WHAT?!

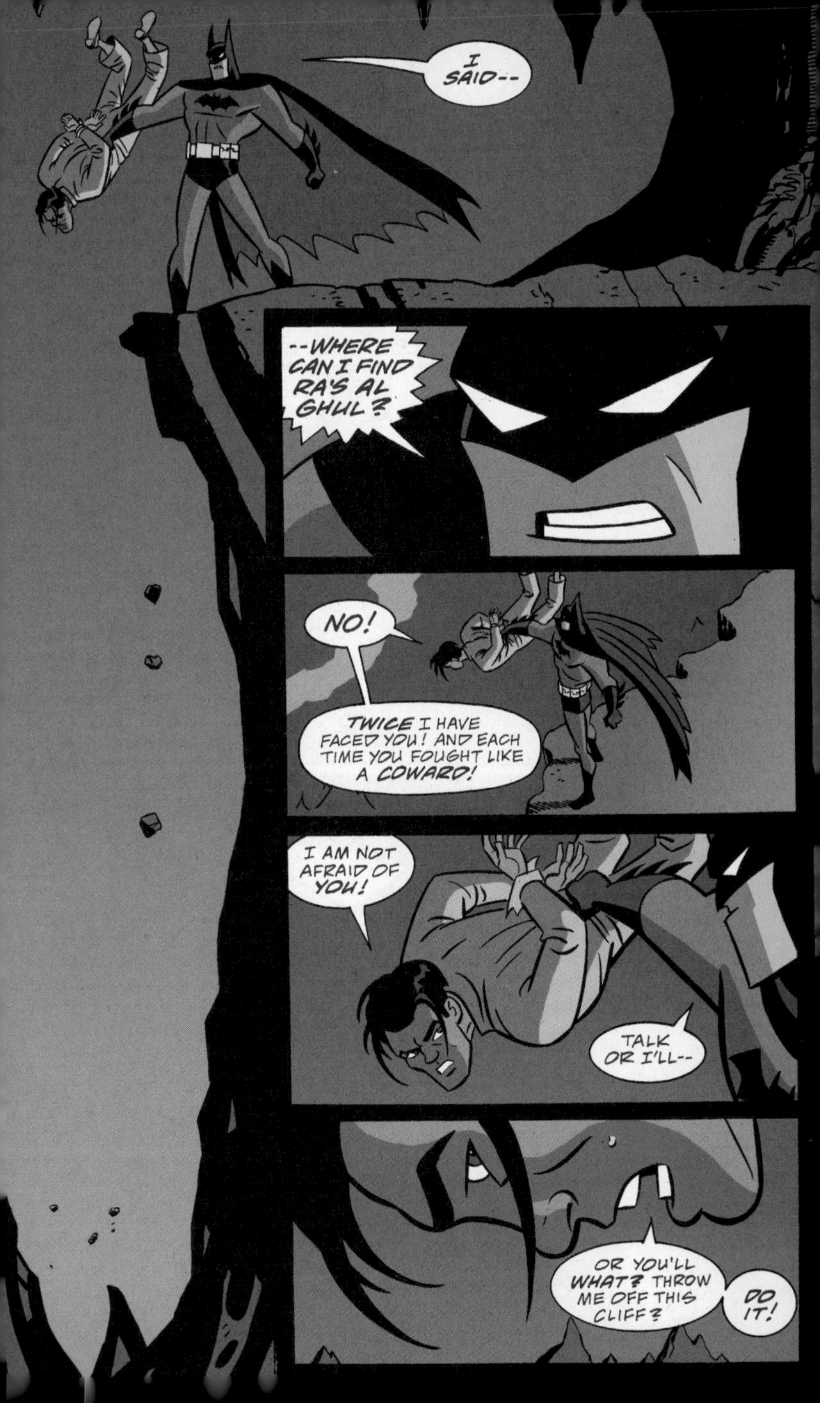
I SAID--
--WHERE CAN I FIND RA'S AL GHUL?
NO!
TWICE I HAVE FACED YOU! AND EACH TIME YOU FOUGHT LIKE A COWARD!
I AM NOT AFRAID OF YOU!
TALK OR I'LL--
OR YOU'LL WHAT? THROW ME OFF THIS CLIFF?
DO IT!

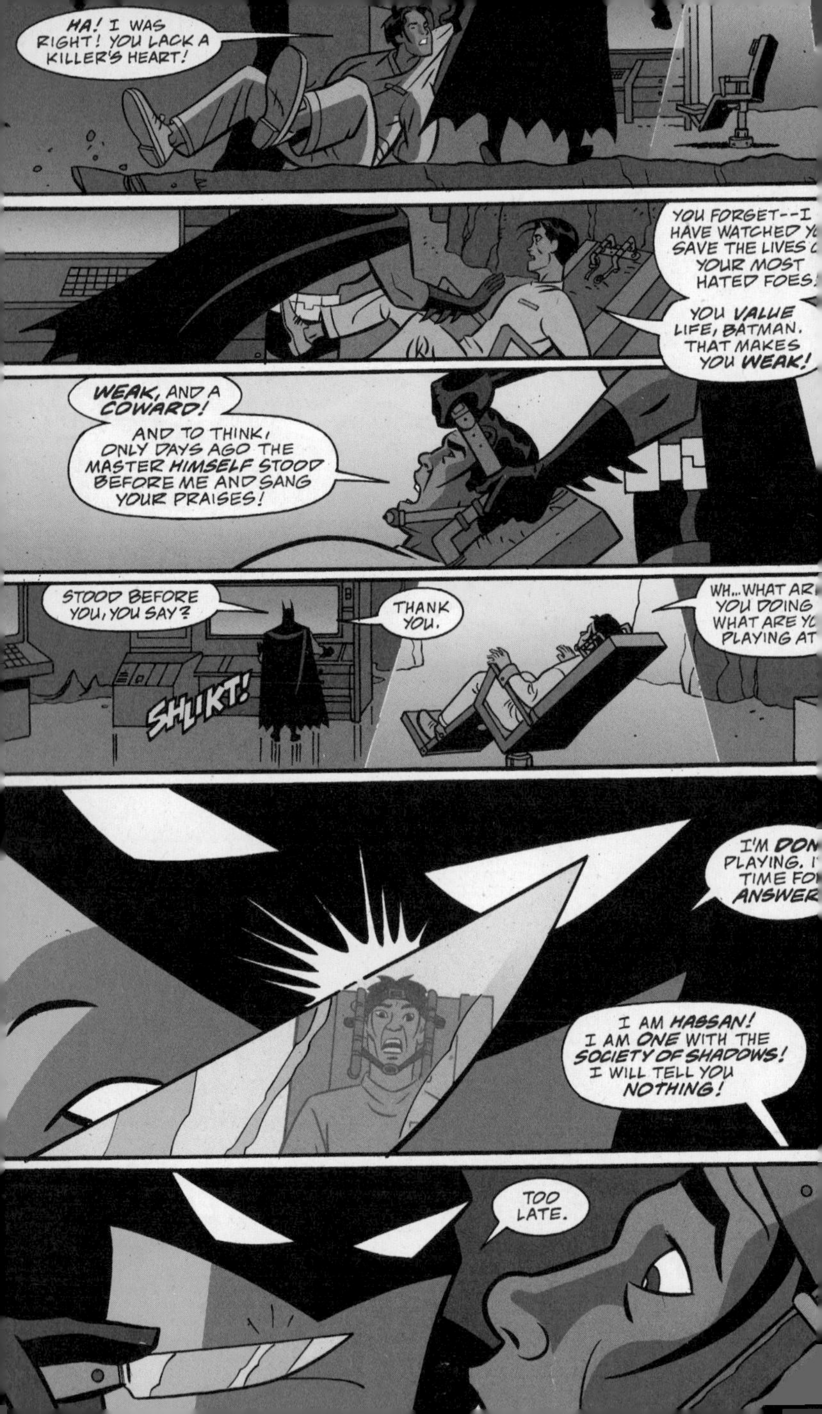
HA! I WAS RIGHT! YOU LACK A KILLER'S HEART!
YOU FORGET--I HAVE WATCHED YO SAVE THE LIVES O YOUR MOST HATED FOES!
YOU VALUE LIFE, BATMAN. THAT MAKES YOU WEAK!
WEAK, AND A COWARD!
AND TO THINK, ONLY DAYS AGO THE MASTER HIMSELF STOOD BEFORE ME AND SANG YOUR PRAISES!
STOOD BEFORE YOU, YOU SAY?
THANK YOU.
SHLIKT!
WH...WHAT AR YOU DOING WHAT ARE YO PLAYING AT
I'M DON PLAYING. I' TIME FO ANSWER
I AM HASSAN! I AM ONE WITH THE SOCIETY OF SHADOWS! I WILL TELL YOU NOTHING!
TOO LATE.

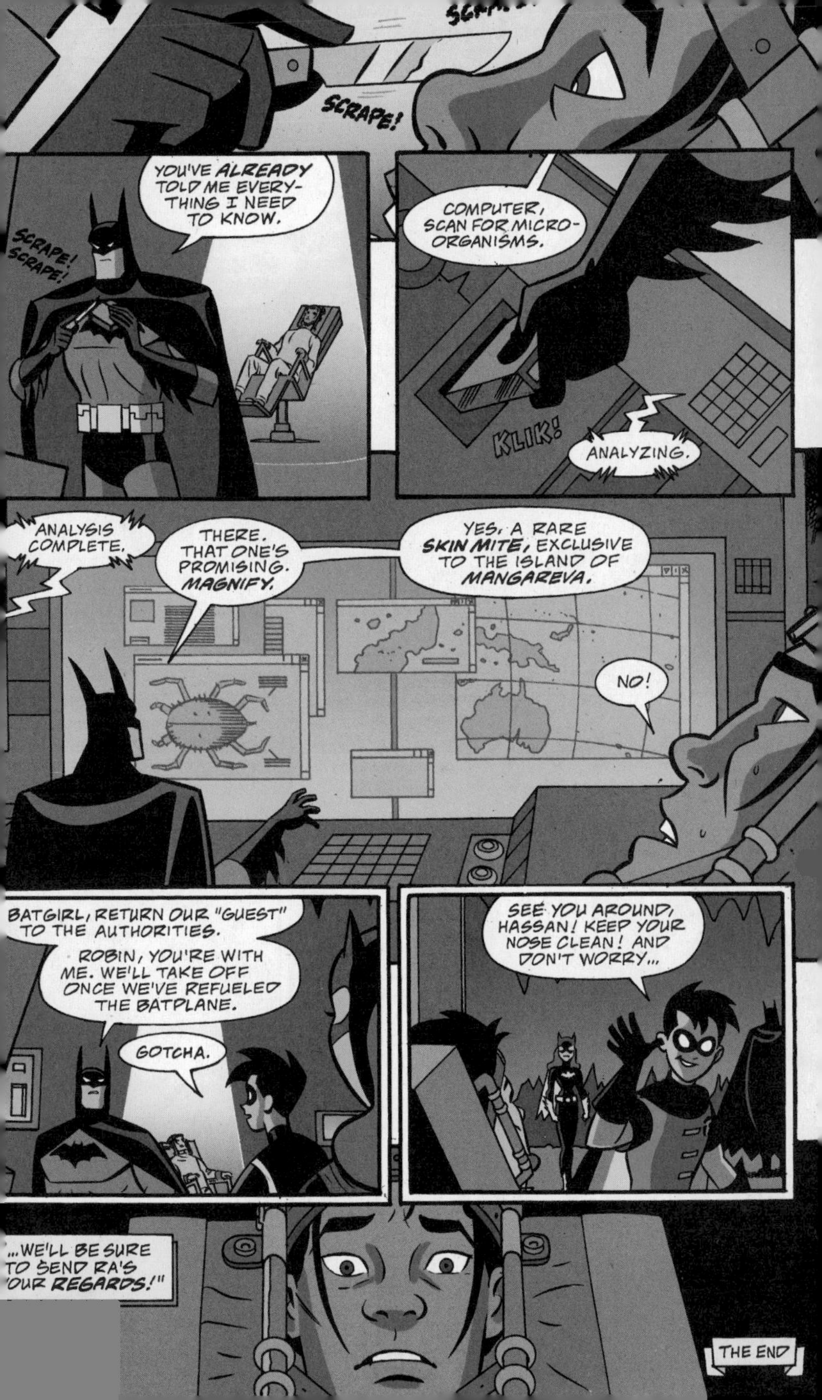
SCRAPE!
YOU'VE ALREADY TOLD ME EVERY-THING I NEED TO KNOW.
SCRAPE! SCRAPE!
COMPUTER, SCAN FOR MICRO-ORGANISMS.
KLIK!
ANALYZING.
ANALYSIS COMPLETE.
THERE. THAT ONE'S PROMISING. MAGNIFY.
YES, A RARE SKIN MITE, EXCLUSIVE TO THE ISLAND OF MANGAREVA.
NO!
BATGIRL, RETURN OUR "GUEST" TO THE AUTHORITIES.
ROBIN, YOU'RE WITH ME. WE'LL TAKE OFF ONCE WE'VE REFUELED THE BATPLANE.
GOTCHA.
SEE YOU AROUND, HASSAN! KEEP YOUR NOSE CLEAN! AND DON'T WORRY...
...WE'LL BE SURE TO SEND RA'S 'OUR REGARDS!"
THE END

DING DONG!

HEY, ALF! TELL BRUCE I'M READY.

READY, MS. MADISON...

AH, YES. READY FOR YOUR *DATE*, THIS EVENING.

DANCING AT THE X-RAY TERRACE, IF I RECALL.

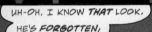

UH-OH, I KNOW *THAT* LOOK.

HE'S *FORGOTTEN*, HASN'T HE?

NOT AT ALL.

BUT I'M AFRAID MASTER BRUCE *HAS* BEEN CALLED AWAY... ON *EXTREMELY* IMPORTANT BUSINESS.

I AM TO CONVEY HIS *DEEP* REGRETS.

WHY DOES HE KEEP *DOING* T

WHAT' MORE IMPORTA THAN ME

THE BALANCE

TY TEMPLETON ——— WRITER
RICK BURCHETT ——— PENCILLER
TERRY BEATTY ——— INKER
LEE LOUGHRIDGE ——— COLORIST
PHIL FELIX ——— LETTERER
HARVEY RICHARDS — ASSISTANT
JOAN HILTY ——— EDITOR
BATMAN CREATED BY BOB KANE

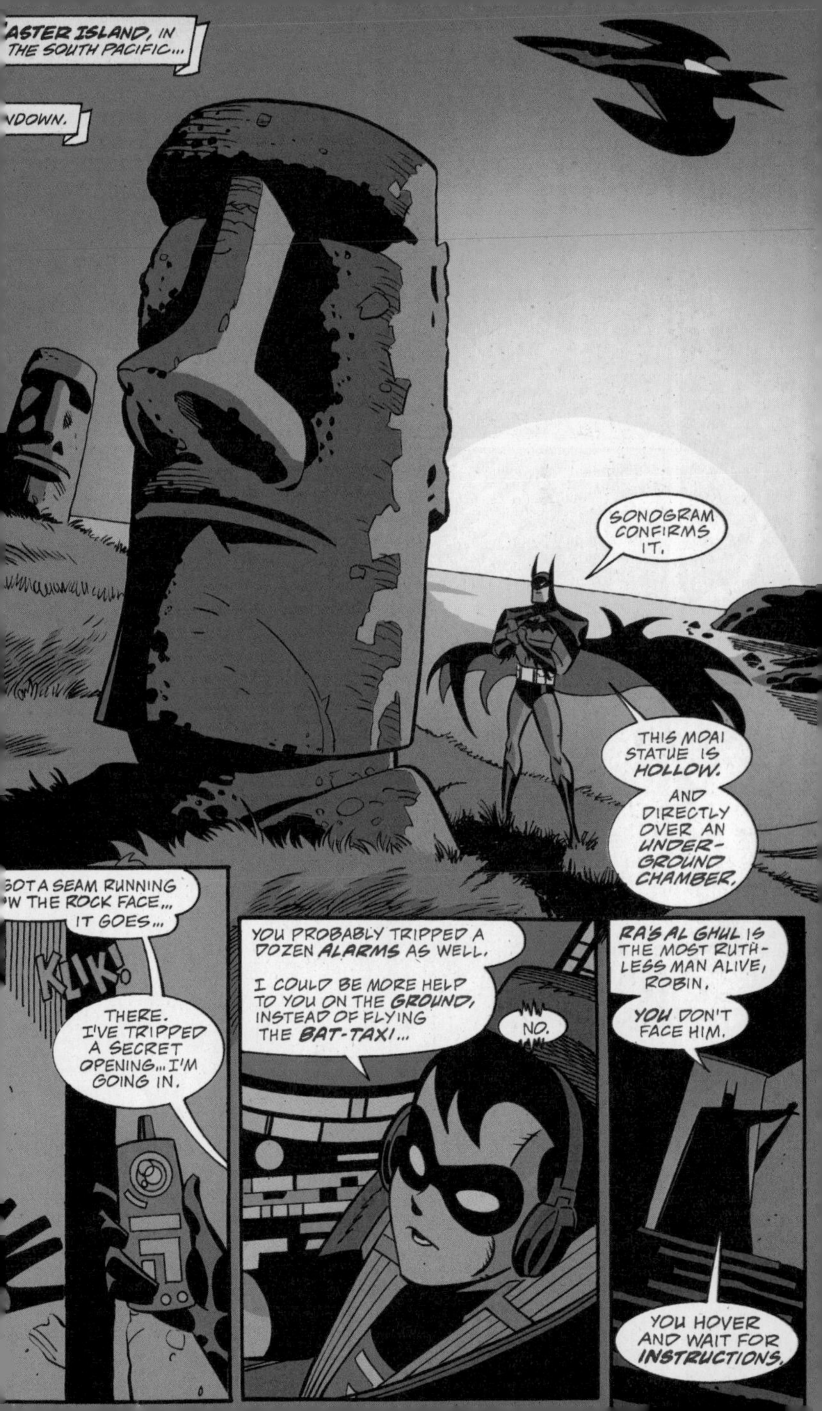
EASTER ISLAND, IN THE SOUTH PACIFIC...
NDOWN.
SONOGRAM CONFIRMS IT.
THIS MOAI STATUE IS HOLLOW.
AND DIRECTLY OVER AN UNDER-GROUND CHAMBER.
GOT A SEAM RUNNING OW THE ROCK FACE... IT GOES...
KLIK!
THERE. I'VE TRIPPED A SECRET OPENING...I'M GOING IN.
YOU PROBABLY TRIPPED A DOZEN ALARMS AS WELL.
I COULD BE MORE HELP TO YOU ON THE GROUND, INSTEAD OF FLYING THE BAT-TAXI...
NO.
RA'S AL GHUL IS THE MOST RUTH-LESS MAN ALIVE, ROBIN.
YOU DON'T FACE HIM.
YOU HOVER AND WAIT FOR INSTRUCTIONS.

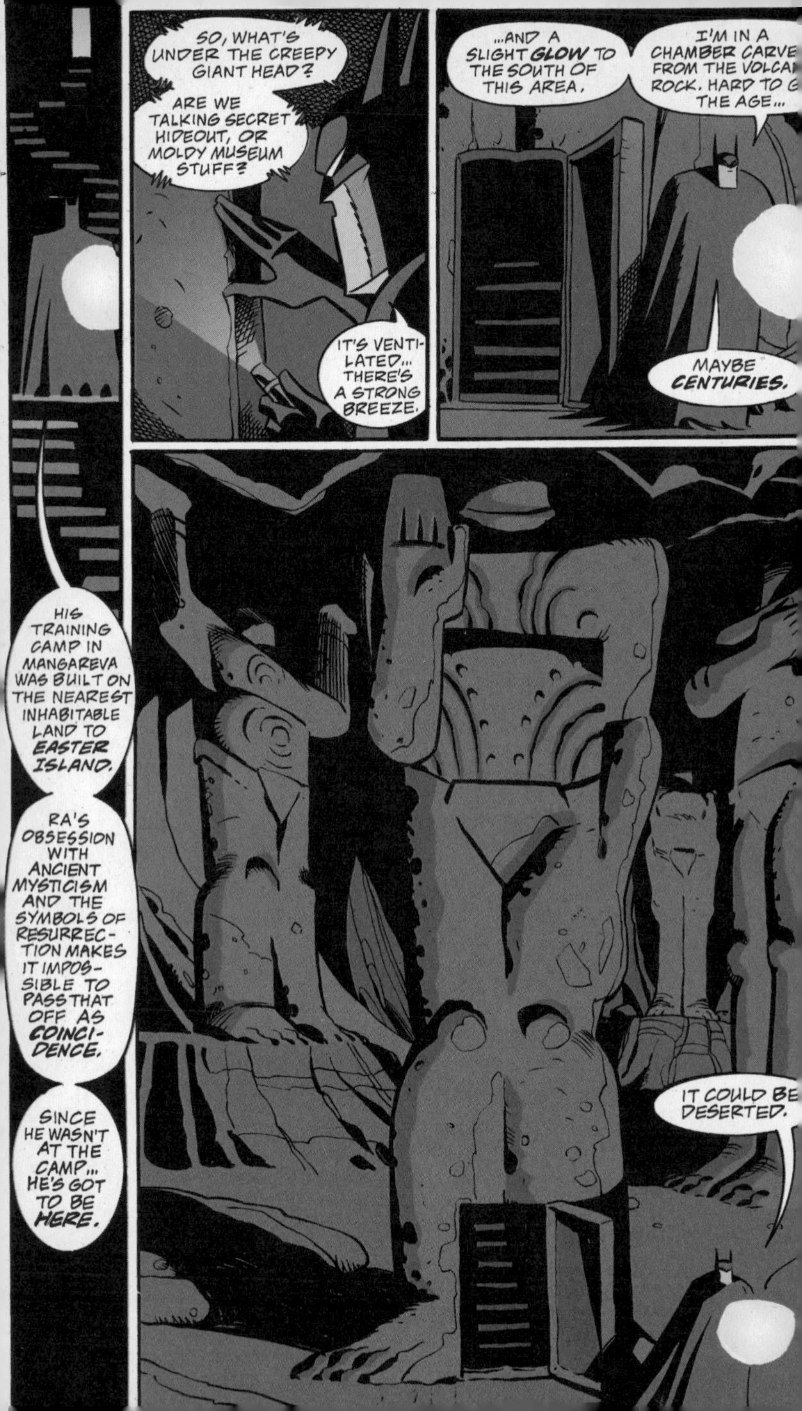
SO, WHAT'S UNDER THE CREEPY GIANT HEAD?
ARE WE TALKING SECRET HIDEOUT, OR MOLDY MUSEUM STUFF?
IT'S VENTI-LATED... THERE'S A STRONG BREEZE.
...AND A SLIGHT GLOW TO THE SOUTH OF THIS AREA.
I'M IN A CHAMBER CARVE FROM THE VOLCA ROCK. HARD TO G THE AGE...
MAYBE CENTURIES.
HIS TRAINING CAMP IN MANGAREVA WAS BUILT ON THE NEAREST INHABITABLE LAND TO EASTER ISLAND.
RA'S OBSESSION WITH ANCIENT MYSTICISM AND THE SYMBOLS OF RESURREC-TION MAKES IT IMPOS-SIBLE TO PASS THAT OFF AS COINCI-DENCE.
SINCE HE WASN'T AT THE CAMP... HE'S GOT TO BE HERE.
IT COULD BE DESERTED.

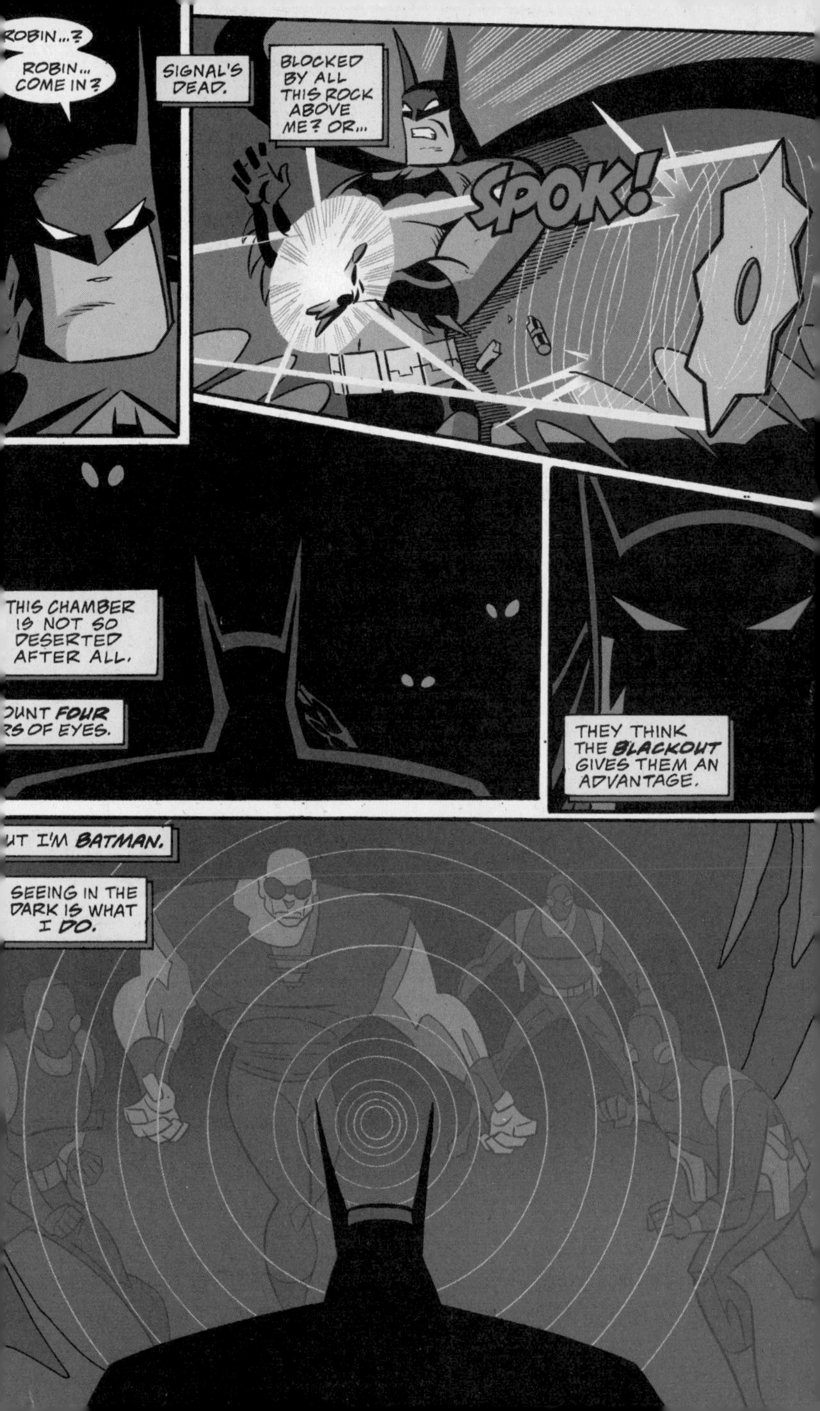
ROBIN...?
ROBIN... COME IN?
SIGNAL'S DEAD.
BLOCKED BY ALL THIS ROCK ABOVE ME? OR...
SPOK!
THIS CHAMBER IS NOT SO DESERTED AFTER ALL.
OUNT FOUR RS OF EYES.
THEY THINK THE BLACKOUT GIVES THEM AN ADVANTAGE.
UT I'M BATMAN.
SEEING IN THE DARK IS WHAT I DO.

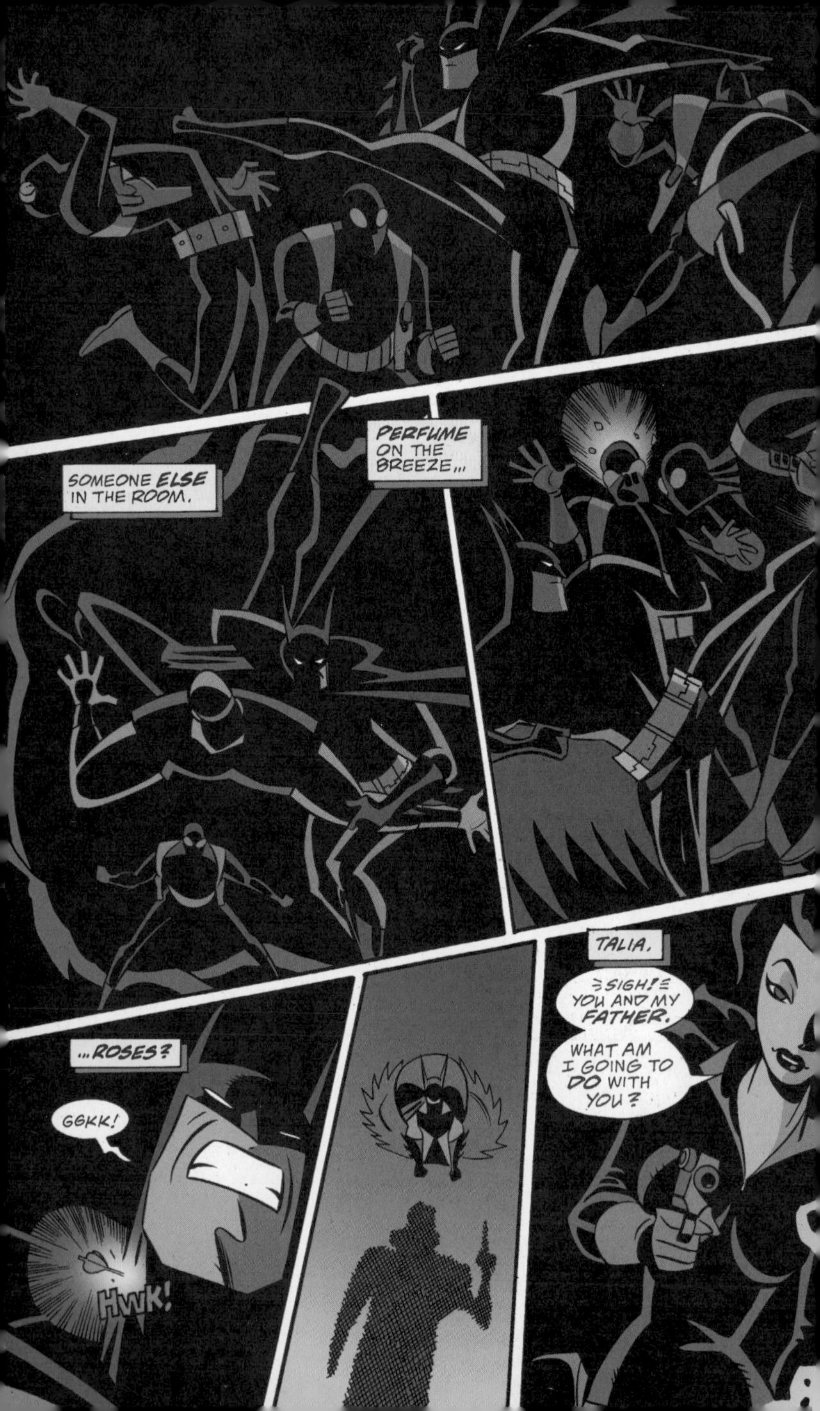
SOMEONE ELSE IN THE ROOM.
PERFUME ON THE BREEZE...
...ROSES?
GGKK!
HWK!
TALIA.
=SIGH!= YOU AND MY FATHER.
WHAT AM I GOING TO DO WITH YOU?

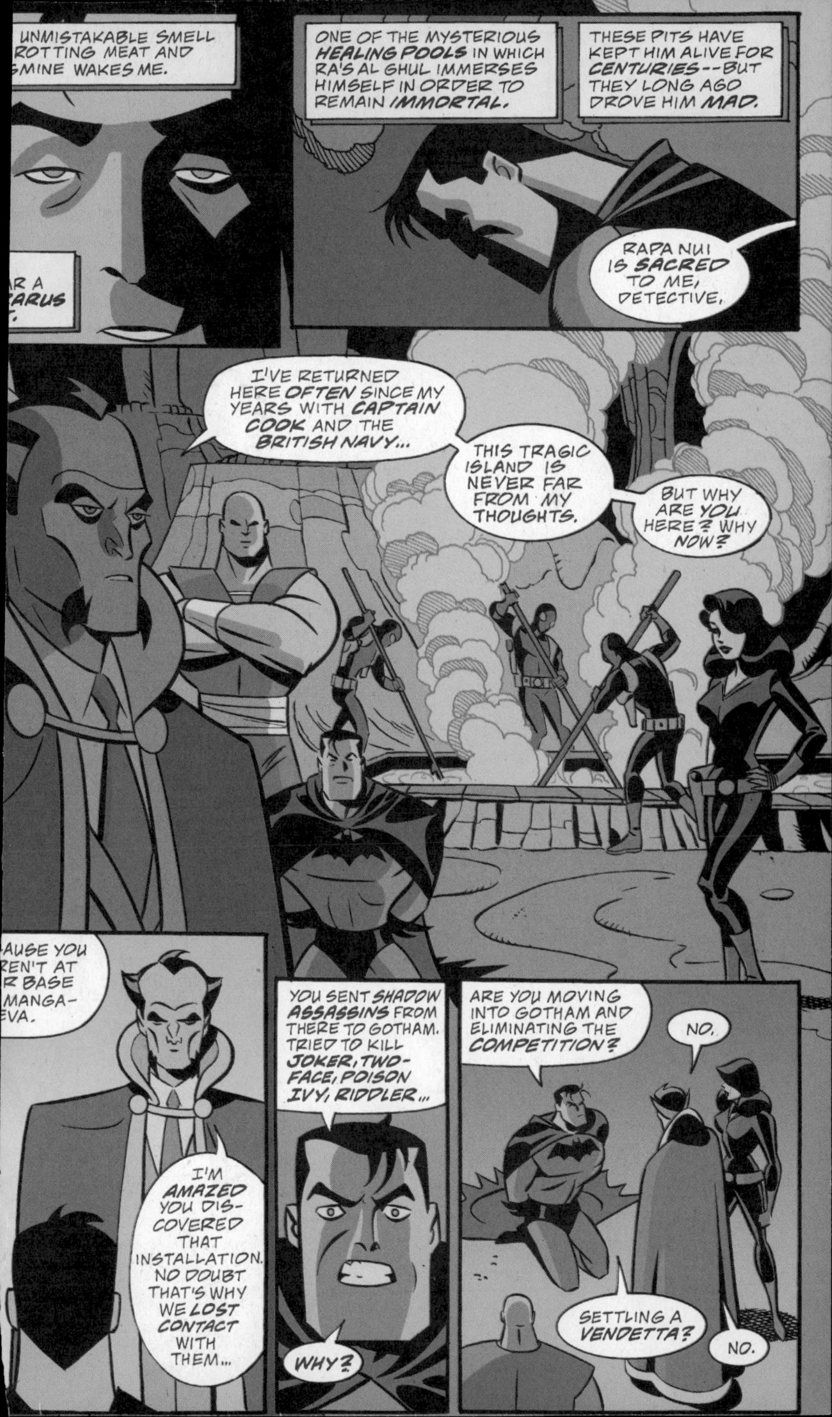

UNMISTAKABLE SMELL ROTTING MEAT AND SMINE WAKES ME.
ONE OF THE MYSTERIOUS HEALING POOLS IN WHICH RA'S AL GHUL IMMERSES HIMSELF IN ORDER TO REMAIN IMMORTAL.
THESE PITS HAVE KEPT HIM ALIVE FOR CENTURIES--BUT THEY LONG AGO DROVE HIM MAD.
AR A ARUS
RAPA NUI IS SACRED TO ME, DETECTIVE.
I'VE RETURNED HERE OFTEN SINCE MY YEARS WITH CAPTAIN COOK AND THE BRITISH NAVY...
THIS TRAGIC ISLAND IS NEVER FAR FROM MY THOUGHTS.
BUT WHY ARE YOU HERE? WHY NOW?
AUSE YOU RENT AT R BASE MANGA- EVA.
I'M AMAZED YOU DISCOVERED THAT INSTALLATION. NO DOUBT THAT'S WHY WE LOST CONTACT WITH THEM...
YOU SENT SHADOW ASSASSINS FROM THERE TO GOTHAM. TRIED TO KILL JOKER, TWO-FACE, POISON IVY, RIDDLER...
WHY?
ARE YOU MOVING INTO GOTHAM AND ELIMINATING THE COMPETITION?
NO.
SETTLING A VENDETTA?
NO.

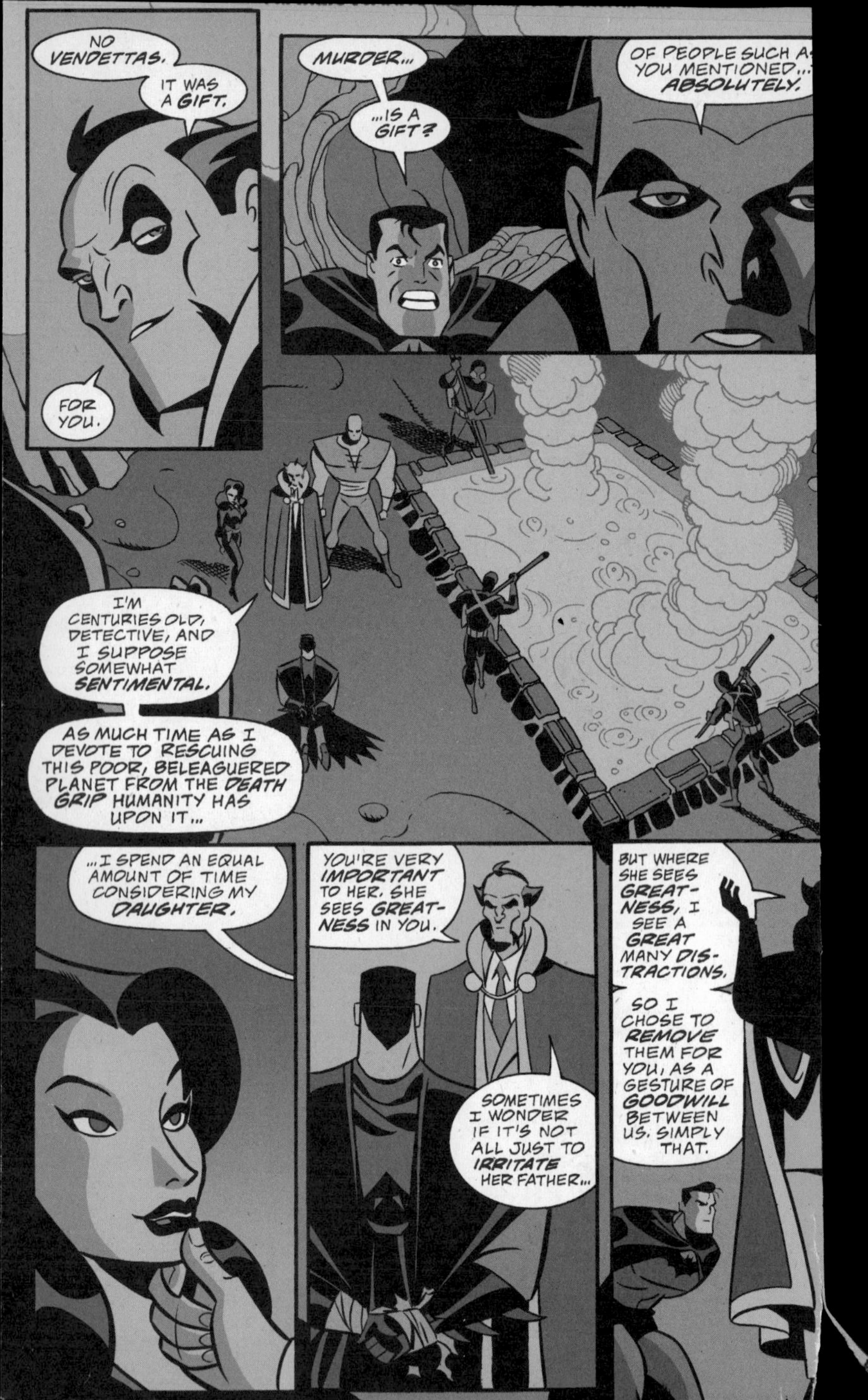
NO VENDETTAS.
IT WAS A GIFT.
FOR YOU.
MURDER...
...IS A GIFT?
OF PEOPLE SUCH AS YOU MENTIONED...? ABSOLUTELY.
I'M CENTURIES OLD, DETECTIVE, AND I SUPPOSE SOMEWHAT SENTIMENTAL.
AS MUCH TIME AS I DEVOTE TO RESCUING THIS POOR, BELEAGUERED PLANET FROM THE DEATH GRIP HUMANITY HAS UPON IT...
...I SPEND AN EQUAL AMOUNT OF TIME CONSIDERING MY DAUGHTER.
YOU'RE VERY IMPORTANT TO HER. SHE SEES GREAT-NESS IN YOU.
SOMETIMES I WONDER IF IT'S NOT ALL JUST TO IRRITATE HER FATHER...
BUT WHERE SHE SEES GREAT-NESS, I SEE A GREAT MANY DIS-TRACTIONS.
SO I CHOSE TO REMOVE THEM FOR YOU, AS A GESTURE OF GOODWILL BETWEEN US. SIMPLY THAT.

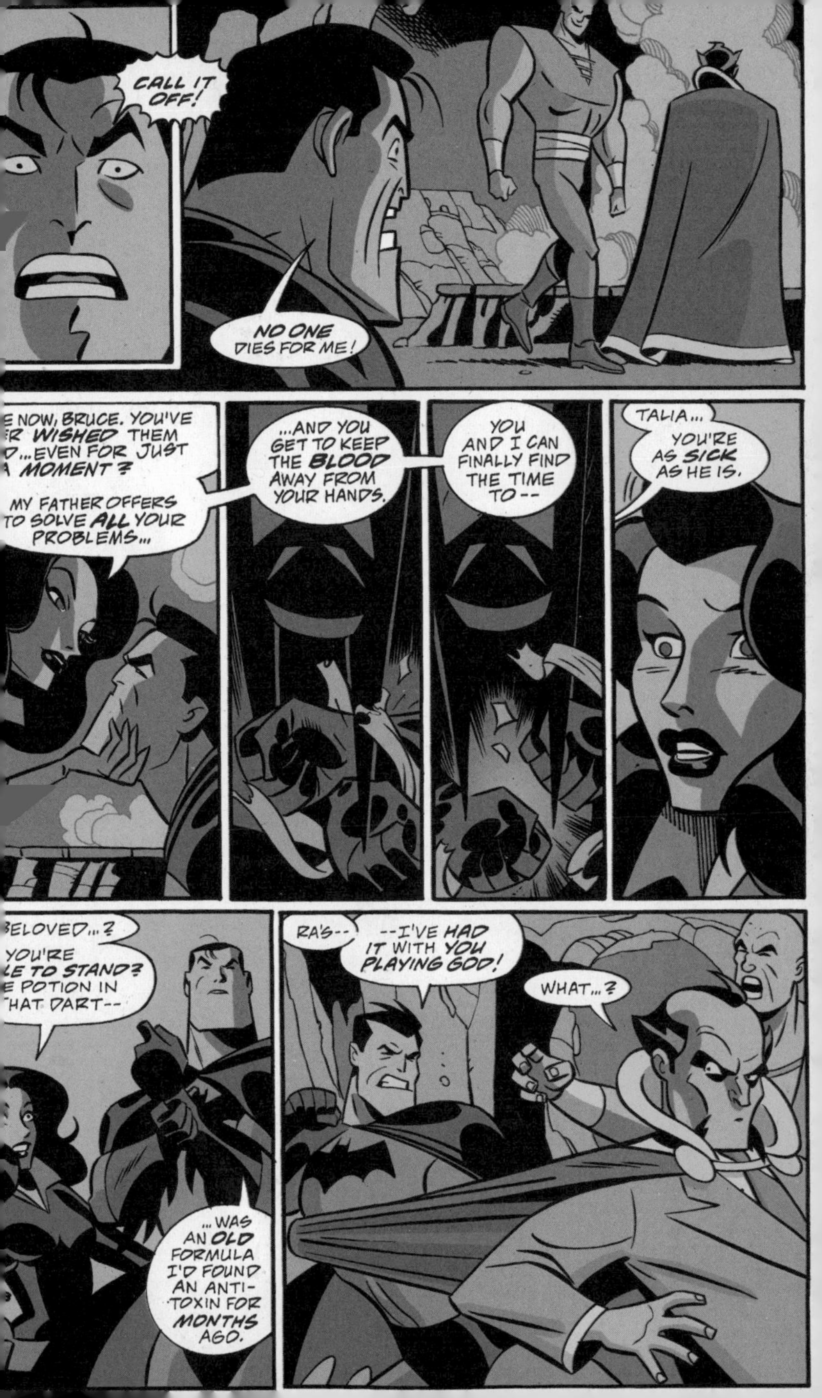
CALL IT OFF!
NO ONE DIES FOR ME!
E NOW, BRUCE. YOU'VE
R WISHED THEM
D...EVEN FOR JUST
A MOMENT?
MY FATHER OFFERS TO SOLVE ALL YOUR PROBLEMS...
...AND YOU GET TO KEEP THE BLOOD AWAY FROM YOUR HANDS.
YOU AND I CAN FINALLY FIND THE TIME TO --
TALIA...
YOU'RE AS SICK AS HE IS.
BELOVED...?
YOU'RE
LE TO STAND?
E POTION IN
THAT DART--
...WAS AN OLD FORMULA I'D FOUND AN ANTI-TOXIN FOR MONTHS AGO.
RA'S--
--I'VE HAD IT WITH YOU PLAYING GOD!
WHAT...?

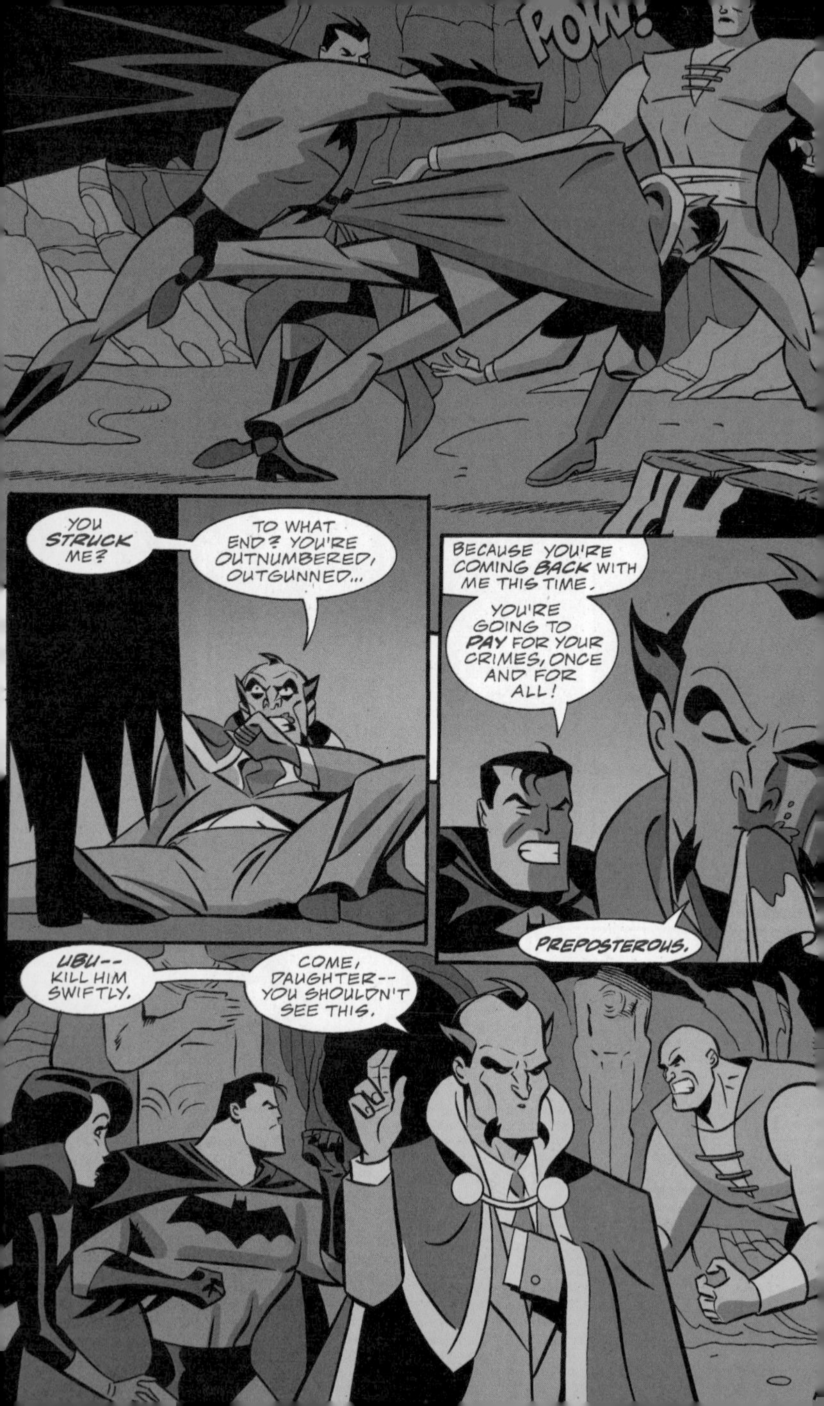
POW!
YOU STRUCK ME?
TO WHAT END? YOU'RE OUTNUMBERED, OUTGUNNED...
BECAUSE YOU'RE COMING BACK WITH ME THIS TIME.
YOU'RE GOING TO PAY FOR YOUR CRIMES, ONCE AND FOR ALL!
PREPOSTEROUS.
UBU-- KILL HIM SWIFTLY.
COME, DAUGHTER-- YOU SHOULDN'T SEE THIS.

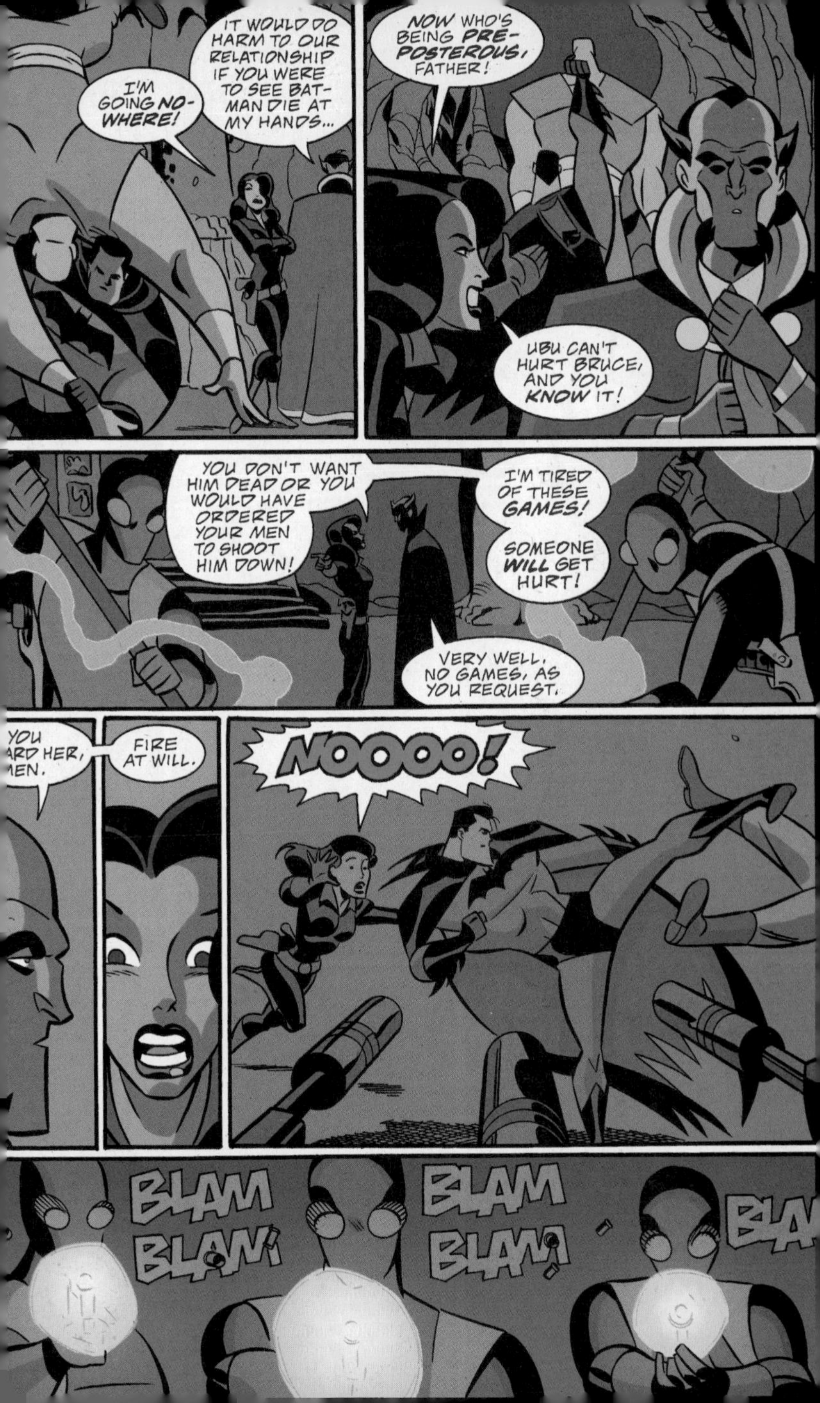
IT WOULD DO HARM TO OUR RELATIONSHIP IF YOU WERE TO SEE BATMAN DIE AT MY HANDS...
I'M GOING NOWHERE!
NOW WHO'S BEING PREPOSTEROUS, FATHER!
UBU CAN'T HURT BRUCE, AND YOU KNOW IT!
YOU DON'T WANT HIM DEAD OR YOU WOULD HAVE ORDERED YOUR MEN TO SHOOT HIM DOWN!
I'M TIRED OF THESE GAMES!
SOMEONE WILL GET HURT!
VERY WELL. NO GAMES, AS YOU REQUEST.
YOU ARD HER, MEN.
FIRE AT WILL.
NOOOO!
BLAM BLAM
BLAM BLAM

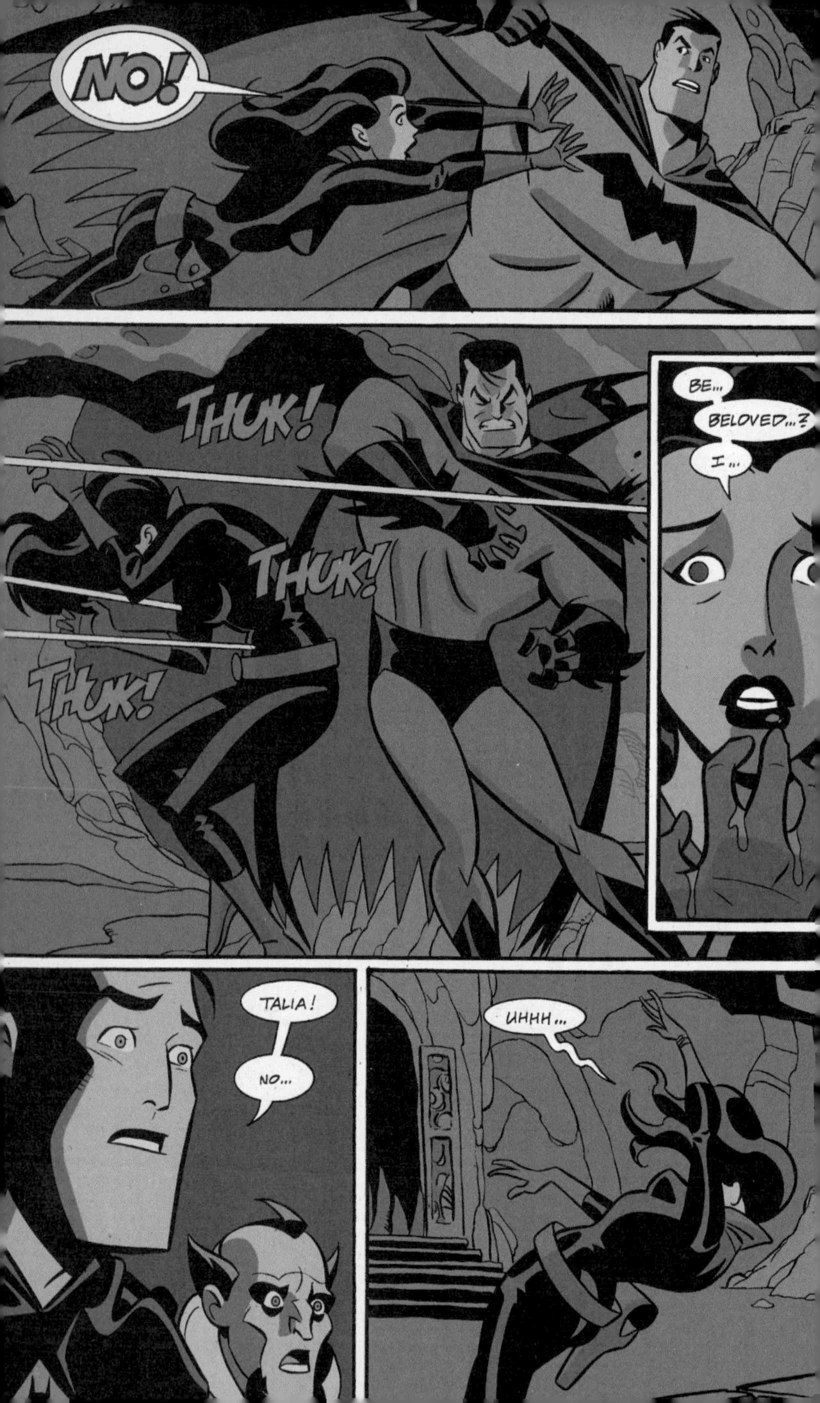
NO!
THUK!
THUK!
THUK!
BE...
BELOVED...?
I...
TALIA!
NO...
UHHH...

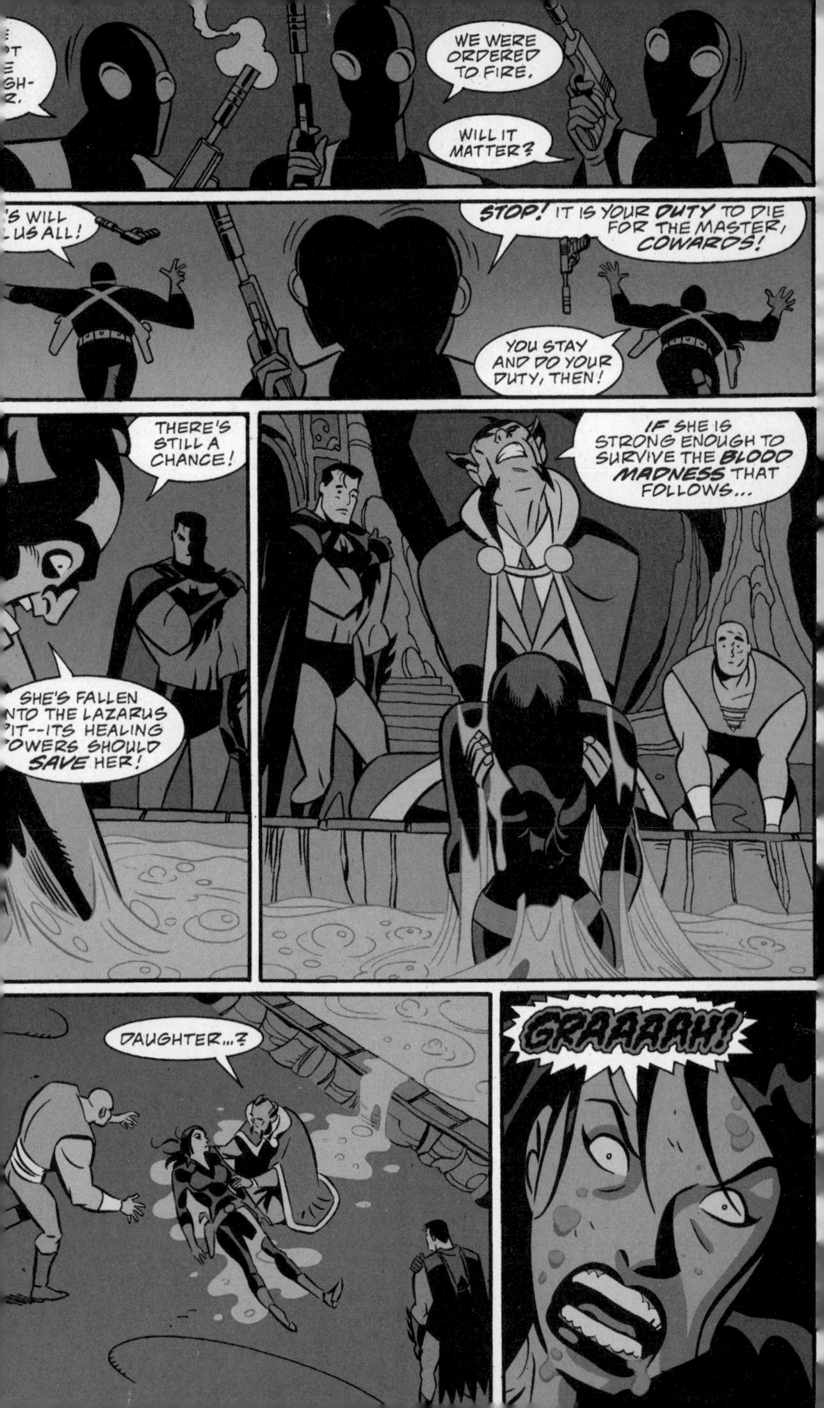
WE WERE ORDERED TO FIRE.
WILL IT MATTER?
'S WILL L US ALL!
STOP! IT IS YOUR DUTY TO DIE FOR THE MASTER, COWARDS!
YOU STAY AND DO YOUR DUTY, THEN!
THERE'S STILL A CHANCE!
SHE'S FALLEN NTO THE LAZARUS PIT--ITS HEALING OWERS SHOULD SAVE HER!
IF SHE IS STRONG ENOUGH TO SURVIVE THE BLOOD MADNESS THAT FOLLOWS...
DAUGHTER...?
GRAAAAH!

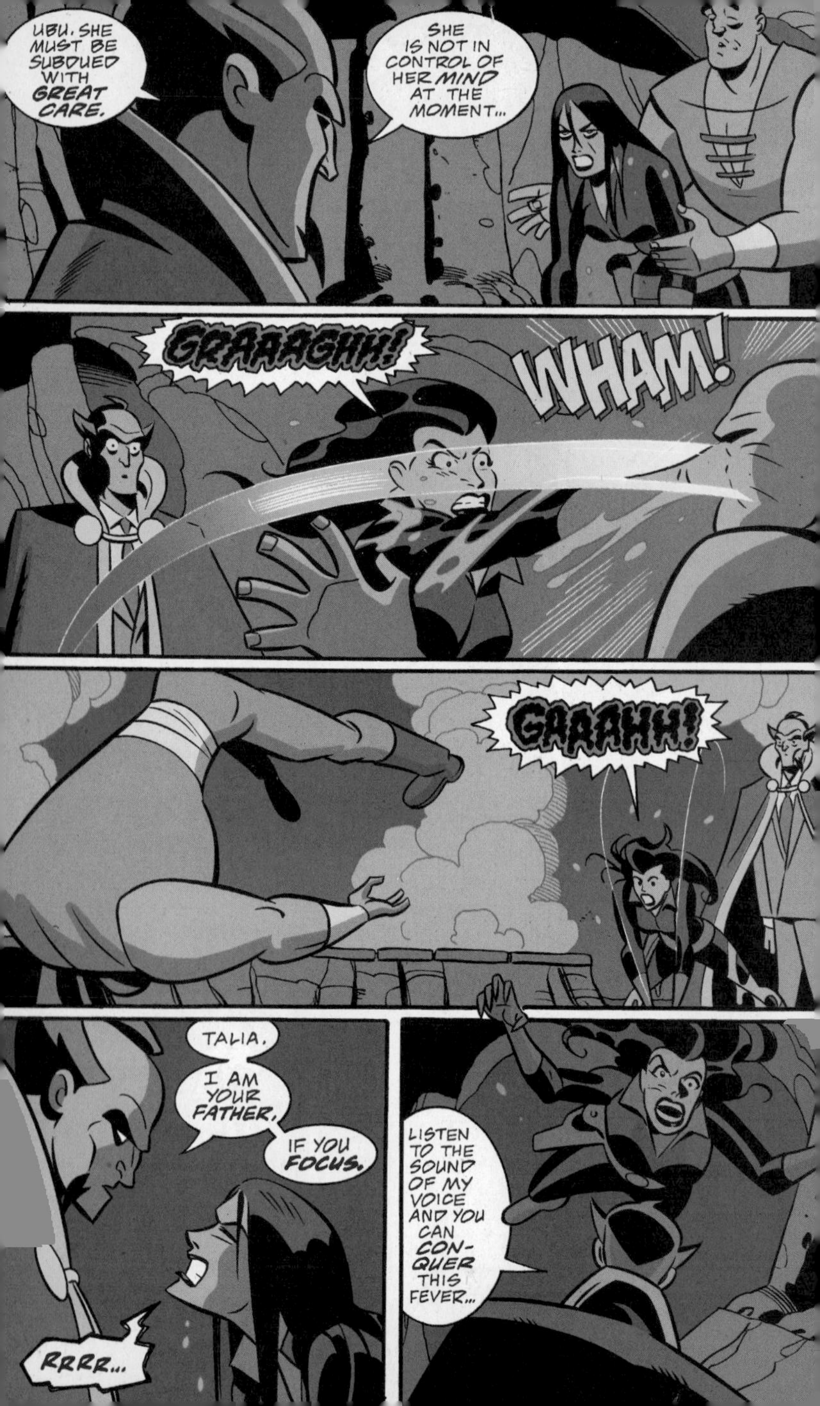
UBU. SHE MUST BE SUBDUED WITH GREAT CARE.
SHE IS NOT IN CONTROL OF HER MIND AT THE MOMENT...
GRAAAGHH!
WHAM!
GAAAHH!
TALIA.
I AM YOUR FATHER.
IF YOU FOCUS.
RRRR...
LISTEN TO THE SOUND OF MY VOICE AND YOU CAN CON-QUER THIS FEVER...

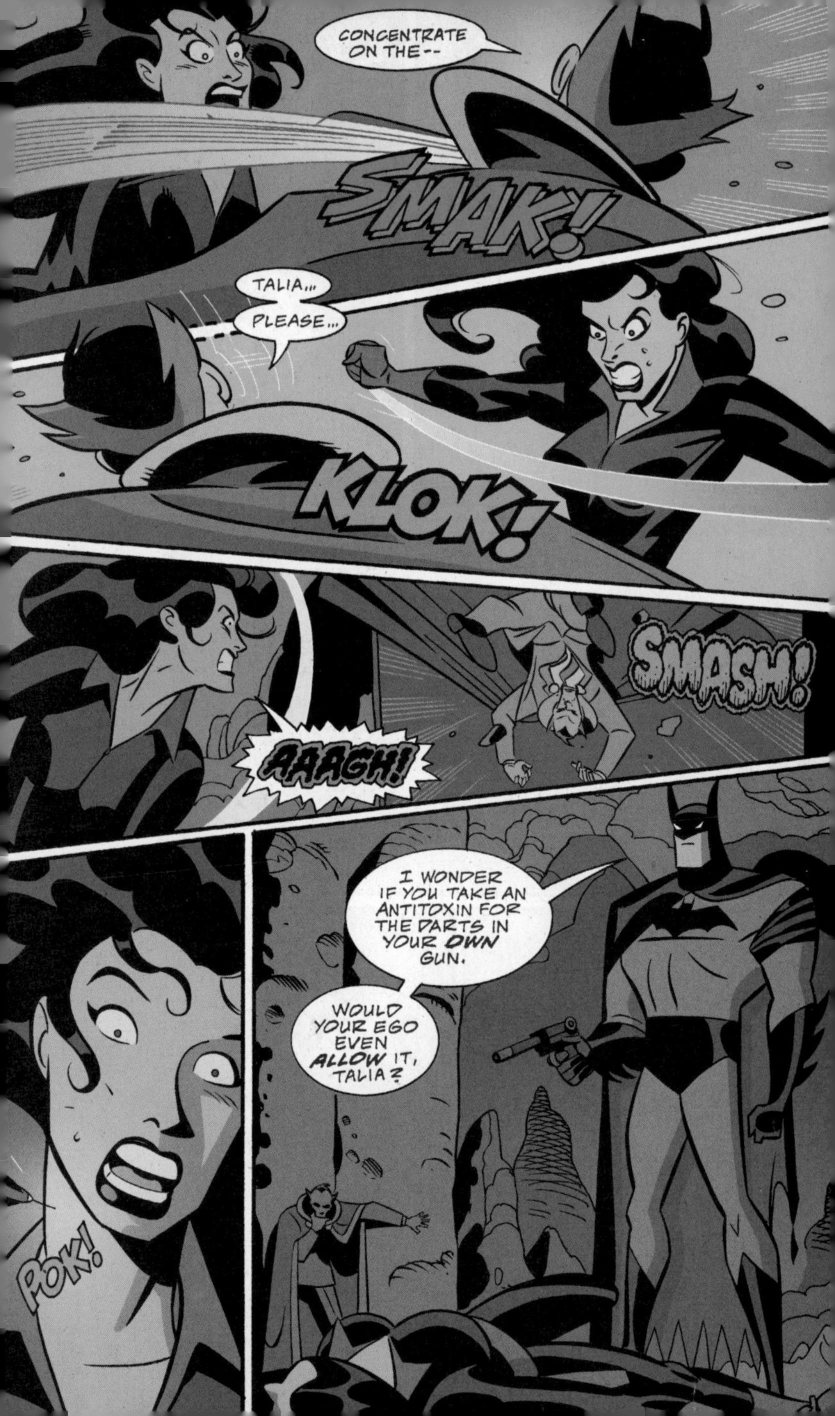
CONCENTRATE ON THE--
SMAK!
TALIA...
PLEASE...
KLOK!
SMASH!
AAAGH!
I WONDER IF YOU TAKE AN ANTITOXIN FOR THE DARTS IN YOUR *OWN* GUN.
WOULD YOUR EGO EVEN *ALLOW* IT, TALIA?
POK!

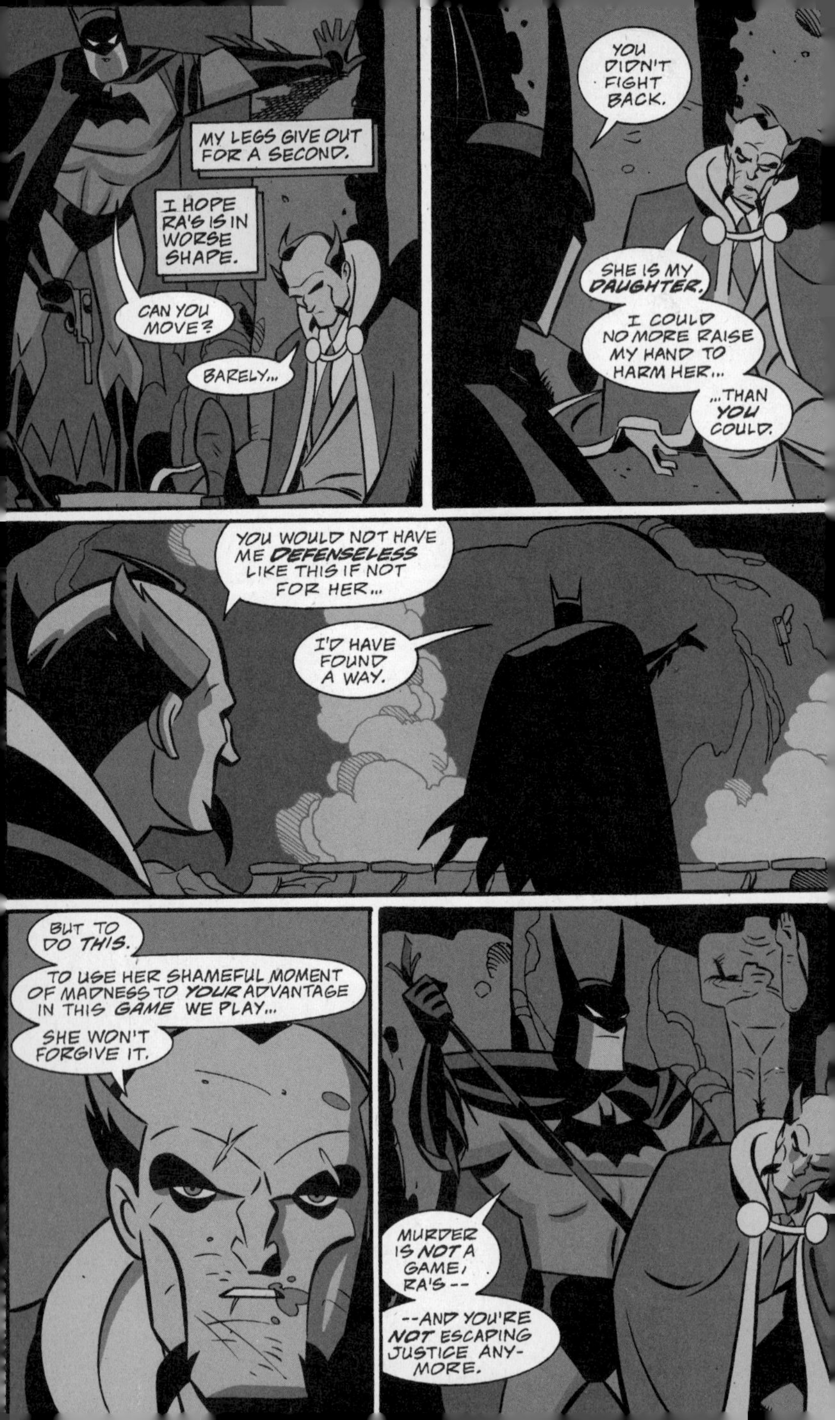
MY LEGS GIVE OUT FOR A SECOND.
I HOPE RA'S IS IN WORSE SHAPE.
CAN YOU MOVE?
BARELY...
YOU DIDN'T FIGHT BACK.
SHE IS MY DAUGHTER.
I COULD NO MORE RAISE MY HAND TO HARM HER...
...THAN YOU COULD.
YOU WOULD NOT HAVE ME DEFENSELESS LIKE THIS IF NOT FOR HER...
I'D HAVE FOUND A WAY.
BUT TO DO THIS.
TO USE HER SHAMEFUL MOMENT OF MADNESS TO YOUR ADVANTAGE IN THIS GAME WE PLAY...
SHE WON'T FORGIVE IT.
MURDER IS NOT A GAME, RA'S --
--AND YOU'RE NOT ESCAPING JUSTICE ANY-MORE.

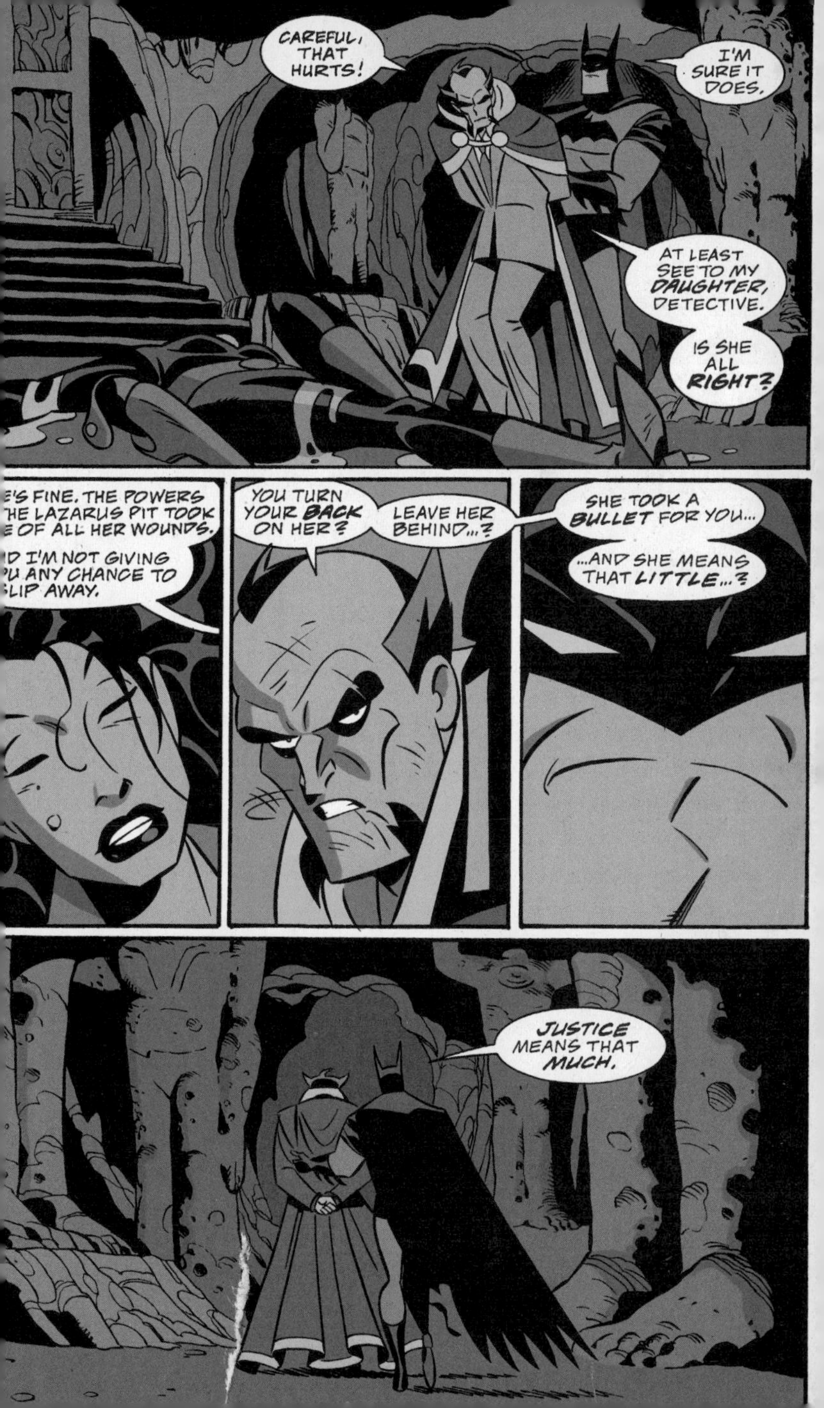
CAREFUL, THAT HURTS!
I'M SURE IT DOES.
AT LEAST SEE TO MY DAUGHTER, DETECTIVE.
IS SHE ALL RIGHT?
E'S FINE. THE POWERS HE LAZARUS PIT TOOK E OF ALL HER WOUNDS.
D I'M NOT GIVING U ANY CHANCE TO LIP AWAY.
YOU TURN YOUR BACK ON HER?
LEAVE HER BEHIND...?
SHE TOOK A BULLET FOR YOU...
...AND SHE MEANS THAT LITTLE...?
JUSTICE MEANS THAT MUCH.

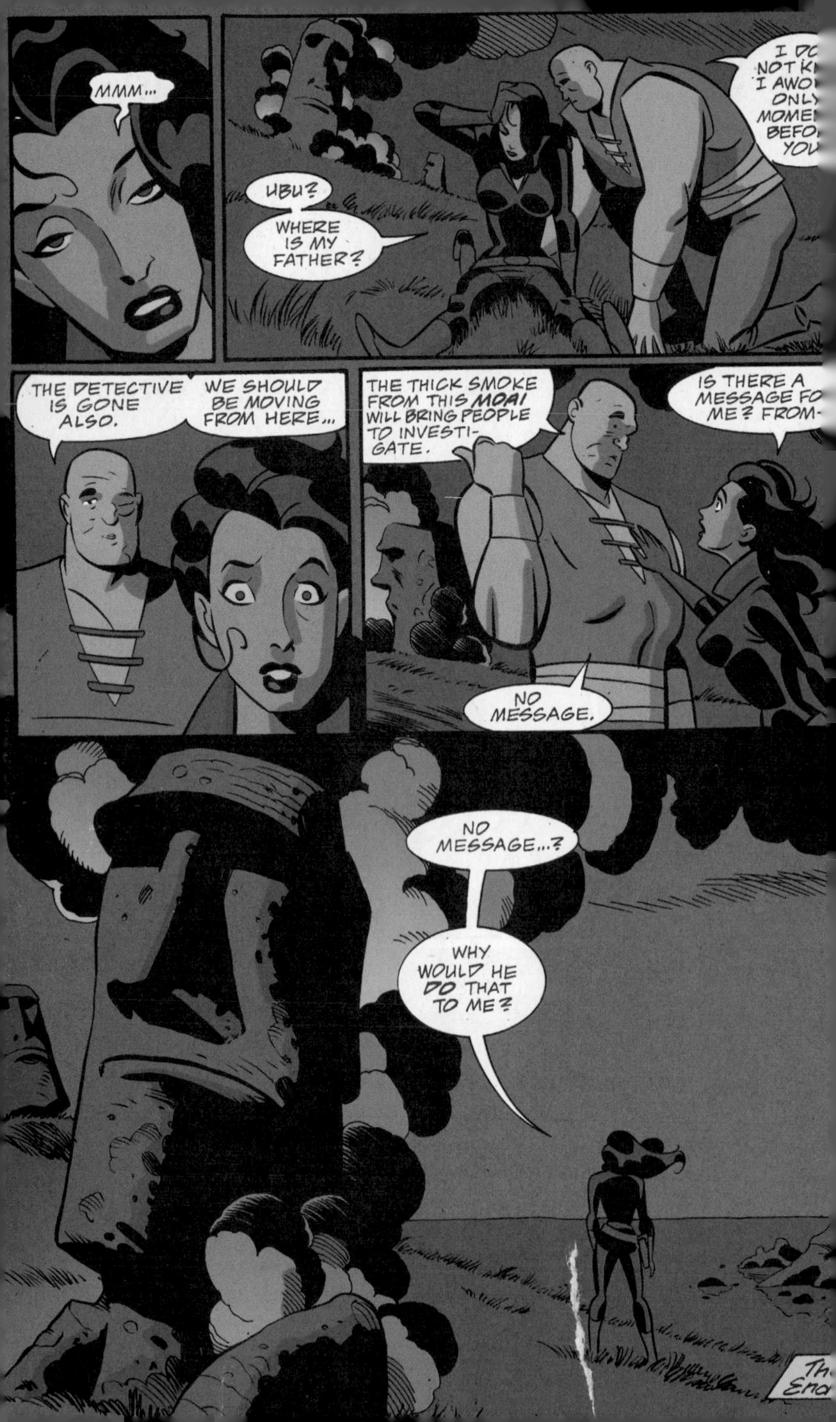
MMM...
UBU?
WHERE IS MY FATHER?
I DO NOT K
I AWO
ONLY
MOME
BEFO
YOU
THE DETECTIVE IS GONE ALSO.
WE SHOULD BE MOVING FROM HERE...
THE THICK SMOKE FROM THIS MOAI WILL BRING PEOPLE TO INVESTI-GATE.
IS THERE A MESSAGE FO ME? FROM-
NO MESSAGE.
NO MESSAGE...?
WHY WOULD HE DO THAT TO ME?
Th
End

MONTVILLE TWP. PUBLIC LIBRARY
90 HORSENECK ROAD
MONTVILLE, NJ 07045